This volume contains INU-YASHA PART 5 #9 through
INU-YASHA PART 6 #2 in their entirety.

STORY AND ART BY
RUMIKO TAKAHASHI

ENGLISH ADAPTATION BY
GERARD JONES

Translation/Mari Morimoto
Touch-Up Art & Lettering/Wayne Truman
Cover Design/Hidemi Sahara
Layout/Sean Lee

Editor/Julie Davis
Managing Editor/ Annette Roman
Sr. V.P. of Sales and Marketing/Rick Bauer
Sr. V.P. of Editorial/Hyoe Narita
Publisher/Seiji Horibuchi

© 1997 Rumiko Takahashi/Shogakukan, Inc.
First Published by Shogakukan, Inc. in Japan as
"Inu-Yasha."

Printed in Canada

Published by VIZ, LLC
P.O. Box 77010 • San Francisco, CA 94107
www.viz.com • store viz.com • www.animerica-mag.com

10 9 8 7 6 5 4
First printing, December 2001
Second printing, June 2002
Third printing, January 2003
Fourth printing, June 2003

<u>INU-YASHA GRAPHIC NOVELS TO DATE:</u>

INU-YASHA VOL. 1
INU-YASHA VOL. 2
INU-YASHA VOL. 3
INU-YASHA VOL. 4
INU-YASHA VOL. 5
INU-YASHA VOL. 6
INU-YASHA VOL. 7
INU-YASHA VOL. 8
INU-YASHA VOL. 9
INU-YASHA VOL. 10
INU-YASHA VOL. 11
INU-YASHA VOL. 12

VIZ GRAPHIC NOVEL

INU-YASHA
A FEUDAL FAIRY TALE™

VOL. 10

STORY AND ART BY
RUMIKO TAKAHASHI

CONTENTS

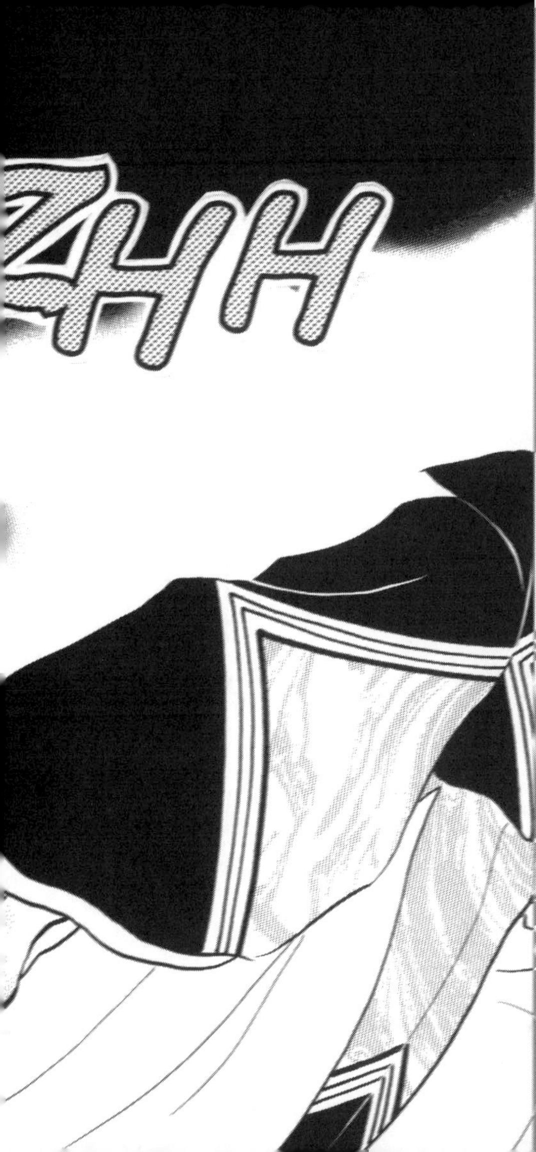
ZHH

THE STORY THUS FAR

Long ago, in the "Warring States" era of Japan's Muromachi period (*Sengoku-jidai*, approximately 1467-1568 CE), a legendary doglike half-demon called "Inu-Yasha" attempted to steal the Shikon Jewel, or "Jewel of Four Souls," from a village, but was stopped by the enchanted arrow of the village priestess, Kikyo. Inu-Yasha fell into a deep sleep, pinned to a tree by Kikyo's arrow, while the mortally wounded Kikyo took the Shikon Jewel with her into the fires of her funeral pyre. Years passed.

Fast forward to the present day. Kagome, a Japanese high school girl, is pulled into a well one day by mysterious centipede monster, and finds herself transported into the past, only to come face to face with the trapped Inu-Yasha. She frees him, and Inu-Yasha easily defeats the centipede monster.

The residents of the village, now fifty years older, readily accept Kagome as the reincarnation of their deceased priestess Kikyo, a claim supported by the fact that the Shikon Jewel emerges from a cut on Kagome's body. Unfortunately, the jewel's rediscovery means that the village is soon under attack by a variety of demons in search of this treasure. Then, the jewel is accidentally shattered into many shards, each of which may have the fearsome power of the entire jewel.

Although Inu-Yasha says he hates Kagome because of her resemblance to Kikyo, the woman who "killed" him, he is forced to team up with her when Kaede, the village leader, binds him to Kagome with a powerful spell. Now the two grudging companions must fight to reclaim and reassemble the shattered shards of the Shikon Jewel before they fall into the wrong hands.

INU-YASHA
A half-human, half-demon hybrid son of a human mother and a demon father, Inu-Yasha resembles a human but has the claws of a demon, a thick mane of white hair, and ears rather like a dog's. The necklace he wears carries a powerful spell which allows Kagome to control him with a single word. Because of his human half, Inu-Yasha's powers are different from those of full-blooded monsters—a fact that the Shikon Jewel has the power to change.

KIKYO
A powerful priestess, Kikyo was charged with the awesome responsibility of protecting the Shikon Jewel from demons and humans who coveted its power. She died after firing the enchanted arrow that kept Inu-Yasha imprisoned for fifty years.

KAGOME
Working with Inu-Yasha to recover the shattered shards of the Shikon Jewel, Kagome routinely travels into Japan's past through an old, magical well on her family's property. All this time travel means she's stuck with living two separate lives in two separate centuries, and she's beginning to worry that she'll *never* be able to catch up to her schoolwork.

SHIPPÔ
A young fox-demon, orphaned by two other demons whose powers had been boosted by the Shikon Jewel, the mischievous Shippô enjoys goading Inu-Yasha and playing tricks with his shape-changing abilities.

NARAKU
An enigmatic demon, Naraku is the one responsible for both Miroku's curse and for turning Kikyo and Inu-Yasha against one another for reasons that are as yet unknown.

MIROKU
An easygoing Buddhist priest with questionable morals, Miroku is the carrier of a curse passed down from his grandfather. He is searching for the demon Naraku, who first inflicted the curse.

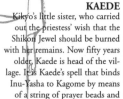

KAEDE
Kikyo's little sister, who carried out the priestess' wish that the Shikon Jewel should be burned with her remains. Now fifty years older, Kaede is head of the village. It is Kaede's spell that binds Inu-Yasha to Kagome by means of a string of prayer beads and Kagome's spoken word—"Sit!"

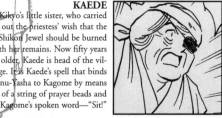

SCROLL ONE

THE MUMMY

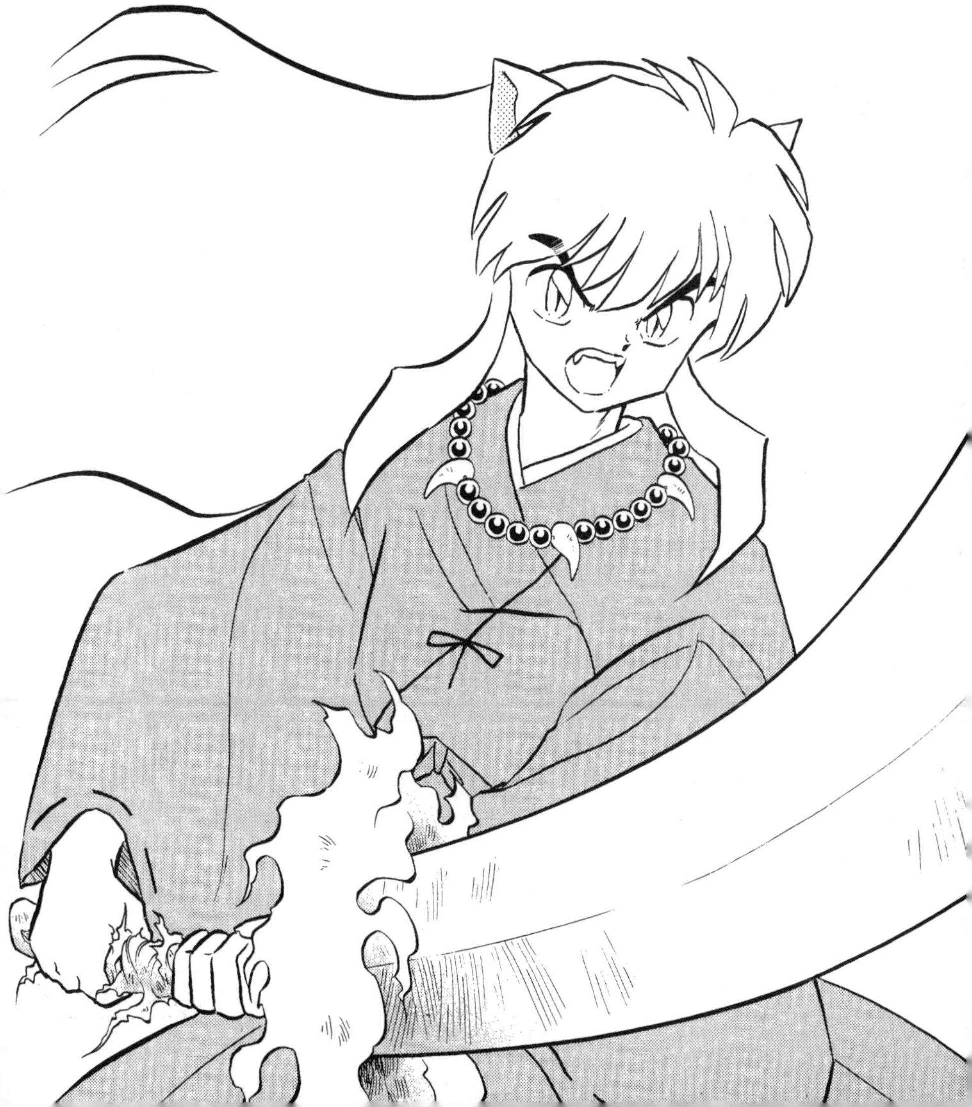

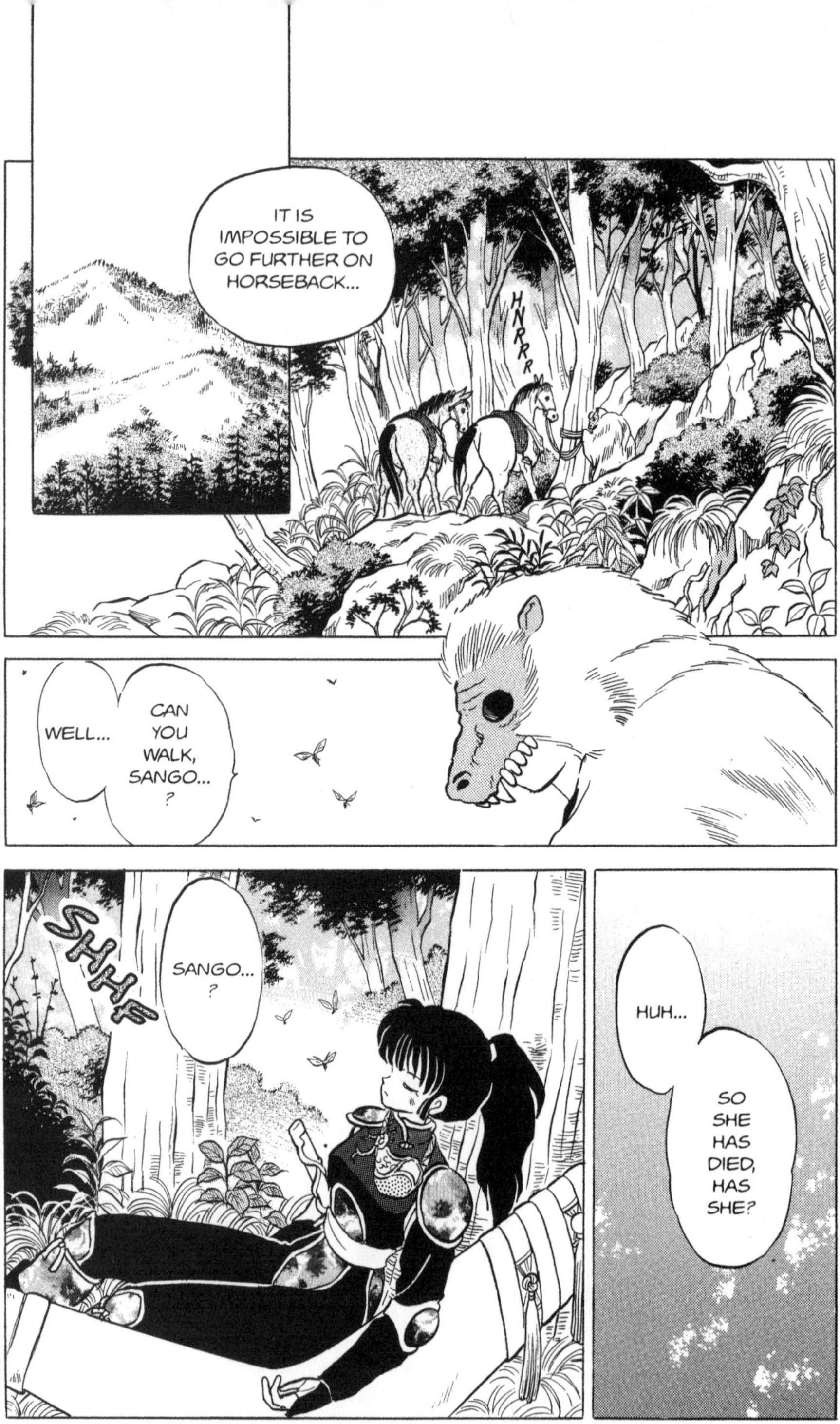
IT IS IMPOSSIBLE TO GO FURTHER ON HORSEBACK...
HNRRR
WELL...
CAN YOU WALK, SANGO...?
SHHF
SANGO...?
HUH...
SO SHE HAS DIED, HAS SHE?

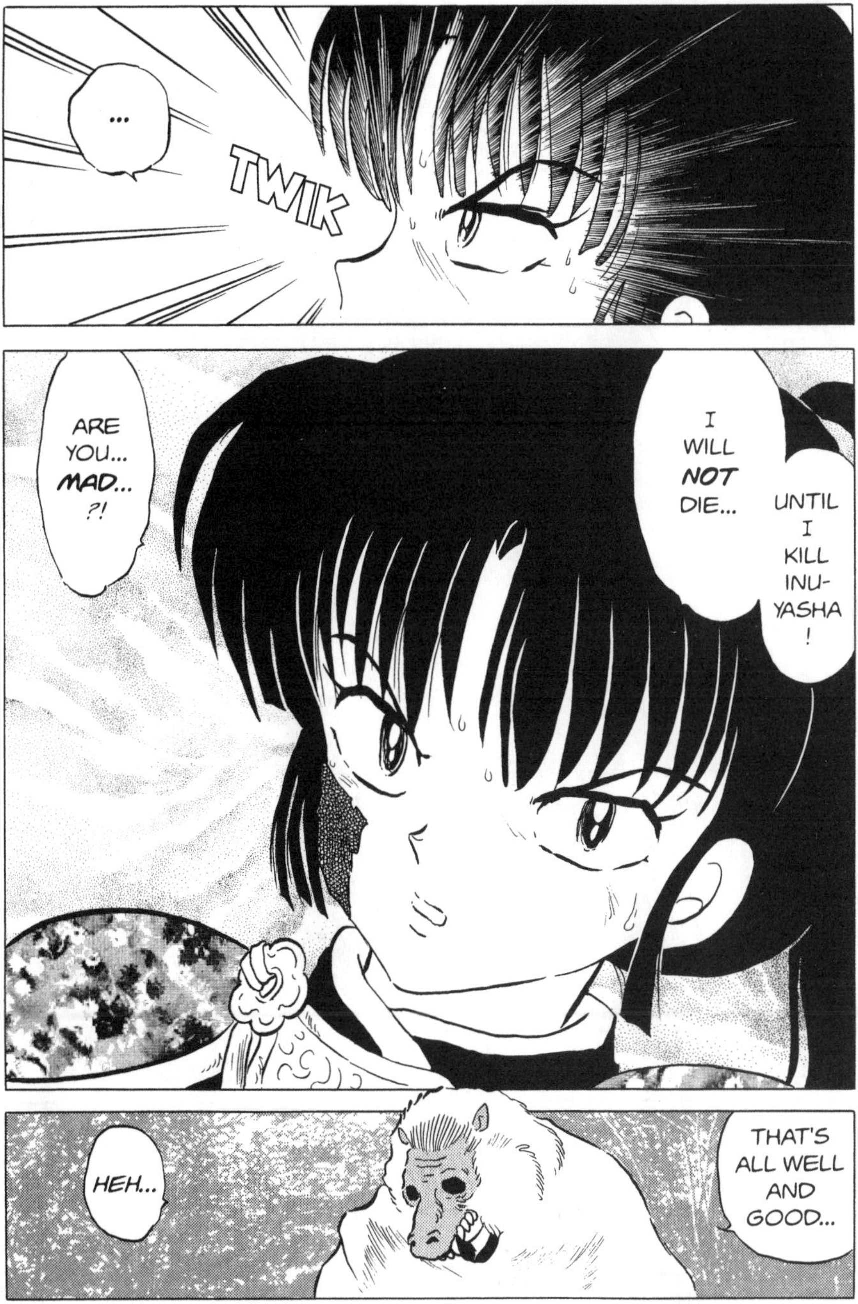
...
TWIK
ARE YOU... MAD... ?!
I WILL NOT DIE...
UNTIL I KILL INU-YASHA!
HEH...
THAT'S ALL WELL AND GOOD...

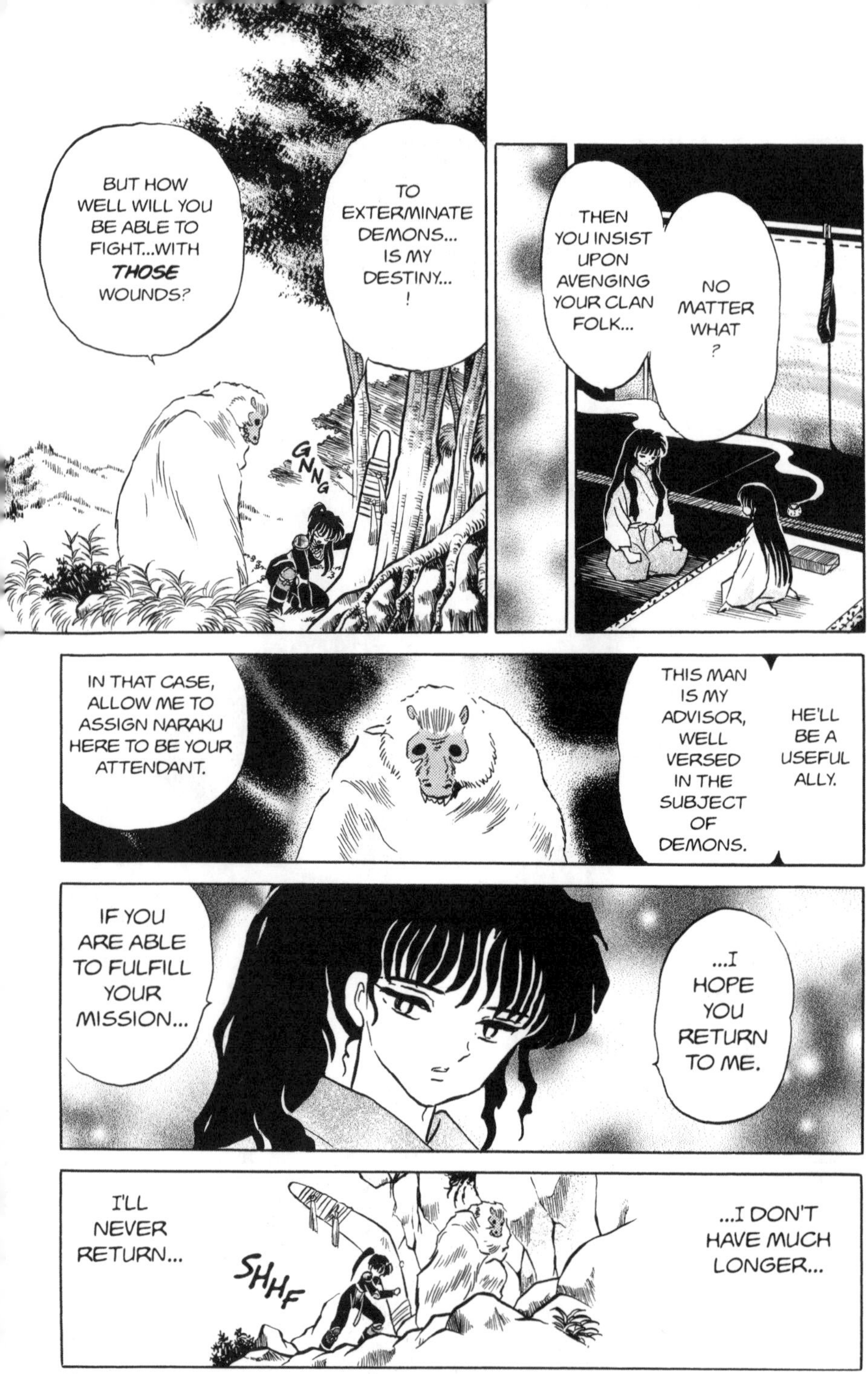
BUT HOW WELL WILL YOU BE ABLE TO FIGHT...WITH ***THOSE*** WOUNDS?
TO EXTERMINATE DEMONS... IS MY DESTINY... !
GNNG
THEN YOU INSIST UPON AVENGING YOUR CLAN FOLK...
NO MATTER WHAT ?
IN THAT CASE, ALLOW ME TO ASSIGN NARAKU HERE TO BE YOUR ATTENDANT.
THIS MAN IS MY ADVISOR, WELL VERSED IN THE SUBJECT OF DEMONS.
HE'LL BE A USEFUL ALLY.
IF YOU ARE ABLE TO FULFILL YOUR MISSION...
...I HOPE YOU RETURN TO ME.
I'LL NEVER RETURN...
SHHF
...I DON'T HAVE MUCH LONGER...

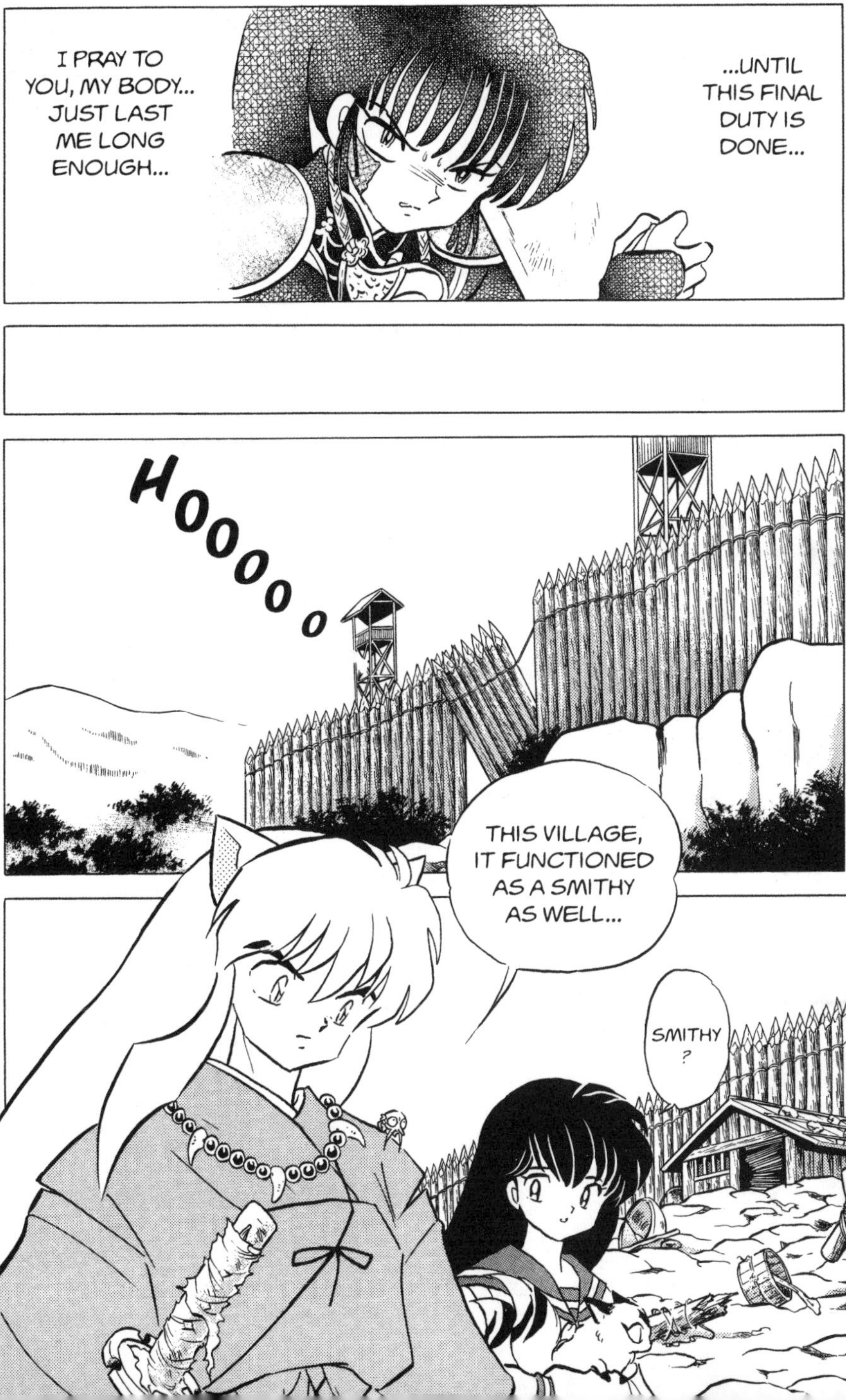
I PRAY TO YOU, MY BODY... JUST LAST ME LONG ENOUGH...
...UNTIL THIS FINAL DUTY IS DONE...
HOOOOOO
THIS VILLAGE, IT FUNCTIONED AS A SMITHY AS WELL...
SMITHY?

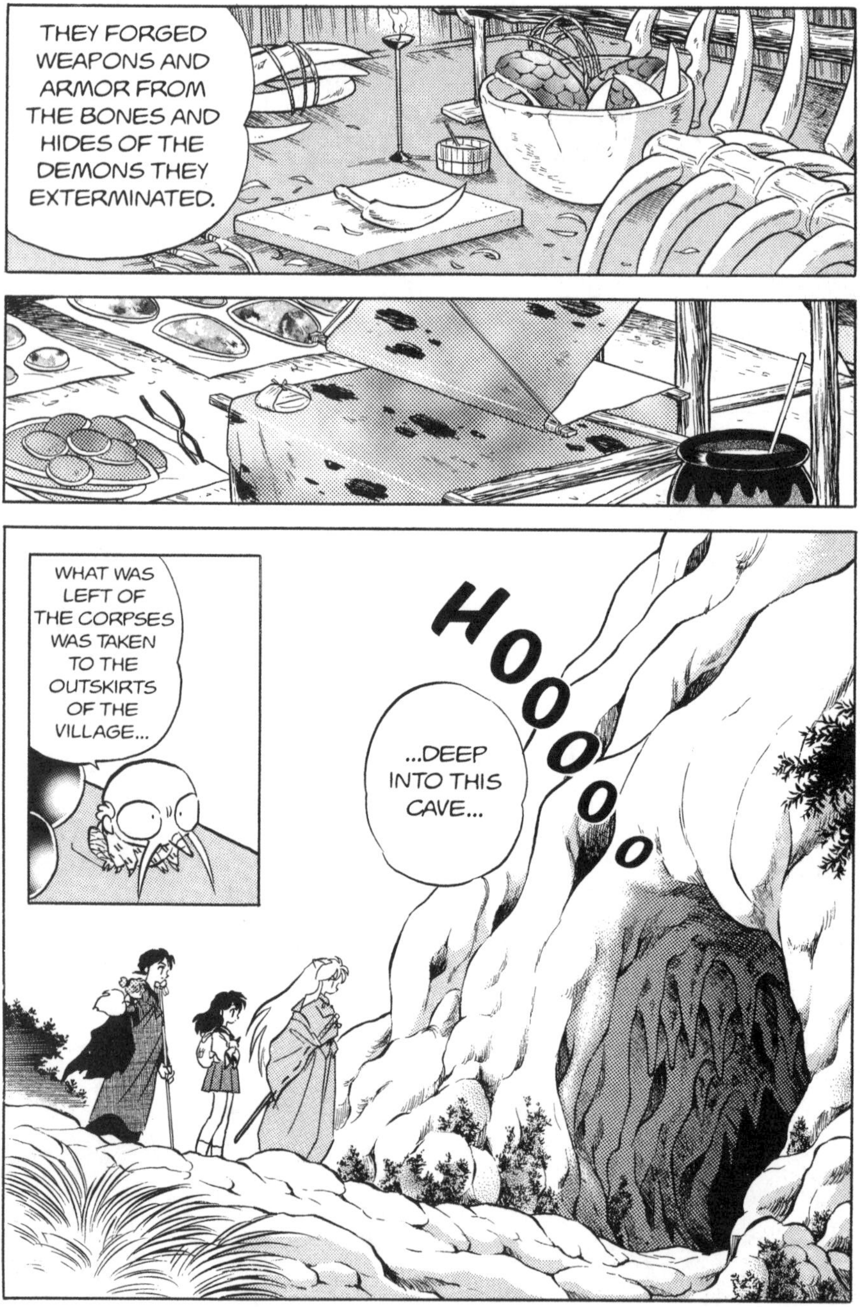
THEY FORGED WEAPONS AND ARMOR FROM THE BONES AND HIDES OF THE DEMONS THEY EXTERMINATED.
WHAT WAS LEFT OF THE CORPSES WAS TAKEN TO THE OUTSKIRTS OF THE VILLAGE...
HOOOOO
...DEEP INTO THIS CAVE...

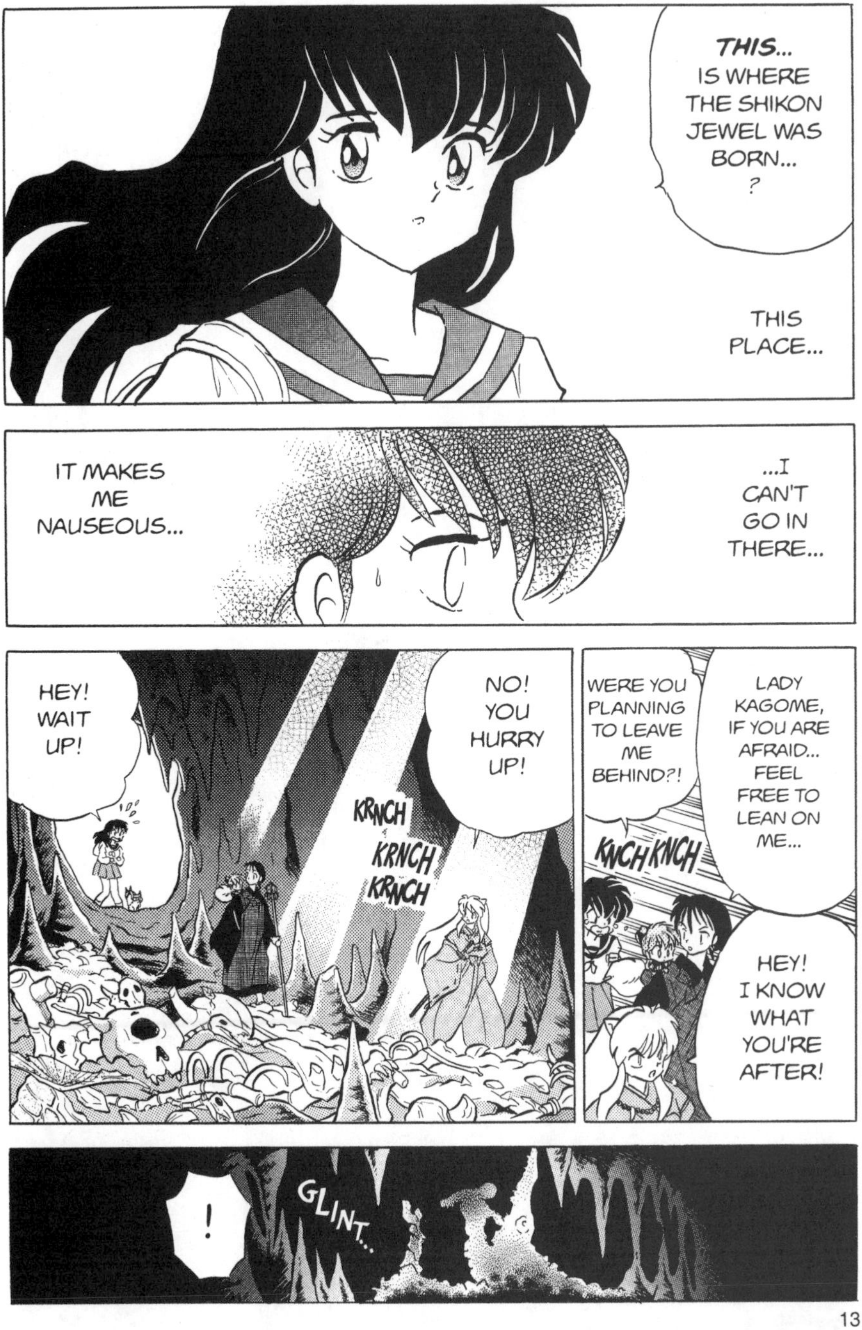
THIS... IS WHERE THE SHIKON JEWEL WAS BORN...?
THIS PLACE...
IT MAKES ME NAUSEOUS...
...I CAN'T GO IN THERE...
HEY! WAIT UP!
NO! YOU HURRY UP!
KRNCH
KRNCH
KRNCH
WERE YOU PLANNING TO LEAVE ME BEHIND?!
LADY KAGOME, IF YOU ARE AFRAID... FEEL FREE TO LEAN ON ME...
KNCH KNCH
HEY! I KNOW WHAT YOU'RE AFTER!
!
GLINT...

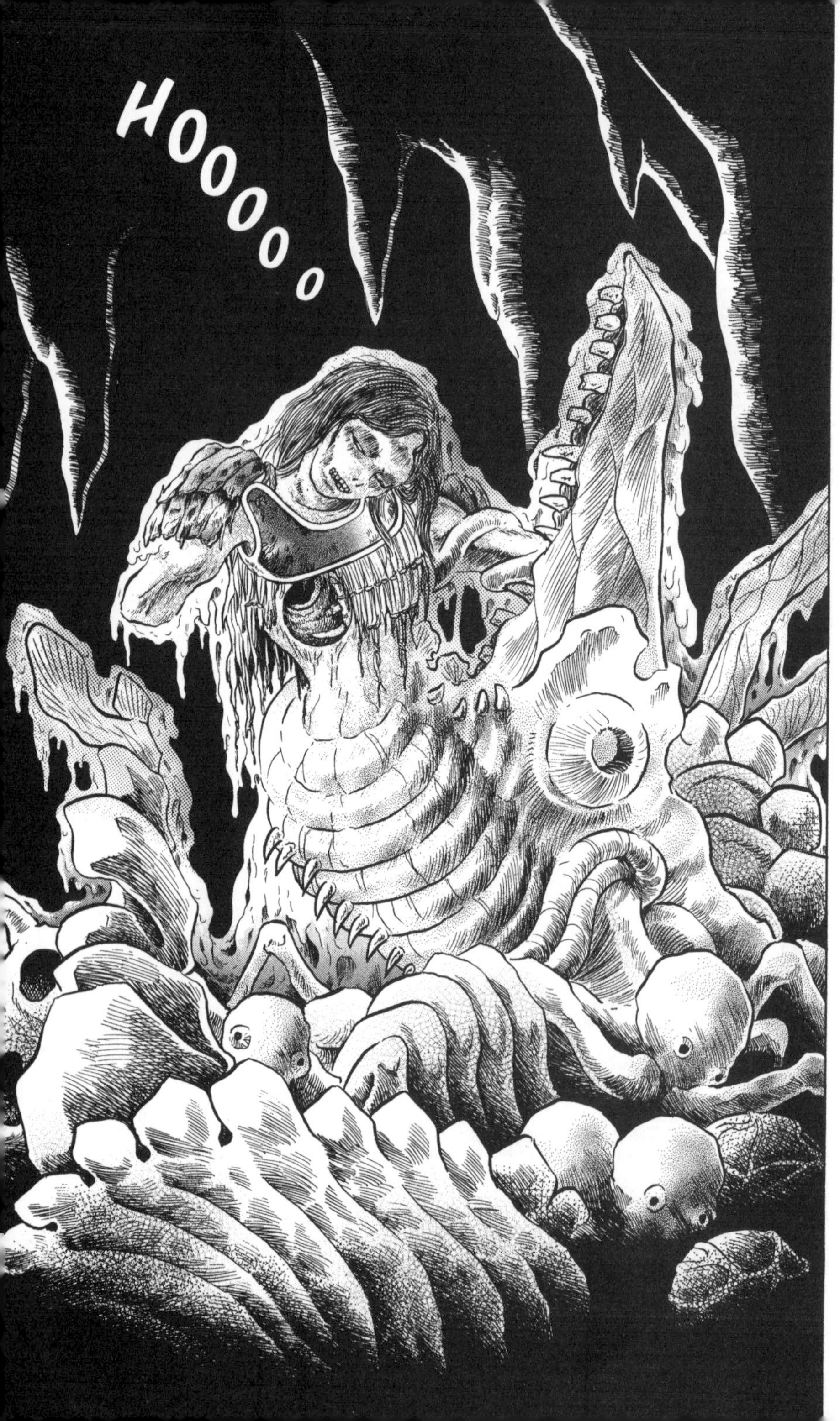
HOOOOOO

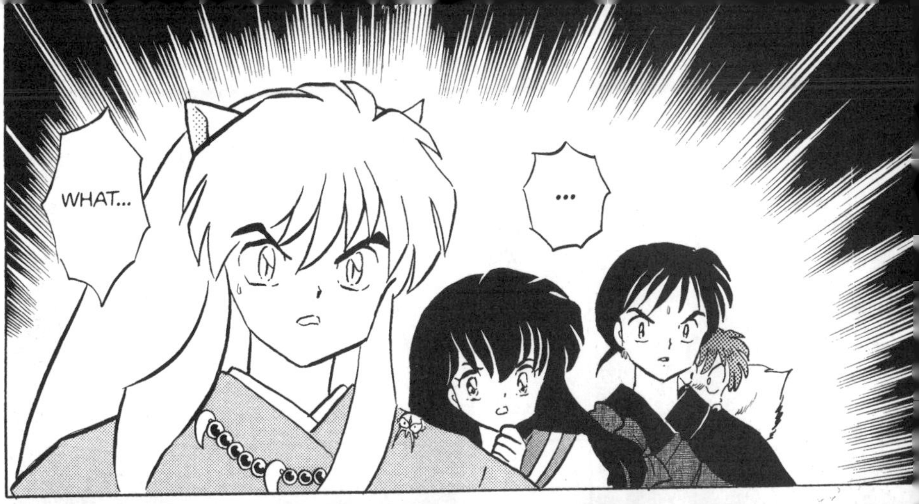
WHAT...
...

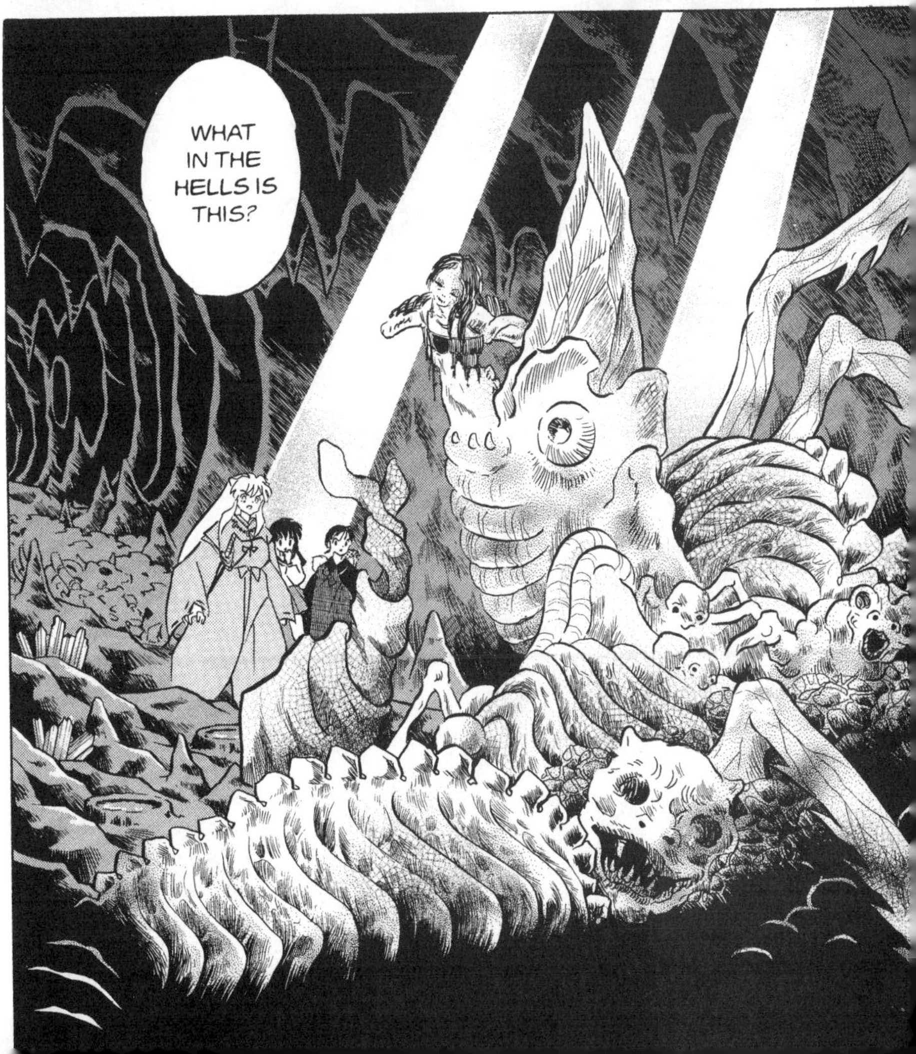
WHAT IN THE HELLS IS THIS?

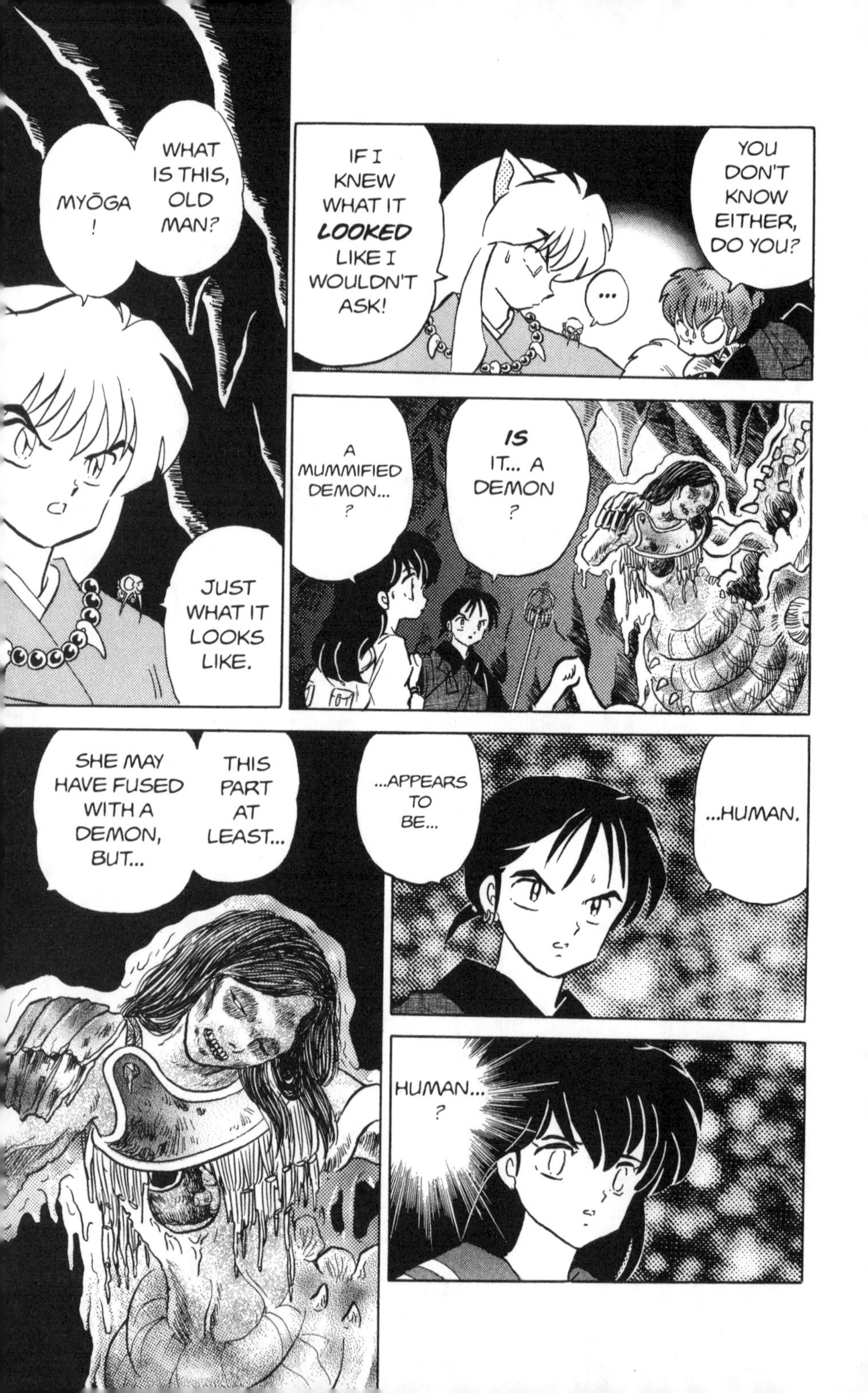
MYŌGA!
WHAT IS THIS, OLD MAN?
JUST WHAT IT LOOKS LIKE.
IF I KNEW WHAT IT LOOKED LIKE I WOULDN'T ASK!
...
YOU DON'T KNOW EITHER, DO YOU?
A MUMMIFIED DEMON...?
IS IT... A DEMON?
SHE MAY HAVE FUSED WITH A DEMON, BUT...
THIS PART AT LEAST...
...APPEARS TO BE...
...HUMAN.
HUMAN...?

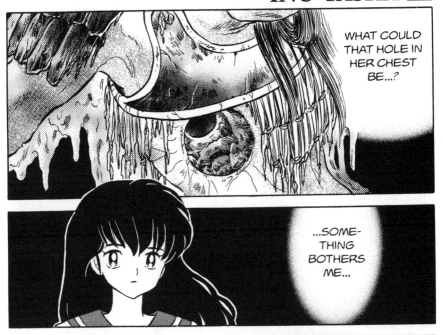

WHAT COULD THAT HOLE IN HER CHEST BE...?

...SOME- THING BOTHERS ME...

IN THE END, IT SEEMS...

WE WILL NEED TO ASK A VILLAGER AFTER ALL.

CRUMPLE

ARE YOU IN PAIN, SANGO... ?

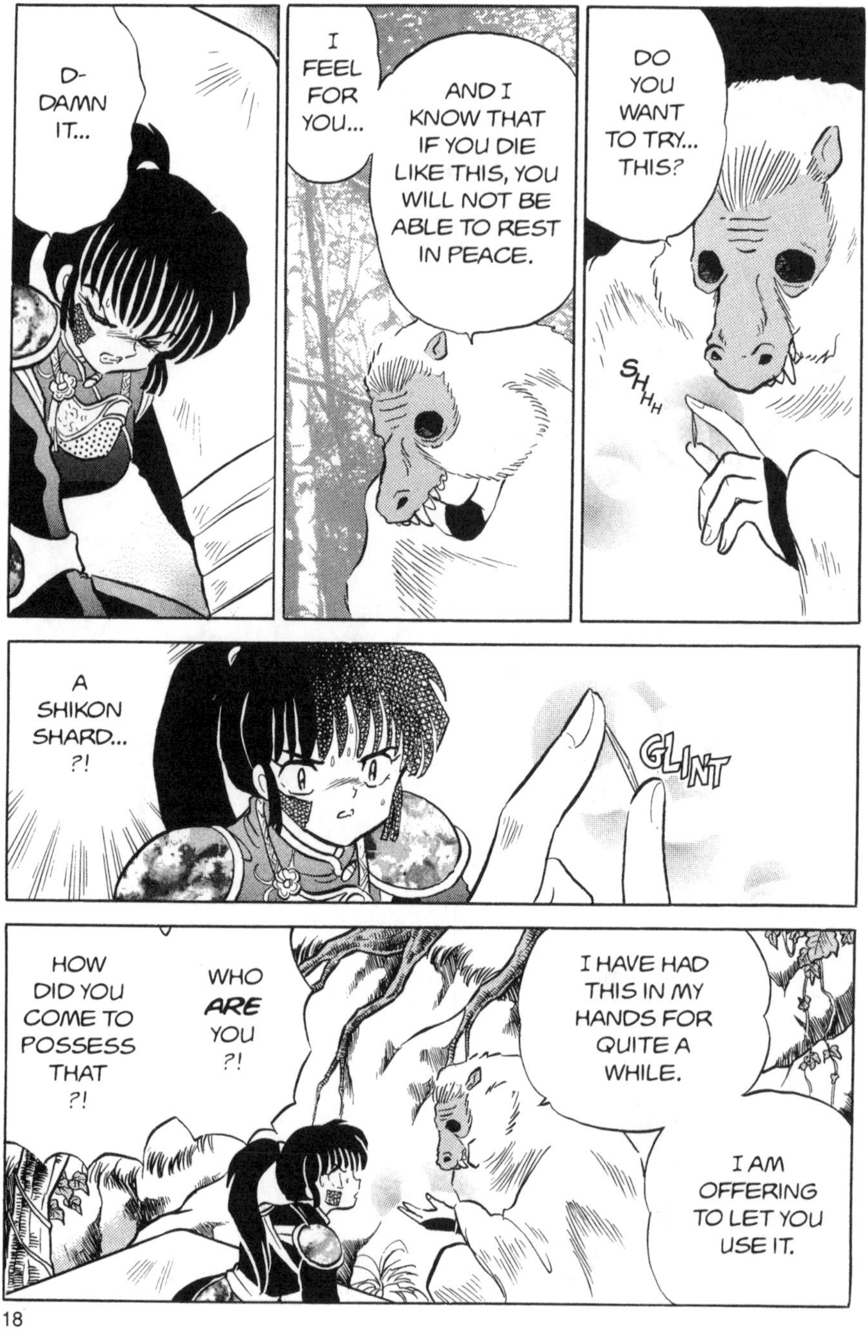
D-DAMN IT...
I FEEL FOR YOU...
AND I KNOW THAT IF YOU DIE LIKE THIS, YOU WILL NOT BE ABLE TO REST IN PEACE.
DO YOU WANT TO TRY... THIS?
SHHH
A SHIKON SHARD...?!
GLINT
HOW DID YOU COME TO POSSESS THAT?!
WHO **ARE** YOU?!
I HAVE HAD THIS IN MY HANDS FOR QUITE A WHILE.
I AM OFFERING TO LET YOU USE IT.

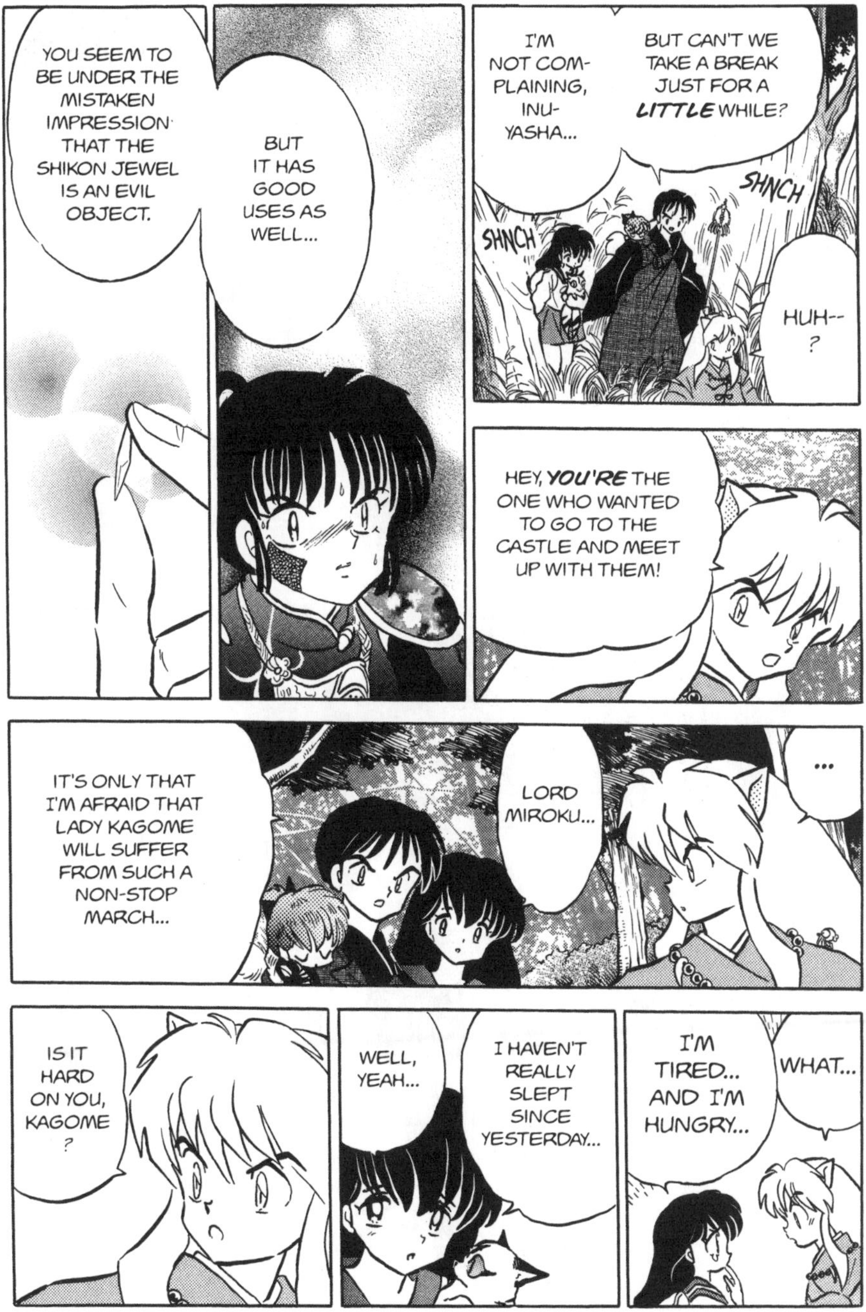
YOU SEEM TO BE UNDER THE MISTAKEN IMPRESSION THAT THE SHIKON JEWEL IS AN EVIL OBJECT.
BUT IT HAS GOOD USES AS WELL...
I'M NOT COM-PLAINING, INU-YASHA...
BUT CAN'T WE TAKE A BREAK JUST FOR A LITTLE WHILE?
SHNCH
SHNCH
HUH-- ?
HEY, YOU'RE THE ONE WHO WANTED TO GO TO THE CASTLE AND MEET UP WITH THEM!
IT'S ONLY THAT I'M AFRAID THAT LADY KAGOME WILL SUFFER FROM SUCH A NON-STOP MARCH...
LORD MIROKU...
...
IS IT HARD ON YOU, KAGOME ?
WELL, YEAH...
I HAVEN'T REALLY SLEPT SINCE YESTERDAY...
I'M TIRED... AND I'M HUNGRY...
WHAT...

WHAT A SPOILED LITTLE PRINCESS!

HEY!

I'VE BEEN HOLDING MY OWN PRETTY WELL UNTIL NOW, YOU KNOW!

BUT I **AM** JUST A HUMAN!

TRYING TO KEEP UP WITH YOUR **DEMON** POWER IS GOING TO KILL ME!

YOU MIGHT SHOW A LITTLE MORE CARE FOR HER, INU-YASHA.

IT ISN'T ENOUGH MERELY TO **SAY** YOU LIKE HER.

CLAP CLAP CLAP

EH ?!

LORD INU-YASHA...HOW LONG HAVE THE TWO OF YOU BEEN **THAT WAY** ?!

OH, SHUT UP!

TWIK

KSSSHHH

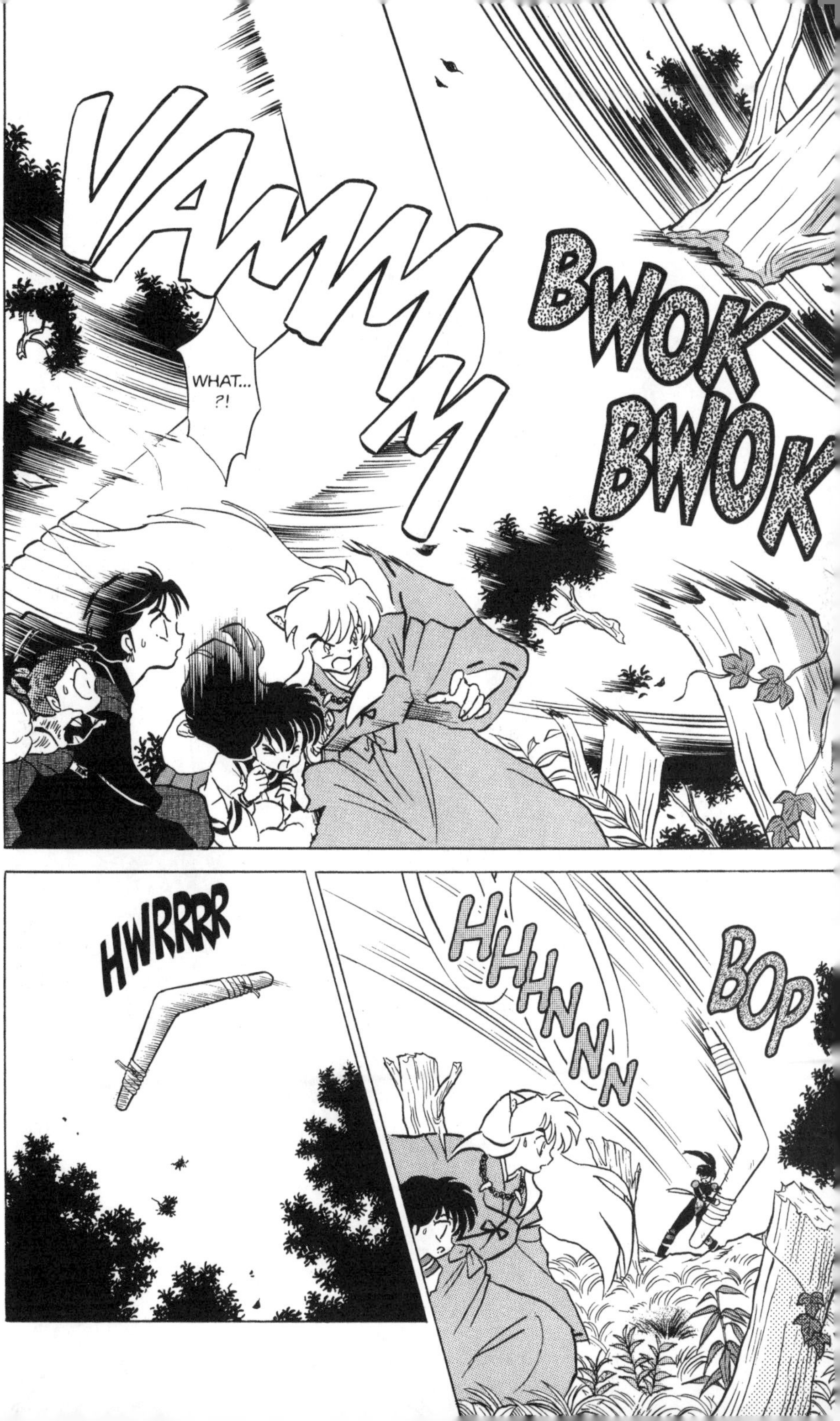
VAMMMM
WHAT... ?!
BWOK BWOK
HWRRRR
HHHHNNNN
BOP

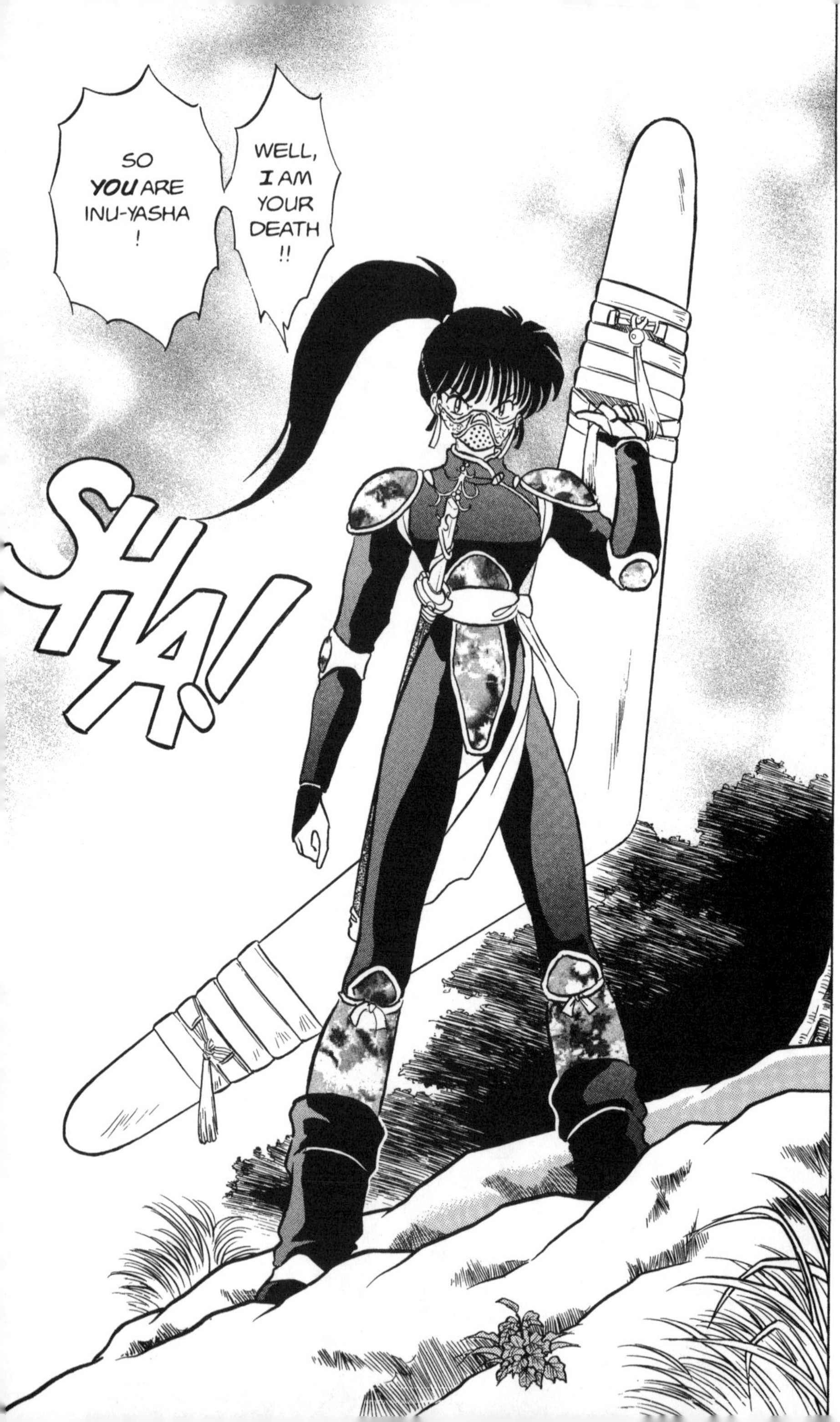
SO **YOU** ARE INU-YASHA !
WELL, **I** AM YOUR DEATH !!
SHA!

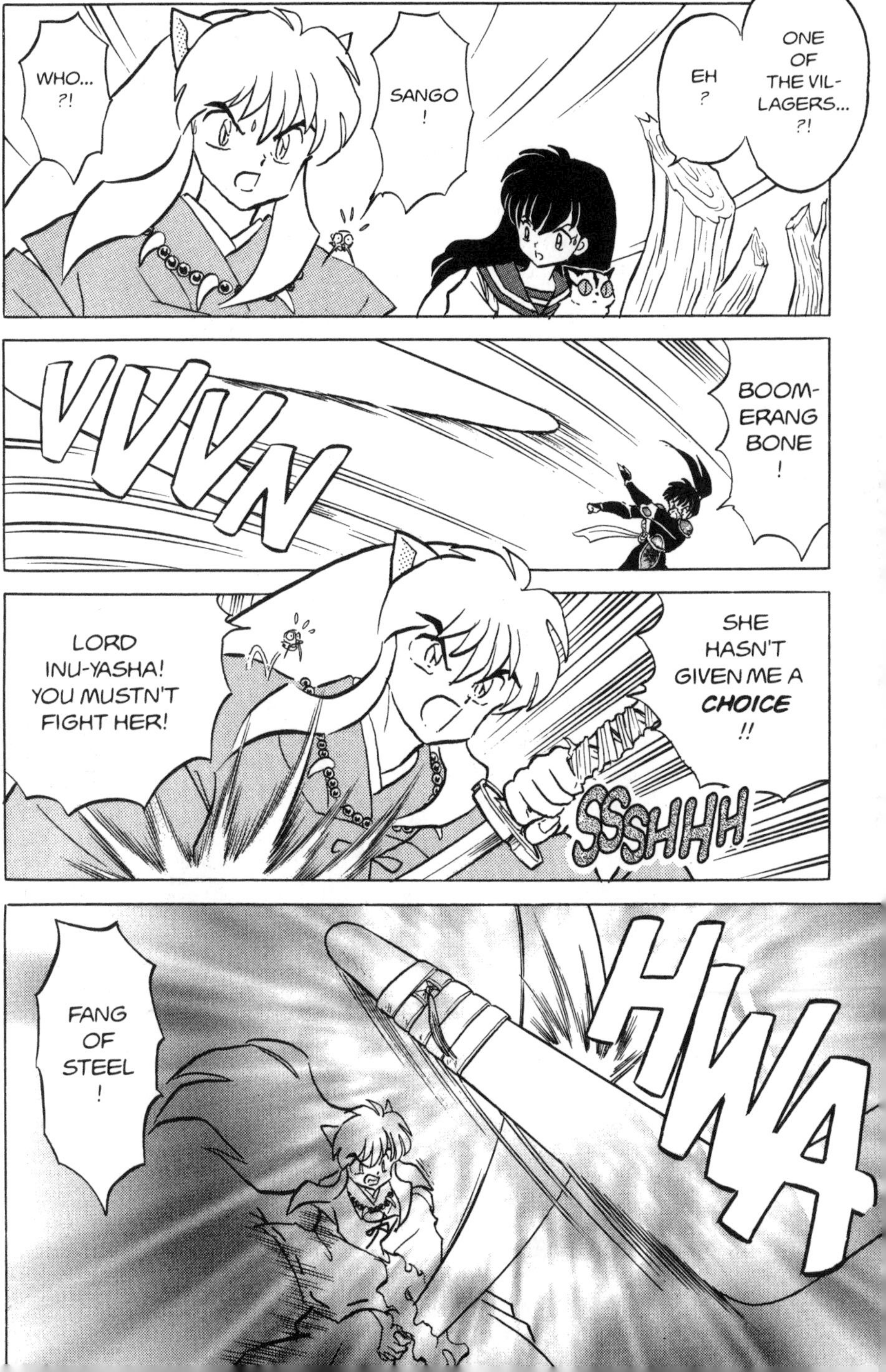
WHO... ?!
SANGO !
EH ?
ONE OF THE VIL- LAGERS... ?!
VVVN
BOOM- ERANG BONE !
LORD INU-YASHA! YOU MUSTN'T FIGHT HER!
SHE HASN'T GIVEN ME A CHOICE !!
SSSHHH
FANG OF STEEL !
HWA

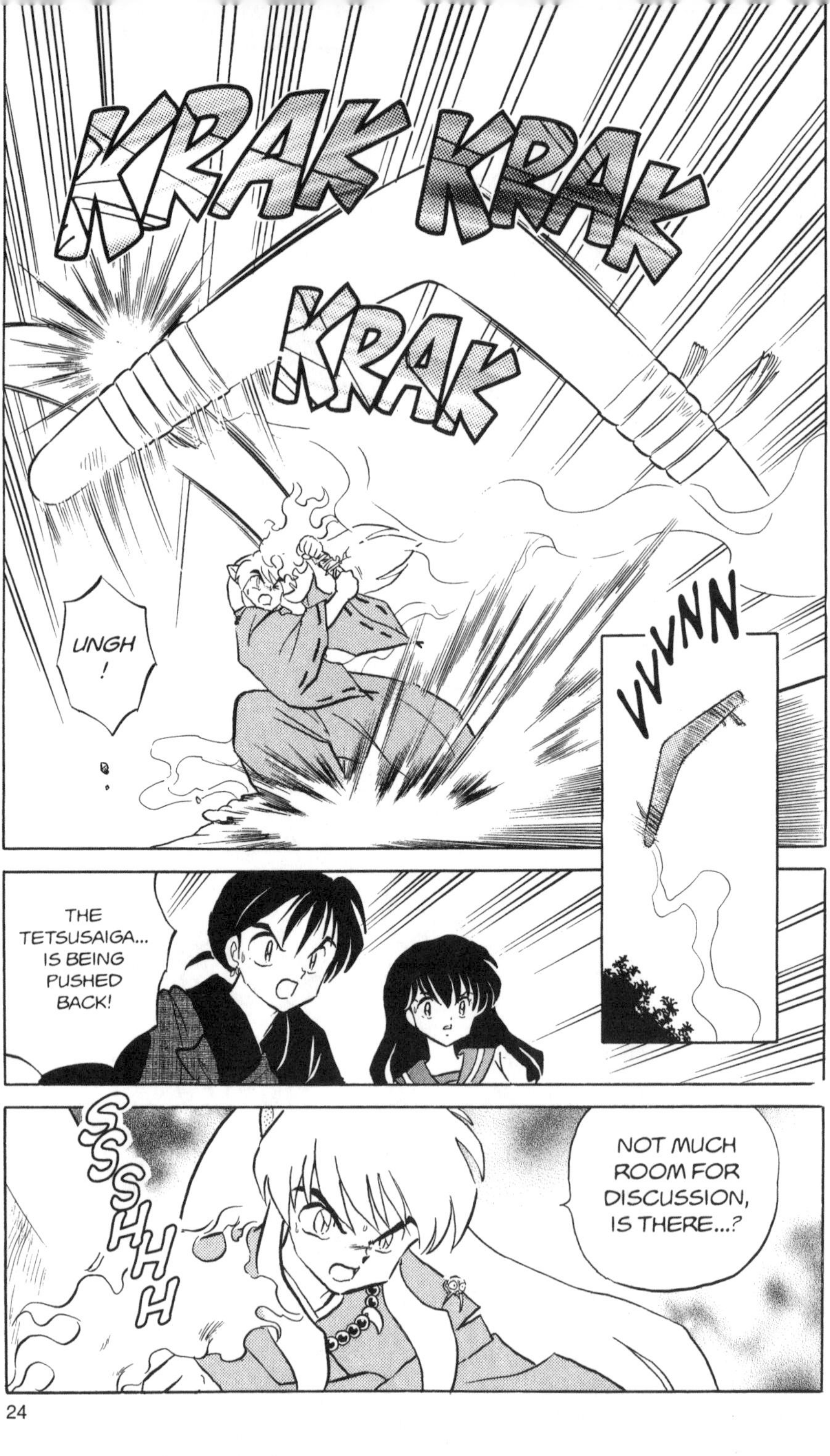
KRAK KRAK
KRAK
UNGH!
THE TETSUSAIGA... IS BEING PUSHED BACK!
VVVNN
SSSHHHH
NOT MUCH ROOM FOR DISCUSSION, IS THERE...?

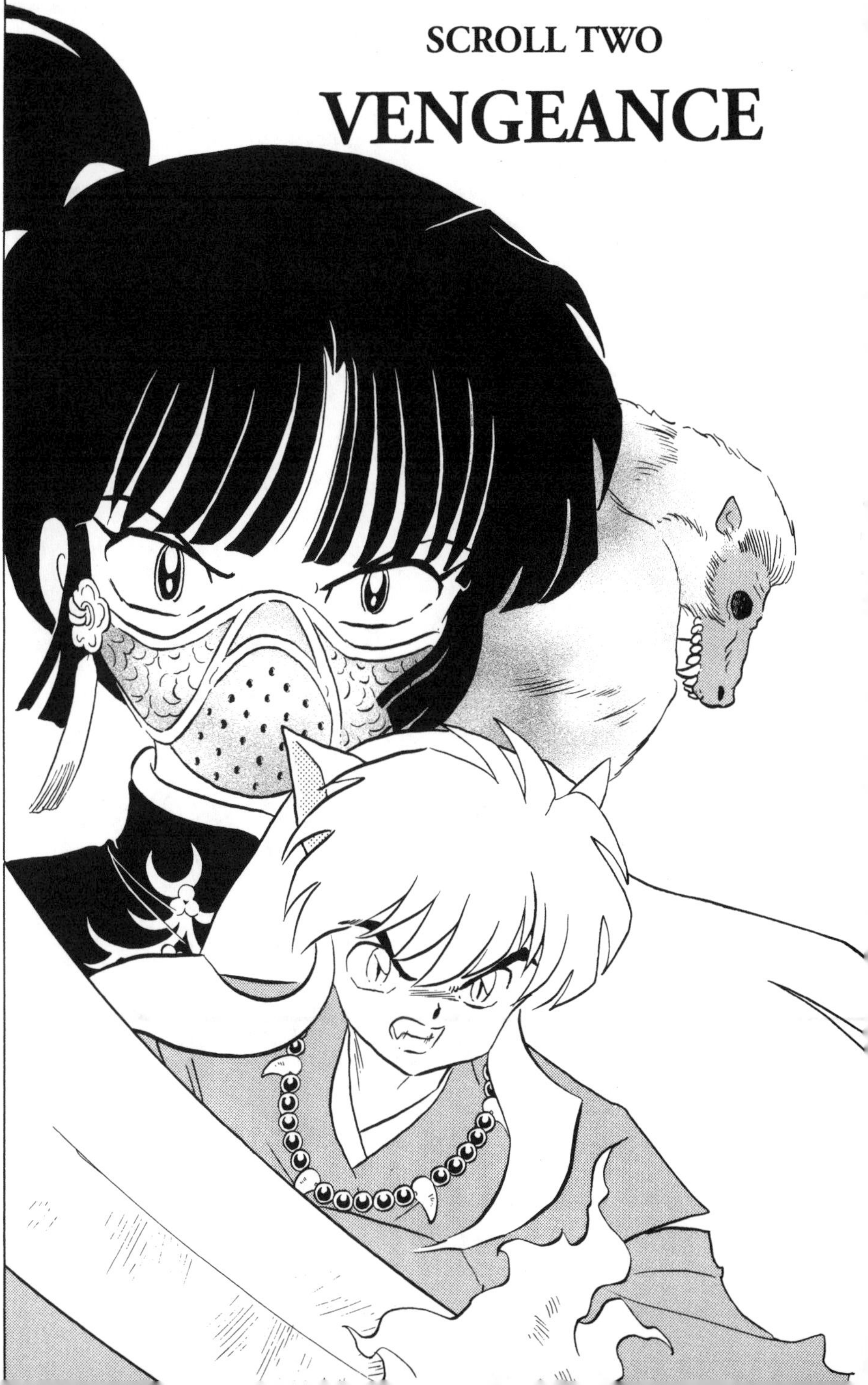
SCROLL TWO
VENGEANCE

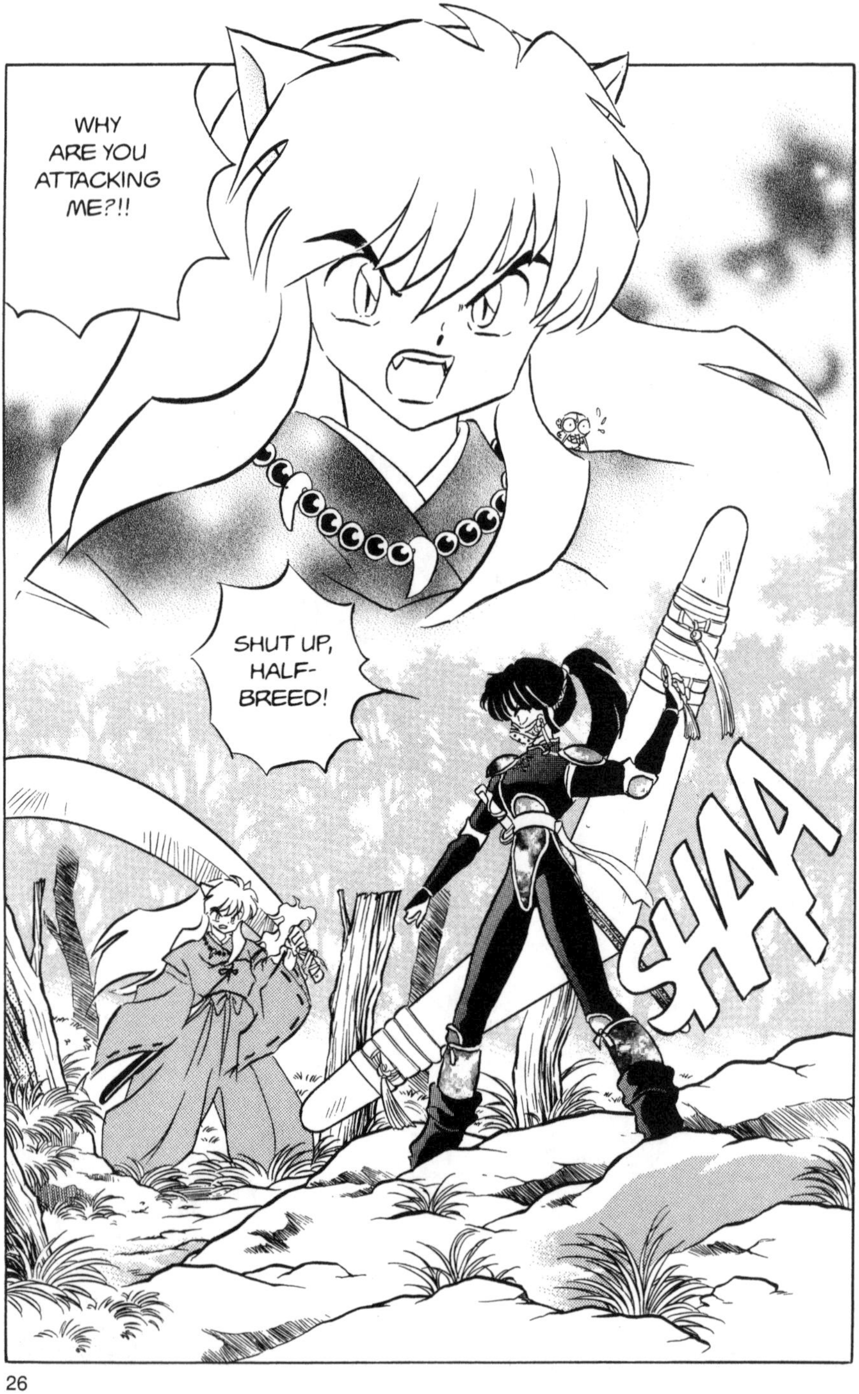
WHY ARE YOU ATTACKING ME?!!
SHUT UP, HALF-BREED!
SHAA

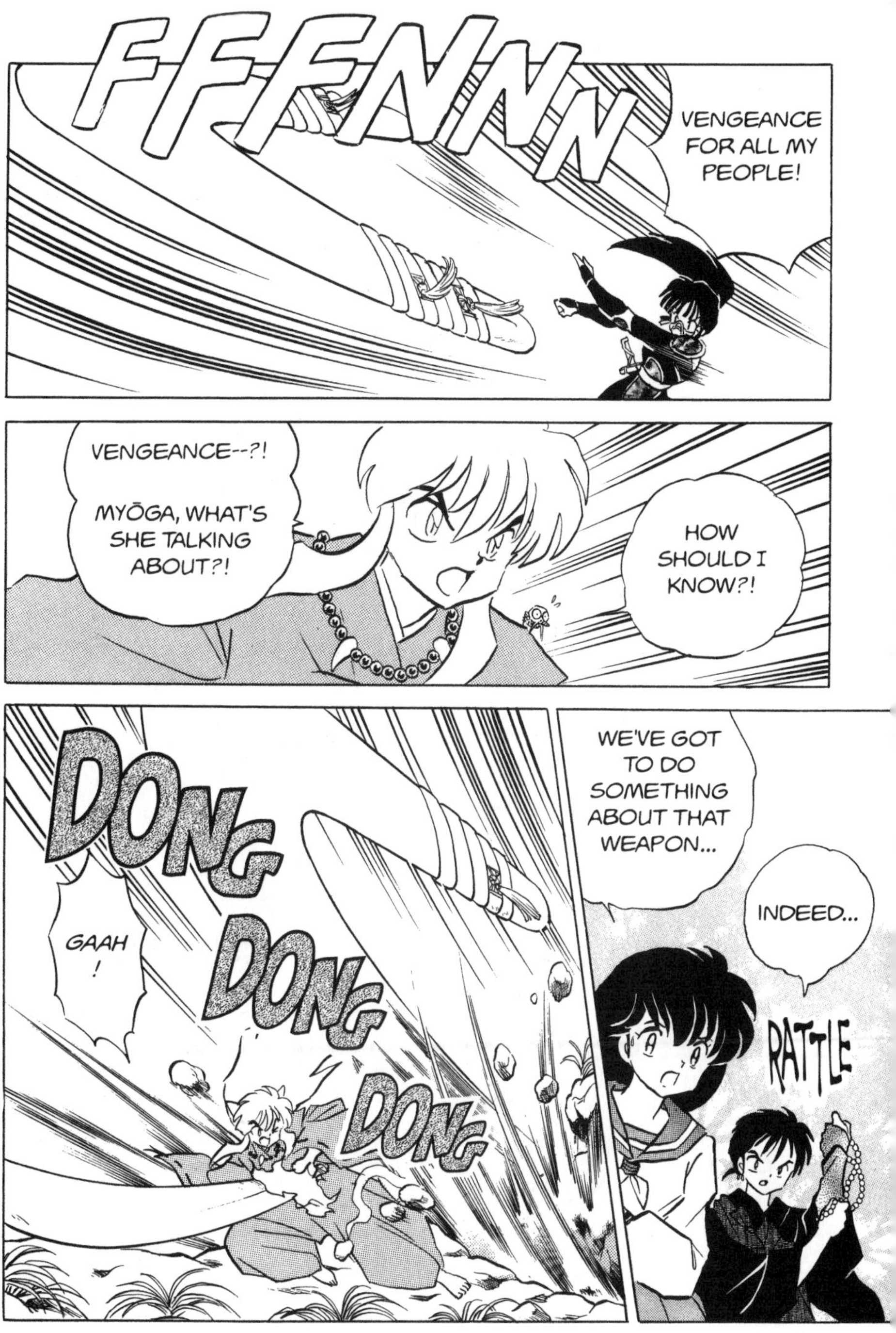
FFFNNN
VENGEANCE FOR ALL MY PEOPLE!
VENGEANCE--?!
MYŌGA, WHAT'S SHE TALKING ABOUT?!
HOW SHOULD I KNOW?!
DONG
GAAH !
DONG
DONG
WE'VE GOT TO DO SOMETHING ABOUT THAT WEAPON...
INDEED...
RATTLE

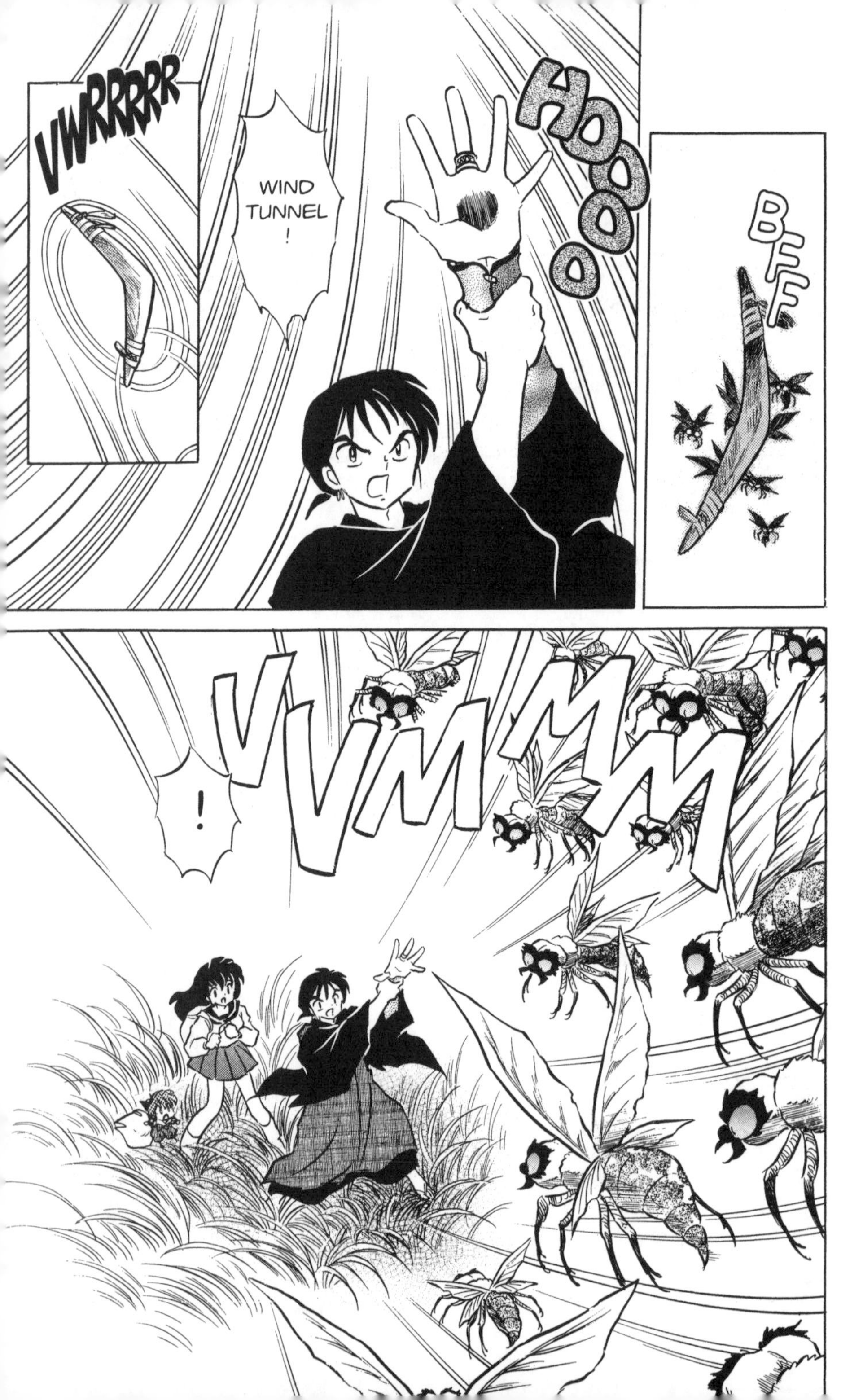
VWRRRRR
WIND TUNNEL !
HOOOOO
BFF
!
VVMMM

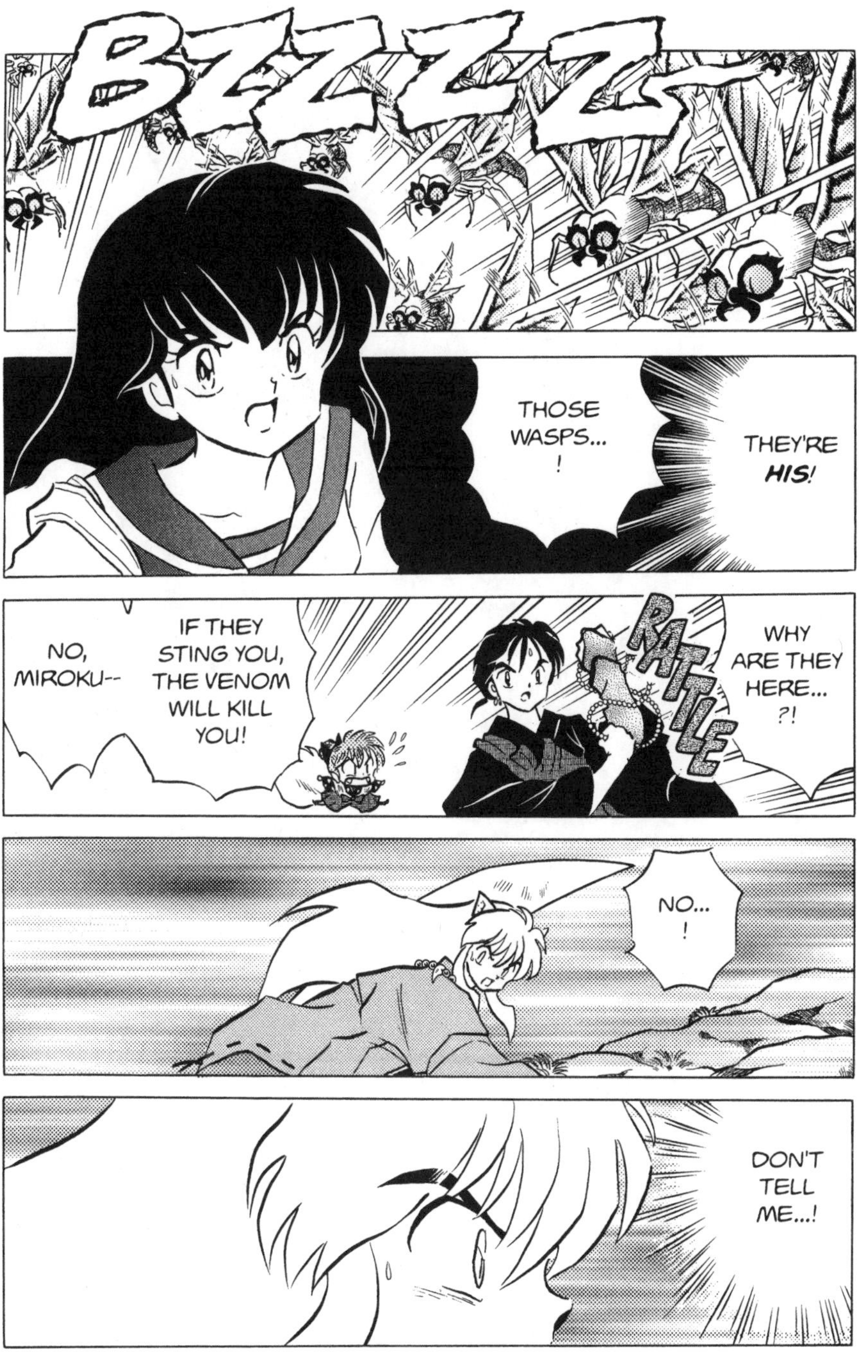
BZZZZ
THOSE WASPS... !
THEY'RE HIS!
NO, MIROKU--
IF THEY STING YOU, THE VENOM WILL KILL YOU!
RATTLE
WHY ARE THEY HERE... ?!
NO... !
DON'T TELL ME...!

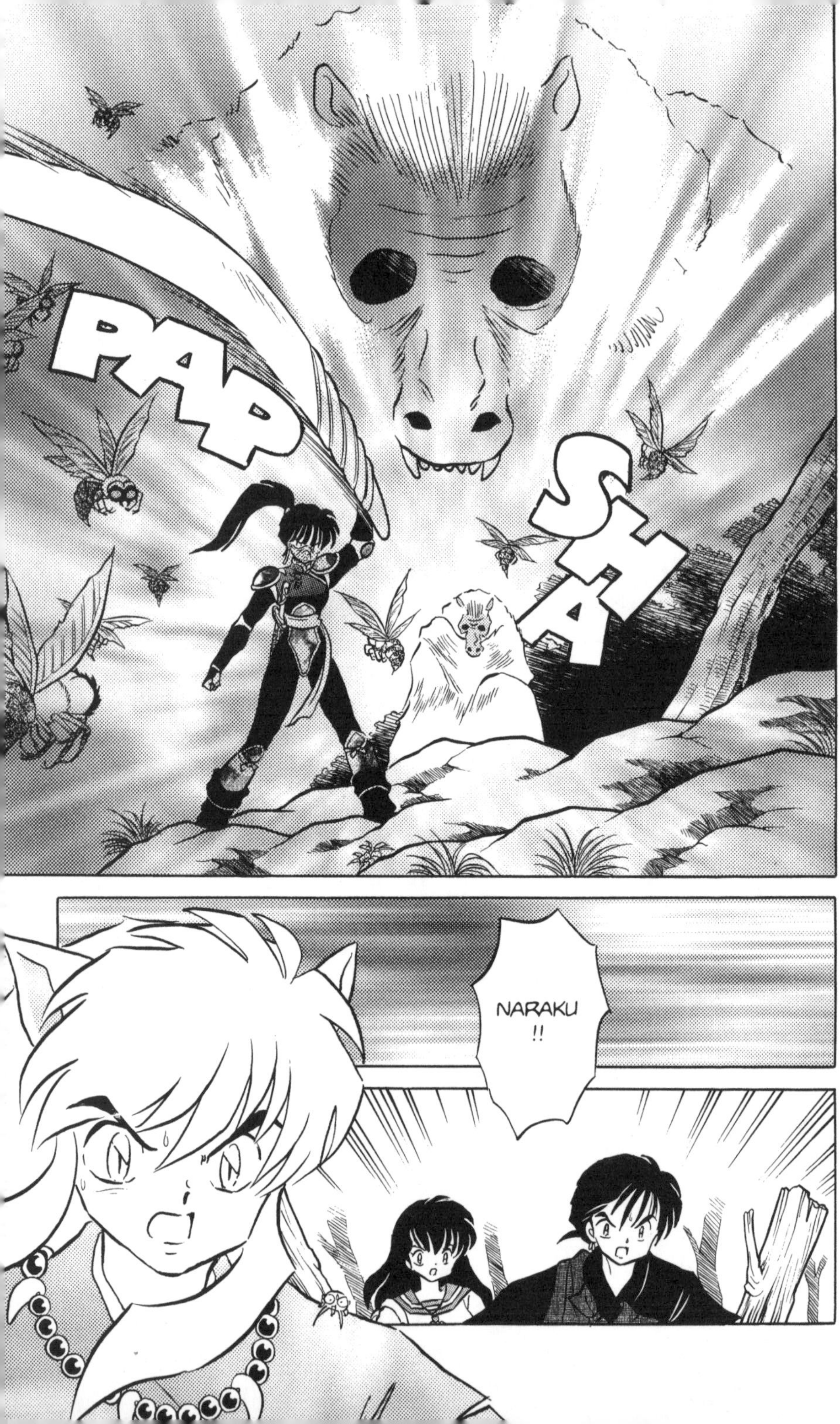
PAP
SHA
NARAKU !!

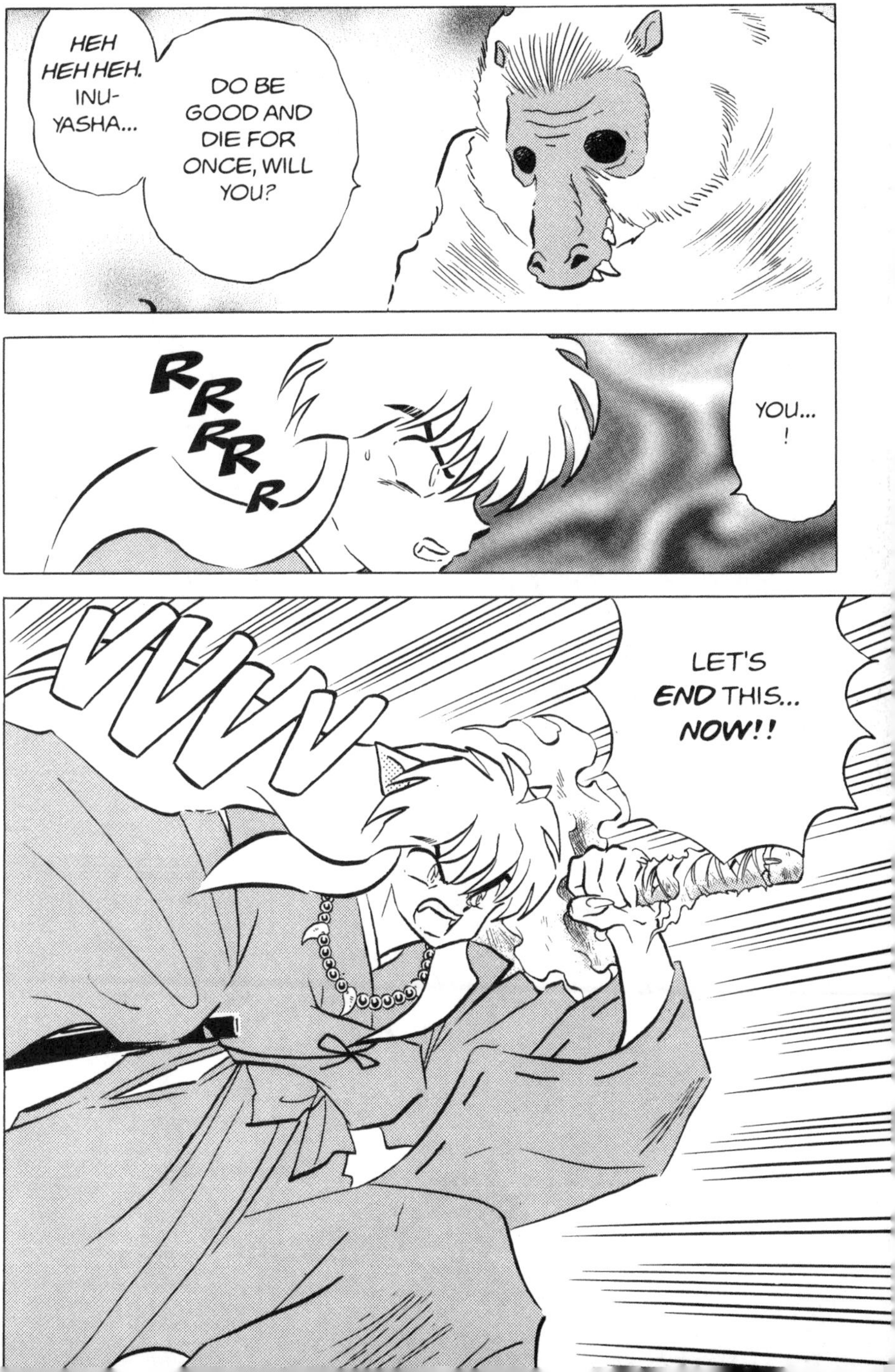
HEH HEH HEH. INU-YASHA...
DO BE GOOD AND DIE FOR ONCE, WILL YOU?
RRRRR
YOU... !
VVVV
LET'S **END** THIS... **NOW!!**

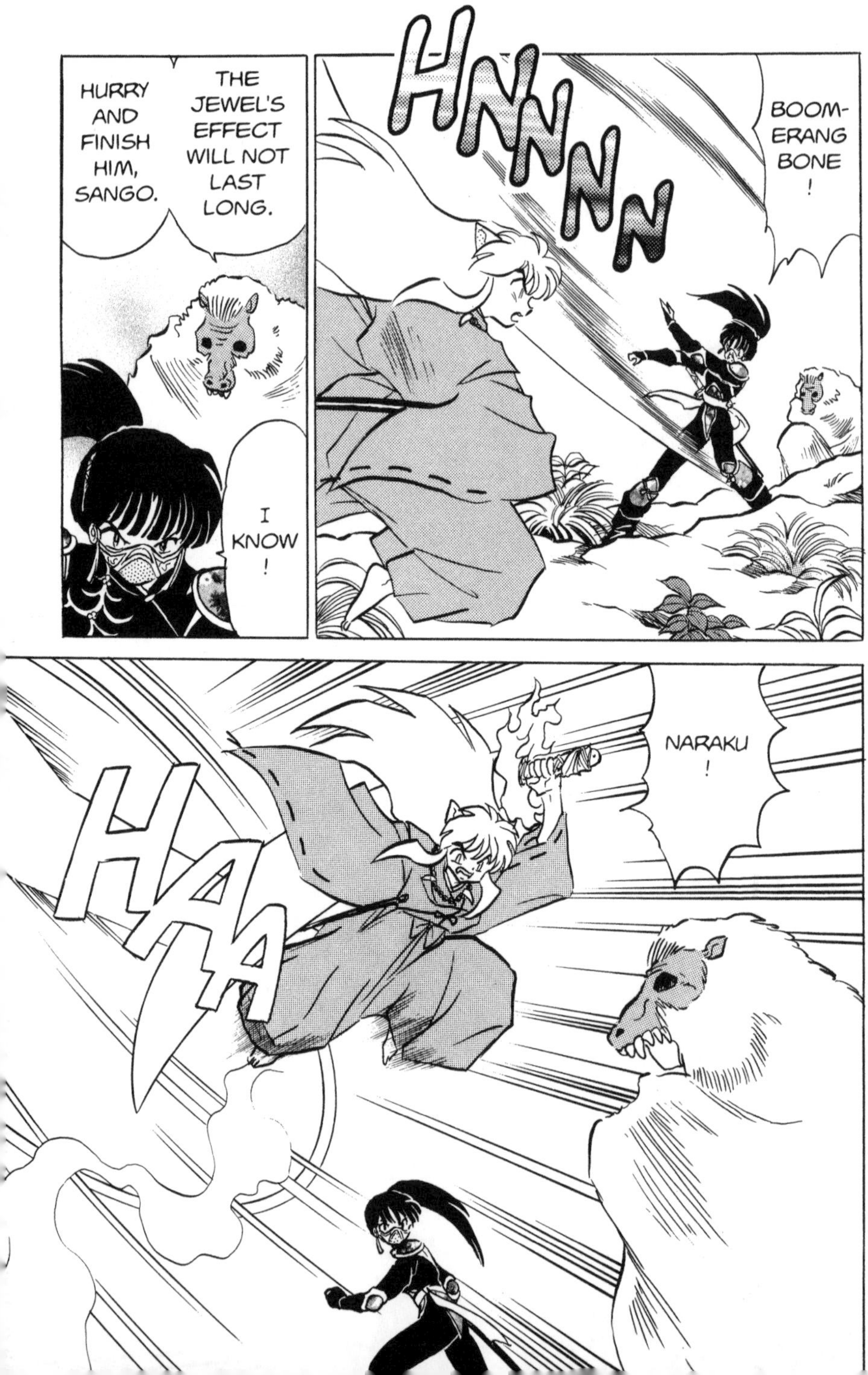
HURRY AND FINISH HIM, SANGO.
THE JEWEL'S EFFECT WILL NOT LAST LONG.
I KNOW!
HNNNNN
BOOM-ERANG BONE!
NARAKU!
HAA

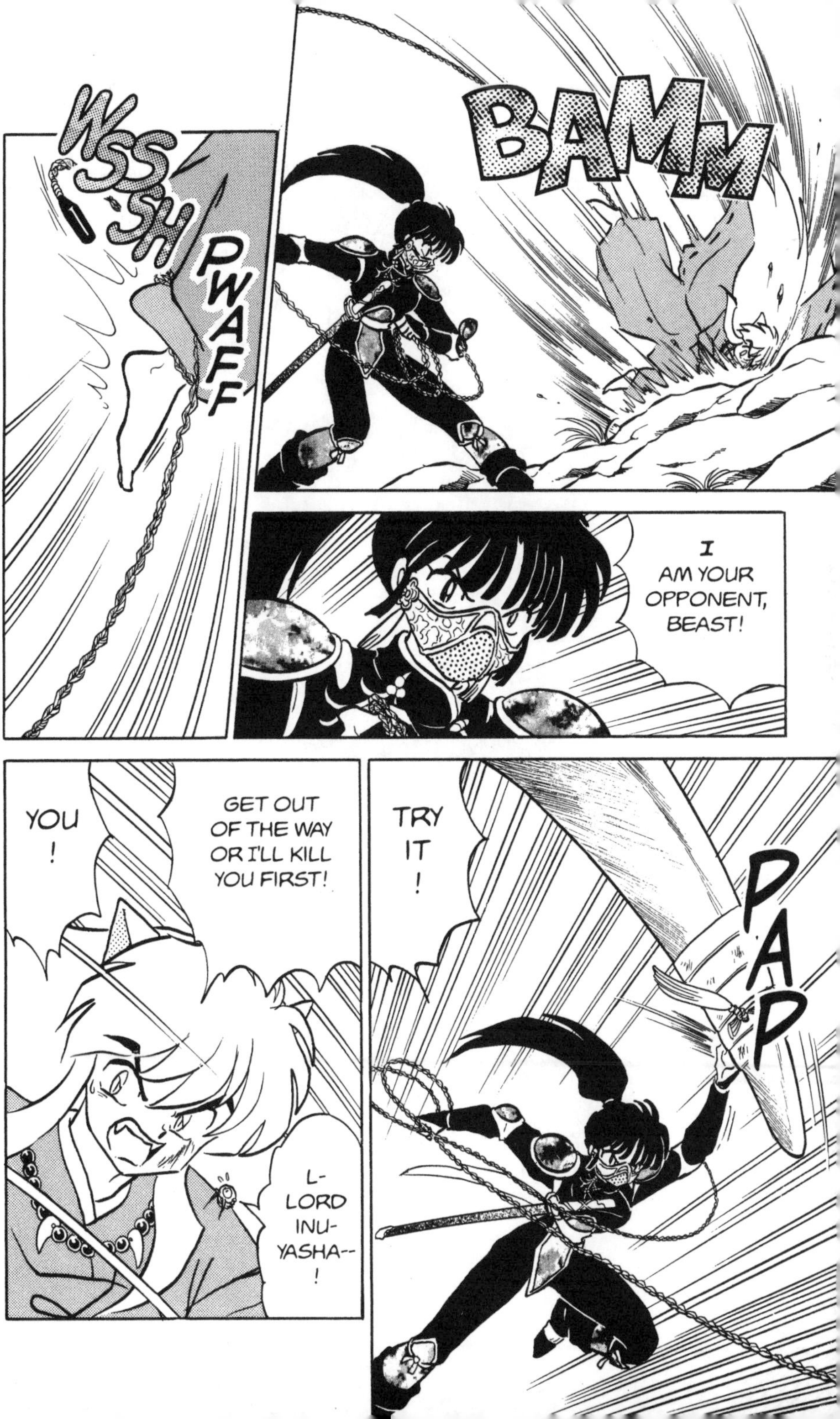
WSSSH
PWAFF
BAMM
I AM YOUR OPPONENT, BEAST!
YOU!
GET OUT OF THE WAY OR I'LL KILL YOU FIRST!
L-LORD INU-YASHA--!
TRY IT!
PAP

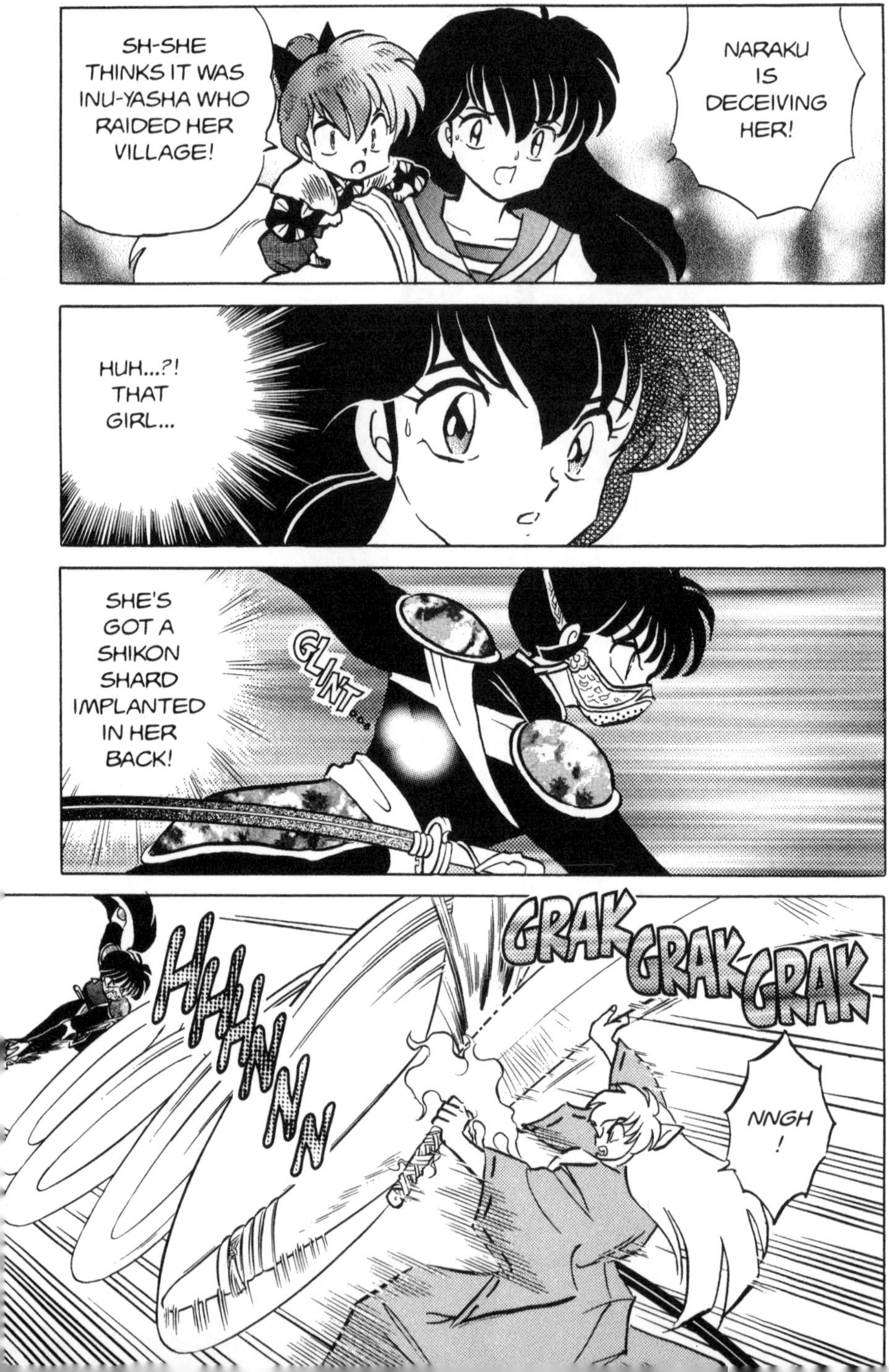
SH-SHE THINKS IT WAS INU-YASHA WHO RAIDED HER VILLAGE!
NARAKU IS DECEIVING HER!
HUH...?! THAT GIRL...
SHE'S GOT A SHIKON SHARD IMPLANTED IN HER BACK!
GLINT
HHHNNNN
GRAK GRAK GRAK
NNGH!

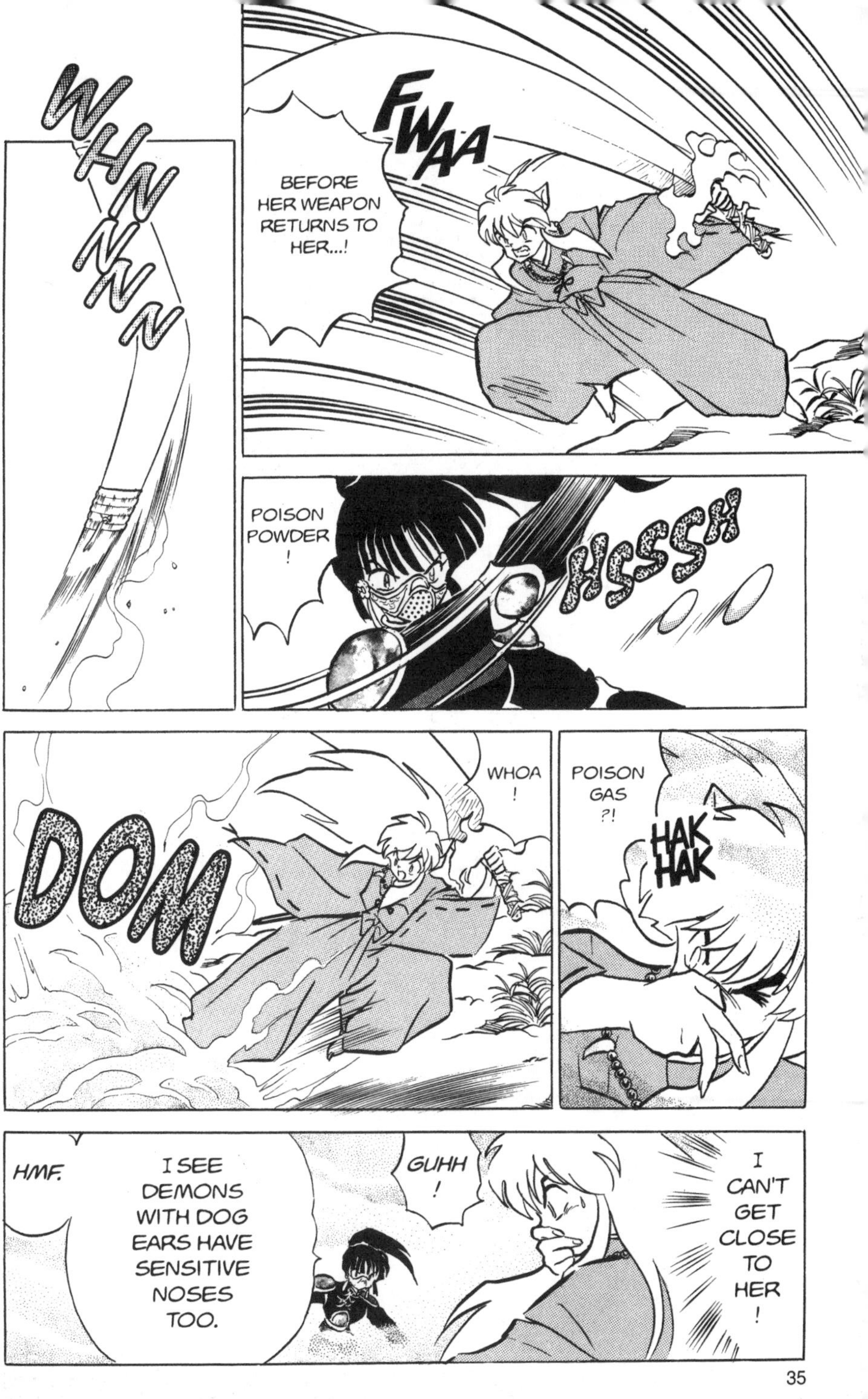
WHNNNNN
FWAA
BEFORE HER WEAPON RETURNS TO HER...!
POISON POWDER!
HSSSH
DOM
WHOA!
POISON GAS?!
HAK HAK
HMF.
I SEE DEMONS WITH DOG EARS HAVE SENSITIVE NOSES TOO.
GUHH!
I CAN'T GET CLOSE TO HER!

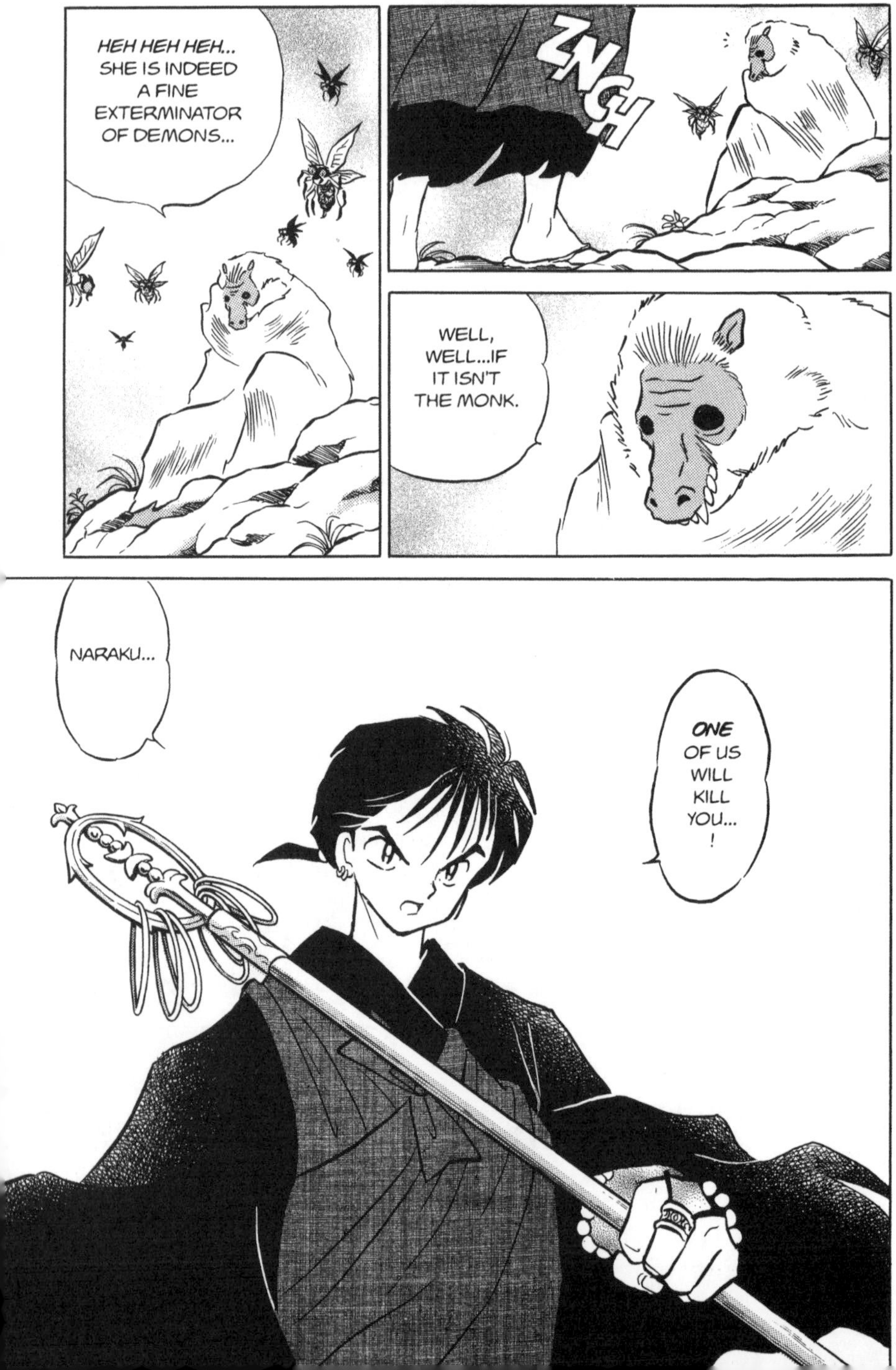
HEH HEH HEH... SHE IS INDEED A FINE EXTERMINATOR OF DEMONS...
ZNCH
WELL, WELL...IF IT ISN'T THE MONK.
NARAKU...
ONE OF US WILL KILL YOU...!

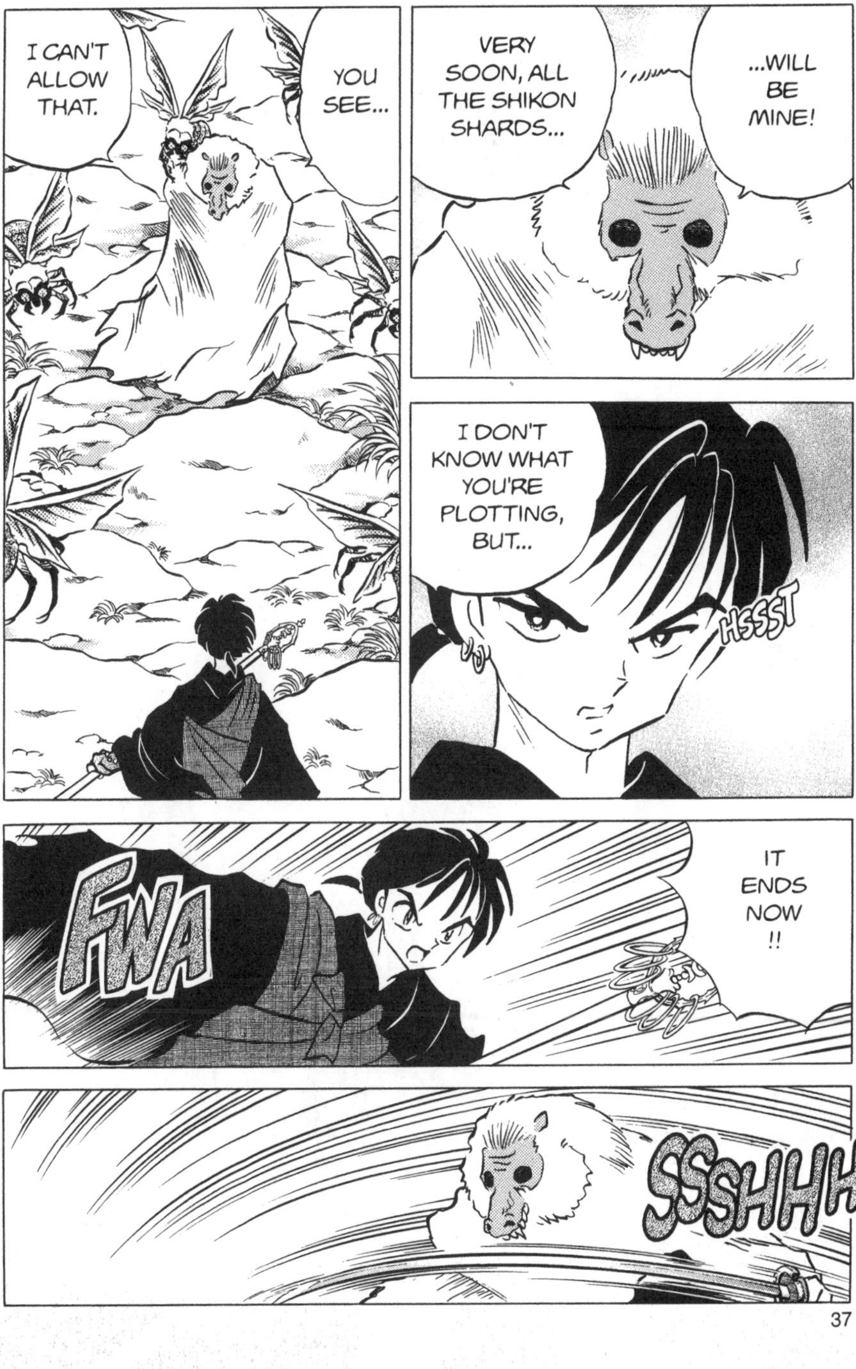
I CAN'T ALLOW THAT.
YOU SEE...
VERY SOON, ALL THE SHIKON SHARDS...
...WILL BE MINE!
I DON'T KNOW WHAT YOU'RE PLOTTING, BUT...
HSSST
FWA
IT ENDS NOW !!
SSSHHH

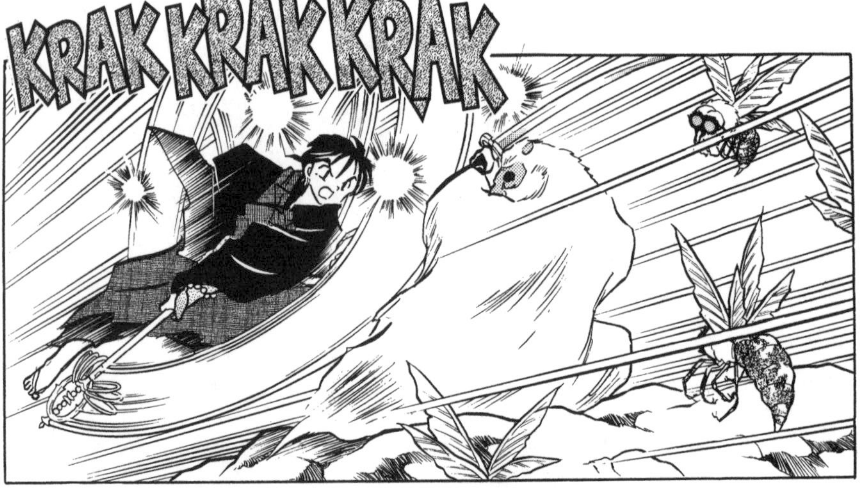
KRAK KRAK KRAK

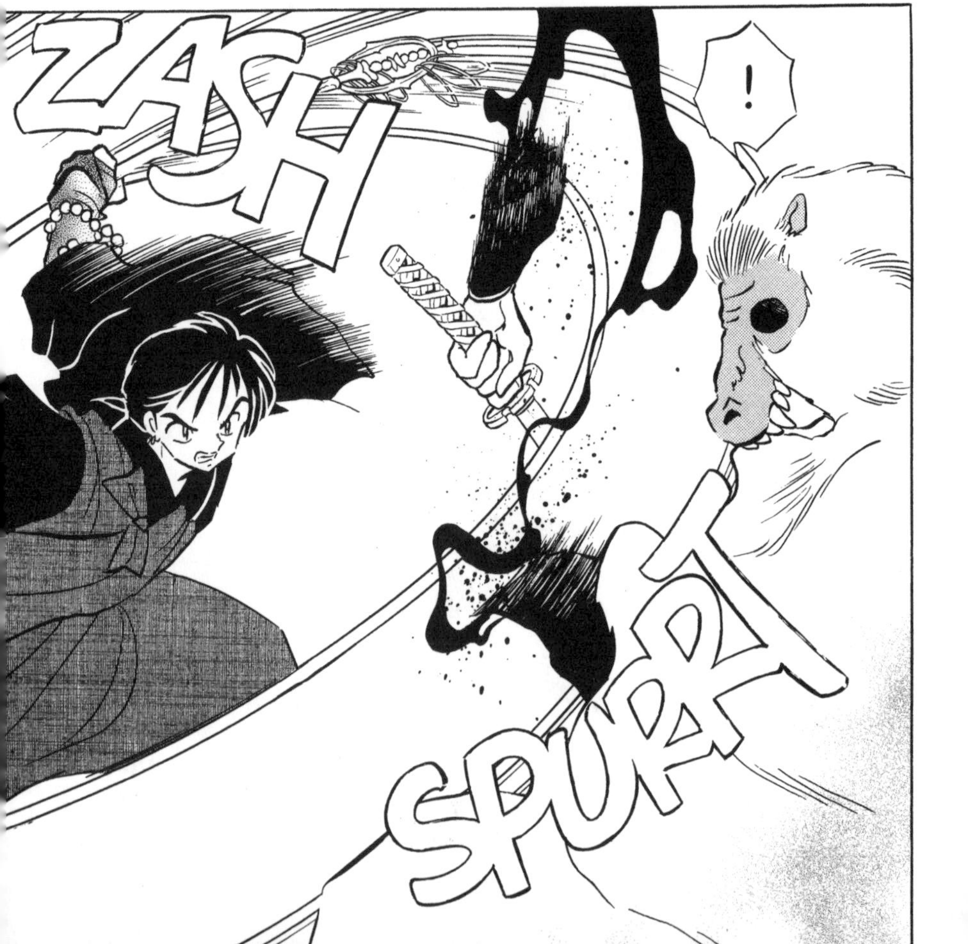
ZASH
!
SPURT

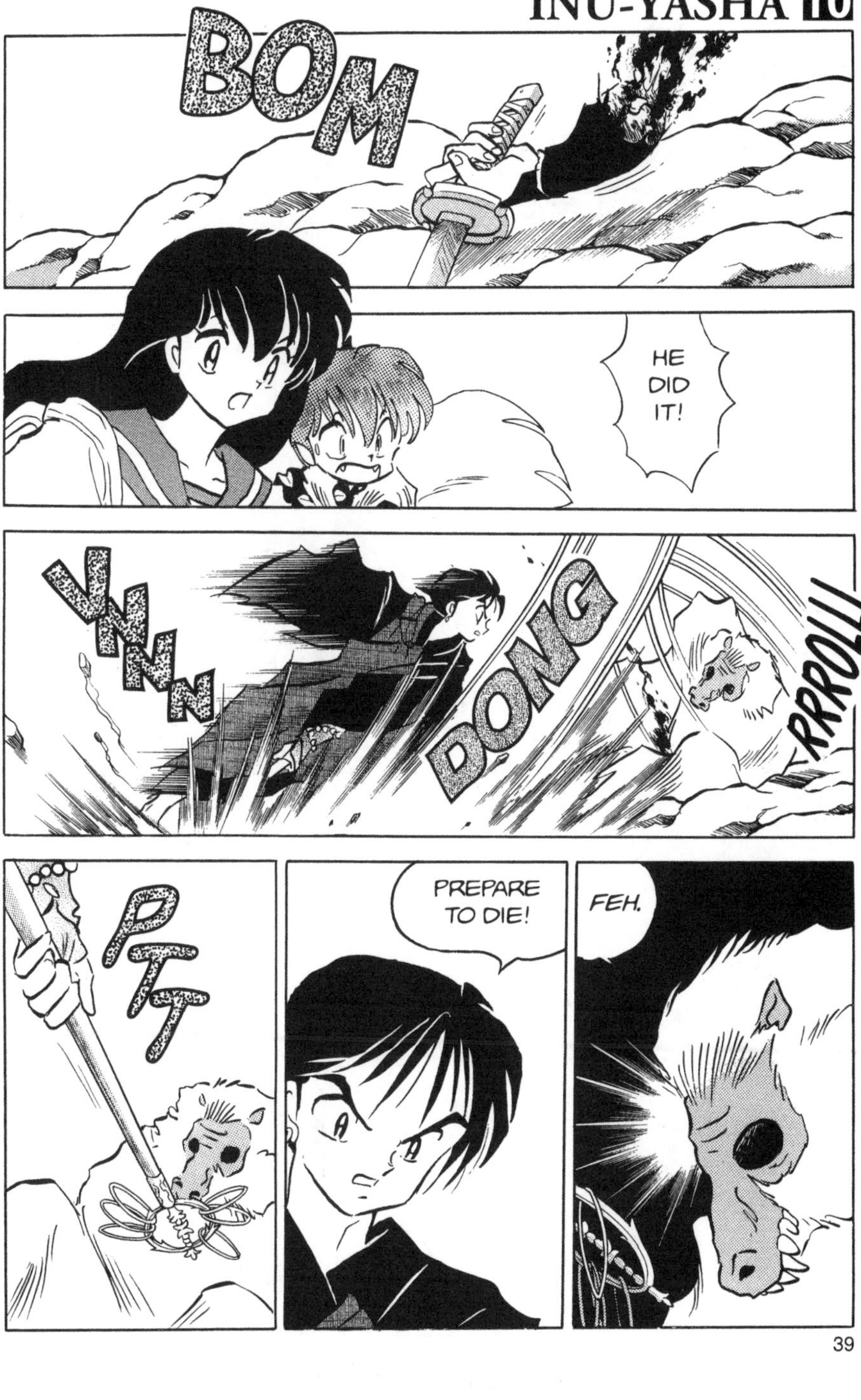
BOM
HE DID IT!
VNNNN
DONG
RRROLLL
PTT
PREPARE TO DIE!
FEH.

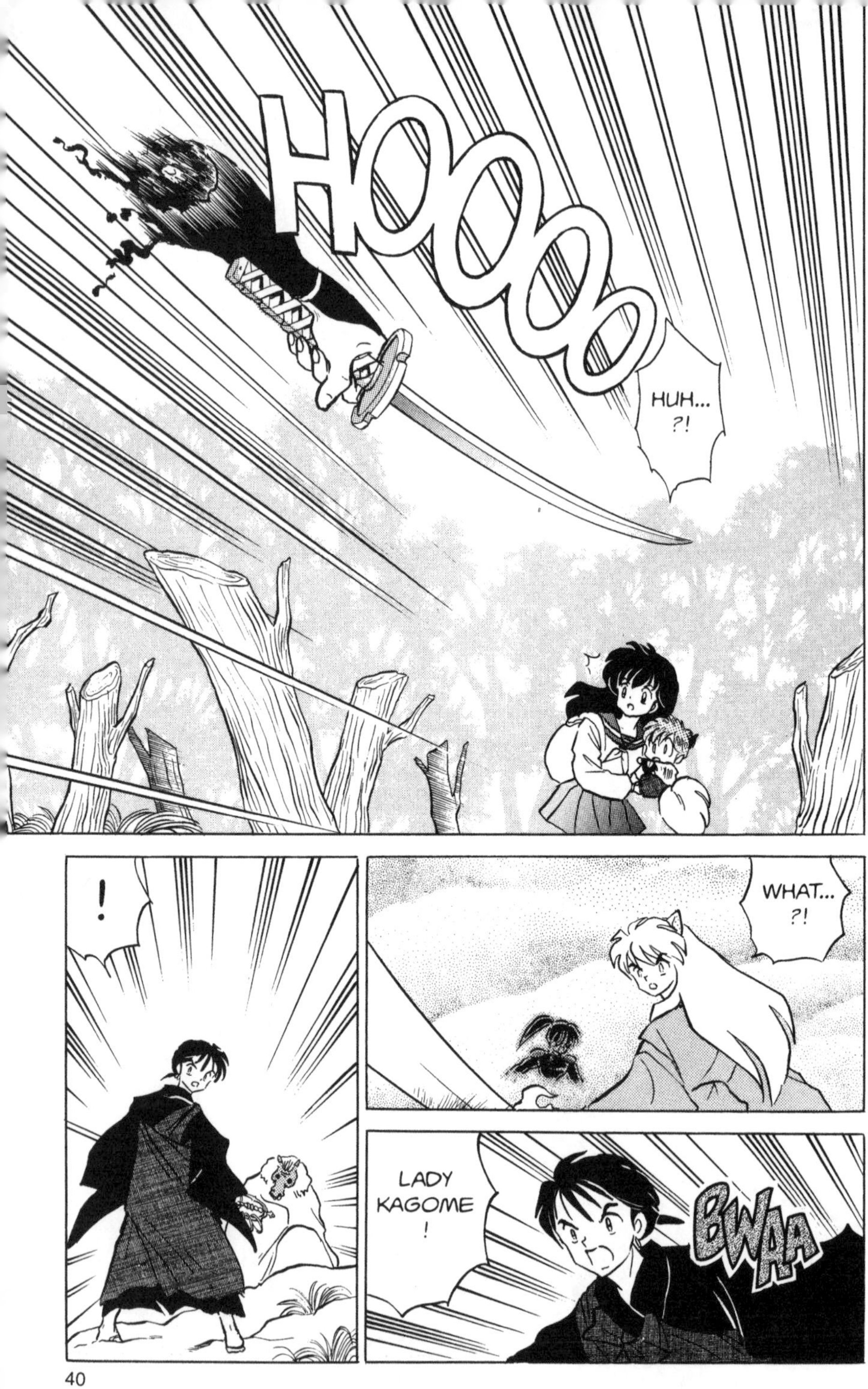
HOOOOO
HUH... ?!
!
WHAT... ?!
LADY KAGOME !
BWAA

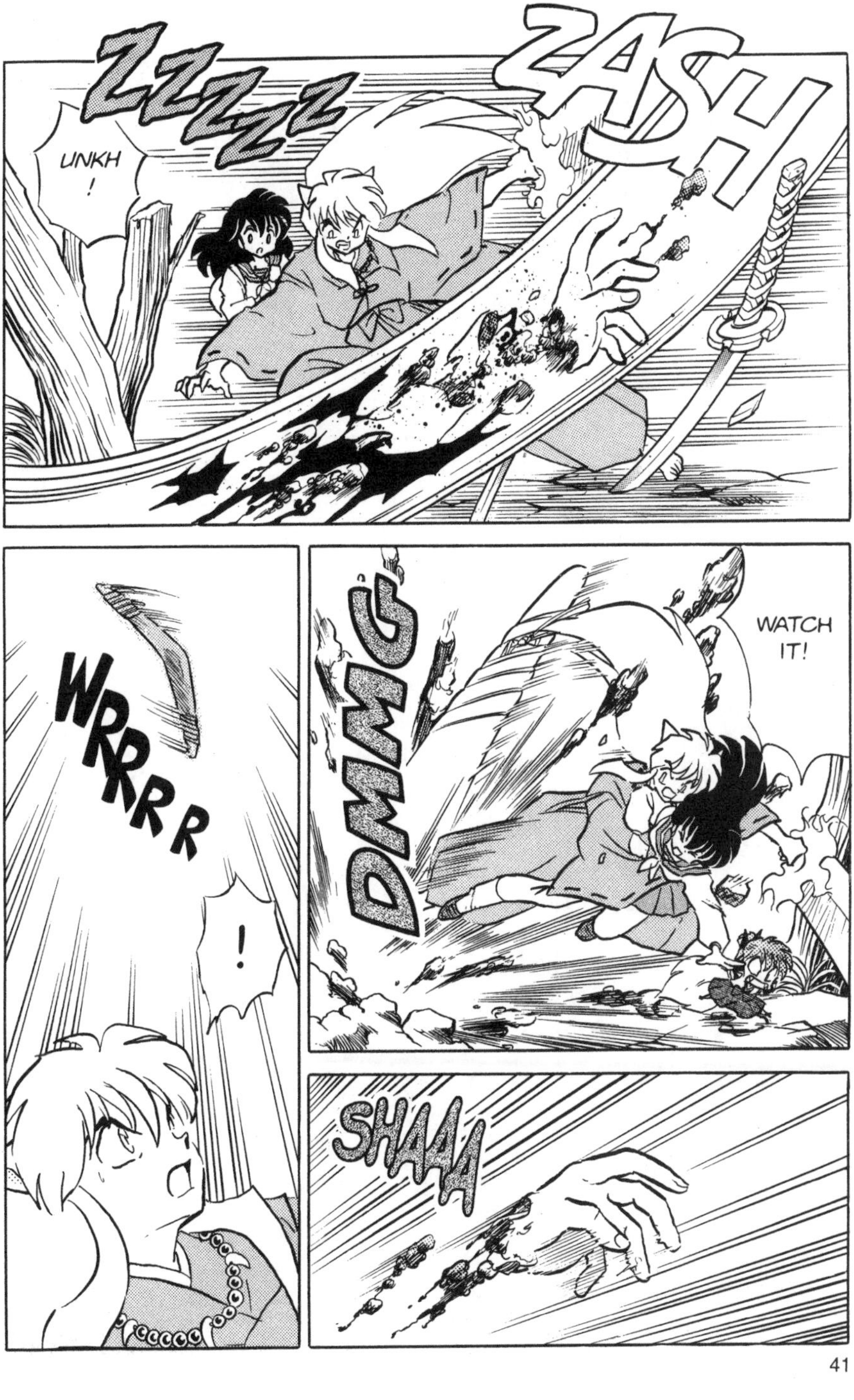
ZZZZZZ
ZASH
UNKH !
WRRRR R
!
DMMG
WATCH IT!
SHAAA

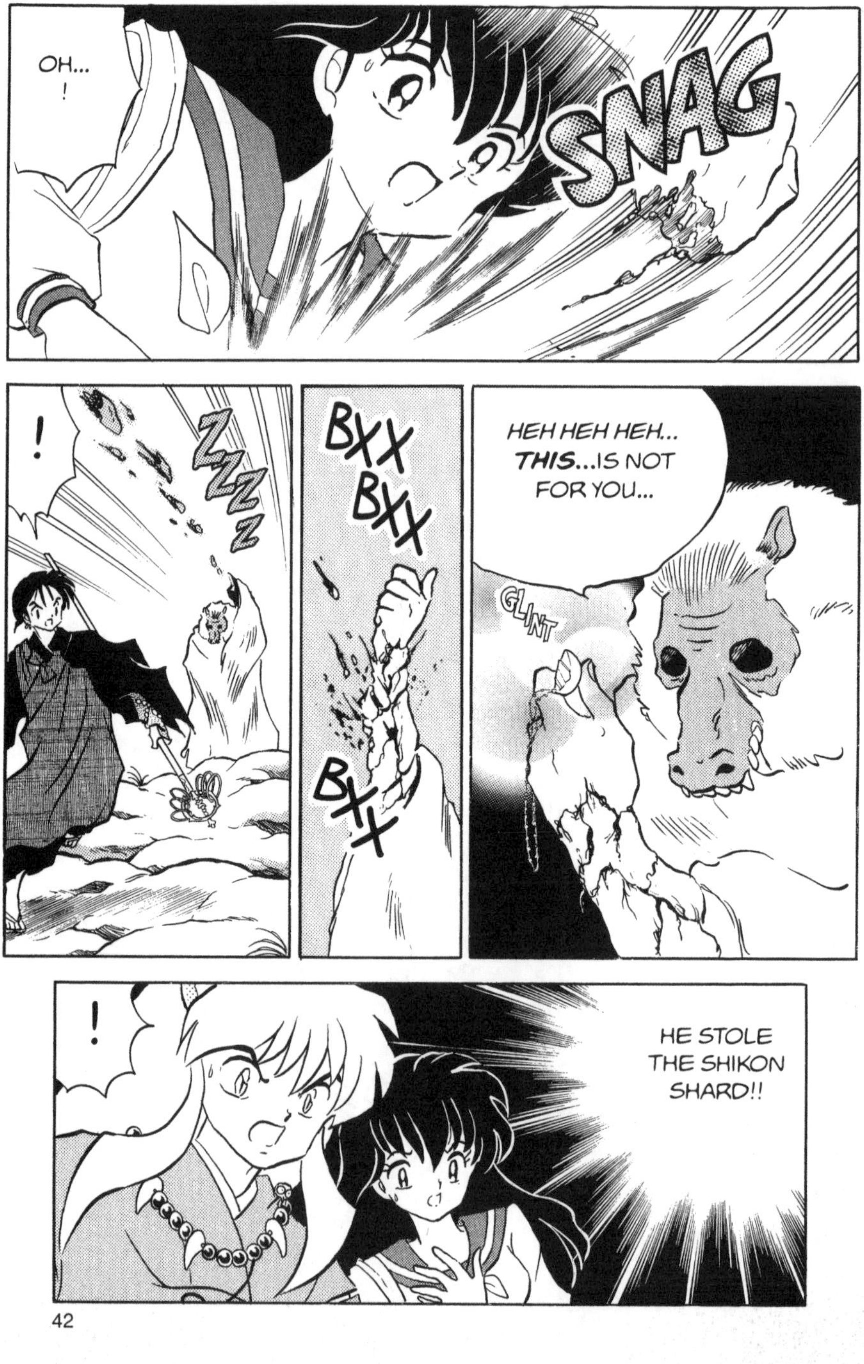
OH... !
SNAG
!
ZZZZZ
BXX BXX
BXX
HEH HEH HEH... **THIS**...IS NOT FOR YOU...
GLINT
!
HE STOLE THE SHIKON SHARD!!

SCROLL THREE

SUSPICIONS

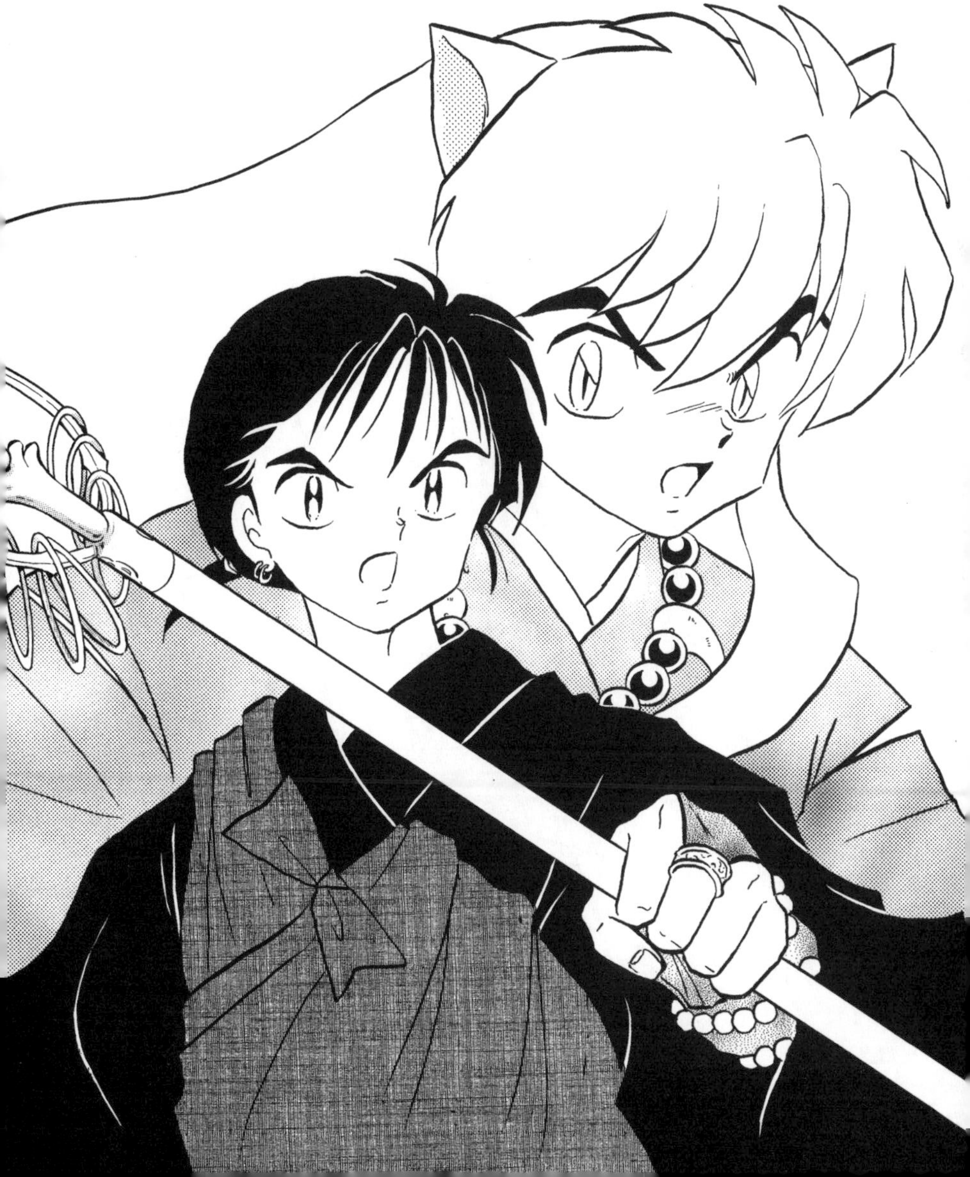

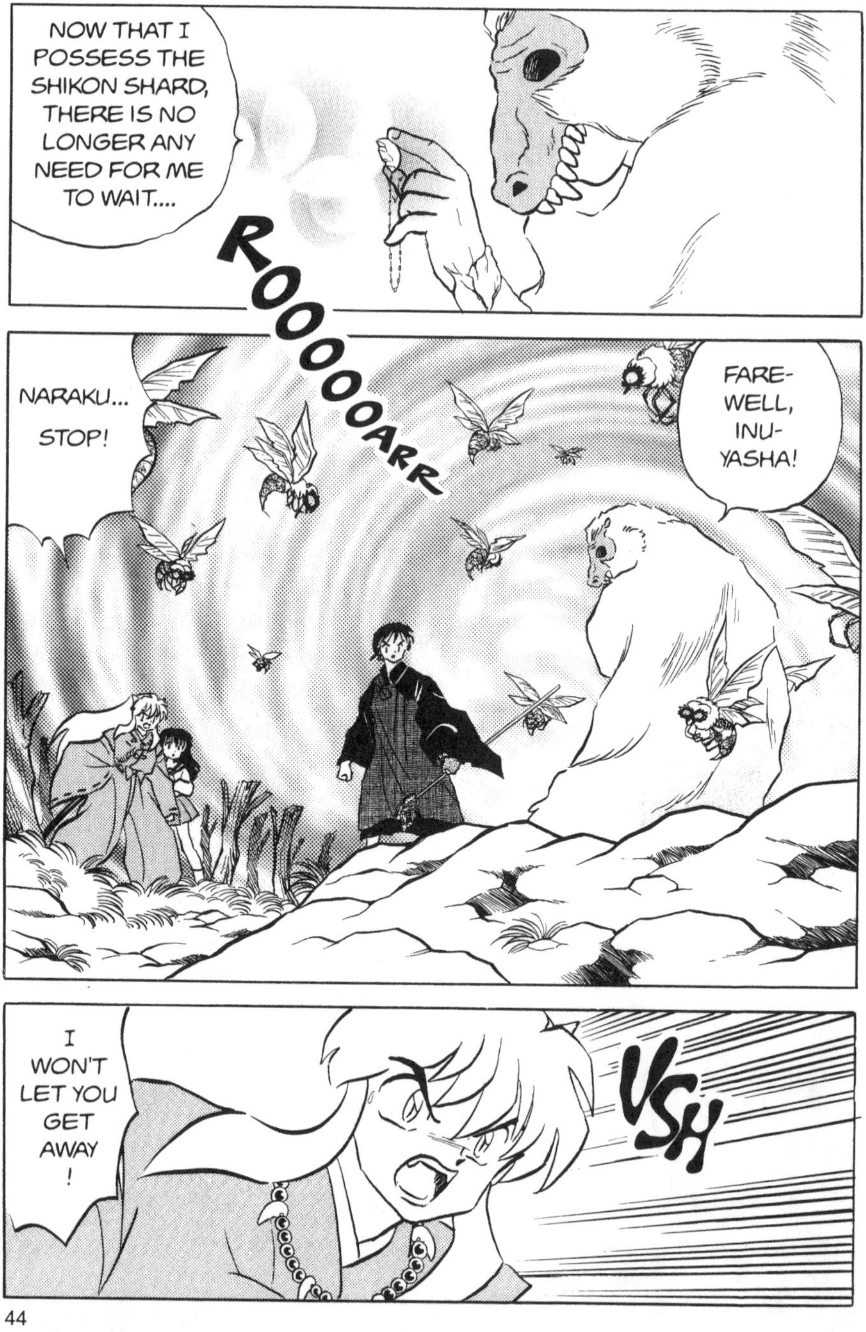
NOW THAT I POSSESS THE SHIKON SHARD, THERE IS NO LONGER ANY NEED FOR ME TO WAIT....
ROOOOOOARR
NARAKU... STOP!
FARE-WELL, INU-YASHA!
I WON'T LET YOU GET AWAY!
VSH

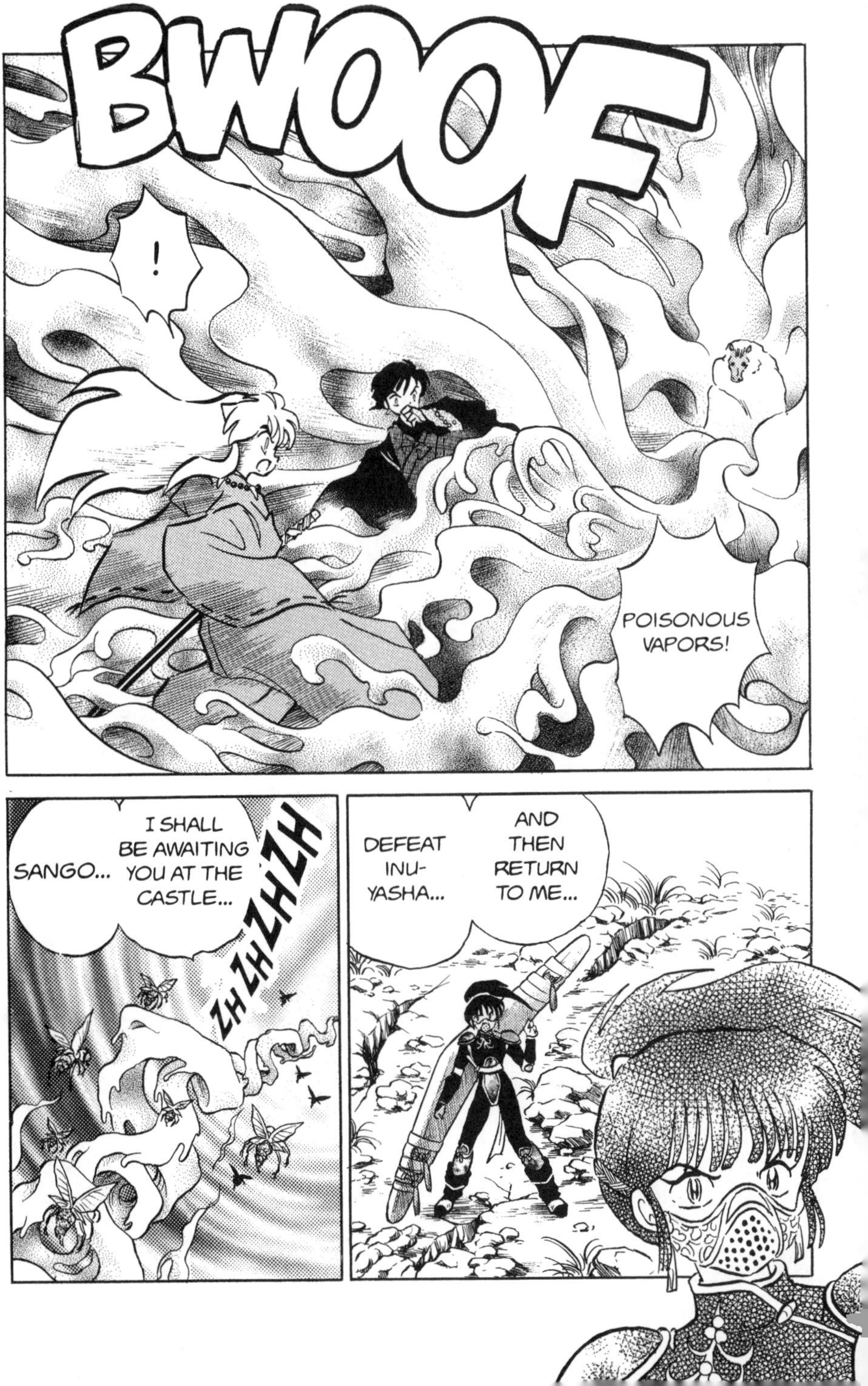
BWOOF
!
POISONOUS VAPORS!
SANGO...
I SHALL BE AWAITING YOU AT THE CASTLE...
ZHZHZHZHZH
DEFEAT INU-YASHA...
AND THEN RETURN TO ME...

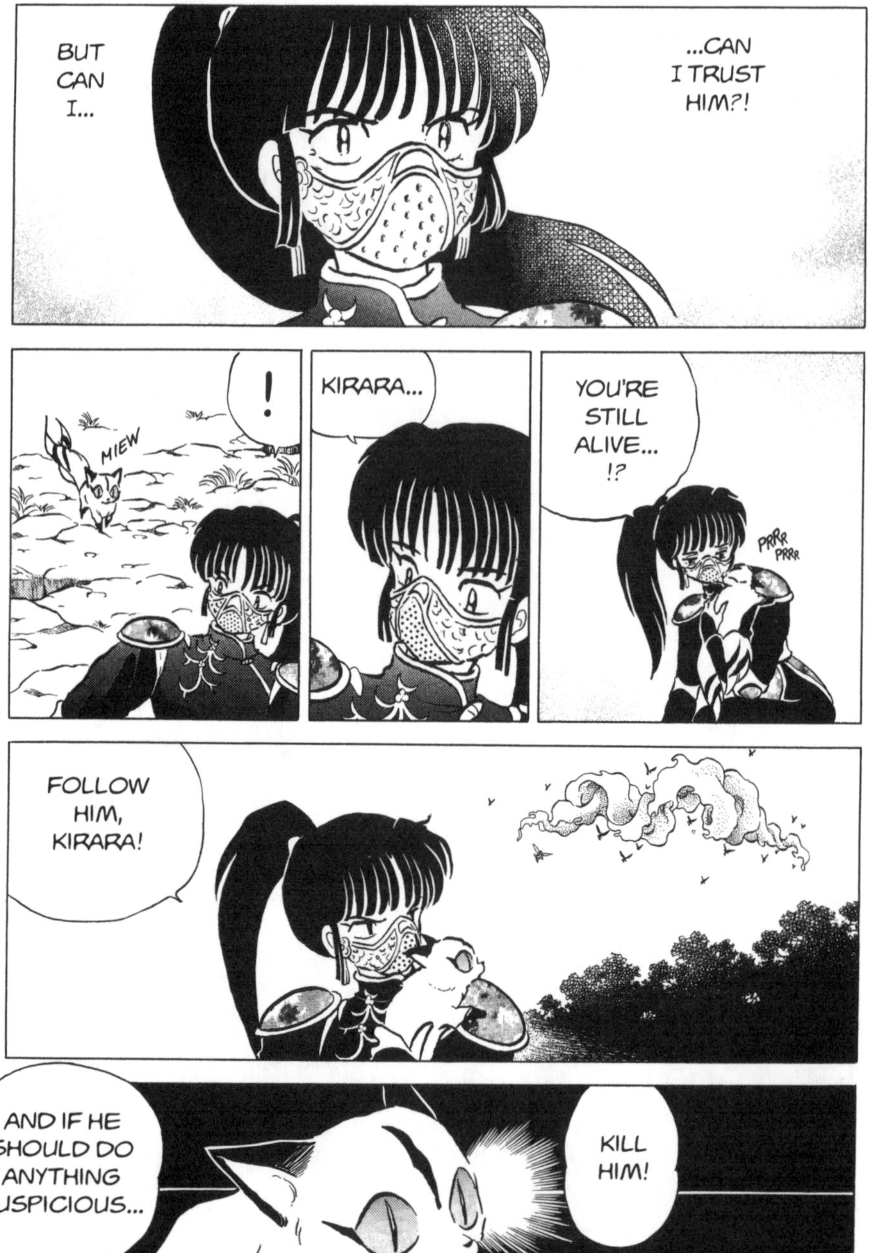
BUT CAN I...
...CAN I TRUST HIM?!
!
MIEW
KIRARA...
YOU'RE STILL ALIVE... !?
PRRR PRRR
FOLLOW HIM, KIRARA!
AND IF HE SHOULD DO ANYTHING SUSPICIOUS...
KILL HIM!

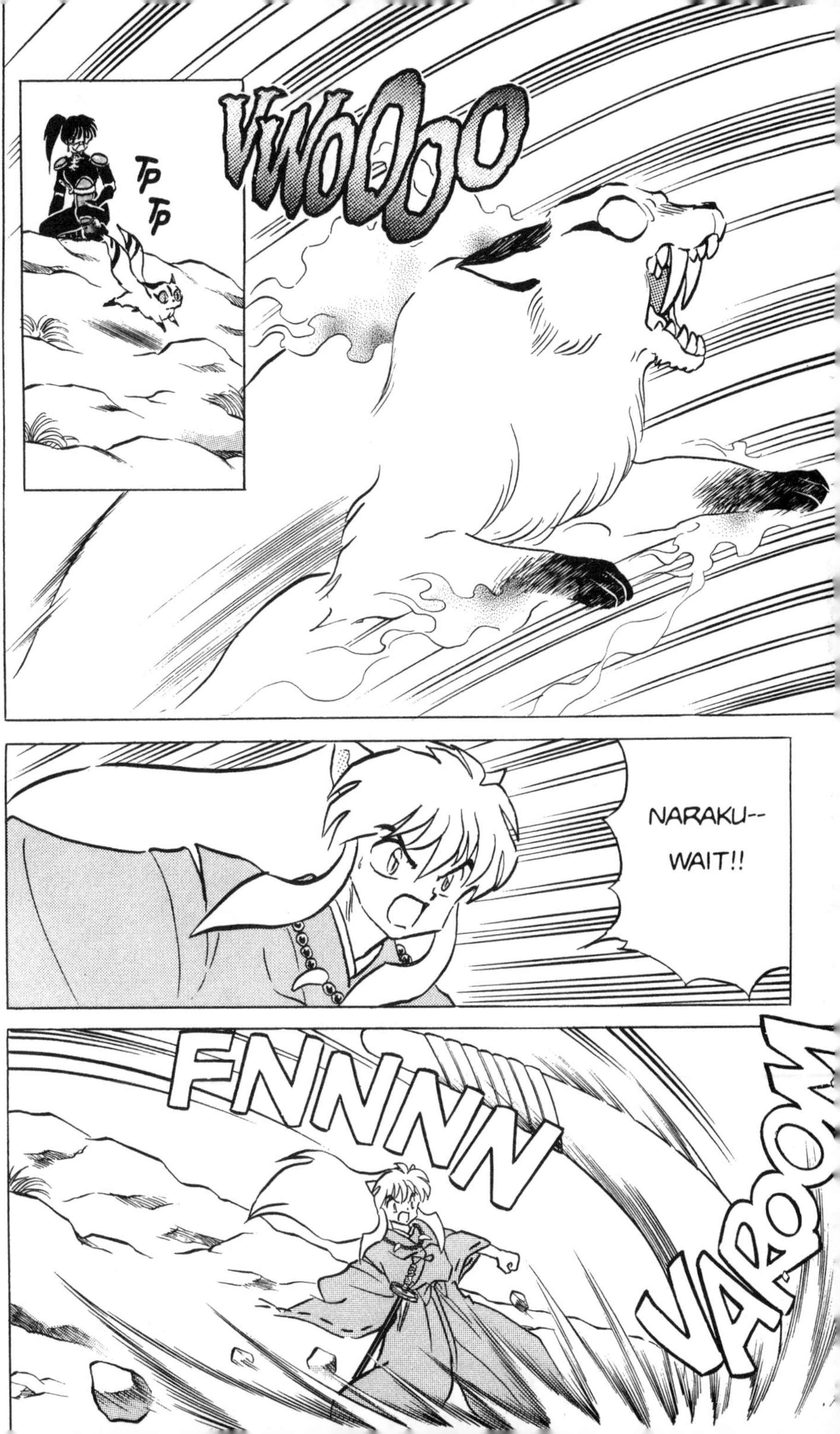
TP TP
VWOOOO
NARAKU--
WAIT!!
FNNNNN
VAROOM

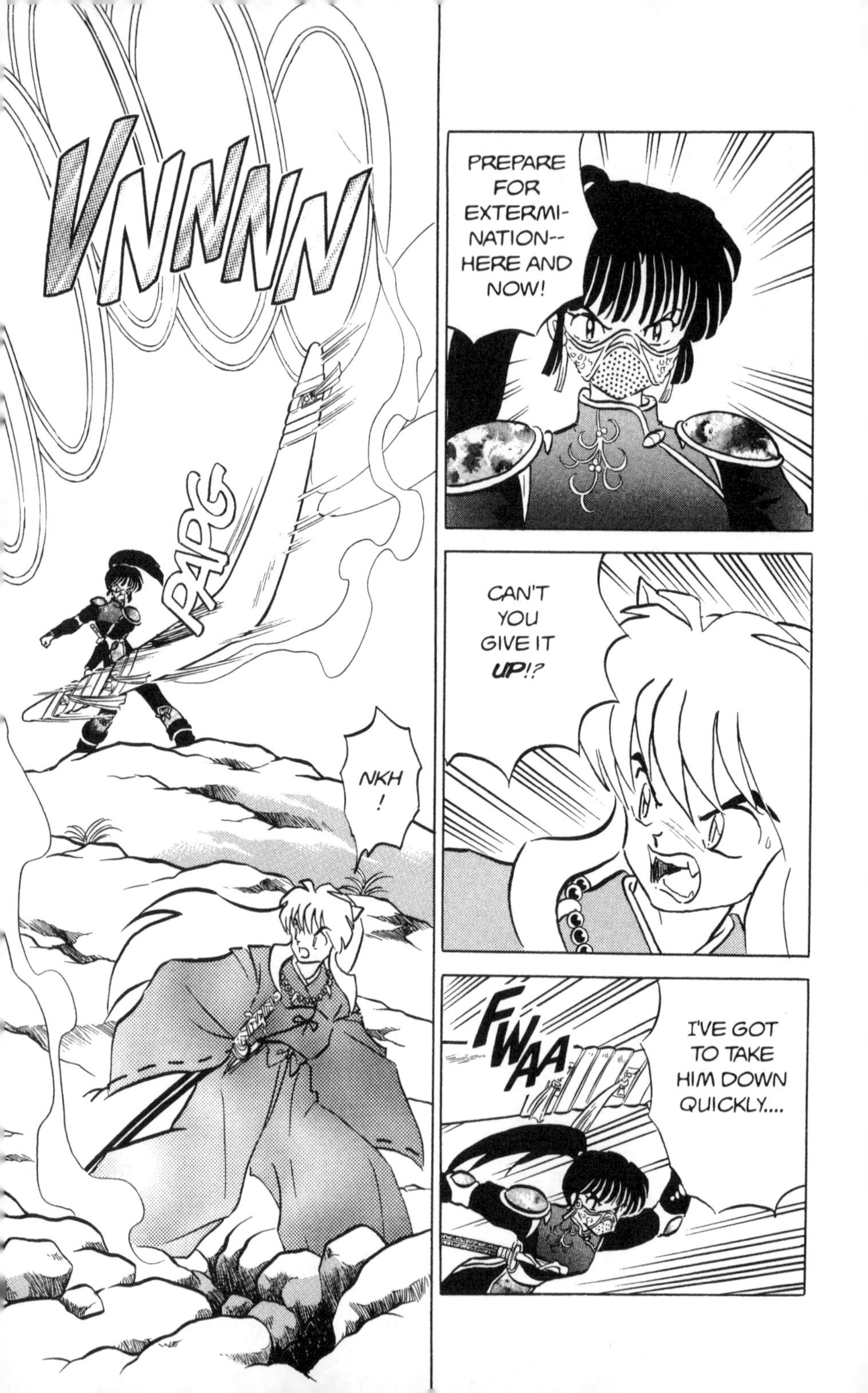
VNNNN
PAPG
NKH!
PREPARE FOR EXTERMINATION--HERE AND NOW!
CAN'T YOU GIVE IT ***UP!?***
FWAA
I'VE GOT TO TAKE HIM DOWN QUICKLY....

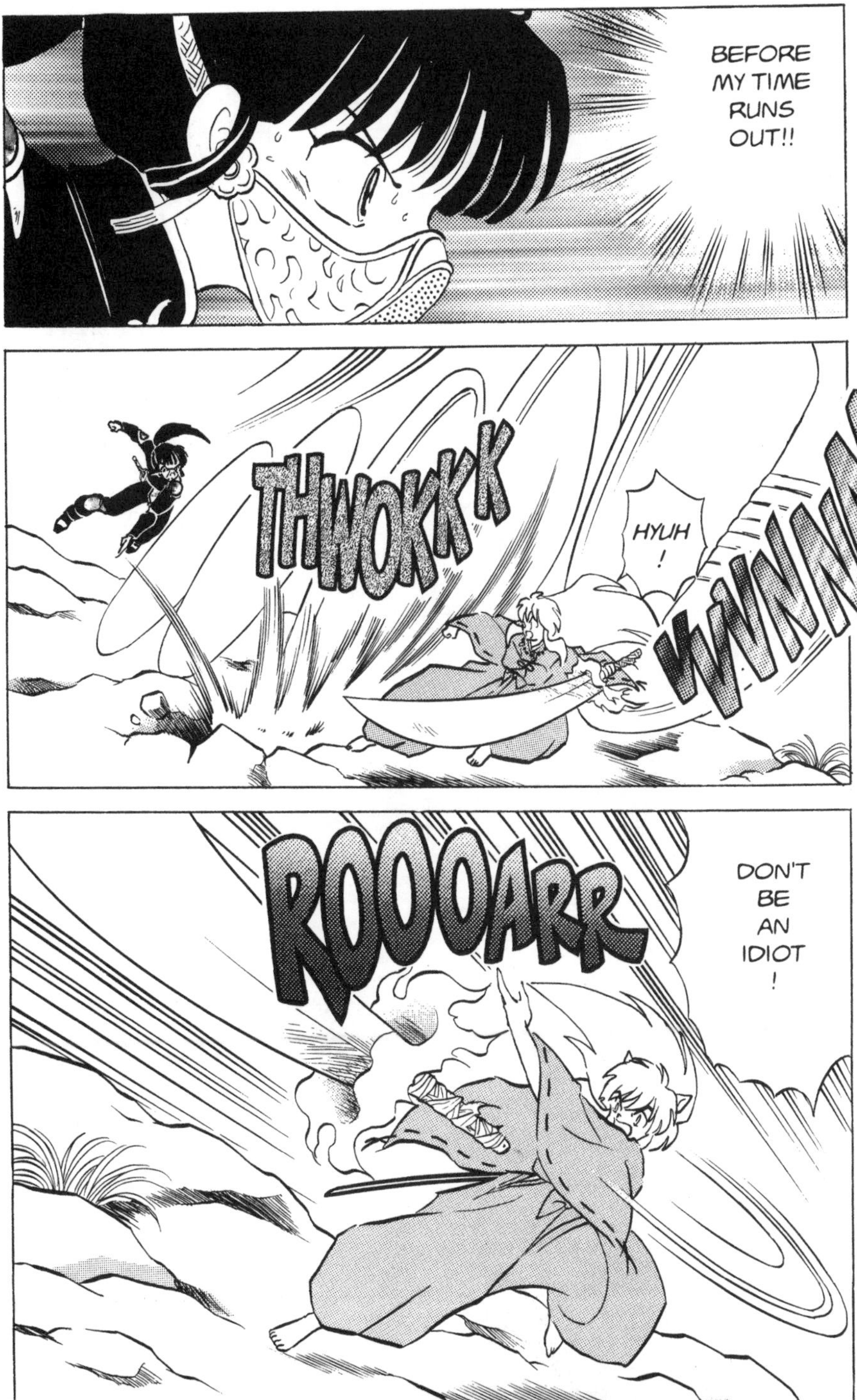
BEFORE MY TIME RUNS OUT!!
THWOKKK
HYUH!
WWNNNN
ROOOARR
DON'T BE AN IDIOT!

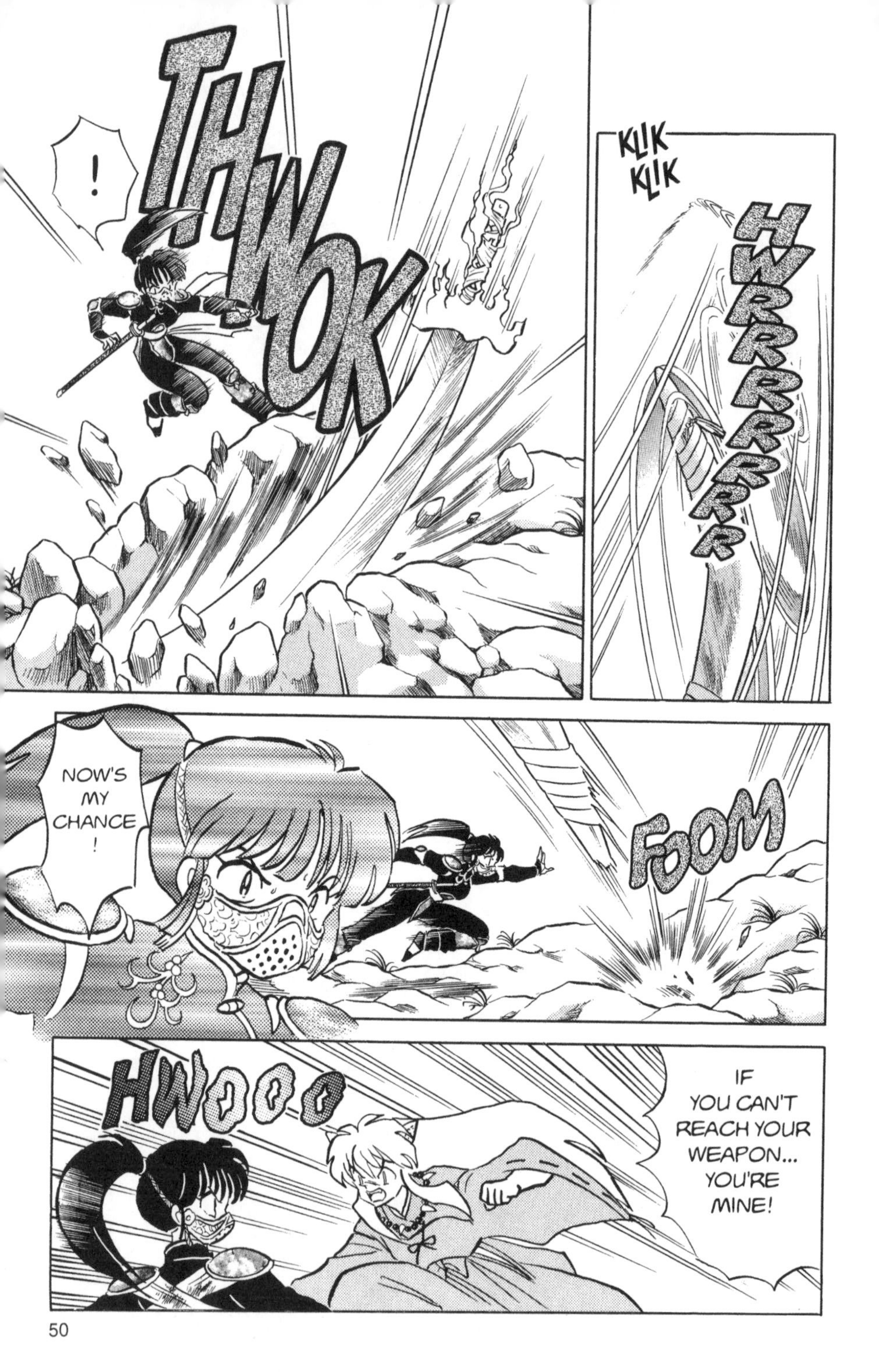
!
THWOK
KLIK
KLIK
HWRRRRRRRR
NOW'S MY CHANCE !
FOOM
HWOOO
IF YOU CAN'T REACH YOUR WEAPON... YOU'RE MINE!

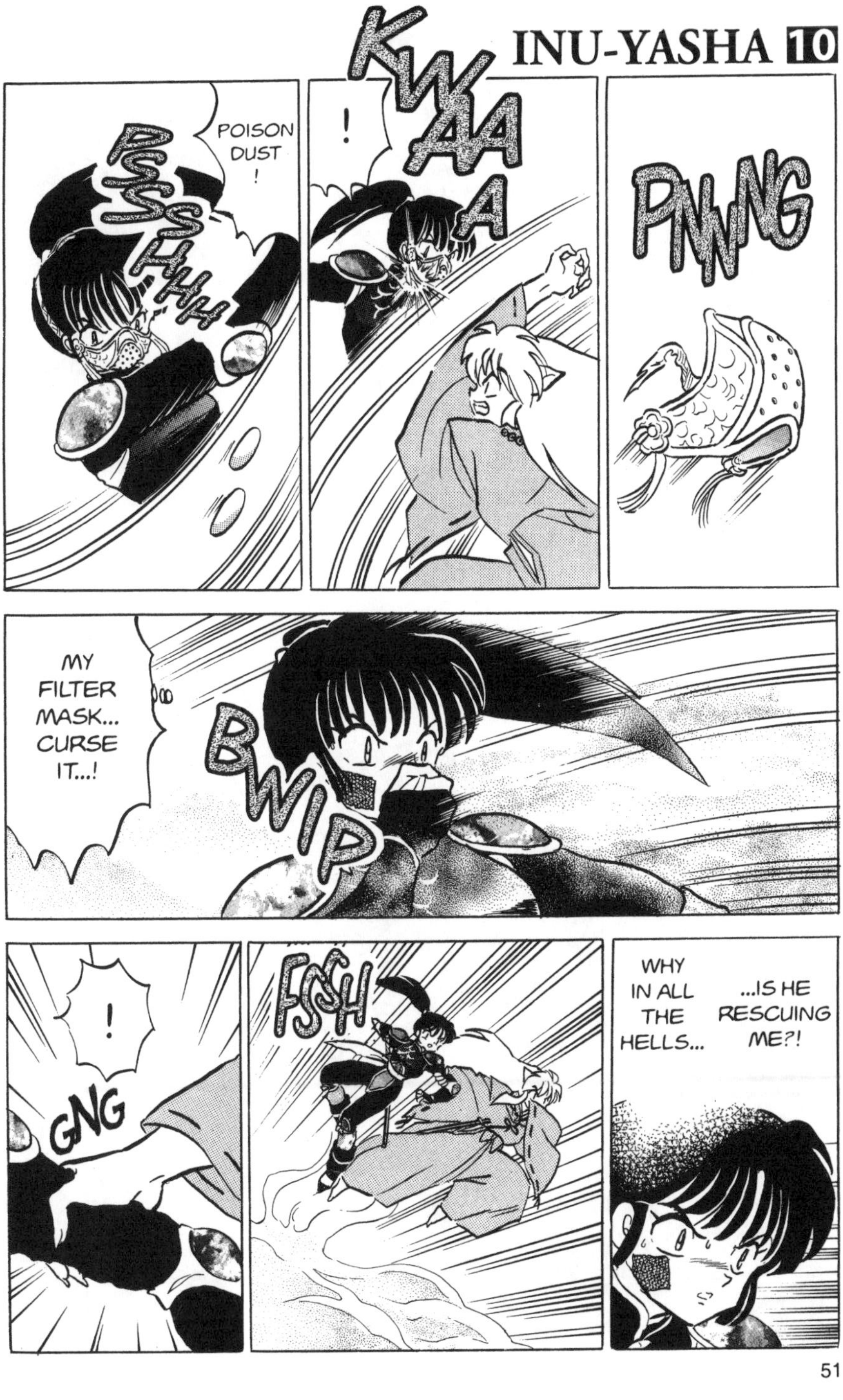
POISON DUST !
PSSSHHH
!
KWAAAA
PNWNG
MY FILTER MASK... CURSE IT...!
BWIP
!
GNG
FSSH
WHY IN ALL THE HELLS...
...IS HE RESCUING ME?!

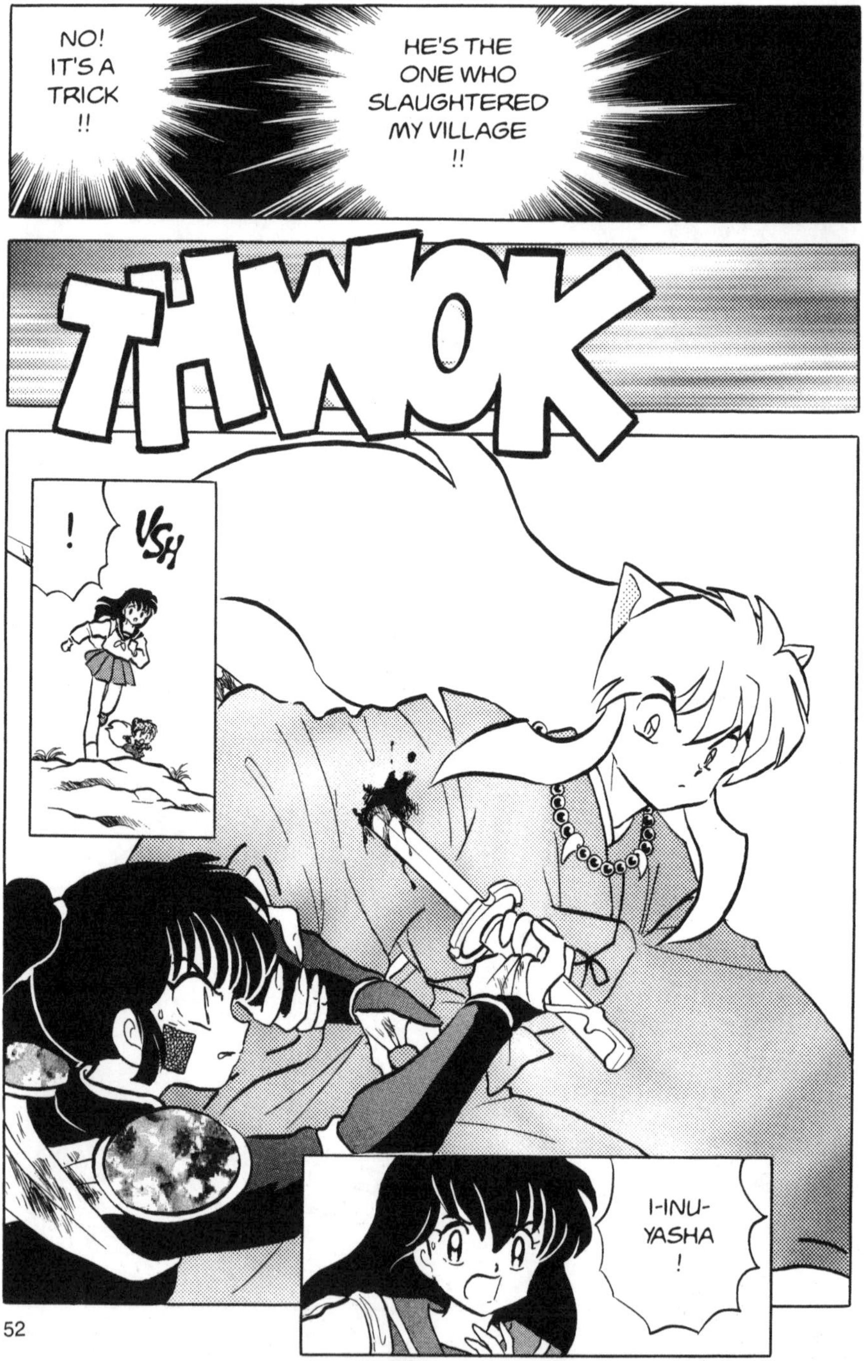
NO! IT'S A TRICK !!
HE'S THE ONE WHO SLAUGHTERED MY VILLAGE !!
THWOK
!
VSH
I-INU-YASHA !

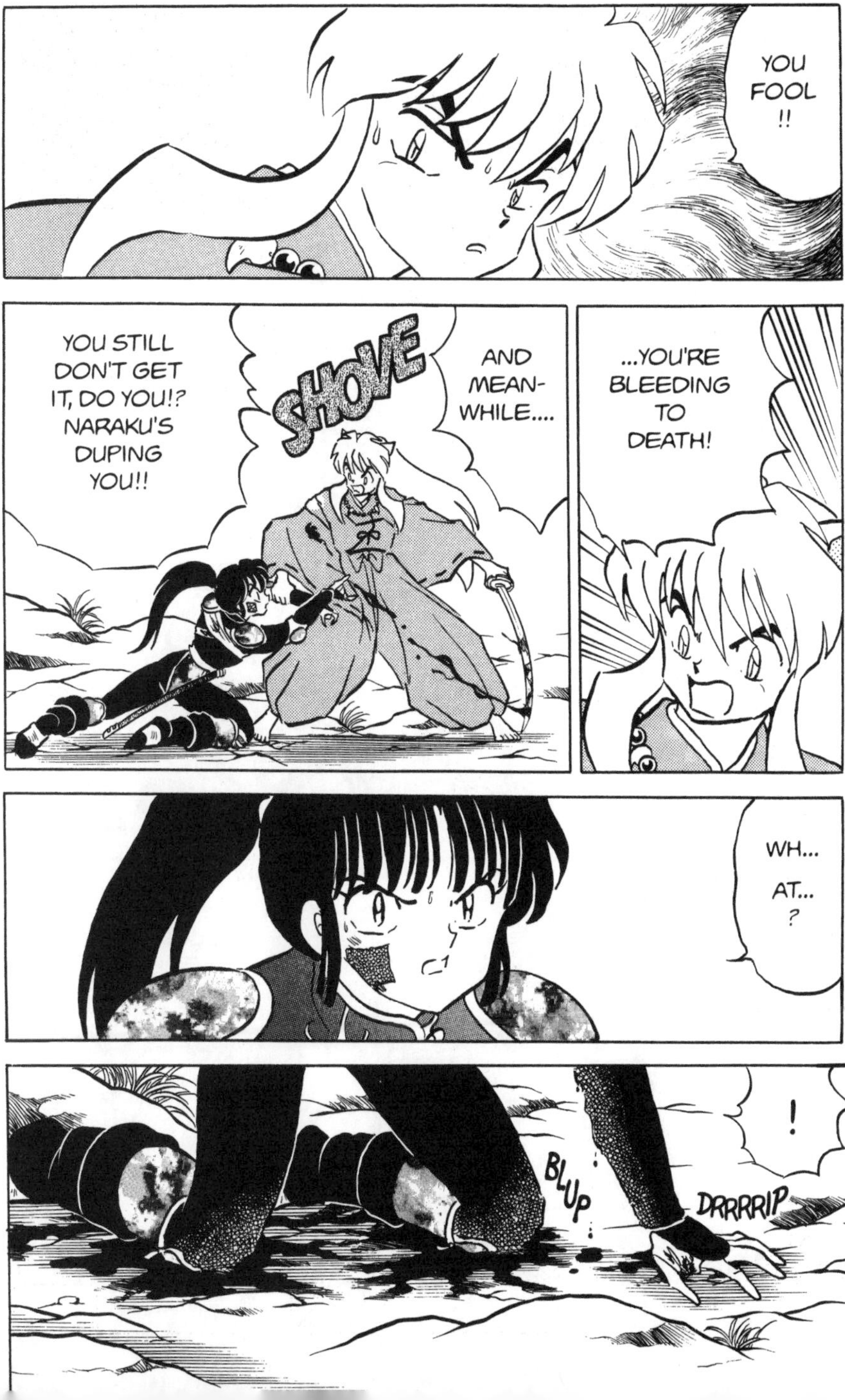
YOU FOOL !!
YOU STILL DON'T GET IT, DO YOU!? NARAKU'S DUPING YOU!!
SHOVE
AND MEAN-WHILE....
...YOU'RE BLEEDING TO DEATH!
WH... AT... ?
BLUP
!
DRRRRIP

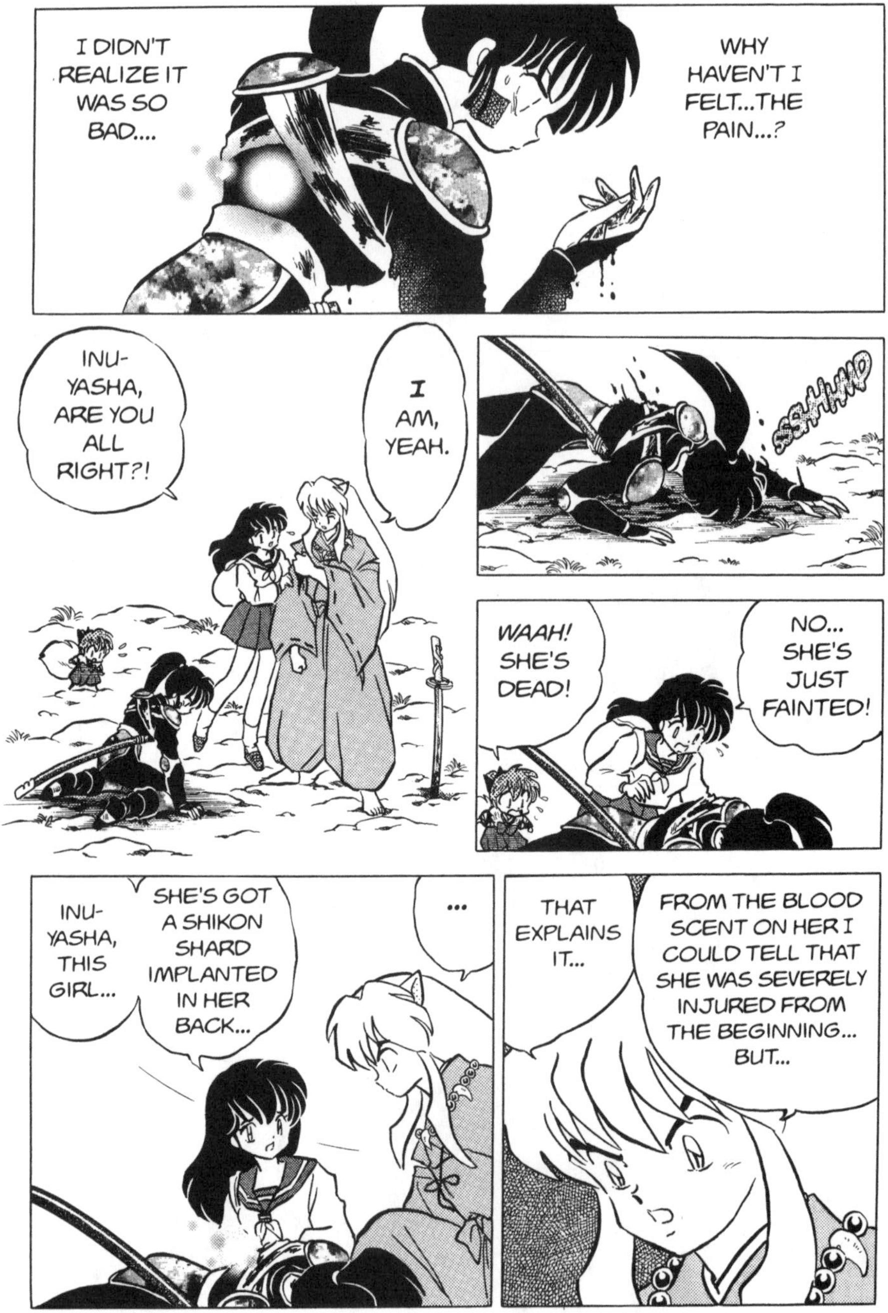
I DIDN'T REALIZE IT WAS SO BAD....
WHY HAVEN'T I FELT...THE PAIN...?
INU-YASHA, ARE YOU ALL RIGHT?!
I AM, YEAH.
SSHHMP
WAAH! SHE'S DEAD!
NO... SHE'S JUST FAINTED!
INU-YASHA, THIS GIRL...
SHE'S GOT A SHIKON SHARD IMPLANTED IN HER BACK...
...
THAT EXPLAINS IT...
FROM THE BLOOD SCENT ON HER I COULD TELL THAT SHE WAS SEVERELY INJURED FROM THE BEGINNING... BUT...

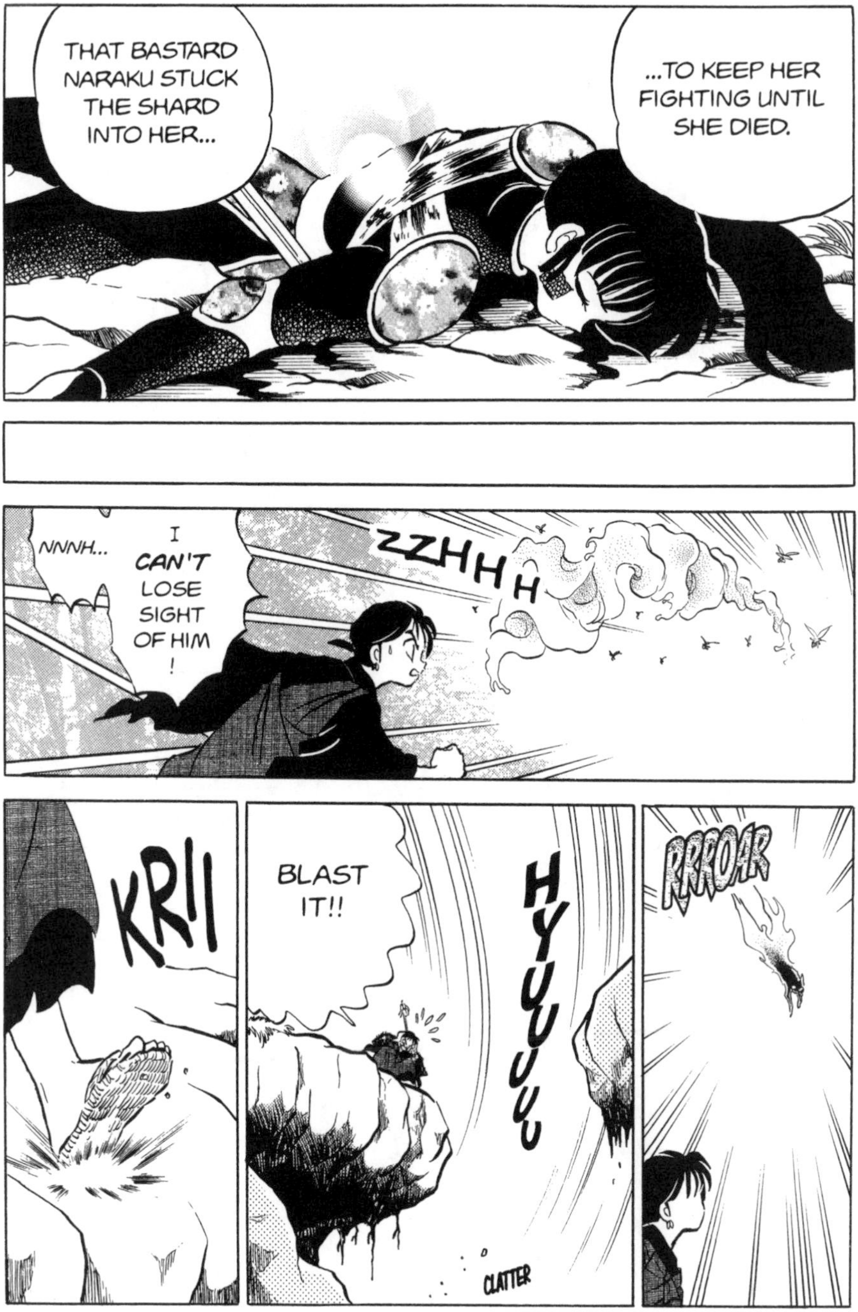
THAT BASTARD NARAKU STUCK THE SHARD INTO HER...
...TO KEEP HER FIGHTING UNTIL SHE DIED.
NNNH...
I CAN'T LOSE SIGHT OF HIM!
ZZHHHH
KRII
BLAST IT!!
HYUUUUUU
CLATTER
RRROAR

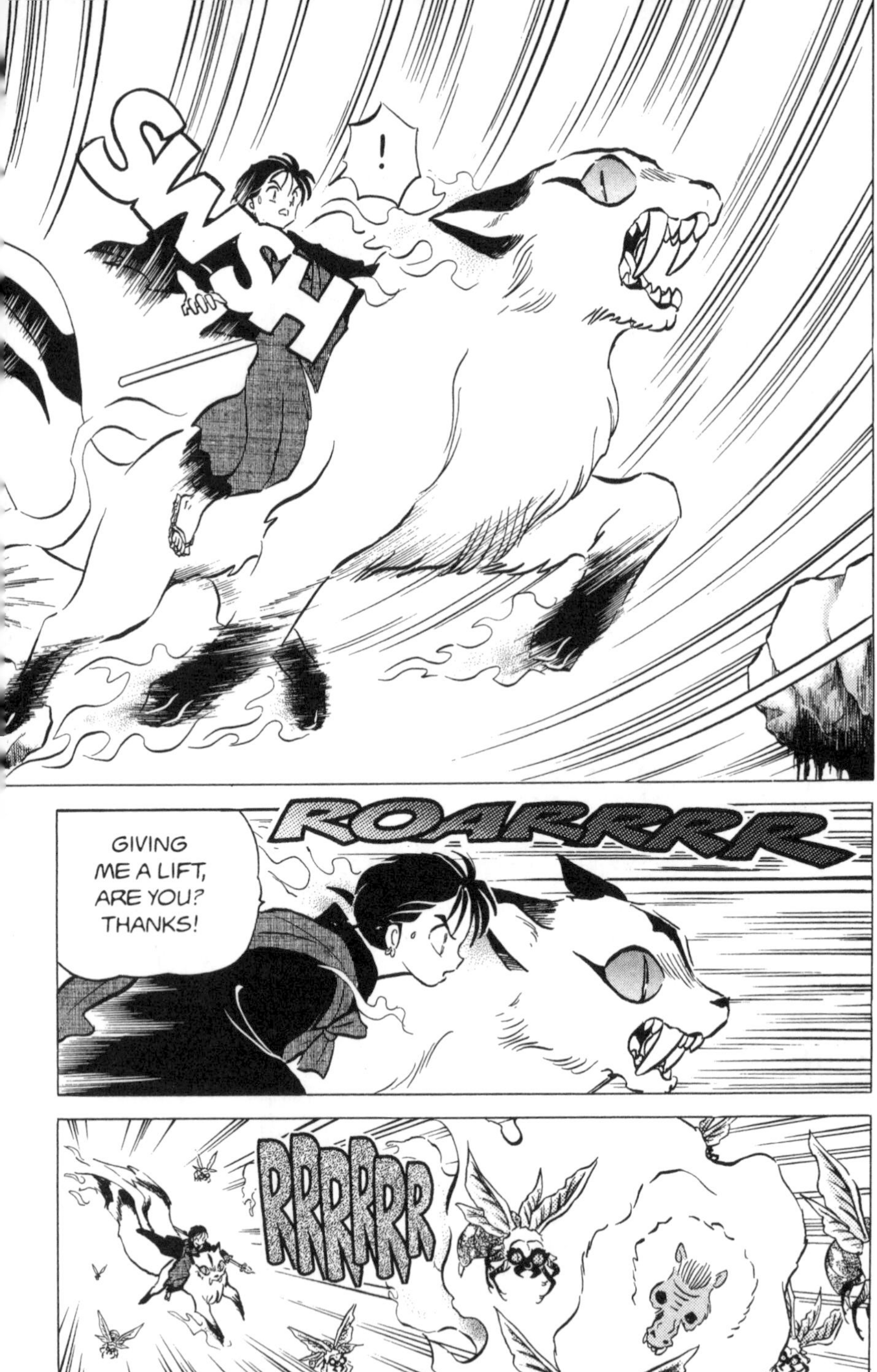
SWSH
!
ROARRRR
GIVING ME A LIFT, ARE YOU? THANKS!
RRRRRR

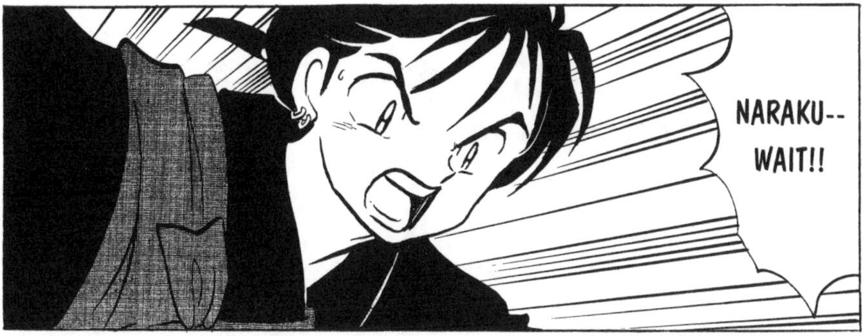
NARAKU--
WAIT!!

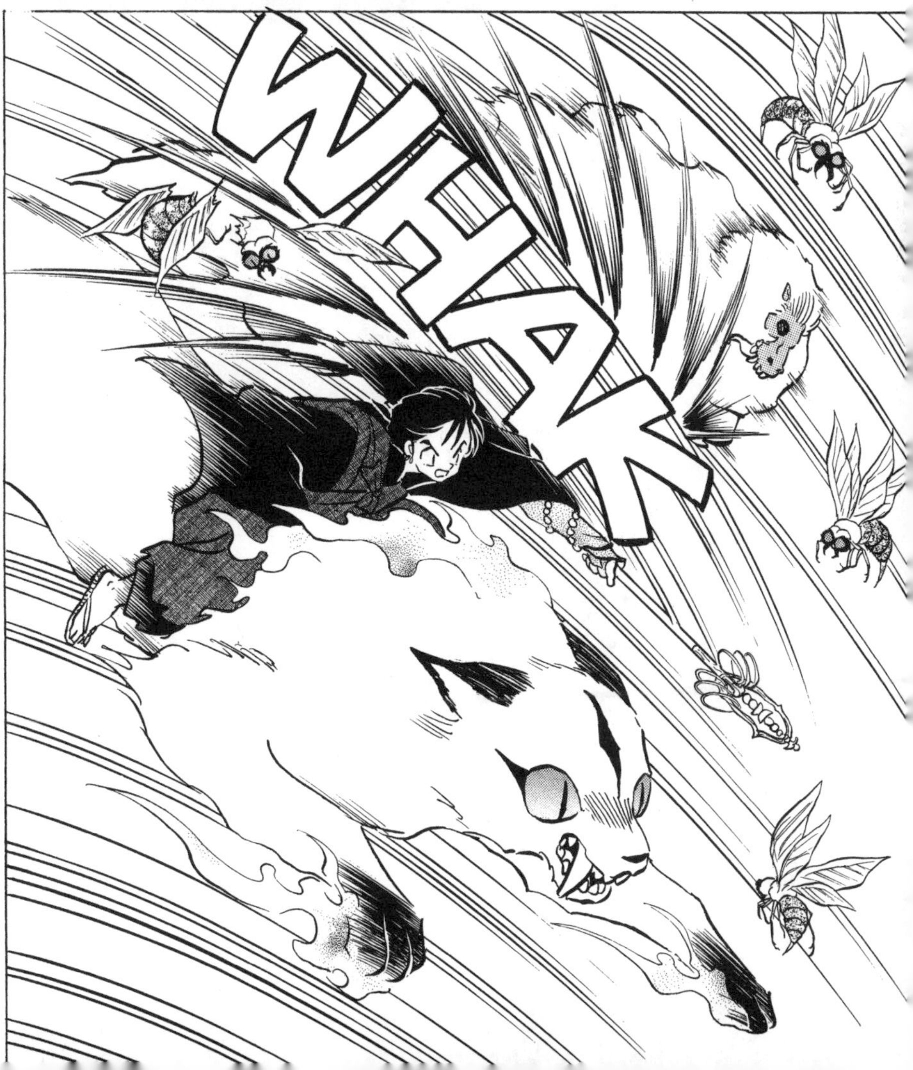
WHAK

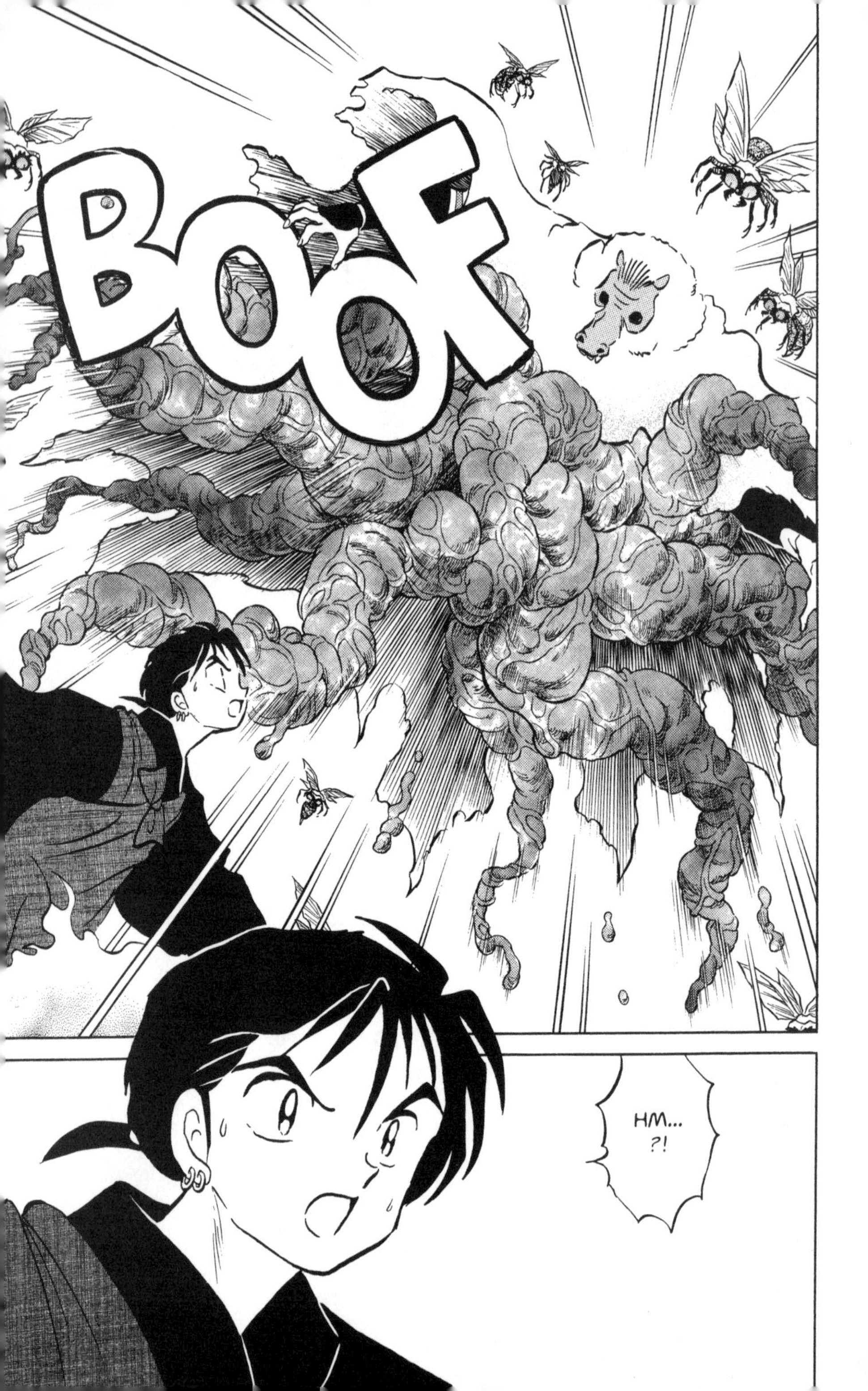
BOOF
HM...
?!

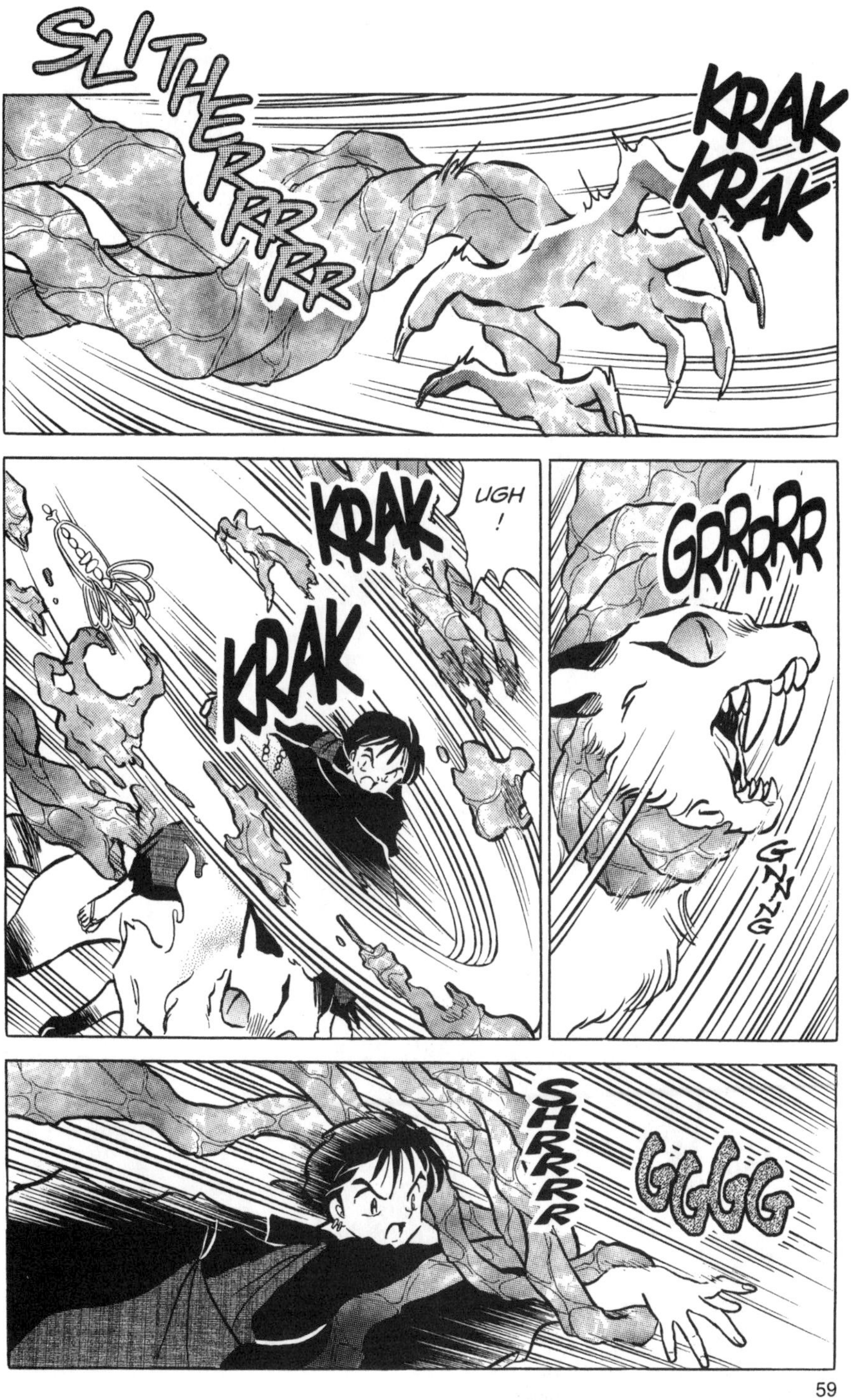
SLITHERRRRRR
KRAK KRAK
KRAK
UGH!
KRAK
GRRRRR
GNNNG
SHRRRR
GGGG

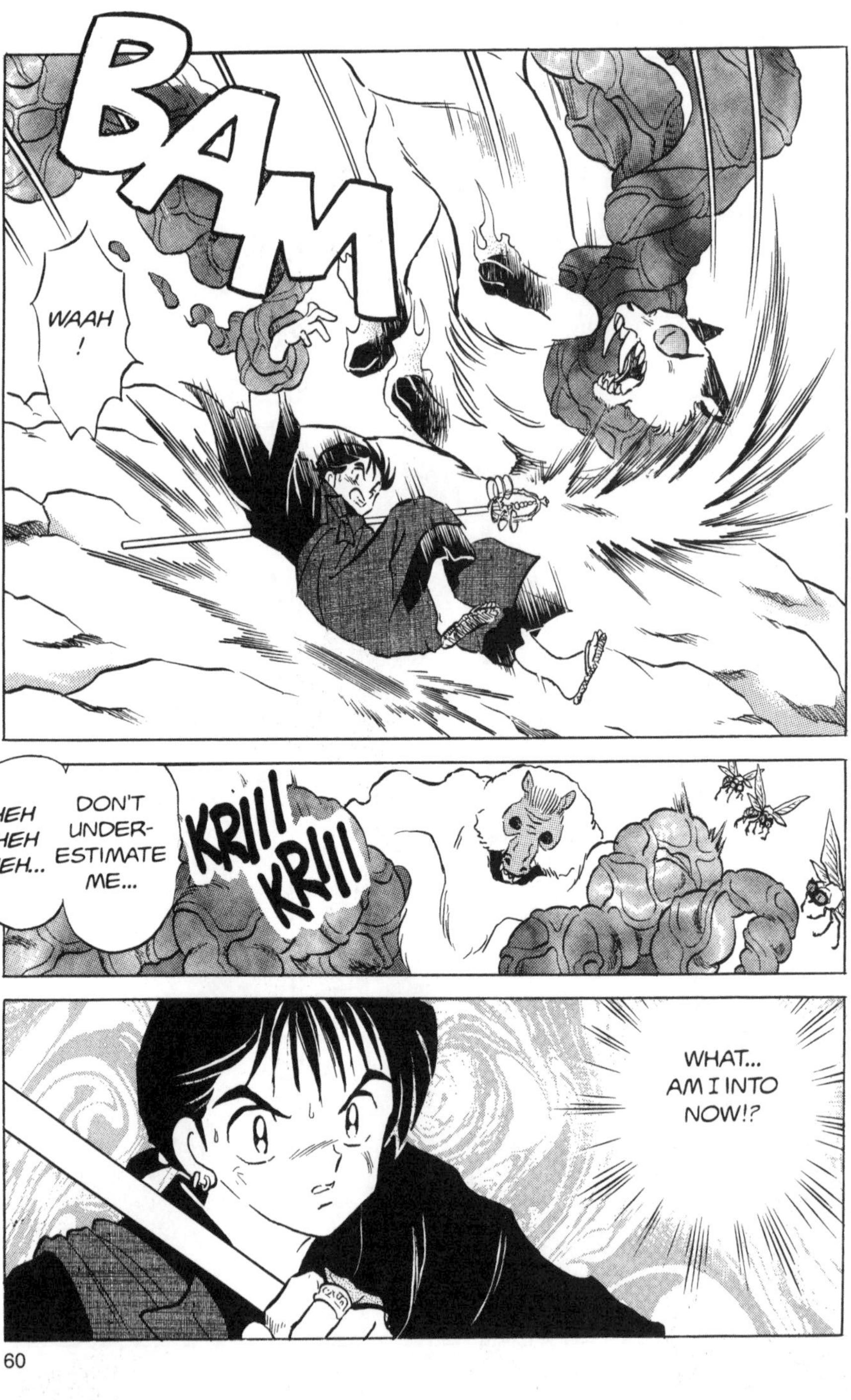
BAM
WAAH!
HEH HEH HEH...
DON'T UNDER-ESTIMATE ME...
KRIII KRIII
WHAT... AM I INTO NOW!?

SCROLL FOUR

STRATEGIES

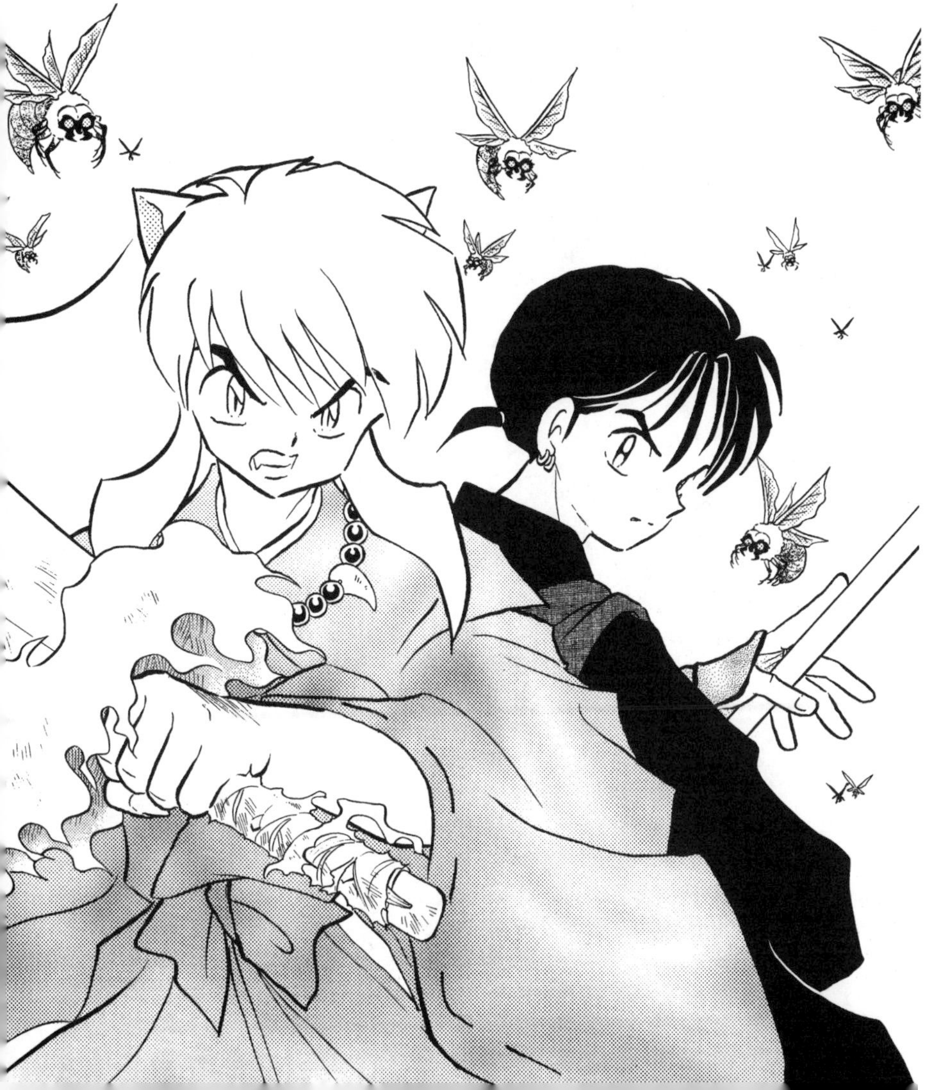

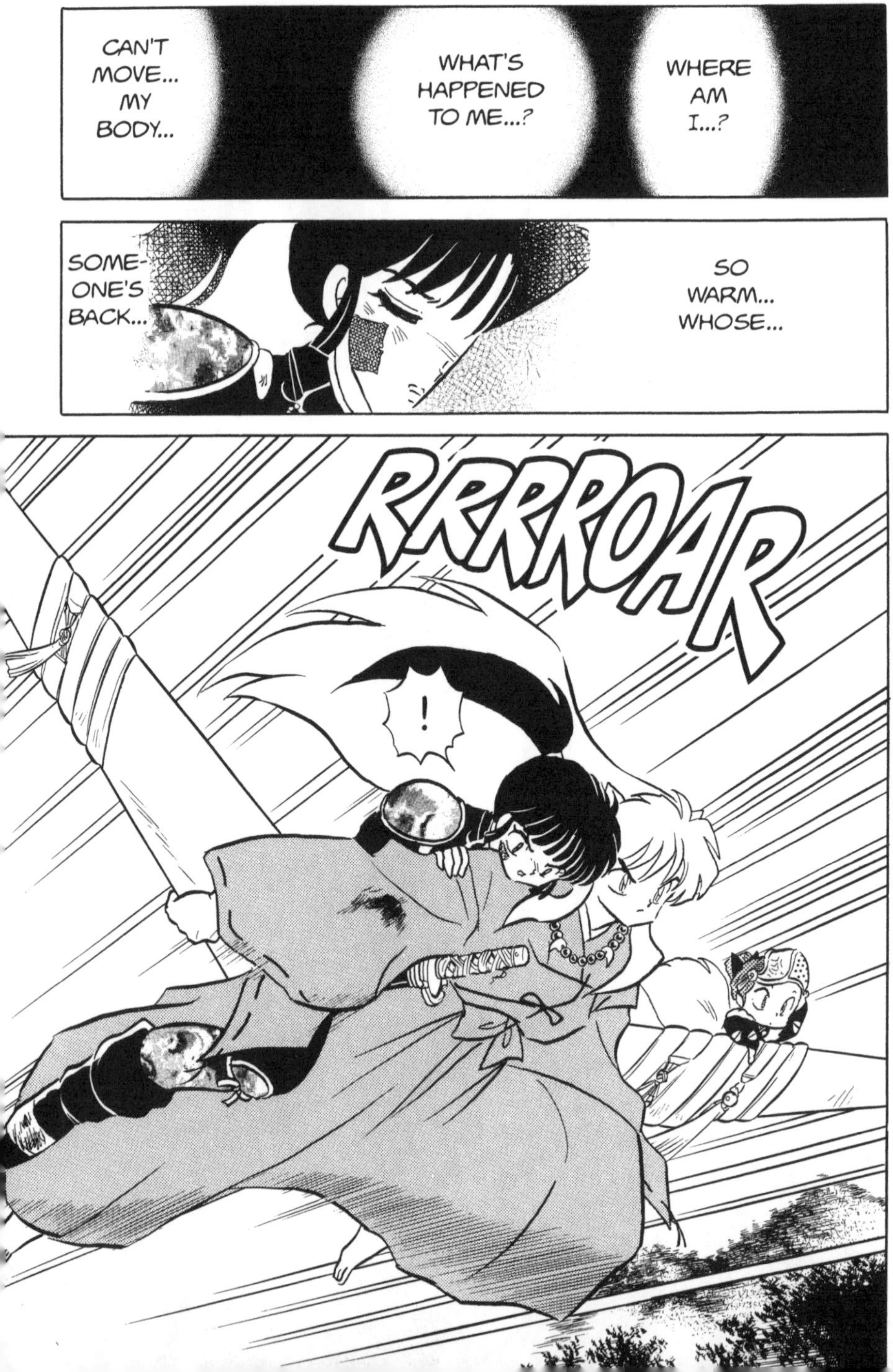
CAN'T MOVE... MY BODY...
WHAT'S HAPPENED TO ME...?
WHERE AM I...?
SOME-ONE'S BACK...
SO WARM... WHOSE...
RRRROAR
!

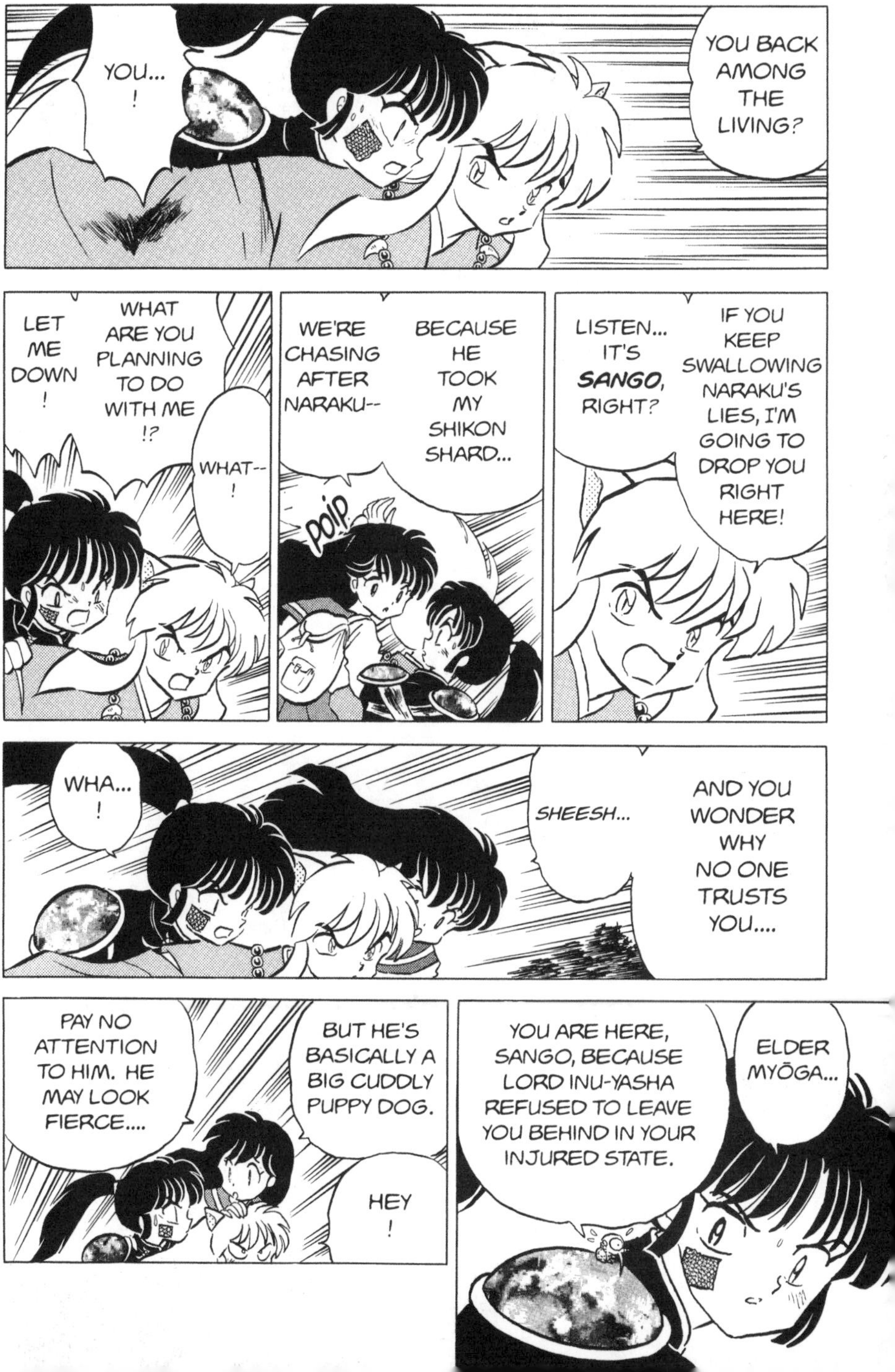
YOU... !
YOU BACK AMONG THE LIVING?
LET ME DOWN !
WHAT ARE YOU PLANNING TO DO WITH ME !?
WHAT-- !
WE'RE CHASING AFTER NARAKU--
BECAUSE HE TOOK MY SHIKON SHARD...
poip
LISTEN... IT'S *SANGO*, RIGHT?
IF YOU KEEP SWALLOWING NARAKU'S LIES, I'M GOING TO DROP YOU RIGHT HERE!
WHA... !
SHEESH...
AND YOU WONDER WHY NO ONE TRUSTS YOU....
PAY NO ATTENTION TO HIM. HE MAY LOOK FIERCE....
BUT HE'S BASICALLY A BIG CUDDLY PUPPY DOG.
HEY !
ELDER MYŌGA...
YOU ARE HERE, SANGO, BECAUSE LORD INU-YASHA REFUSED TO LEAVE YOU BEHIND IN YOUR INJURED STATE.

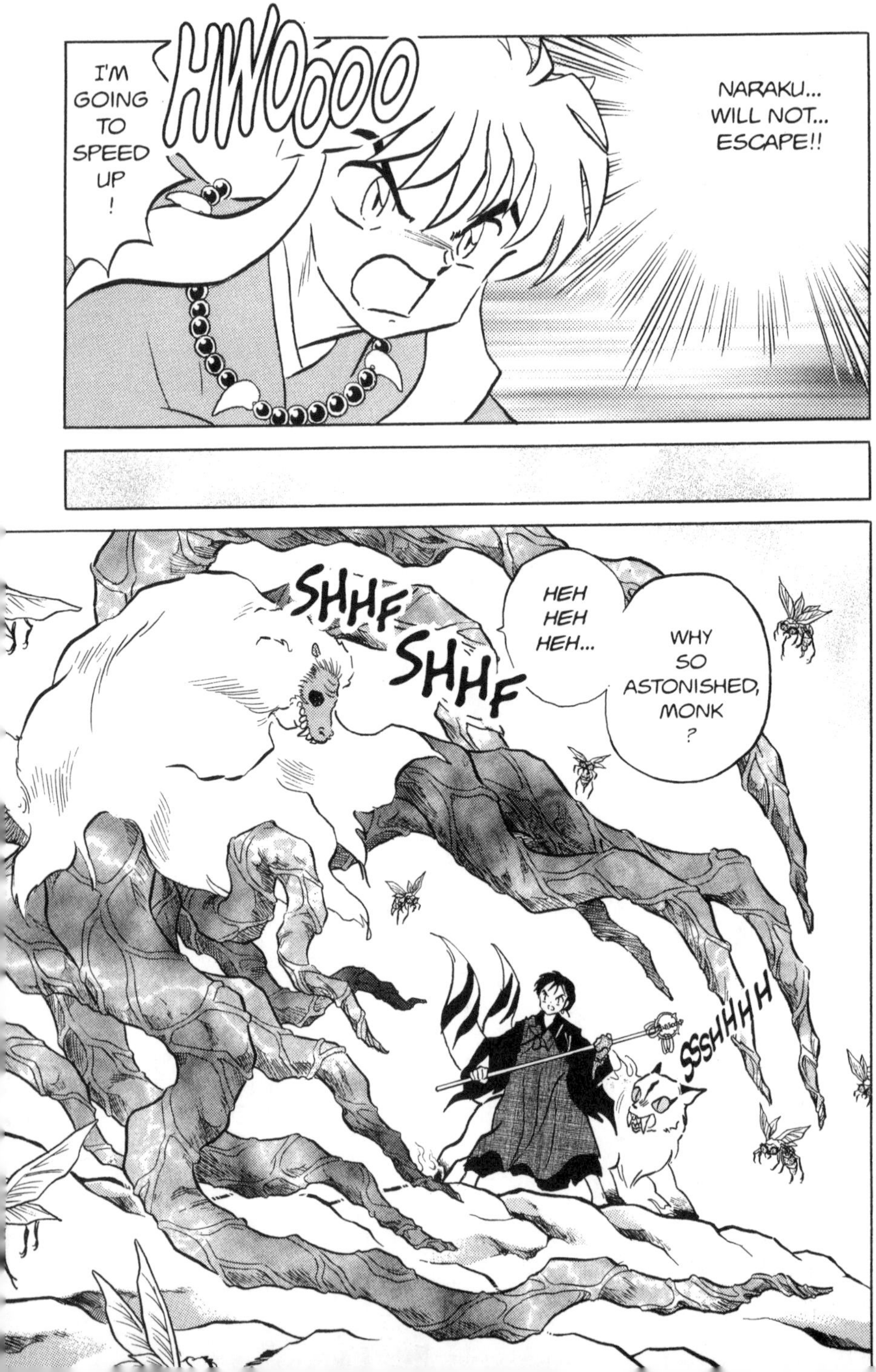
I'M GOING TO SPEED UP!
HWOOOOO
NARAKU... WILL NOT... ESCAPE!!
SHHF SHHF
HEH HEH HEH...
WHY SO ASTONISHED, MONK?
SSSHHHH

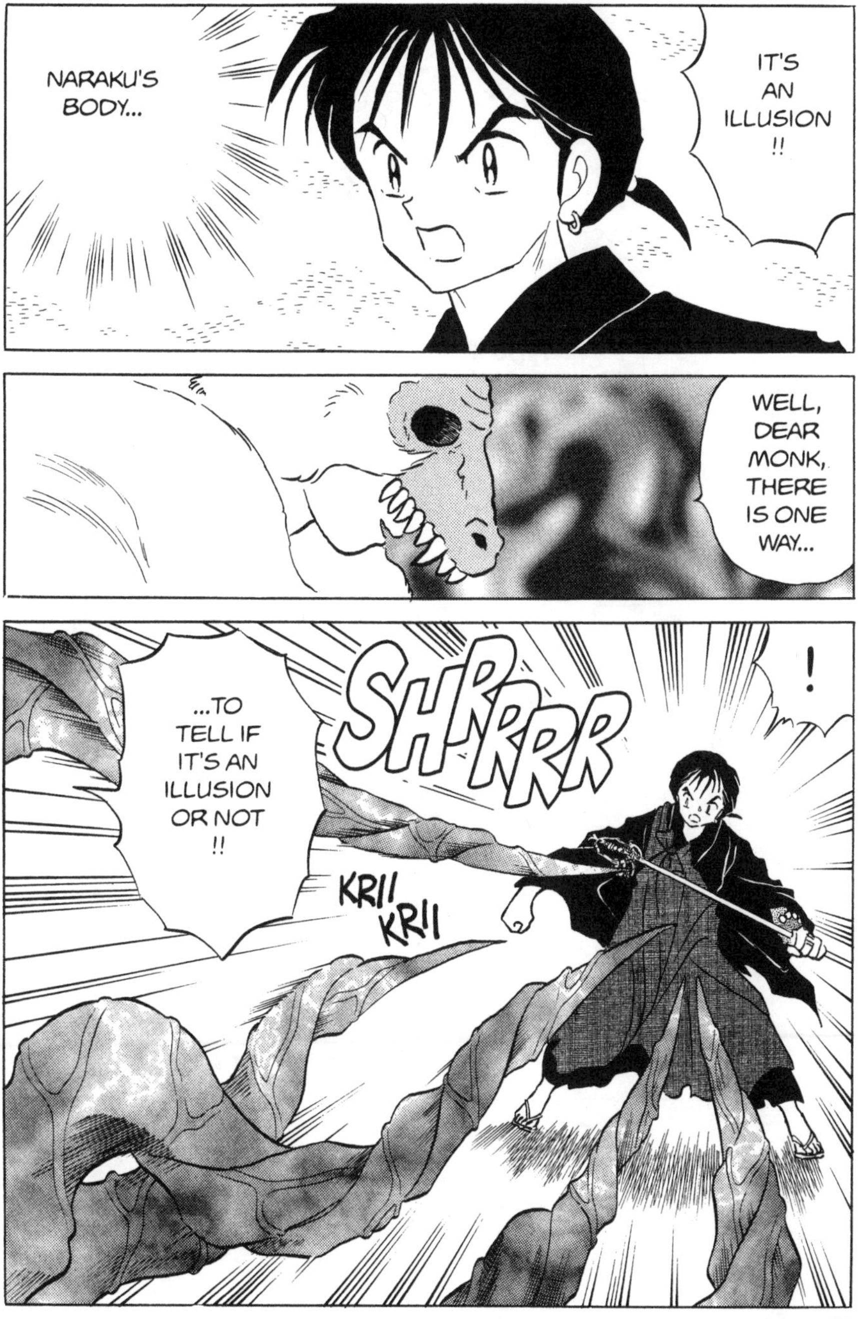
NARAKU'S BODY...
IT'S AN ILLUSION !!
WELL, DEAR MONK, THERE IS ONE WAY...
...TO TELL IF IT'S AN ILLUSION OR NOT !!
SHRRRR
!
KR!I KR!I

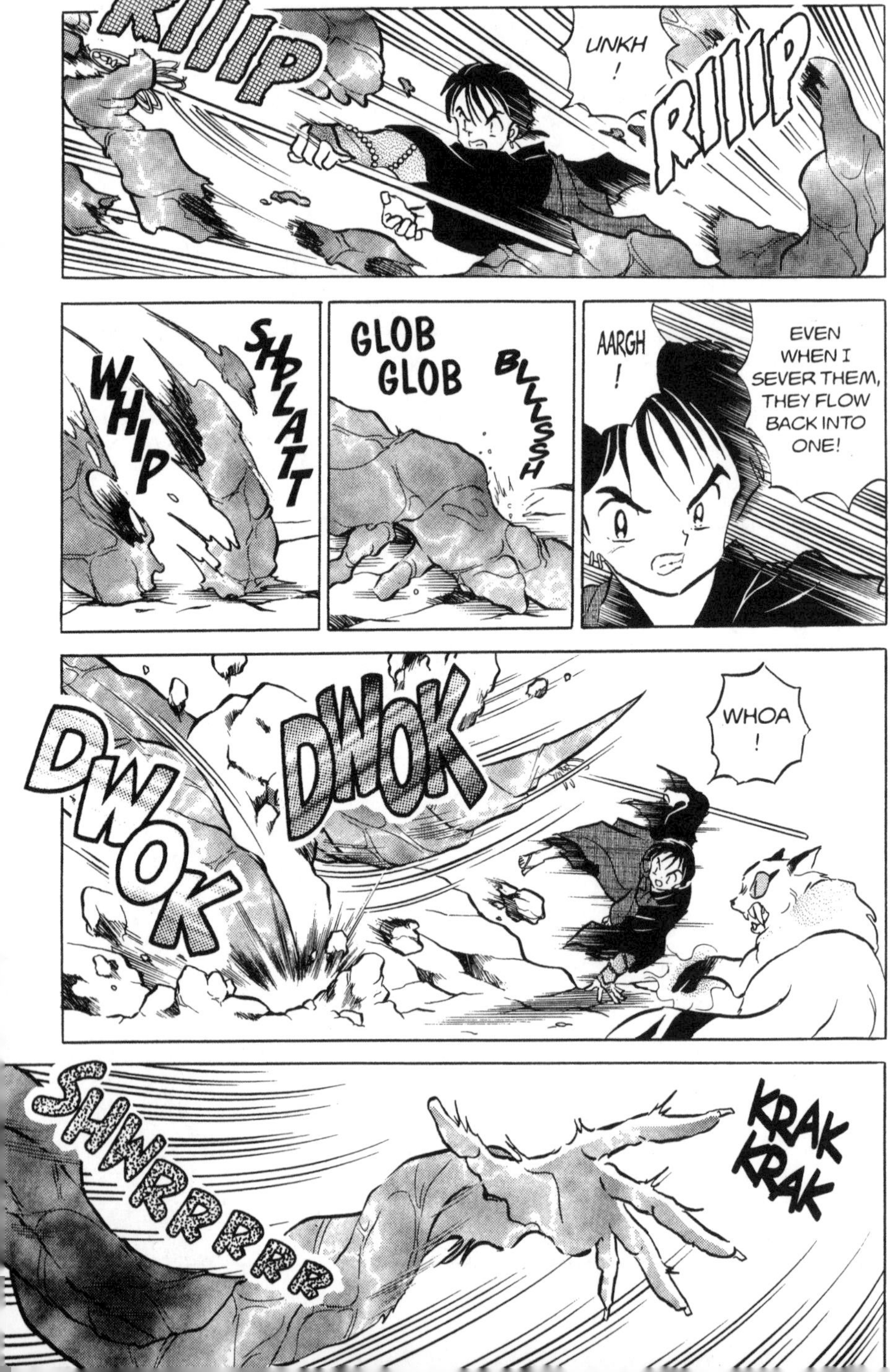
RIIIP
UNKH!
RIIIP
WHIP
SHPLATT
GLOB GLOB
BLLSSH
AARGH!
EVEN WHEN I SEVER THEM, THEY FLOW BACK INTO ONE!
DWOK
DWOK
WHOA!
SHWRRRRR
KRAK KRAK

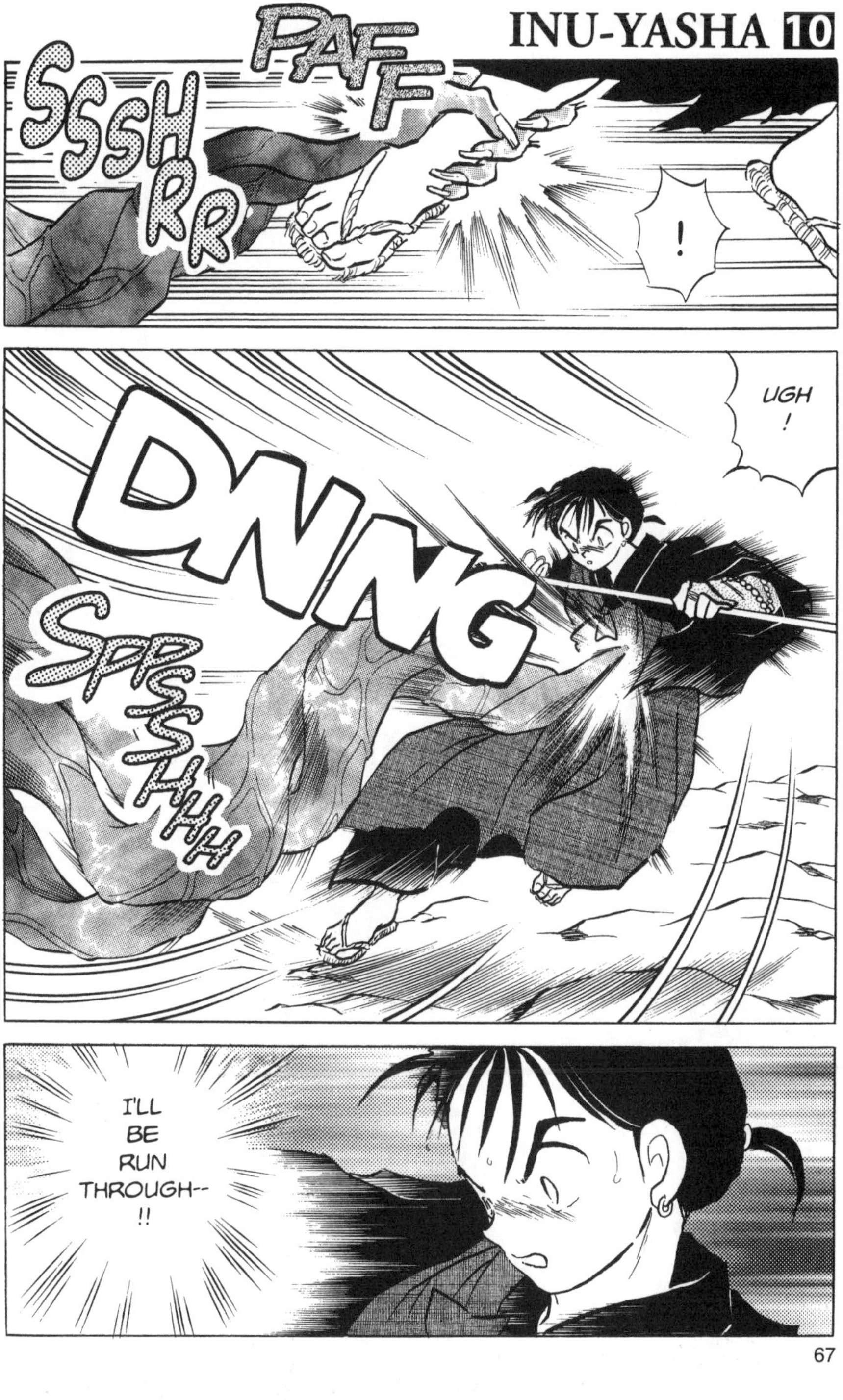
SSSH RR
PAFF
!
DNNG
SPPSSHHH
UGH !
I'LL BE RUN THROUGH-- !!

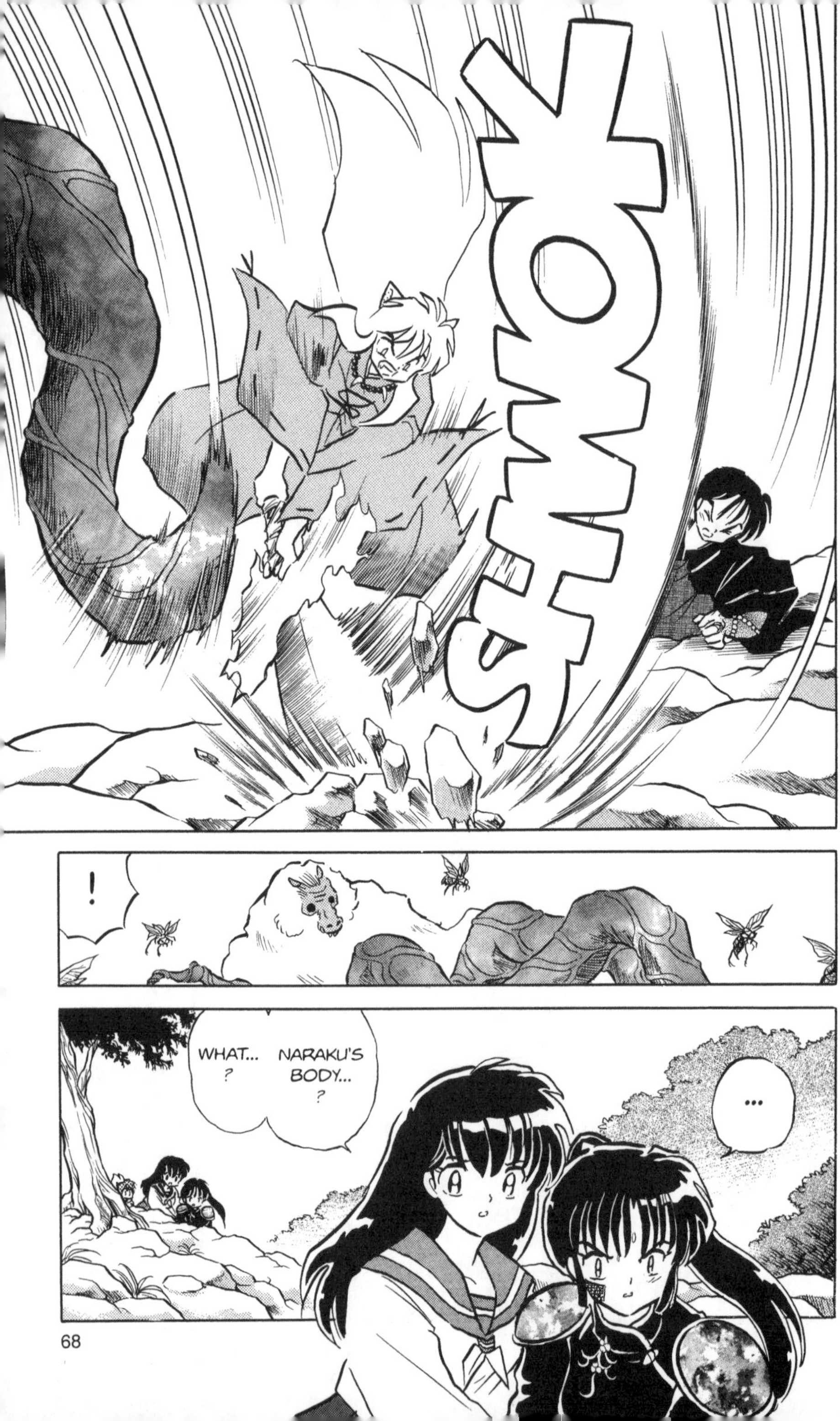
SHWOK
!
WHAT... ?
NARAKU'S BODY... ?
...

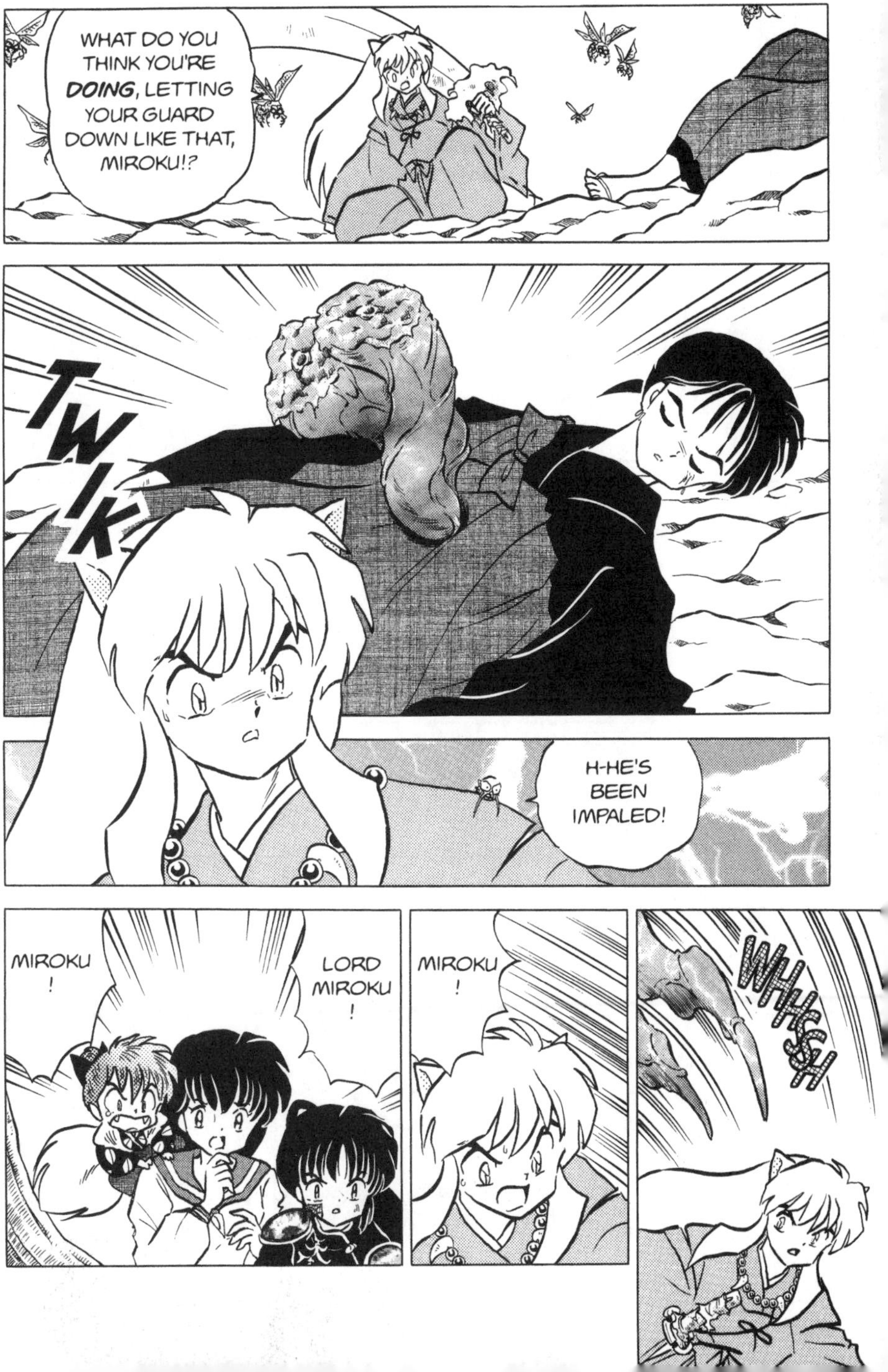
WHAT DO YOU THINK YOU'RE **DOING**, LETTING YOUR GUARD DOWN LIKE THAT, MIROKU!?
TWIK
H-HE'S BEEN IMPALED!
MIROKU!
LORD MIROKU!
MIROKU!
WHHSH

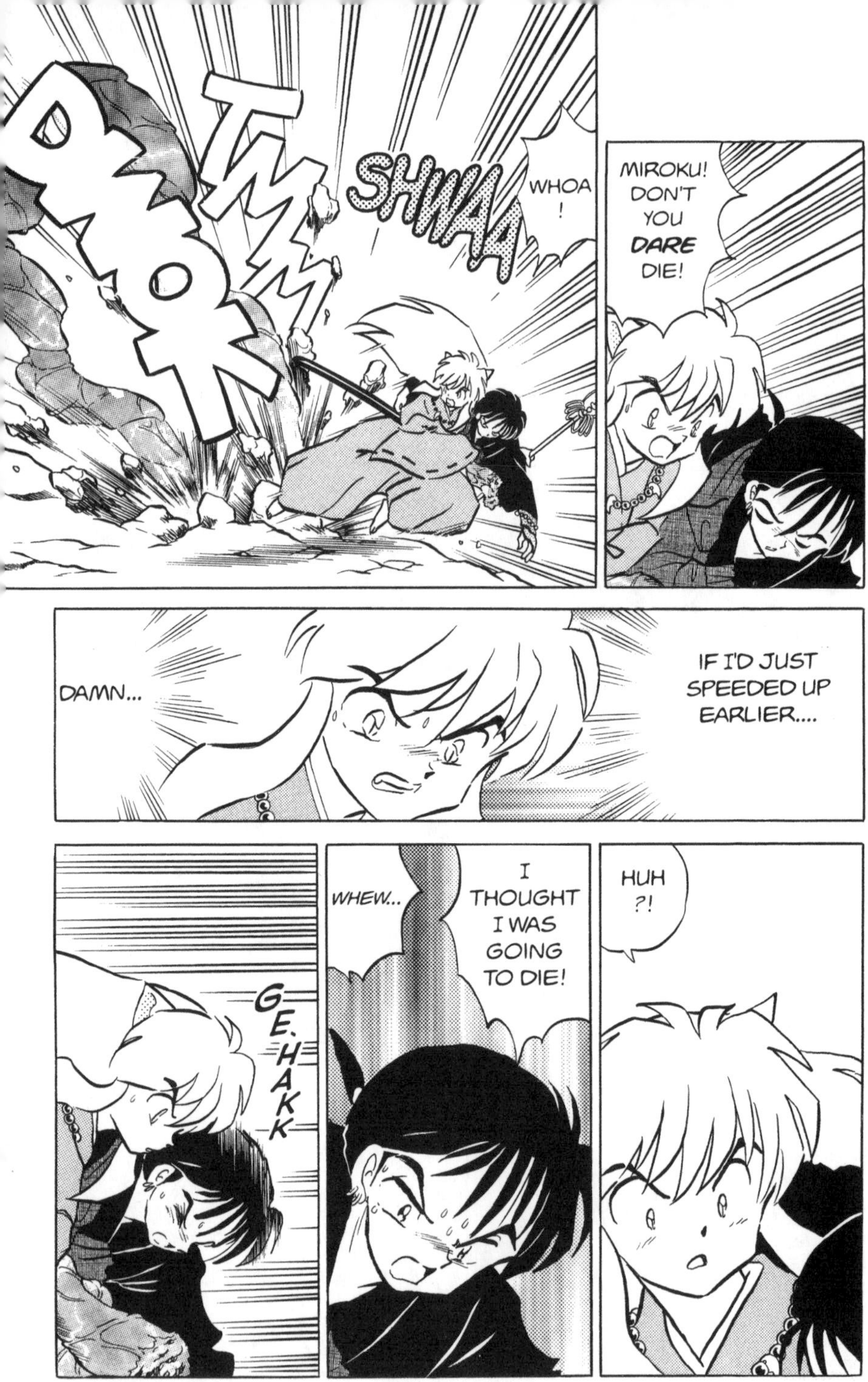
DWOK
TWM
SHWAA
WHOA!
MIROKU! DON'T YOU **DARE** DIE!
DAMN...
IF I'D JUST SPEEDED UP EARLIER....
GE. HAKK
WHEW...
I THOUGHT I WAS GOING TO DIE!
HUH?!

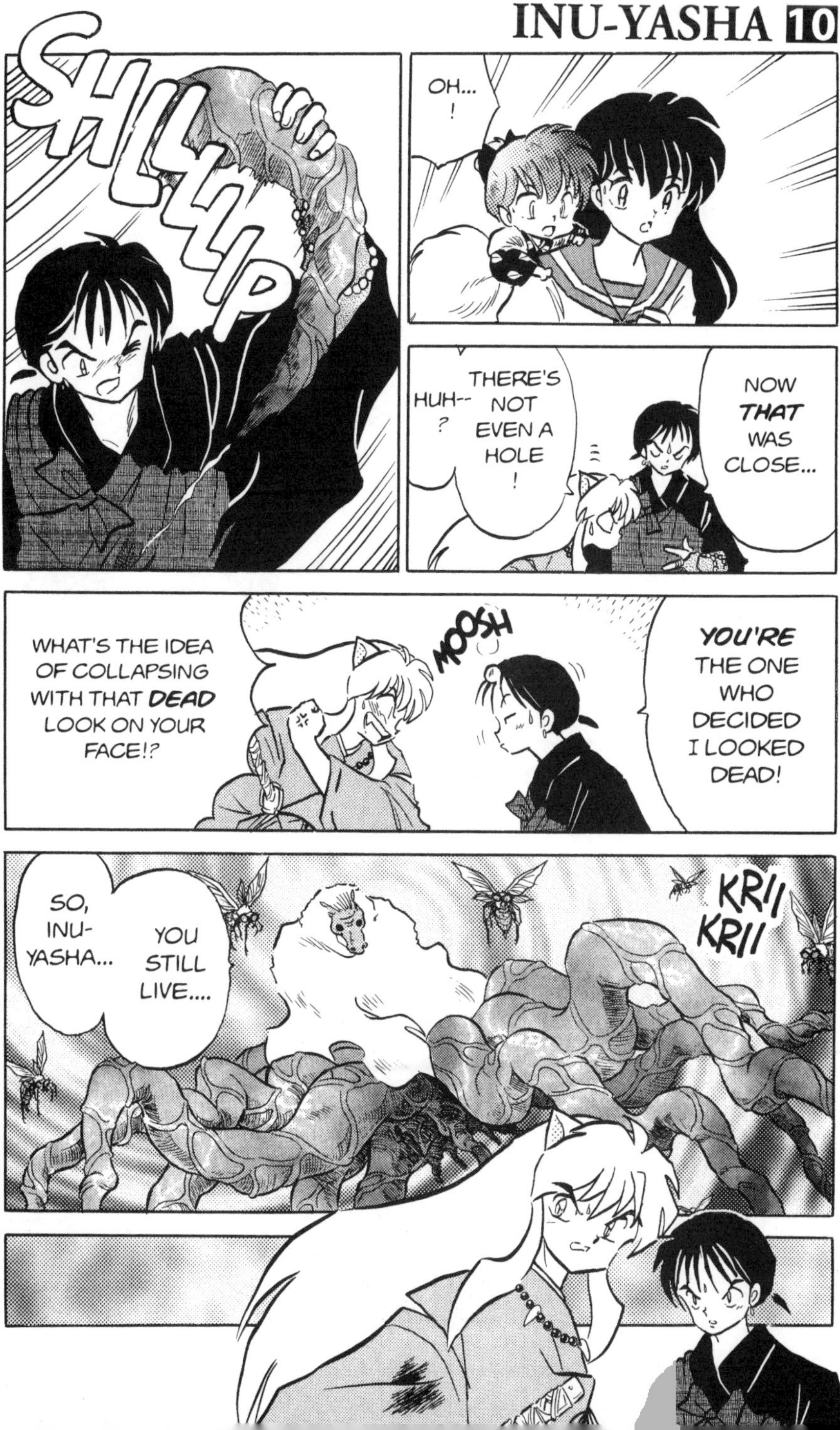
SHLLLIP
OH... !
HUH-- ?
THERE'S NOT EVEN A HOLE !
NOW THAT WAS CLOSE...
WHAT'S THE IDEA OF COLLAPSING WITH THAT DEAD LOOK ON YOUR FACE!?
MOOSH
YOU'RE THE ONE WHO DECIDED I LOOKED DEAD!
SO, INU-YASHA...
YOU STILL LIVE....
KRII KRII

SANGO WAS UNABLE TO TAKE YOU DOWN, EH...?

NARAKU... IT WAS ALL YOUR DOING, WASN'T IT!? YOU'RE THE ONE WHO LED THE DEMON HORDE TO THE EXTERMINATORS' VILLAGE...

AND CAUSED ITS DECIMATION!

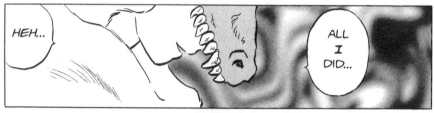

HEH...

ALL *I* DID...

WAS INFORM THE DEMONS THAT THE MOST POWERFUL OF THE EXTERMINATORS WERE SUMMONED TO THE CASTLE...

SO THAT THE VILLAGE'S DEFENSES WERE THIN.

YOU...

AND YOUR GOAL WAS THE SHIKON SHARD LOCATED IN THE VILLAGE?

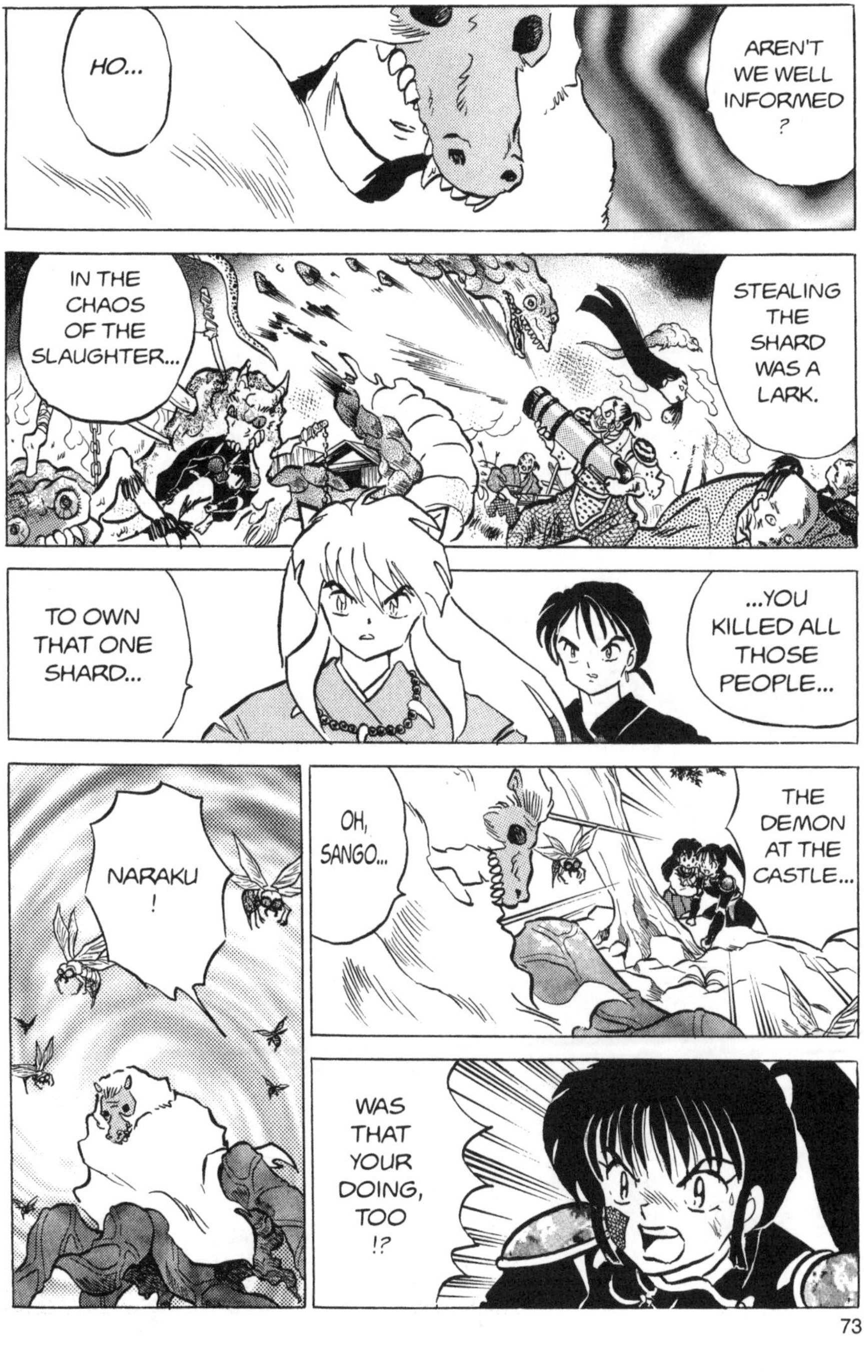
HO...
AREN'T WE WELL INFORMED ?
IN THE CHAOS OF THE SLAUGHTER...
STEALING THE SHARD WAS A LARK.
TO OWN THAT ONE SHARD...
...YOU KILLED ALL THOSE PEOPLE...
NARAKU !
OH, SANGO...
THE DEMON AT THE CASTLE...
WAS THAT YOUR DOING, TOO !?

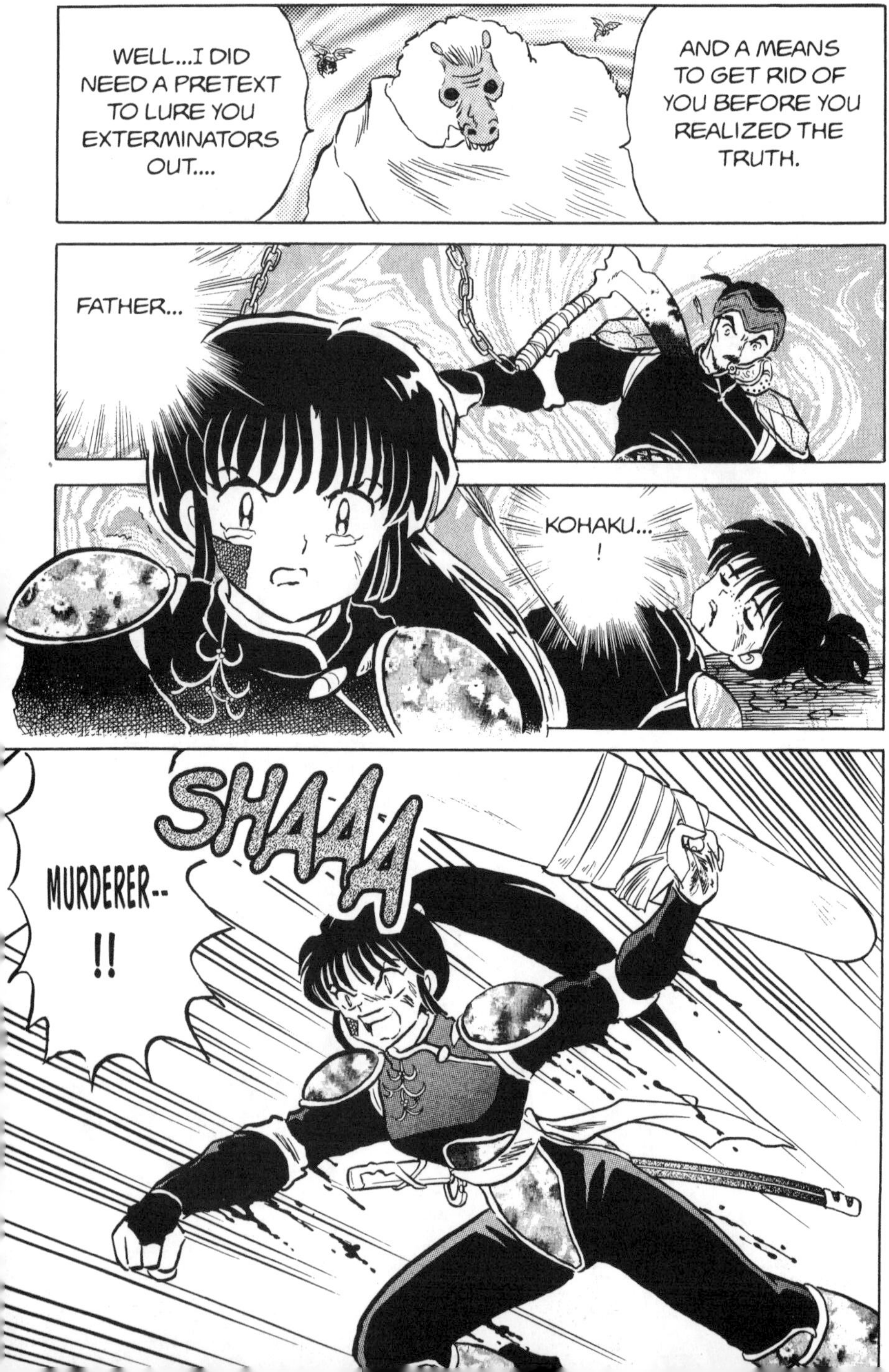
WELL...I DID NEED A PRETEXT TO LURE YOU EXTERMINATORS OUT....
AND A MEANS TO GET RID OF YOU BEFORE YOU REALIZED THE TRUTH.
FATHER...
KOHAKU... !
SHAAA
MURDERER-- !!

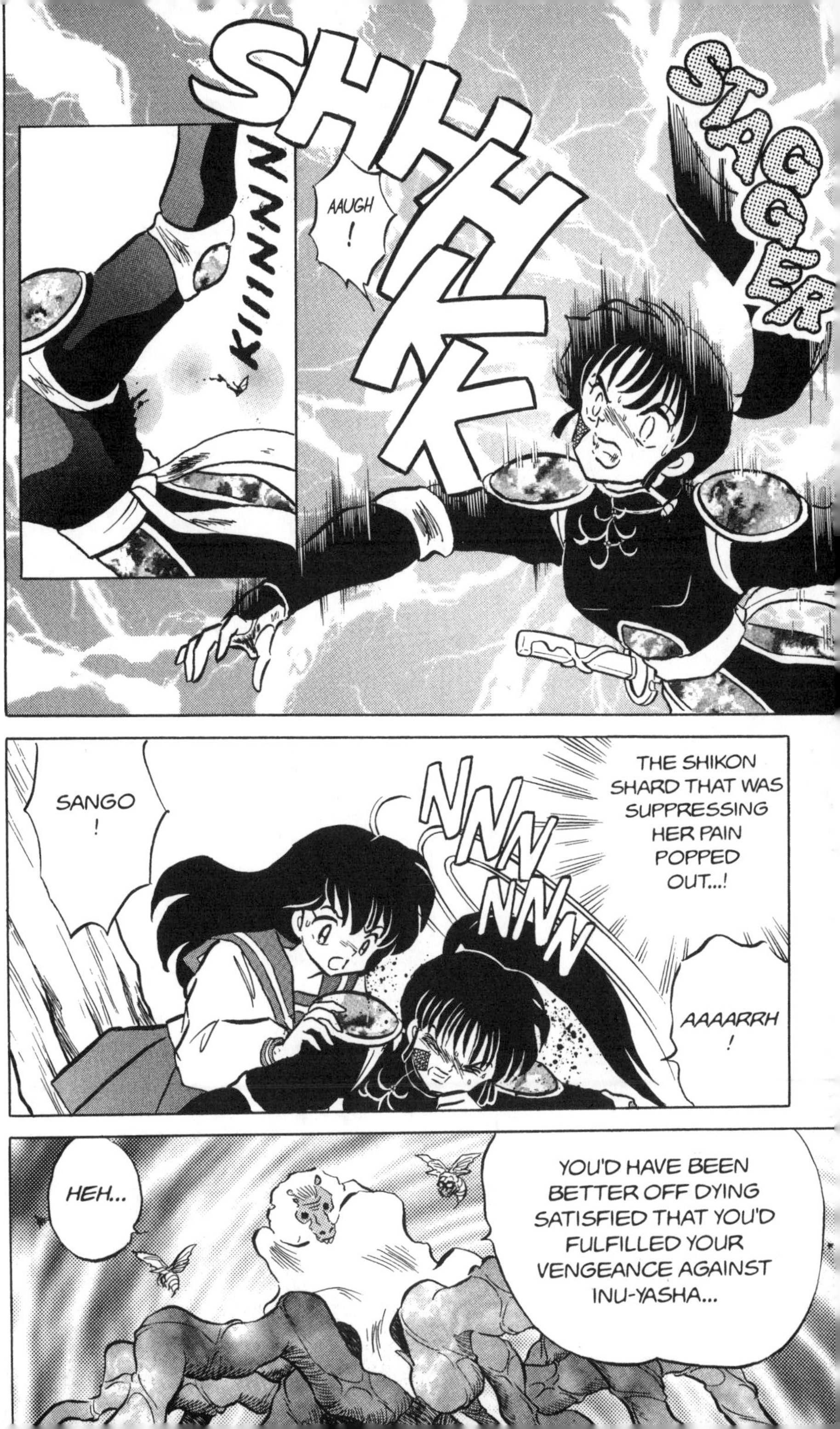
KIIIINNN
SHHHKKK
AAUGH!
STAGGER
SANGO!
NNNNNNN
THE SHIKON SHARD THAT WAS SUPPRESSING HER PAIN POPPED OUT...!
AAAARRH!
HEH...
YOU'D HAVE BEEN BETTER OFF DYING SATISFIED THAT YOU'D FULFILLED YOUR VENGEANCE AGAINST INU-YASHA...

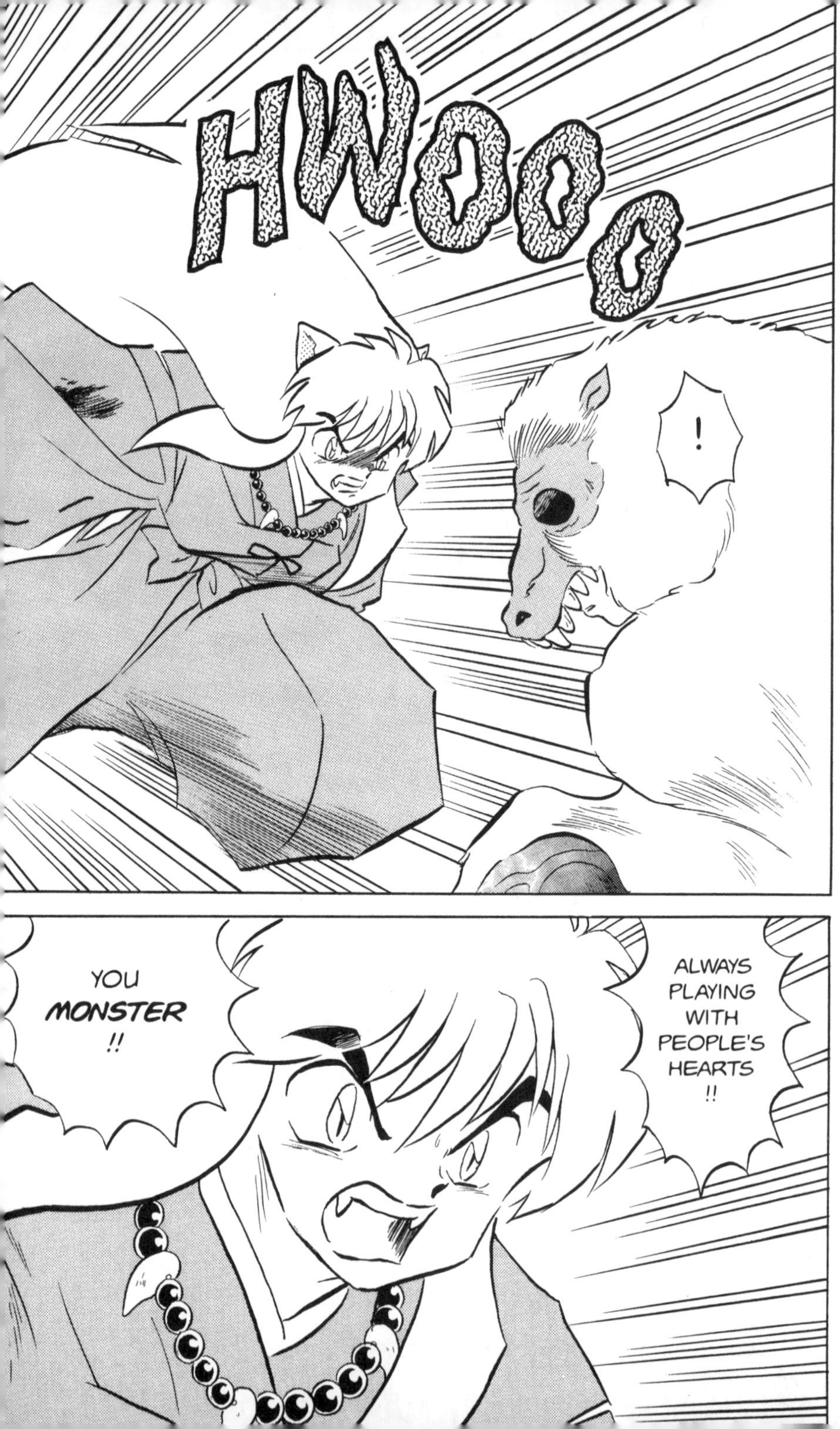
HWOOO
!
YOU MONSTER !!
ALWAYS PLAYING WITH PEOPLE'S HEARTS !!

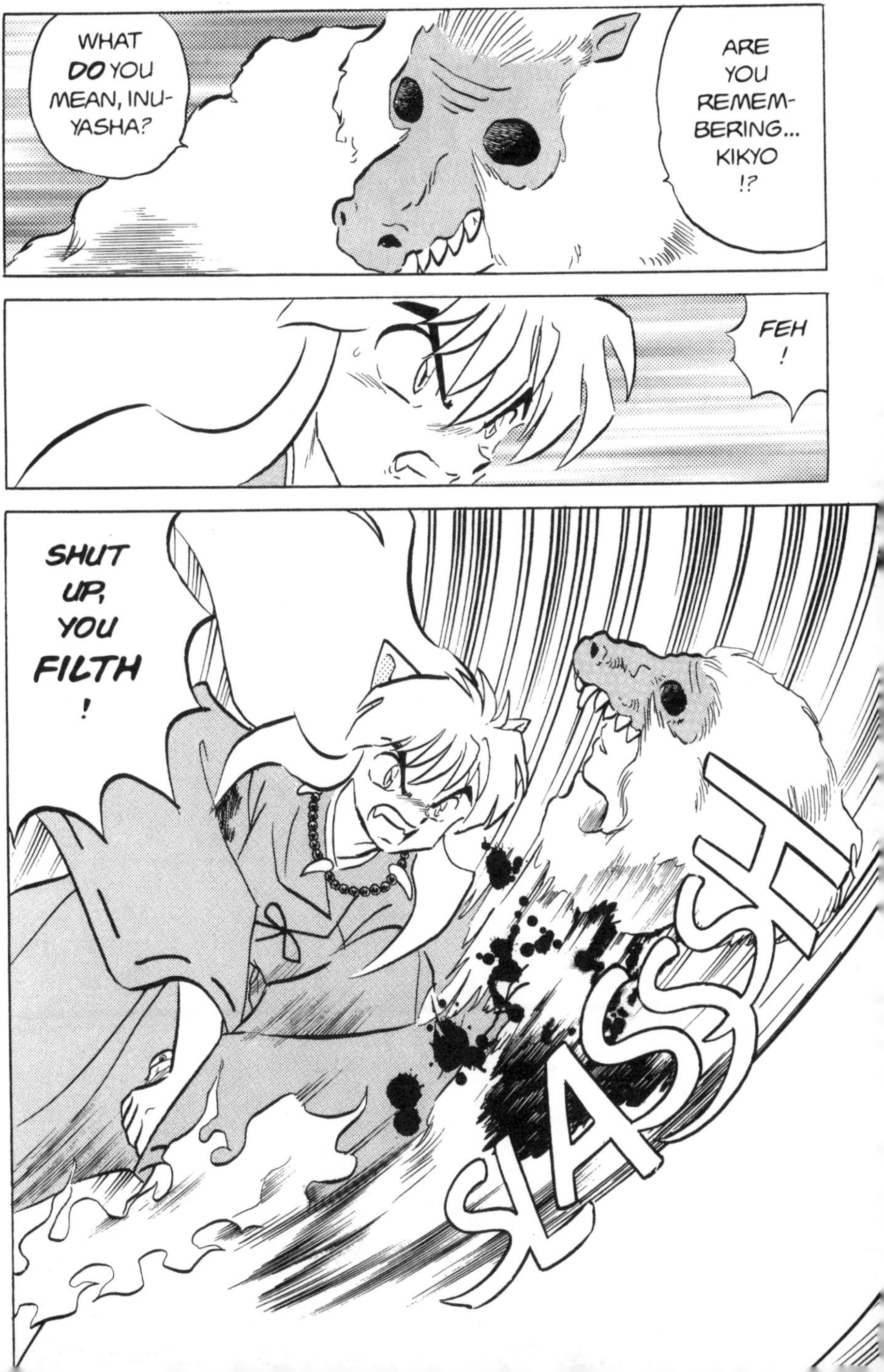
WHAT DO YOU MEAN, INU-YASHA?
ARE YOU REMEMBERING... KIKYO !?
FEH !
SHUT UP, YOU FILTH !
SLASSH

OH...!

HE DID IT...!

DOMP

...

ROLLL

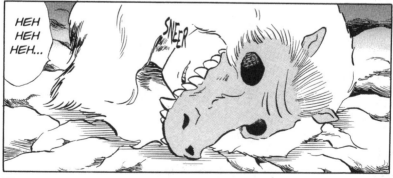

HEH HEH HEH...

SNEER

SCROLL FIVE

GOLEM

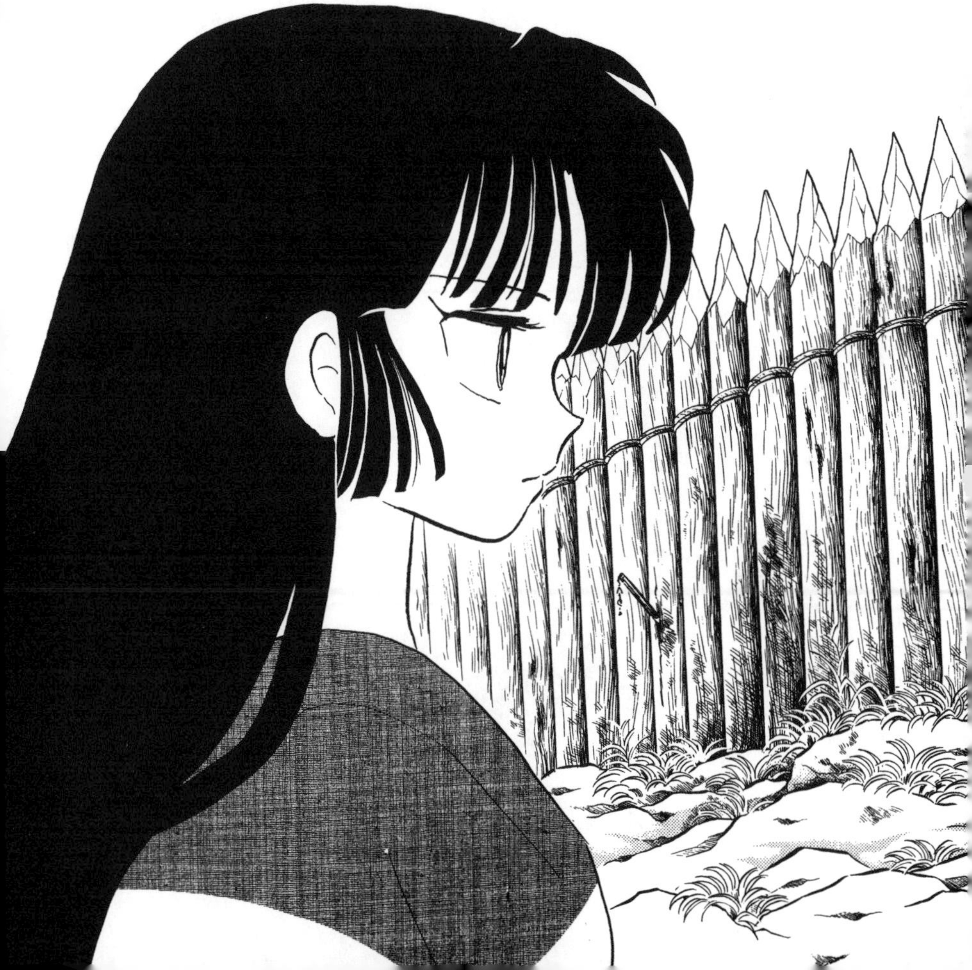

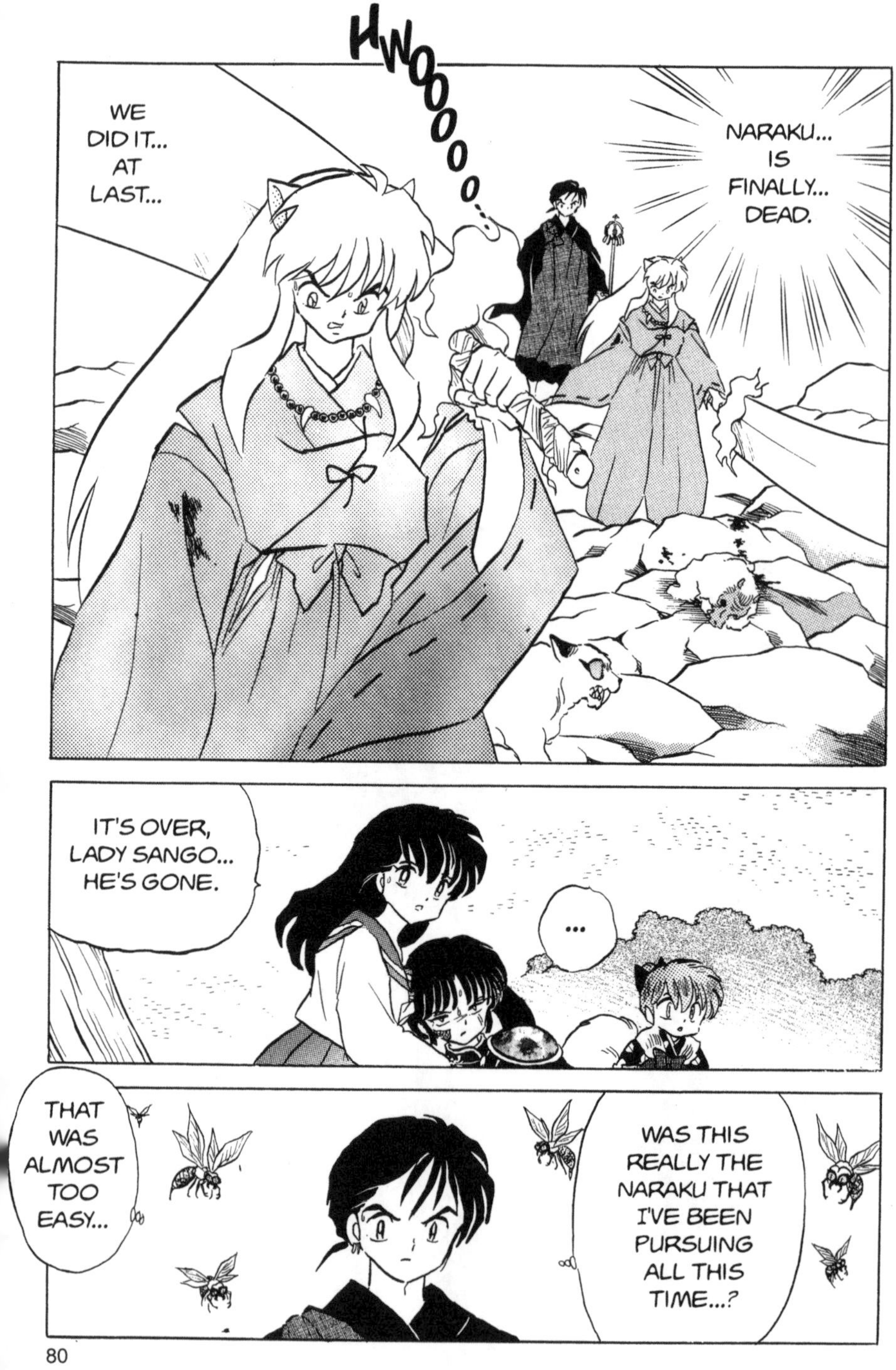
HWOOOOOO...
WE DID IT... AT LAST...
NARAKU... IS FINALLY... DEAD.
IT'S OVER, LADY SANGO... HE'S GONE.
...
THAT WAS ALMOST TOO EASY...
WAS THIS REALLY THE NARAKU THAT I'VE BEEN PURSUING ALL THIS TIME...?

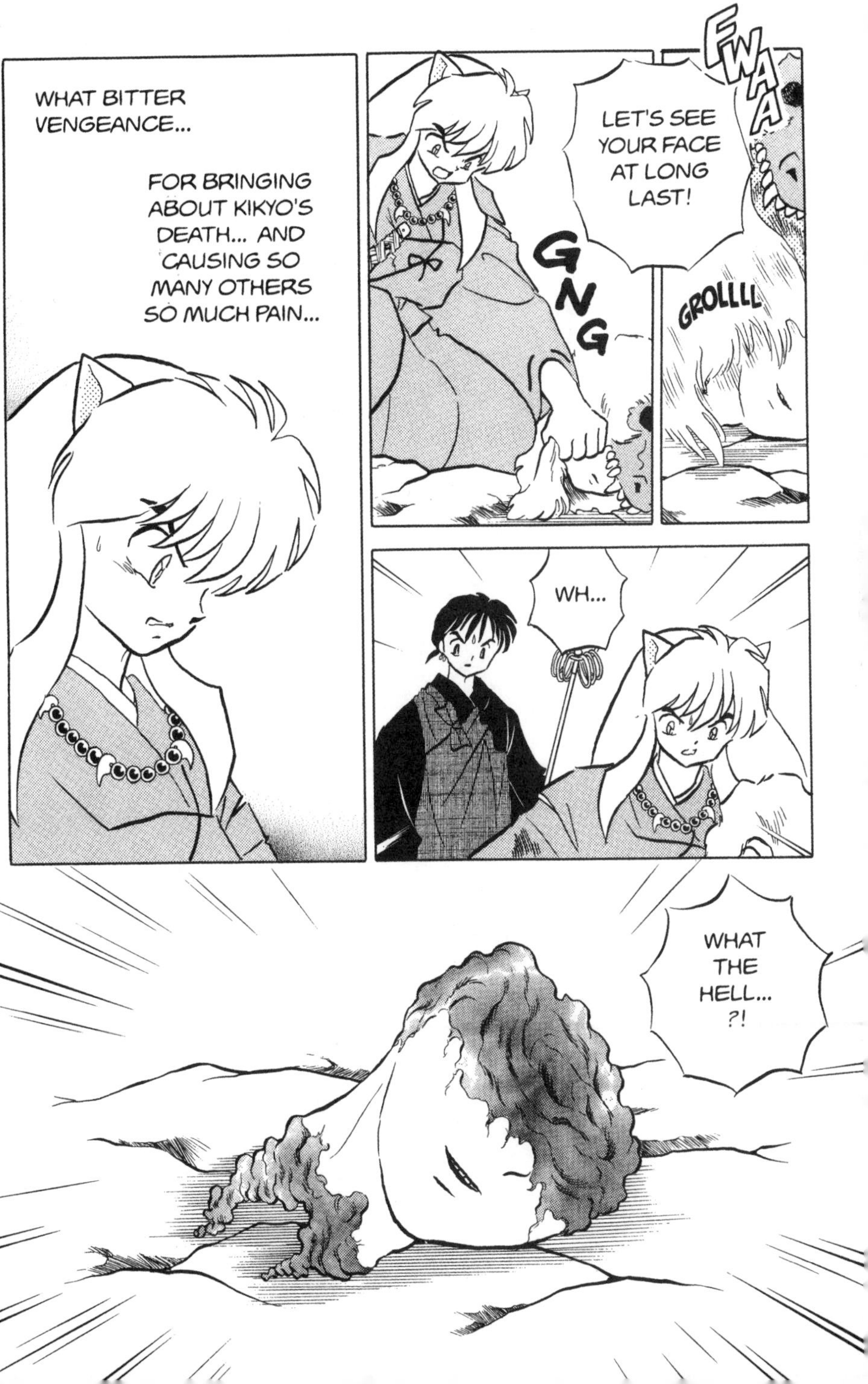
WHAT BITTER VENGEANCE...
FOR BRINGING ABOUT KIKYO'S DEATH... AND CAUSING SO MANY OTHERS SO MUCH PAIN...
LET'S SEE YOUR FACE AT LONG LAST!
GNG
FWAAA
GROLLLL
WH...
WHAT THE HELL... ?!

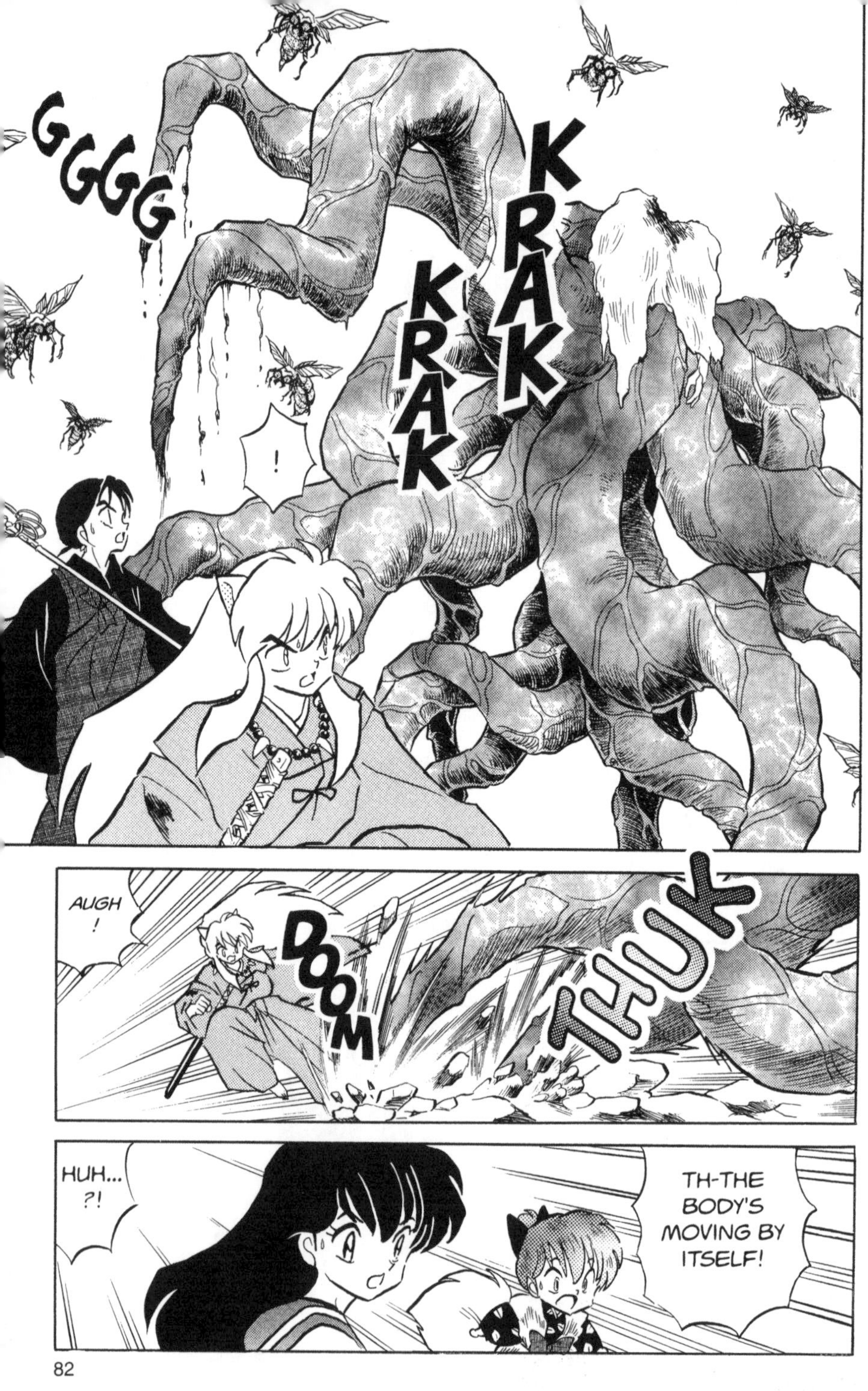

GGGG
KRAK
KRAK
!
AUGH !
DOOM
THUK
HUH... ?!
TH-THE BODY'S MOVING BY ITSELF!

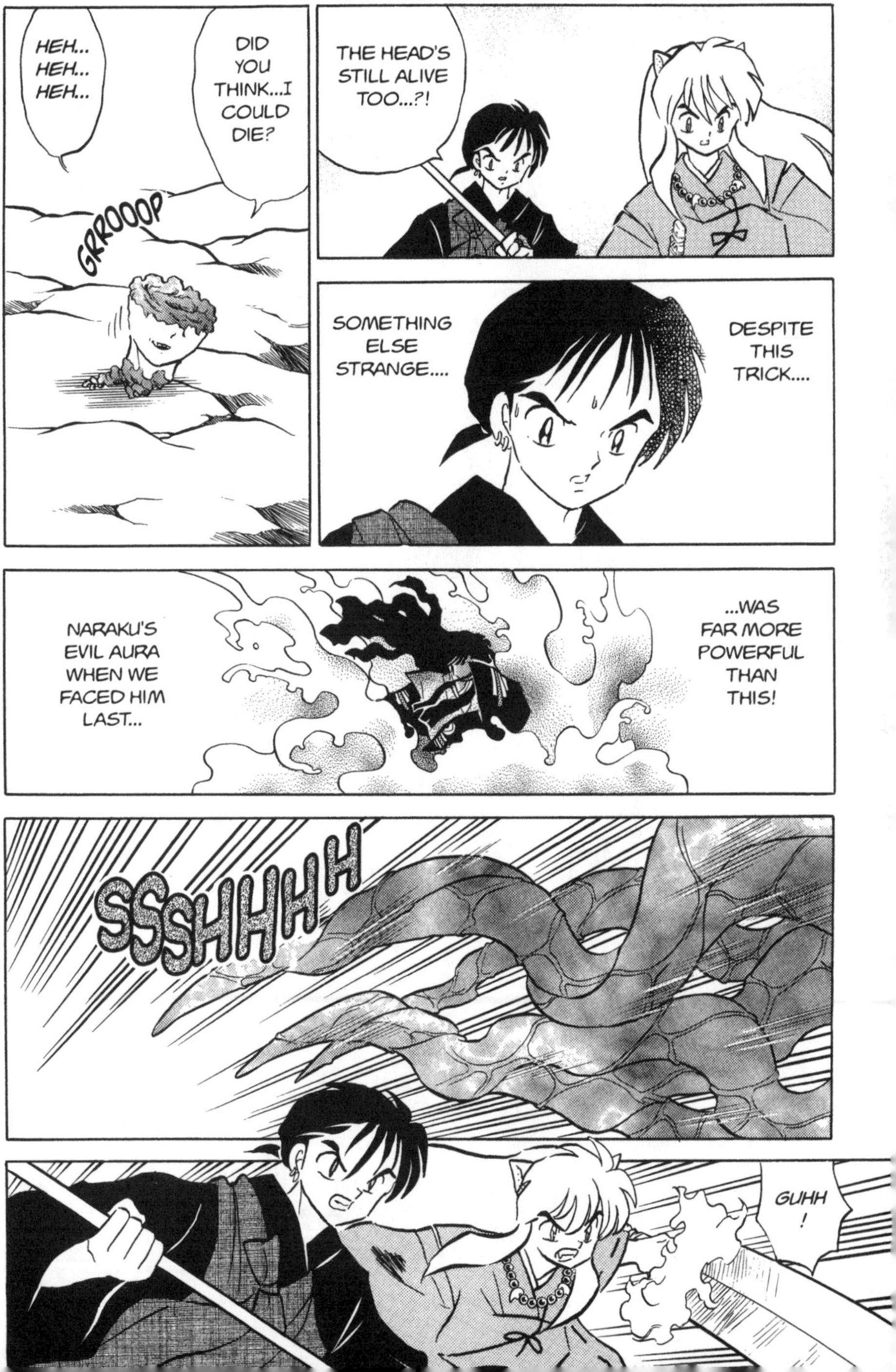
HEH... HEH... HEH...
DID YOU THINK...I COULD DIE?
GRROOOP
THE HEAD'S STILL ALIVE TOO...?!
SOMETHING ELSE STRANGE....
DESPITE THIS TRICK....
NARAKU'S EVIL AURA WHEN WE FACED HIM LAST...
...WAS FAR MORE POWERFUL THAN THIS!
SSSHHHHH
GUHH!

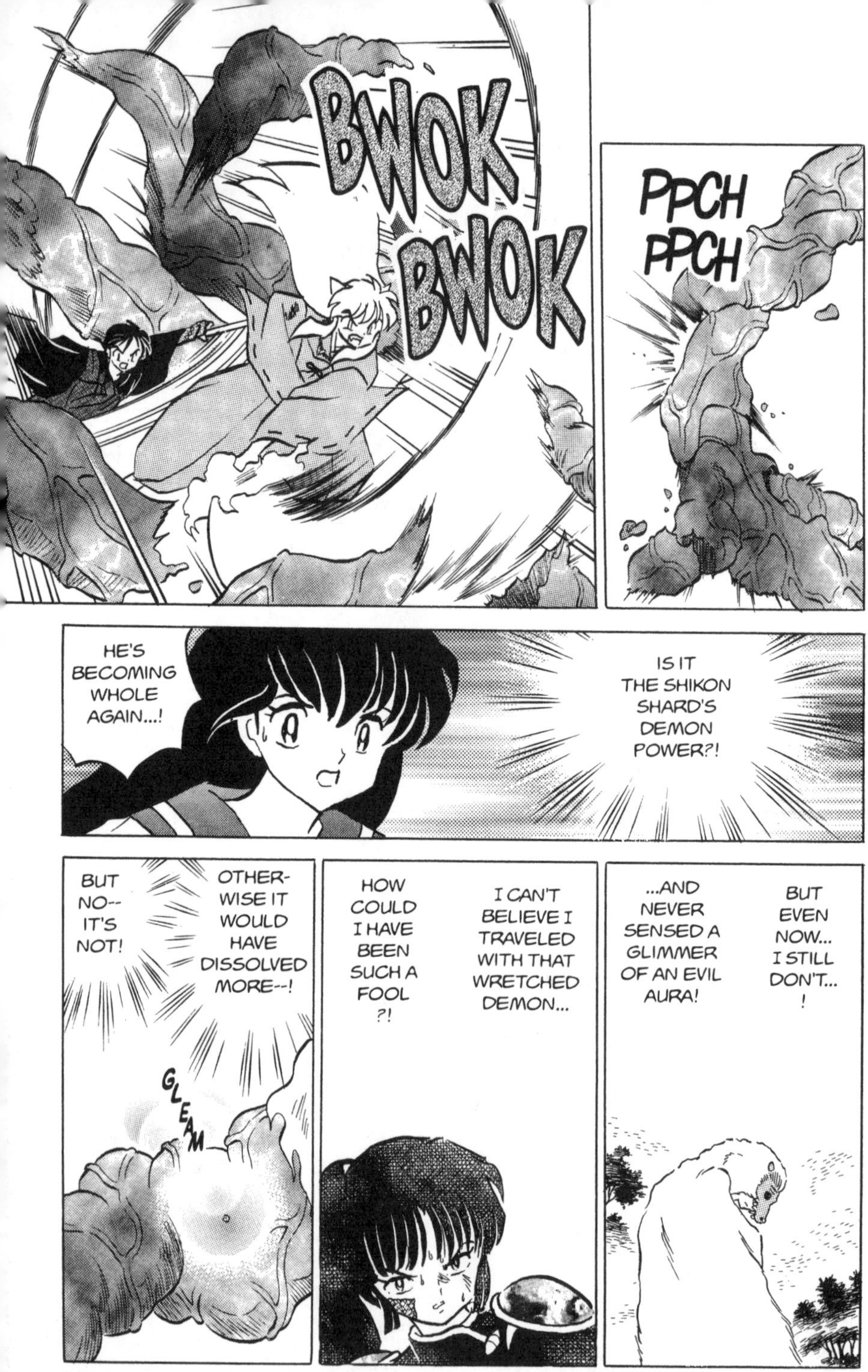
BWOK
BWOK
PPCH
PPCH
HE'S BECOMING WHOLE AGAIN...!
IS IT THE SHIKON SHARD'S DEMON POWER?!
BUT NO-- IT'S NOT!
OTHER-WISE IT WOULD HAVE DISSOLVED MORE--!
GLEAM
HOW COULD I HAVE BEEN SUCH A FOOL ?!
I CAN'T BELIEVE I TRAVELED WITH THAT WRETCHED DEMON...
...AND NEVER SENSED A GLIMMER OF AN EVIL AURA!
BUT EVEN NOW... I STILL DON'T... !

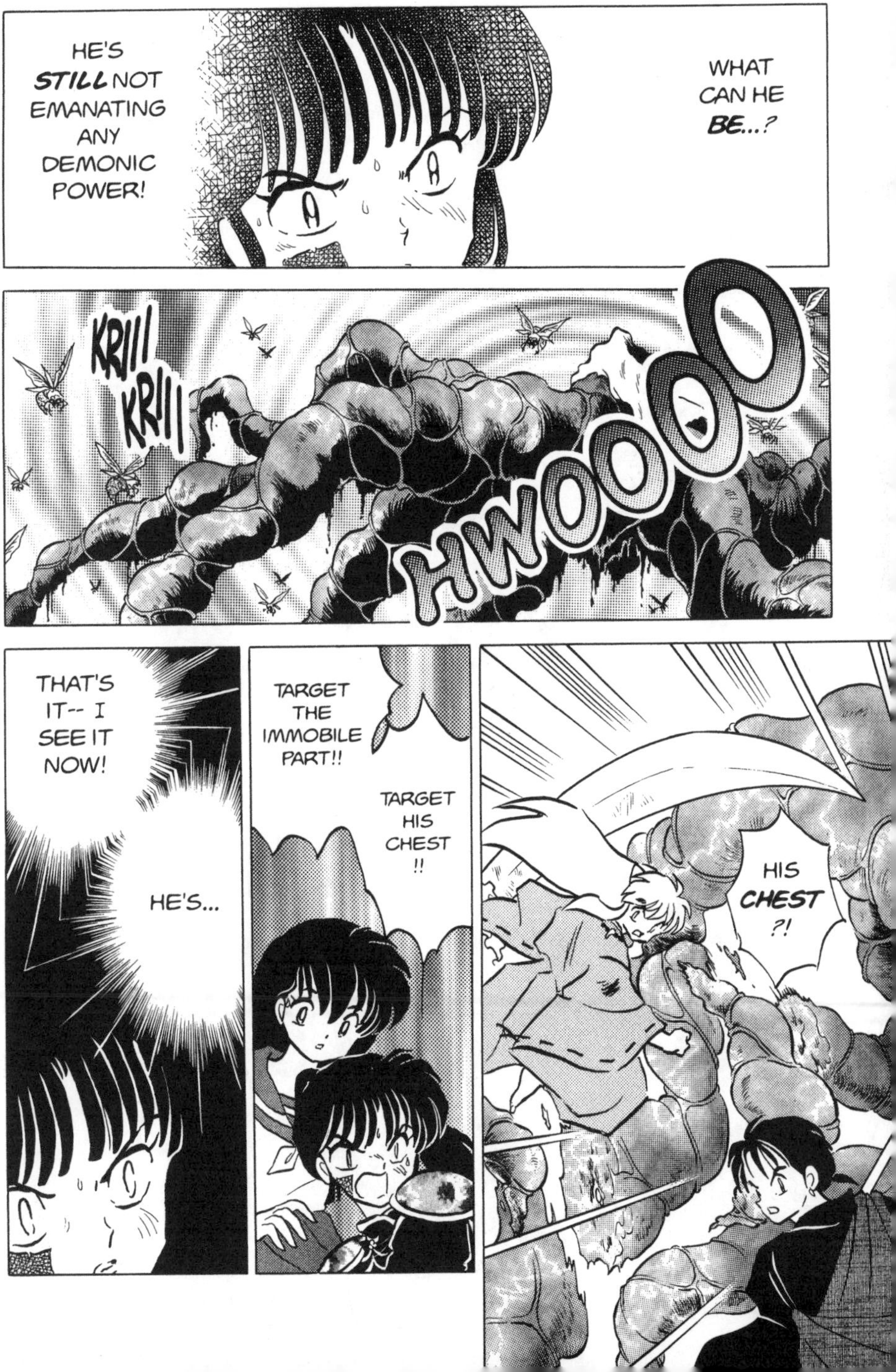
HE'S STILL NOT EMANATING ANY DEMONIC POWER!
WHAT CAN HE BE...?
KRIII KRIII
HWOOOOO
THAT'S IT-- I SEE IT NOW!
HE'S...
TARGET THE IMMOBILE PART!!
TARGET HIS CHEST !!
HIS CHEST ?!

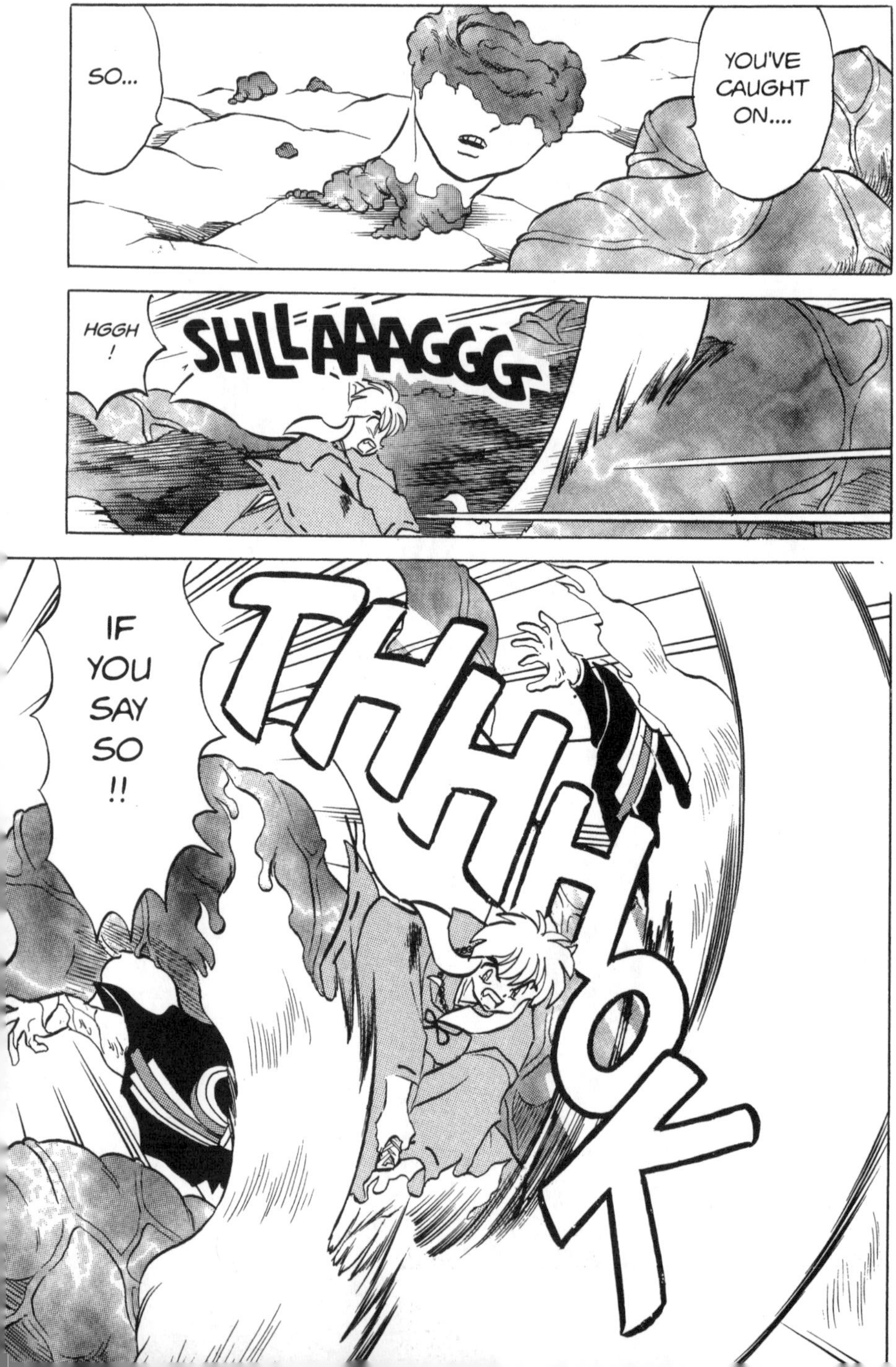
SO...
YOU'VE CAUGHT ON....
HGGH!
SHLLAAAGGG
IF YOU SAY SO!!
THHHHOK

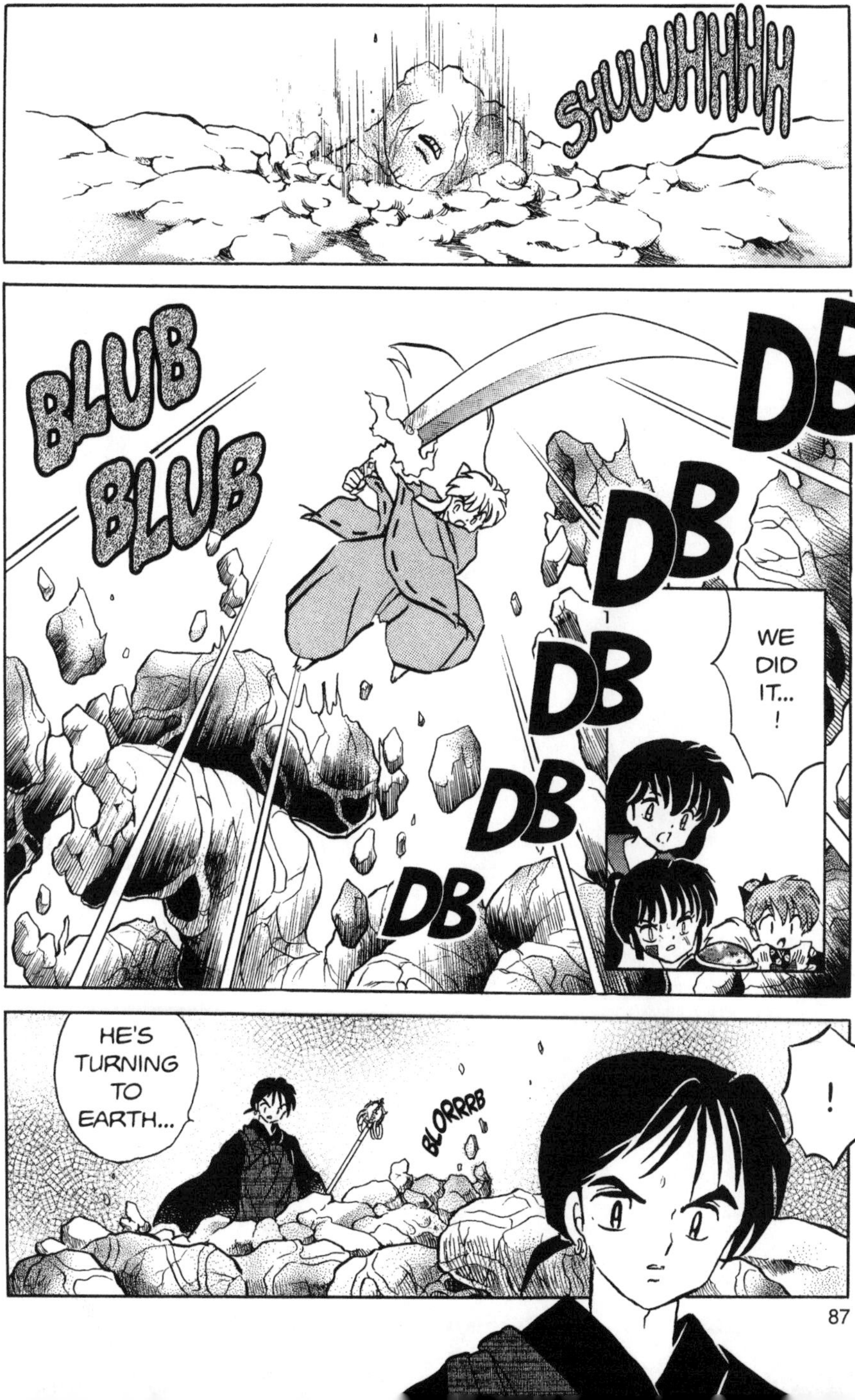
SHUUUHHHH
BLUB BLUB
DB DB DB DB DB
WE DID IT... !
HE'S TURNING TO EARTH...
BLORRRB
!

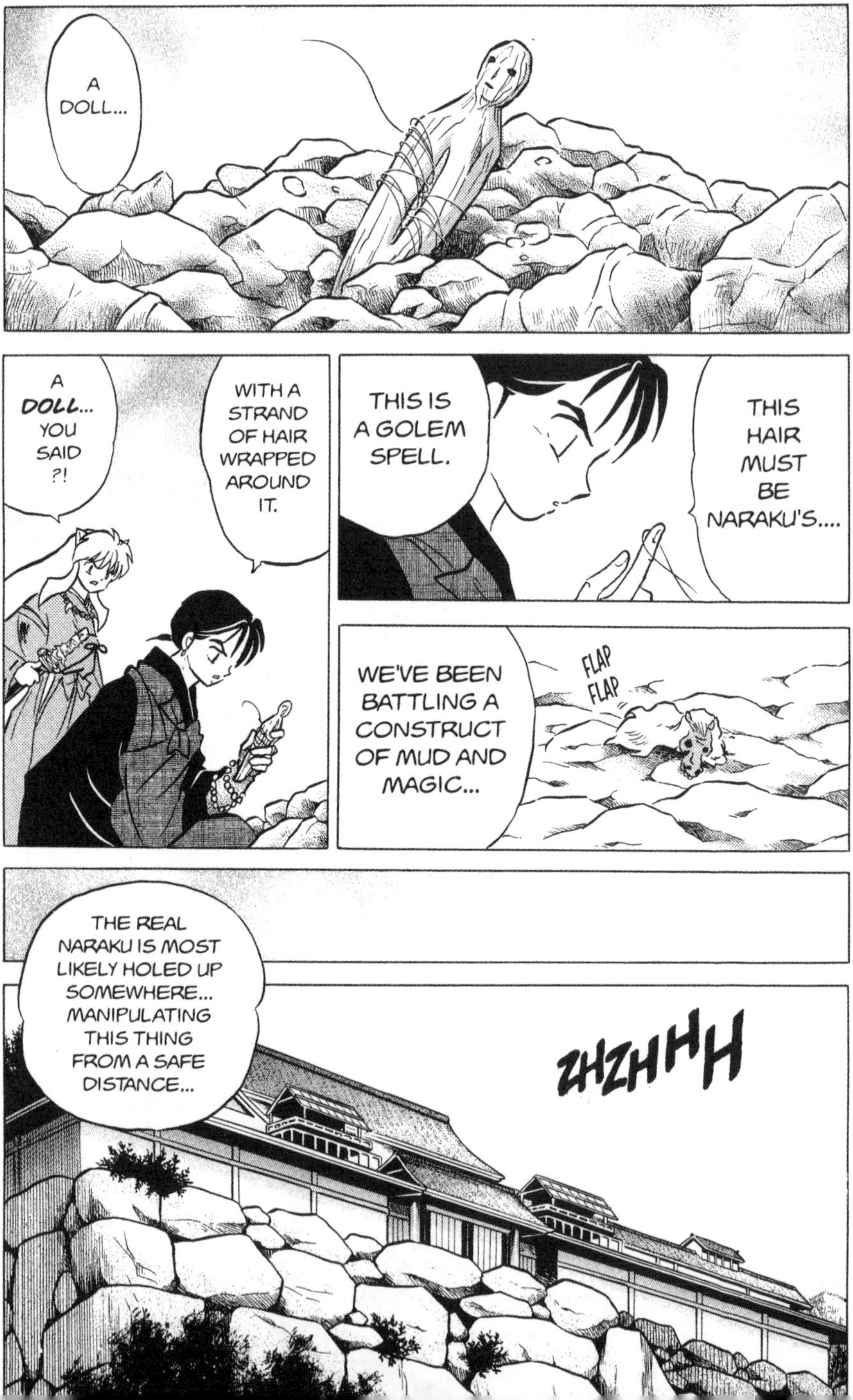
A DOLL...
A DOLL... YOU SAID ?!
WITH A STRAND OF HAIR WRAPPED AROUND IT.
THIS IS A GOLEM SPELL.
THIS HAIR MUST BE NARAKU'S....
WE'VE BEEN BATTLING A CONSTRUCT OF MUD AND MAGIC...
FLAP FLAP
THE REAL NARAKU IS MOST LIKELY HOLED UP SOMEWHERE... MANIPULATING THIS THING FROM A SAFE DISTANCE...
ZHZHHHH

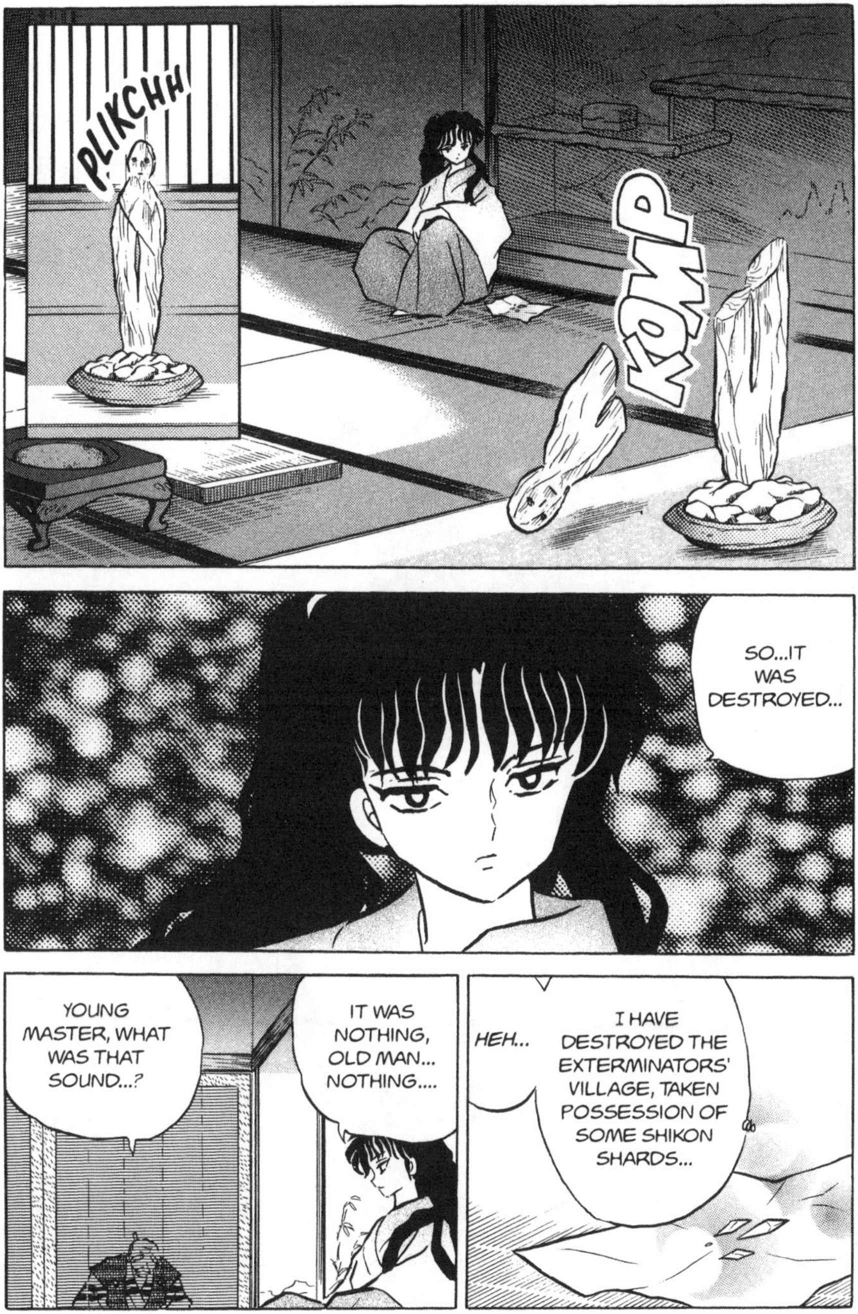
PLIKCHH
KOMP
SO...IT WAS DESTROYED...
YOUNG MASTER, WHAT WAS THAT SOUND...?
IT WAS NOTHING, OLD MAN... NOTHING....
HEH...
I HAVE DESTROYED THE EXTERMINATORS' VILLAGE, TAKEN POSSESSION OF SOME SHIKON SHARDS...

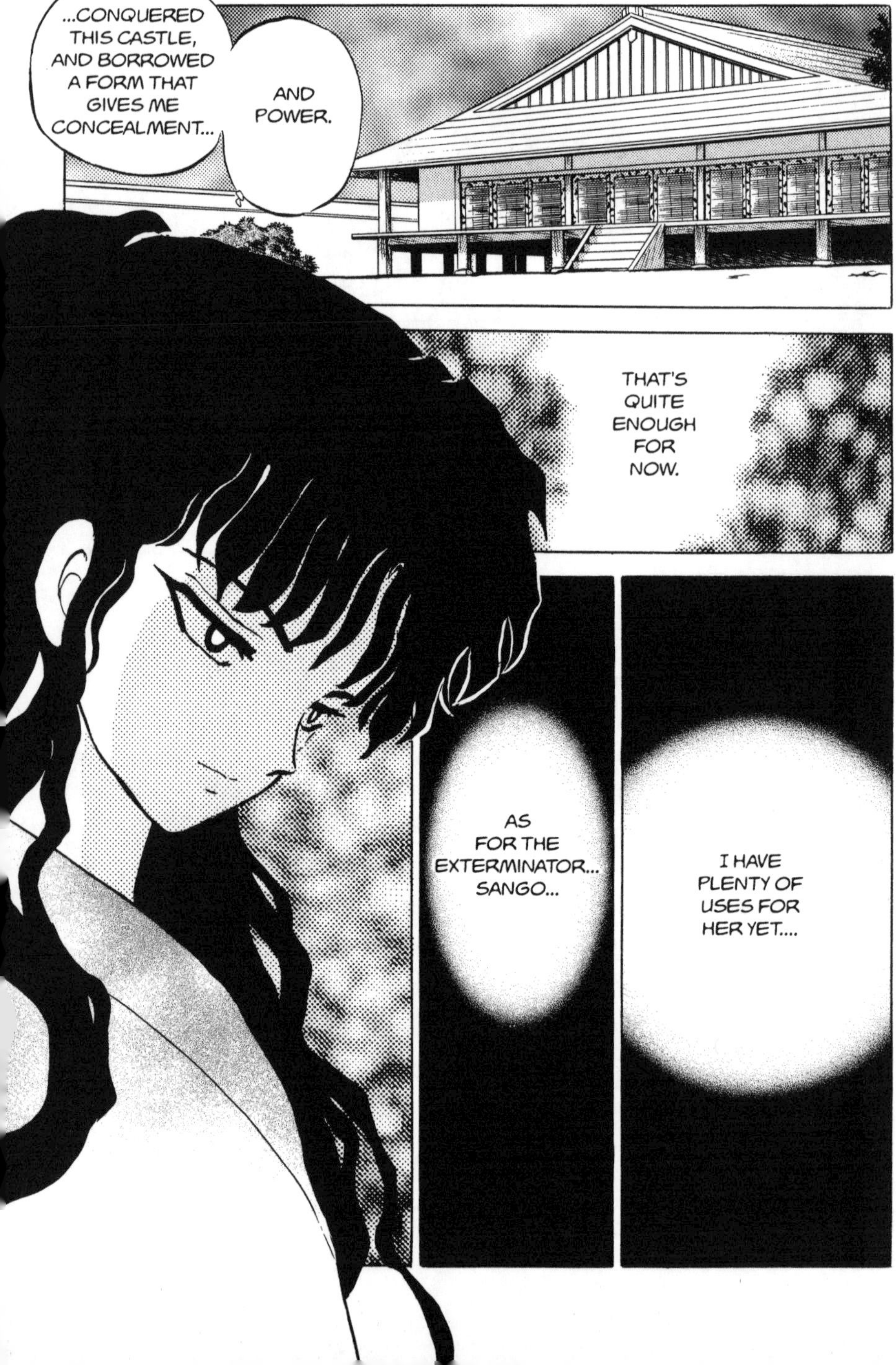
...CONQUERED THIS CASTLE, AND BORROWED A FORM THAT GIVES ME CONCEALMENT...
AND POWER.
THAT'S QUITE ENOUGH FOR NOW.
AS FOR THE EXTERMINATOR... SANGO...
I HAVE PLENTY OF USES FOR HER YET....

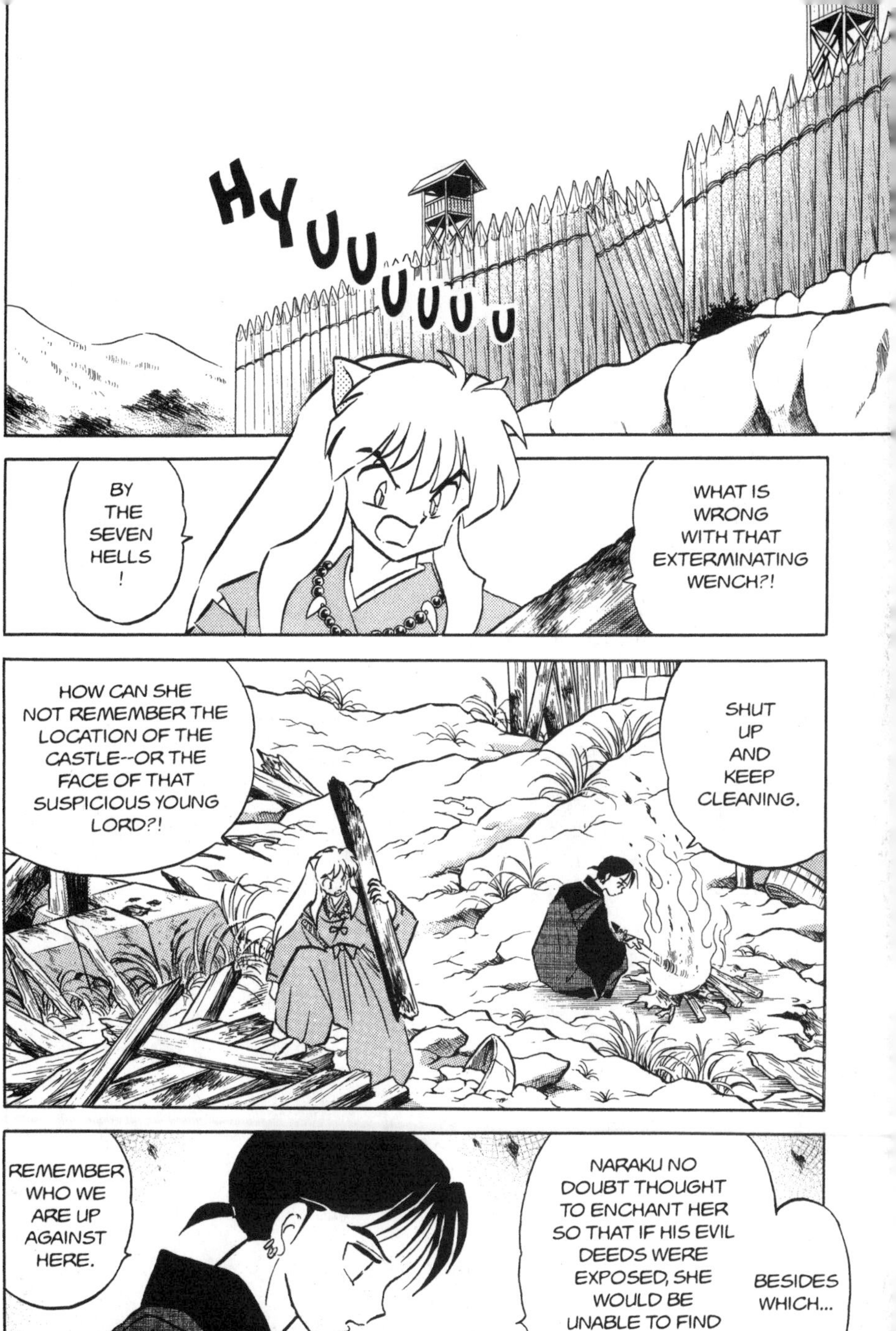
HYUUUUUUU
BY THE SEVEN HELLS!
WHAT IS WRONG WITH THAT EXTERMINATING WENCH?!
HOW CAN SHE NOT REMEMBER THE LOCATION OF THE CASTLE--OR THE FACE OF THAT SUSPICIOUS YOUNG LORD?!
SHUT UP AND KEEP CLEANING.
REMEMBER WHO WE ARE UP AGAINST HERE.
NARAKU NO DOUBT THOUGHT TO ENCHANT HER SO THAT IF HIS EVIL DEEDS WERE EXPOSED, SHE WOULD BE UNABLE TO FIND HER WAY BACK TO HIM.
BESIDES WHICH...

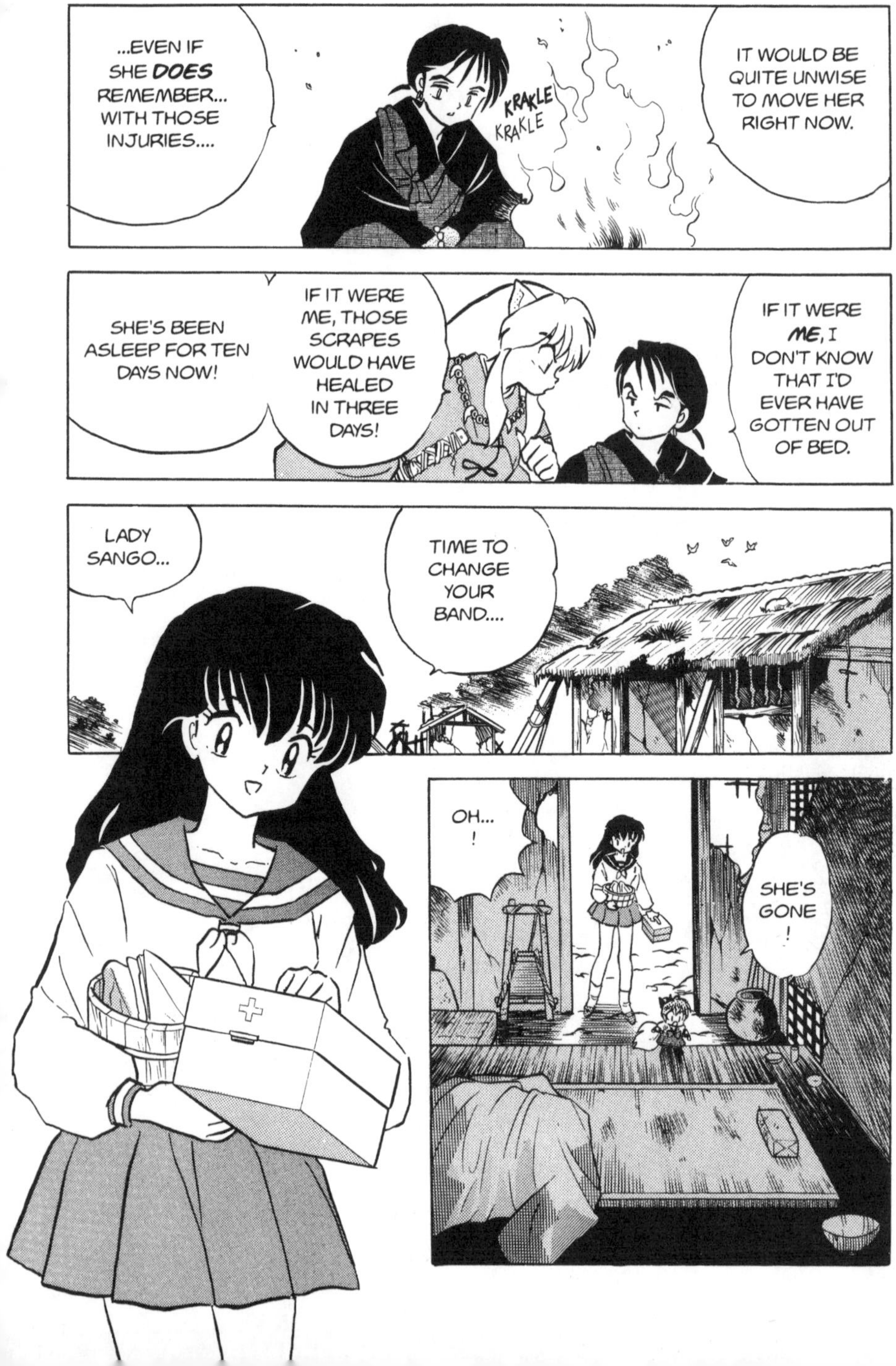
...EVEN IF SHE **DOES** REMEMBER... WITH THOSE INJURIES....
KRAKLE KRAKLE
IT WOULD BE QUITE UNWISE TO MOVE HER RIGHT NOW.
SHE'S BEEN ASLEEP FOR TEN DAYS NOW!
IF IT WERE ME, THOSE SCRAPES WOULD HAVE HEALED IN THREE DAYS!
IF IT WERE **ME**, I DON'T KNOW THAT I'D EVER HAVE GOTTEN OUT OF BED.
LADY SANGO...
TIME TO CHANGE YOUR BAND....
OH... !
SHE'S GONE !

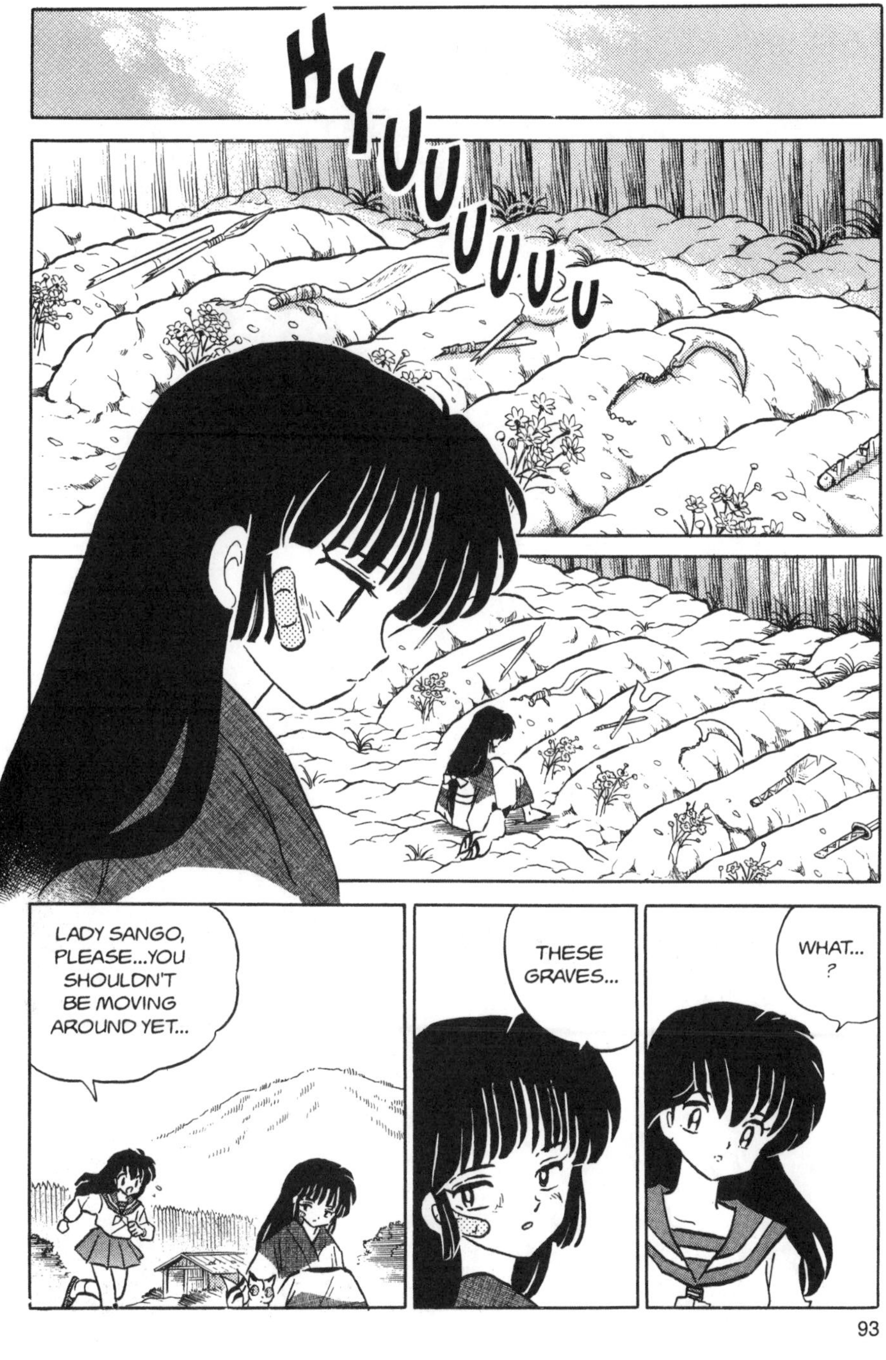
HYUUUUUUU
LADY SANGO, PLEASE...YOU SHOULDN'T BE MOVING AROUND YET...
THESE GRAVES...
WHAT... ?

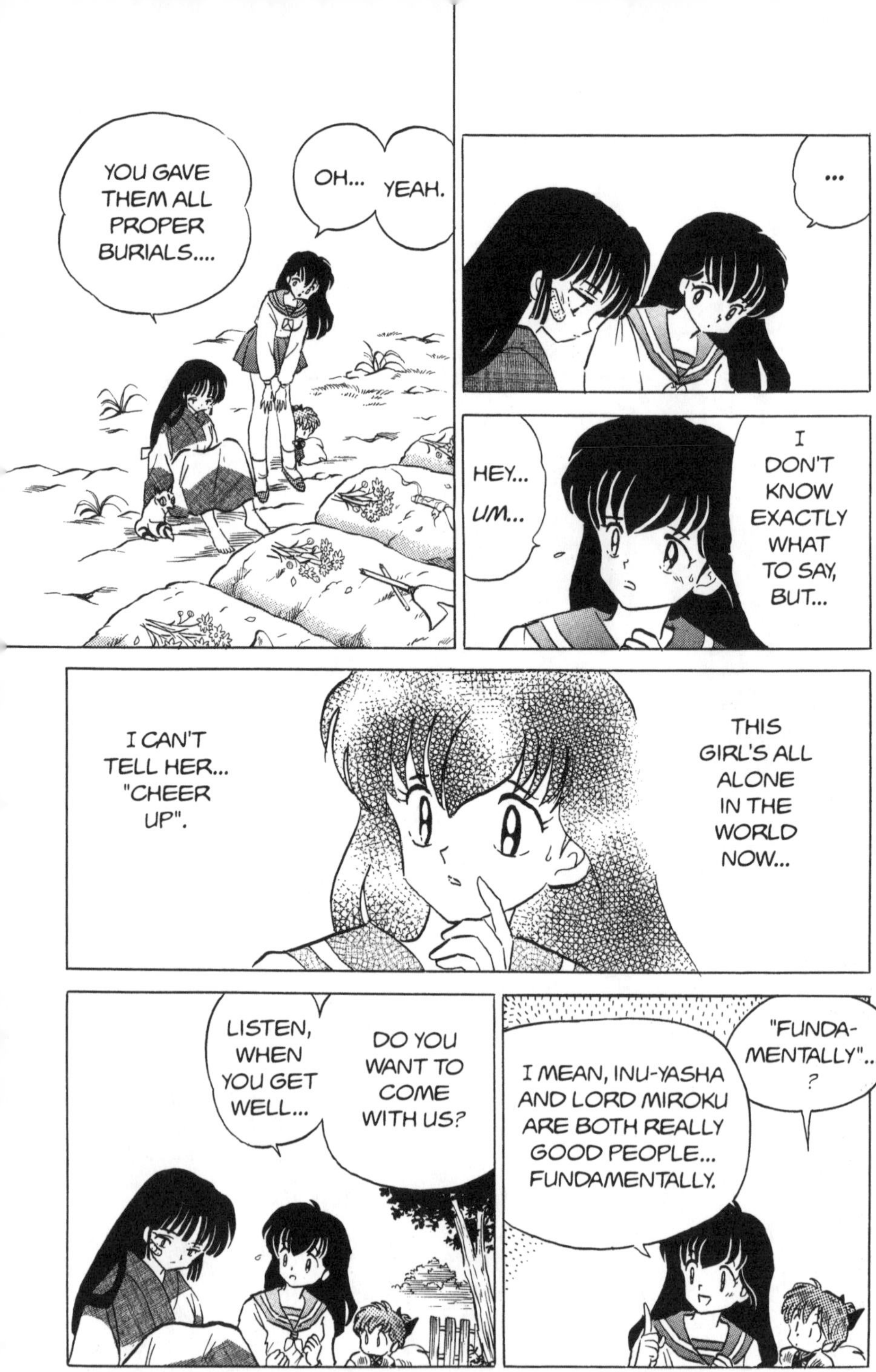
YOU GAVE THEM ALL PROPER BURIALS....
OH...
YEAH.
...
HEY... UM...
I DON'T KNOW EXACTLY WHAT TO SAY, BUT...
I CAN'T TELL HER... "CHEER UP".
THIS GIRL'S ALL ALONE IN THE WORLD NOW...
LISTEN, WHEN YOU GET WELL...
DO YOU WANT TO COME WITH US?
I MEAN, INU-YASHA AND LORD MIROKU ARE BOTH REALLY GOOD PEOPLE... FUNDAMENTALLY.
"FUNDA-MENTALLY"... ?

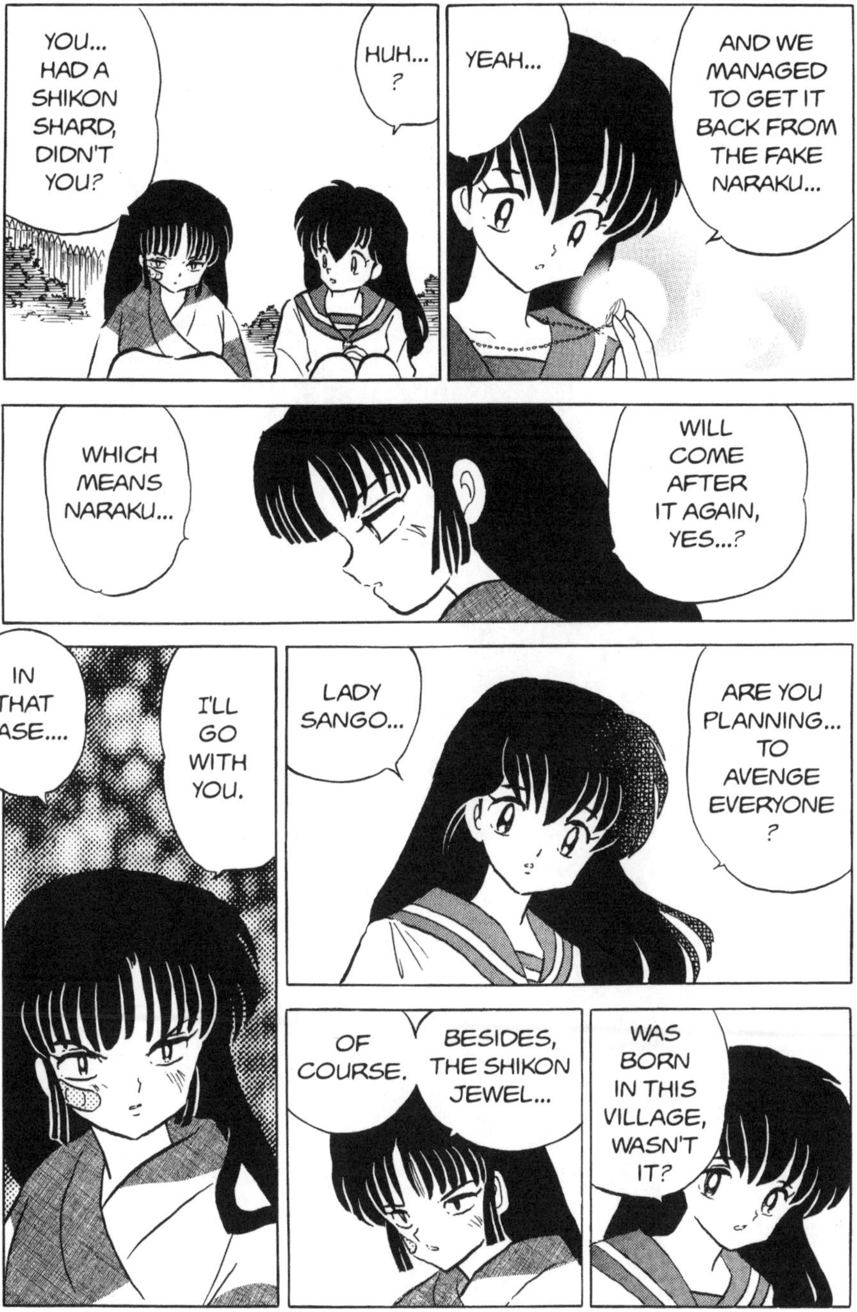
YOU... HAD A SHIKON SHARD, DIDN'T YOU?
HUH... ?
YEAH...
AND WE MANAGED TO GET IT BACK FROM THE FAKE NARAKU...
WHICH MEANS NARAKU...
WILL COME AFTER IT AGAIN, YES...?
IN THAT CASE....
I'LL GO WITH YOU.
LADY SANGO...
ARE YOU PLANNING... TO AVENGE EVERYONE ?
OF COURSE.
BESIDES, THE SHIKON JEWEL...
WAS BORN IN THIS VILLAGE, WASN'T IT?

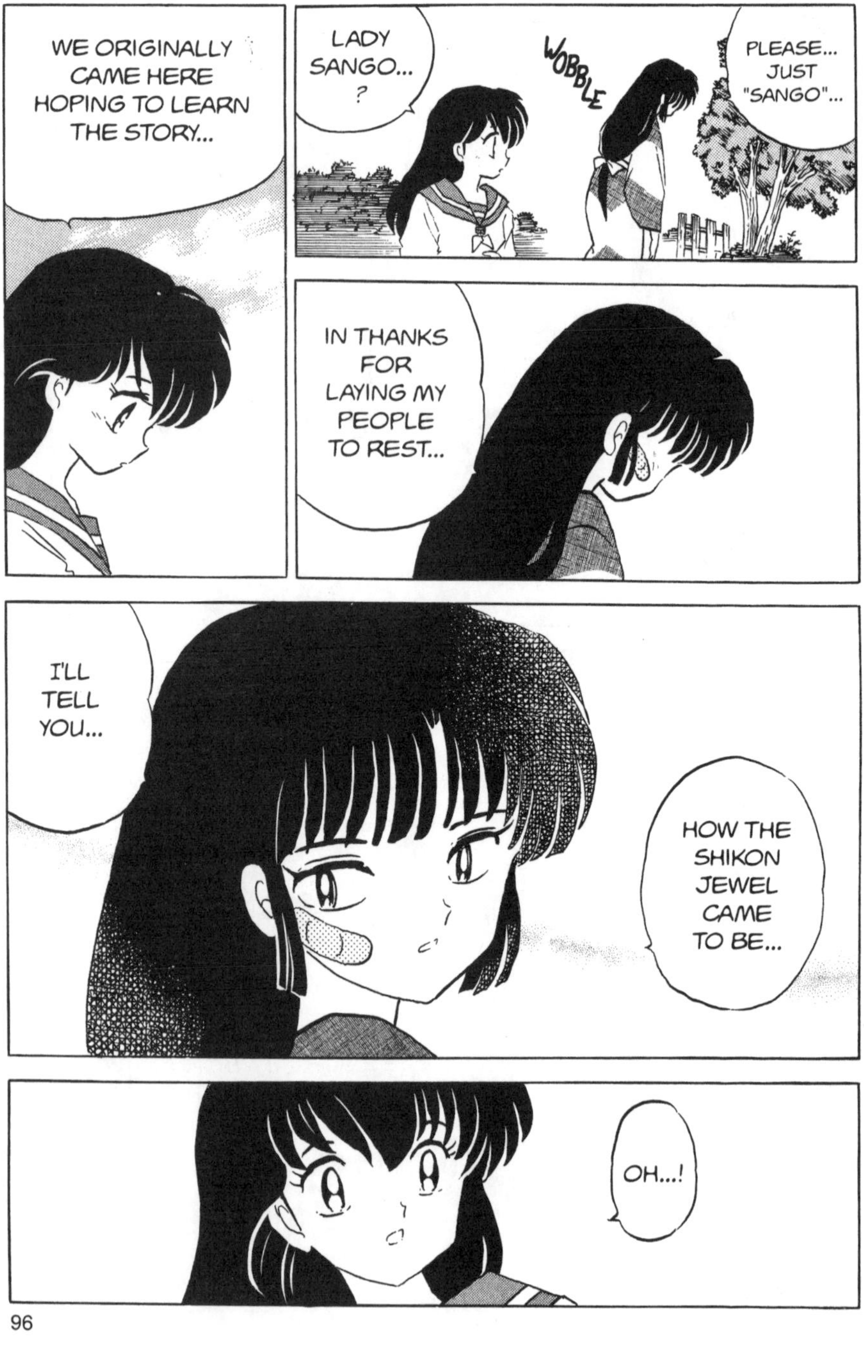
WE ORIGINALLY CAME HERE HOPING TO LEARN THE STORY...
LADY SANGO... ?
WOBBLE
PLEASE... JUST "SANGO"...
IN THANKS FOR LAYING MY PEOPLE TO REST...
I'LL TELL YOU...
HOW THE SHIKON JEWEL CAME TO BE...
OH...!

SCROLL SIX

THE BIRTH OF THE JEWEL

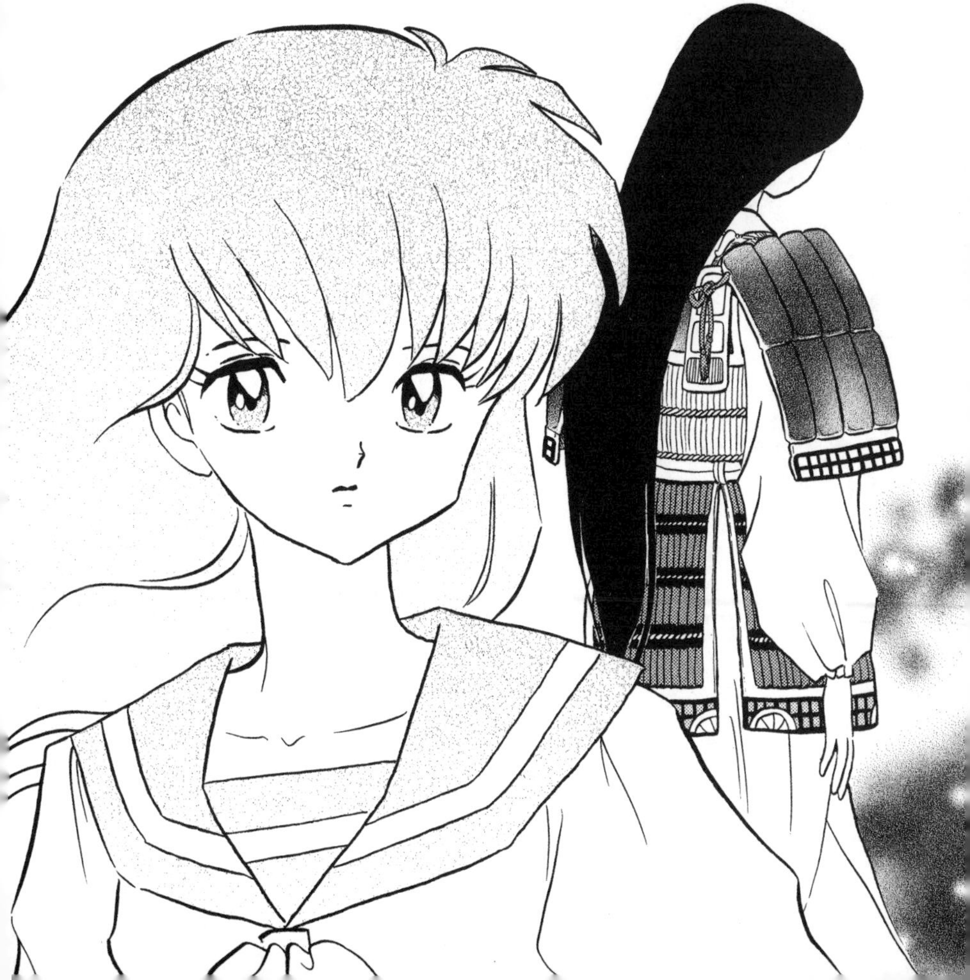

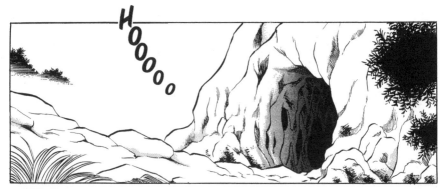

SO YOU **HAVE** SEEN THE THING...

THAT LIES AT THE BACK OF THIS CAVE?

UH-HUH. A MUM-MIFIED DEMON, IS IT?

MMM. BUT MORE THAN THAT...

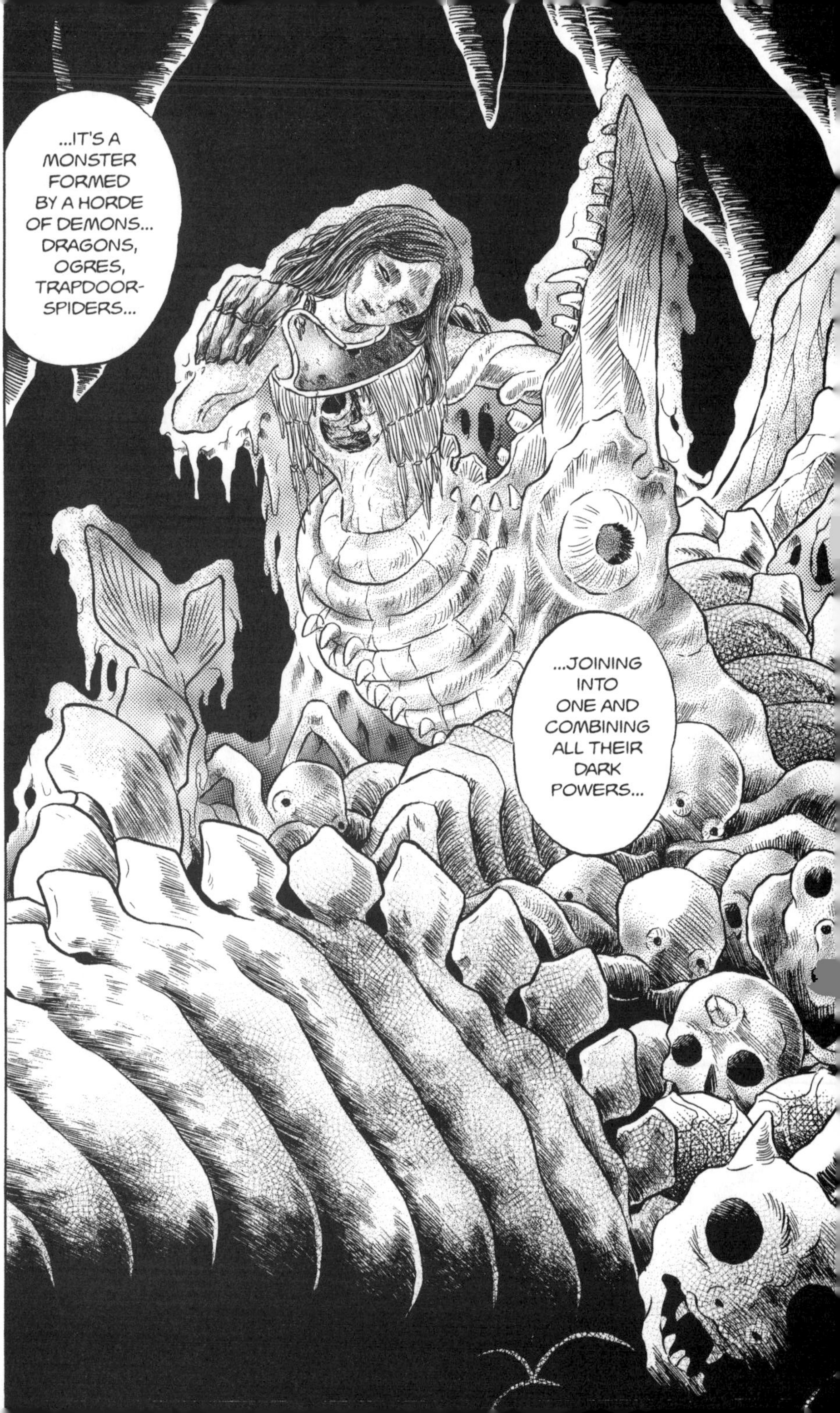
...IT'S A MONSTER FORMED BY A HORDE OF DEMONS... DRAGONS, OGRES, TRAPDOOR-SPIDERS...
...JOINING INTO ONE AND COMBINING ALL THEIR DARK POWERS...

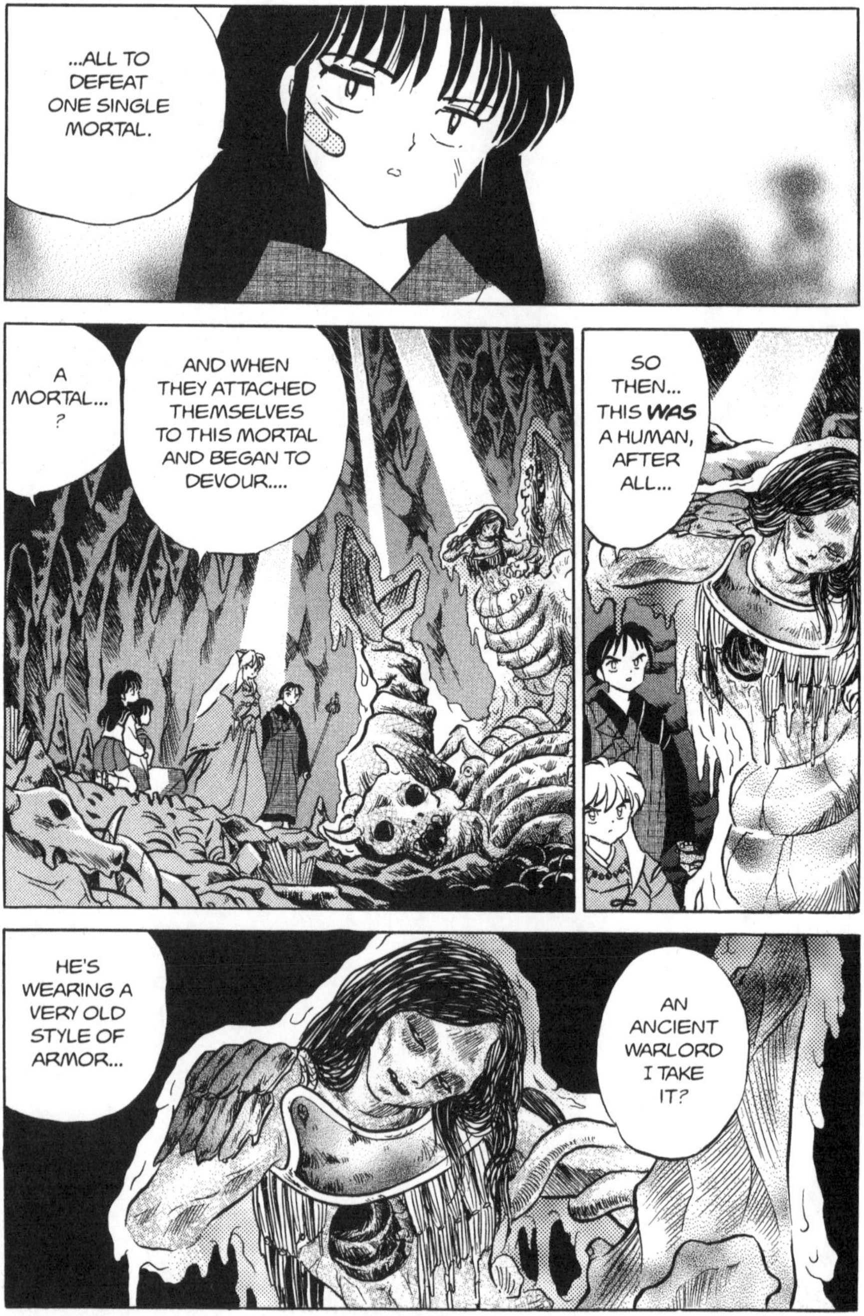
...ALL TO DEFEAT ONE SINGLE MORTAL.
A MORTAL... ?
AND WHEN THEY ATTACHED THEMSELVES TO THIS MORTAL AND BEGAN TO DEVOUR....
SO THEN... THIS **WAS** A HUMAN, AFTER ALL...
HE'S WEARING A VERY OLD STYLE OF ARMOR...
AN ANCIENT WARLORD I TAKE IT?

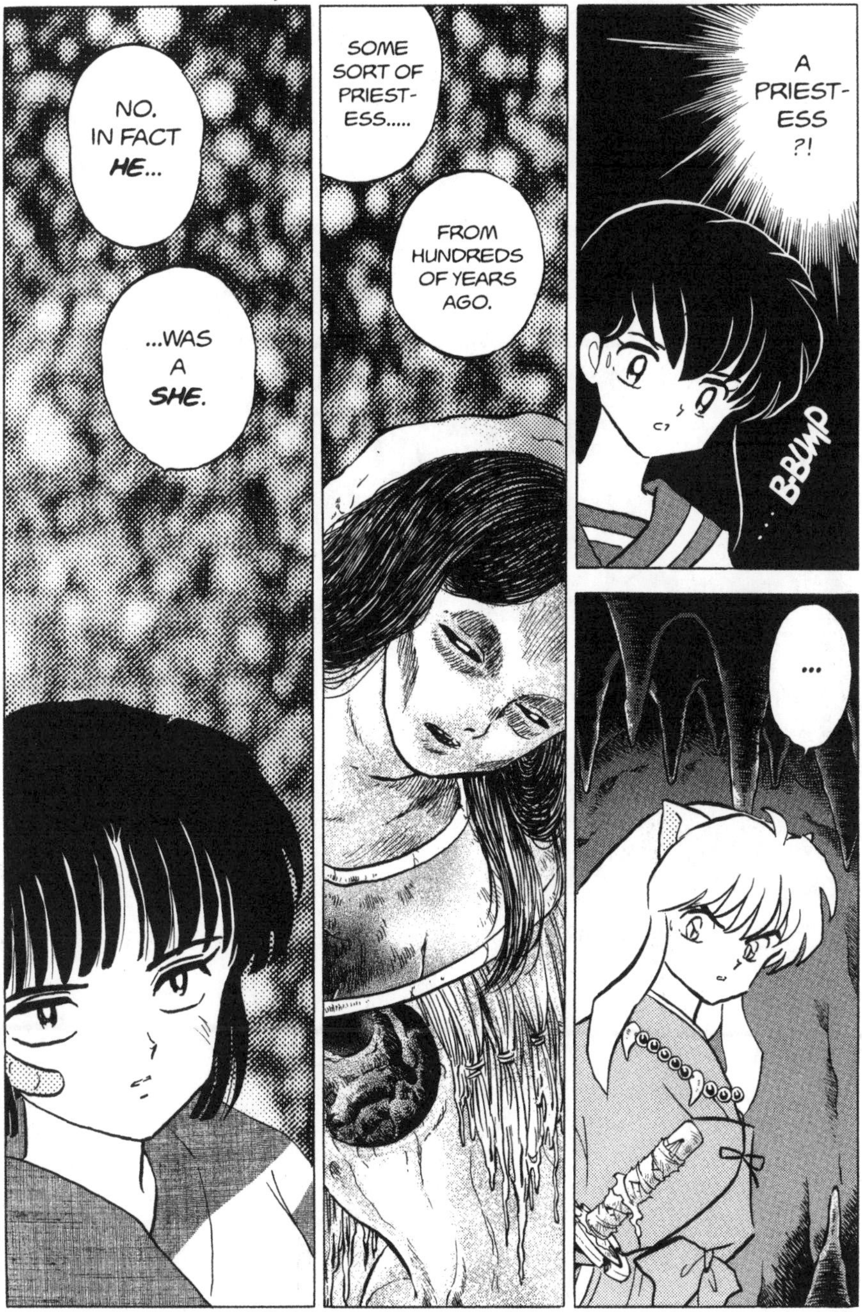
NO. IN FACT **HE**...
...WAS A **SHE**.
SOME SORT OF PRIEST-ESS.....
FROM HUNDREDS OF YEARS AGO.
A PRIEST-ESS ?!
B-BUMP
...

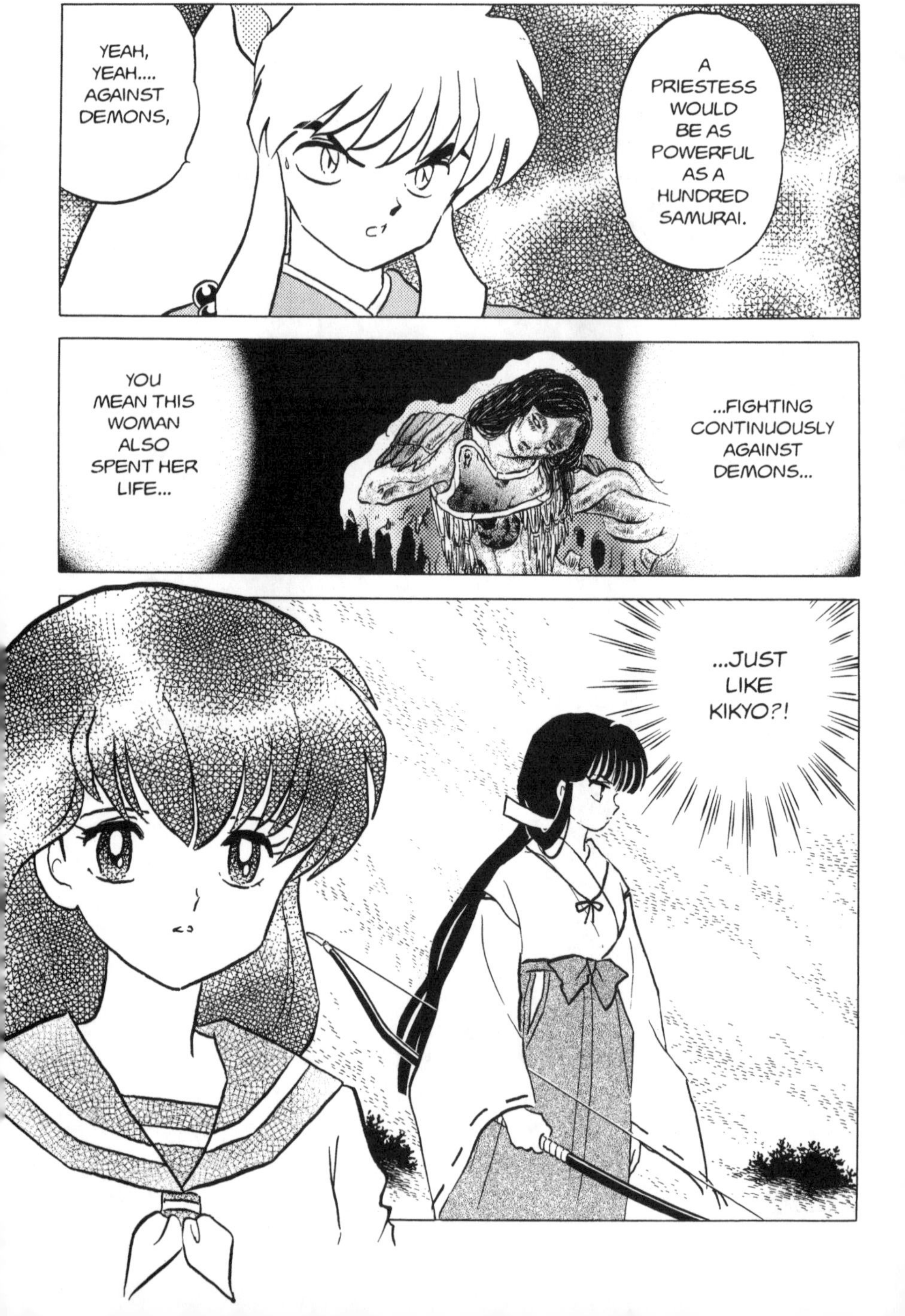
YEAH, YEAH.... AGAINST DEMONS,
A PRIESTESS WOULD BE AS POWERFUL AS A HUNDRED SAMURAI.
YOU MEAN THIS WOMAN ALSO SPENT HER LIFE...
...FIGHTING CONTINUOUSLY AGAINST DEMONS...
...JUST LIKE KIKYO?!

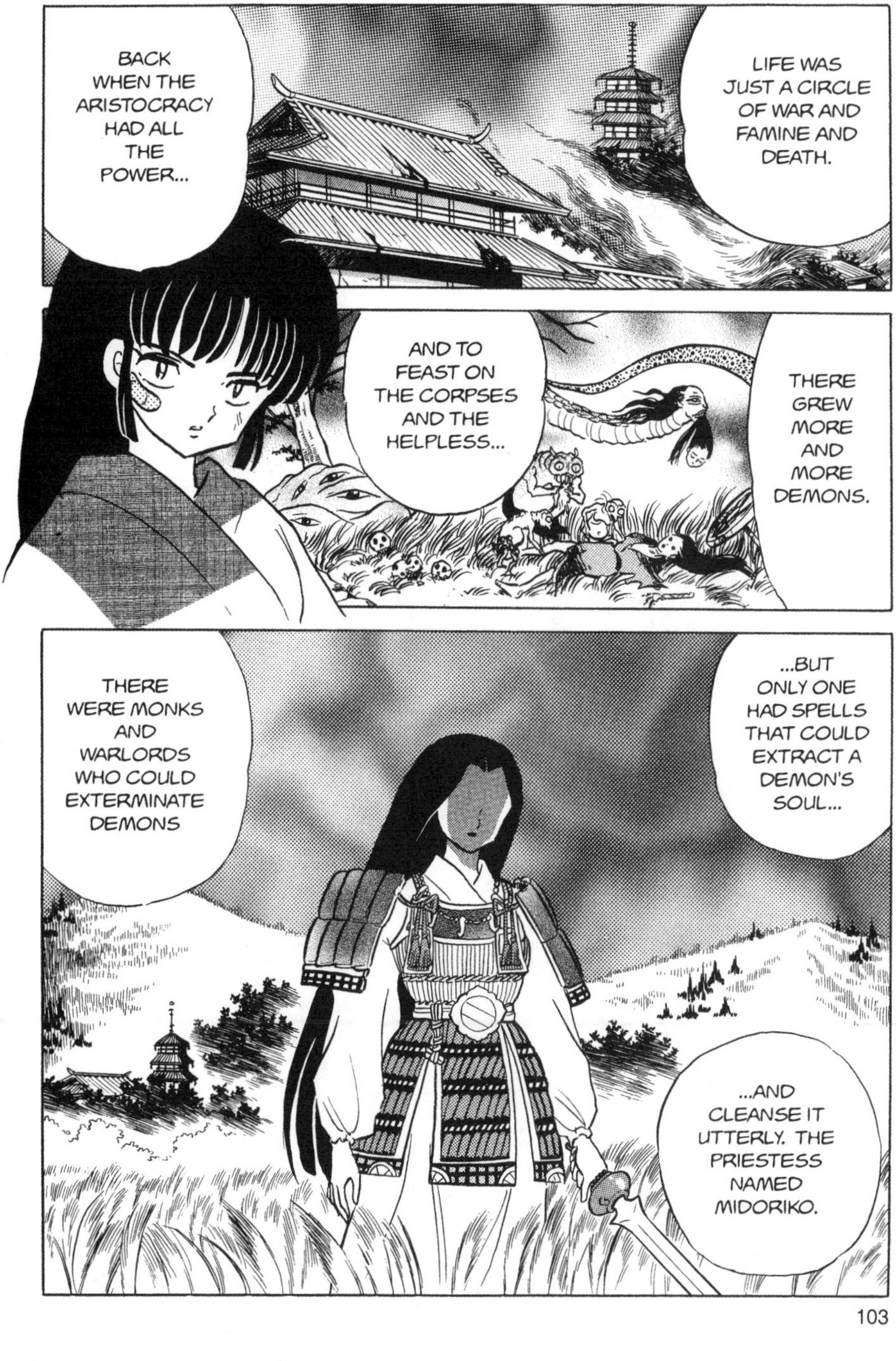
BACK WHEN THE ARISTOCRACY HAD ALL THE POWER...
LIFE WAS JUST A CIRCLE OF WAR AND FAMINE AND DEATH.
AND TO FEAST ON THE CORPSES AND THE HELPLESS...
THERE GREW MORE AND MORE DEMONS.
THERE WERE MONKS AND WARLORDS WHO COULD EXTERMINATE DEMONS
...BUT ONLY ONE HAD SPELLS THAT COULD EXTRACT A DEMON'S SOUL...
...AND CLEANSE IT UTTERLY. THE PRIESTESS NAMED MIDORIKO.

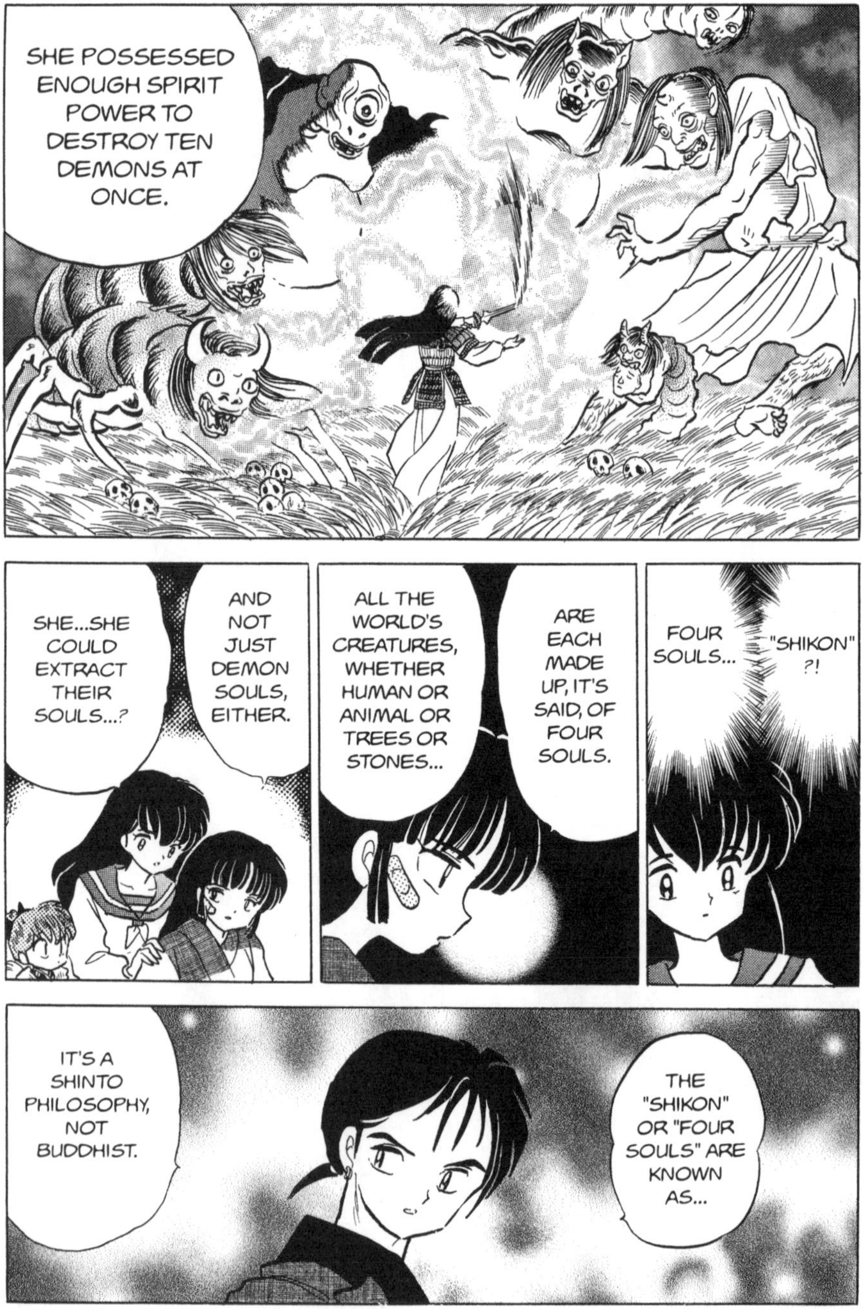

SHE POSSESSED ENOUGH SPIRIT POWER TO DESTROY TEN DEMONS AT ONCE.
SHE...SHE COULD EXTRACT THEIR SOULS...?
AND NOT JUST DEMON SOULS, EITHER.
ALL THE WORLD'S CREATURES, WHETHER HUMAN OR ANIMAL OR TREES OR STONES...
ARE EACH MADE UP, IT'S SAID, OF FOUR SOULS.
FOUR SOULS...
"SHIKON" ?!
IT'S A SHINTO PHILOSOPHY, NOT BUDDHIST.
THE "SHIKON" OR "FOUR SOULS" ARE KNOWN AS...

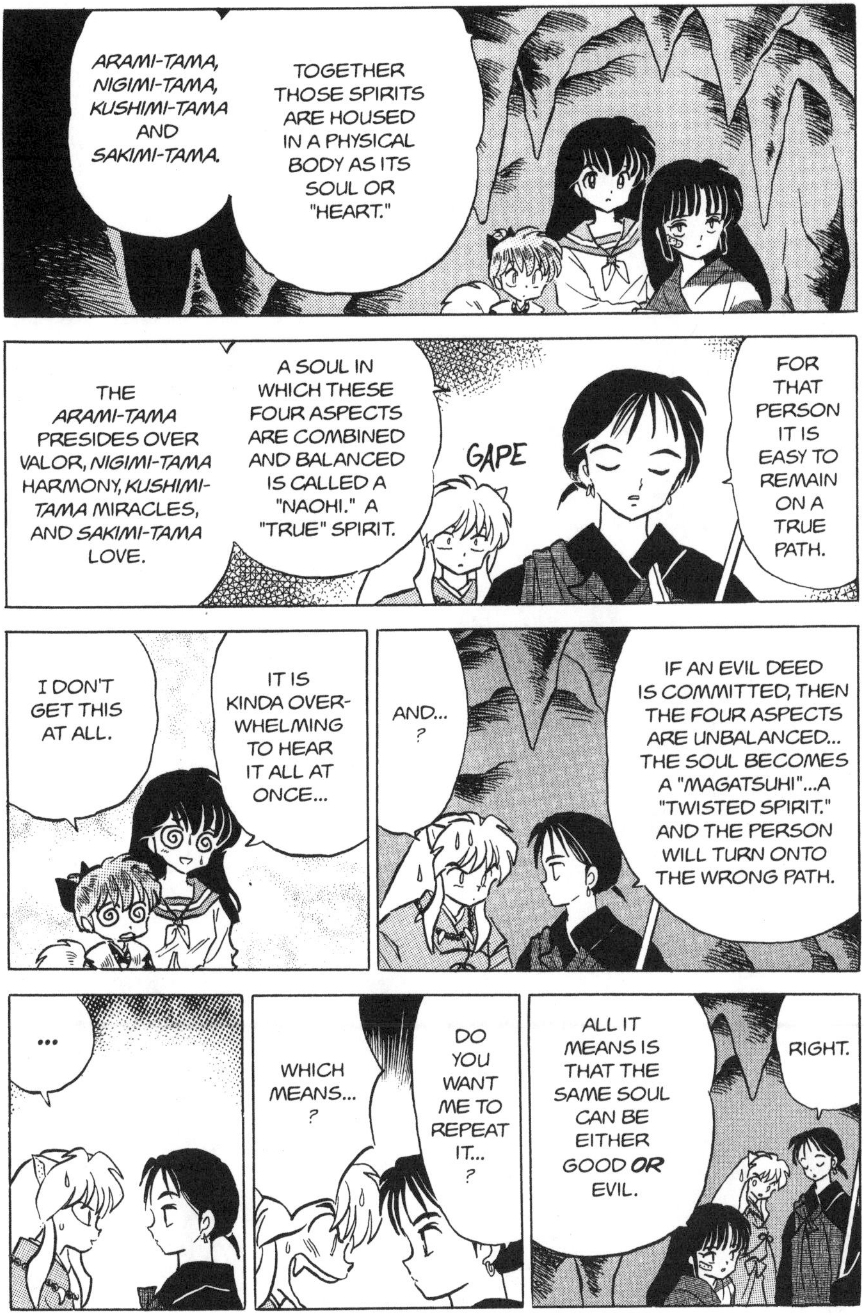
ARAMI-TAMA, NIGIMI-TAMA, KUSHIMI-TAMA AND SAKIMI-TAMA.
TOGETHER THOSE SPIRITS ARE HOUSED IN A PHYSICAL BODY AS ITS SOUL OR "HEART."
THE ARAMI-TAMA PRESIDES OVER VALOR, NIGIMI-TAMA HARMONY, KUSHIMI-TAMA MIRACLES, AND SAKIMI-TAMA LOVE.
A SOUL IN WHICH THESE FOUR ASPECTS ARE COMBINED AND BALANCED IS CALLED A "NAOHI." A "TRUE" SPIRIT.
GAPE
FOR THAT PERSON IT IS EASY TO REMAIN ON A TRUE PATH.
I DON'T GET THIS AT ALL.
IT IS KINDA OVER-WHELMING TO HEAR IT ALL AT ONCE...
AND... ?
IF AN EVIL DEED IS COMMITTED, THEN THE FOUR ASPECTS ARE UNBALANCED... THE SOUL BECOMES A "MAGATSUHI"...A "TWISTED SPIRIT." AND THE PERSON WILL TURN ONTO THE WRONG PATH.
...
WHICH MEANS... ?
DO YOU WANT ME TO REPEAT IT... ?
ALL IT MEANS IS THAT THE SAME SOUL CAN BE EITHER GOOD OR EVIL.
RIGHT.

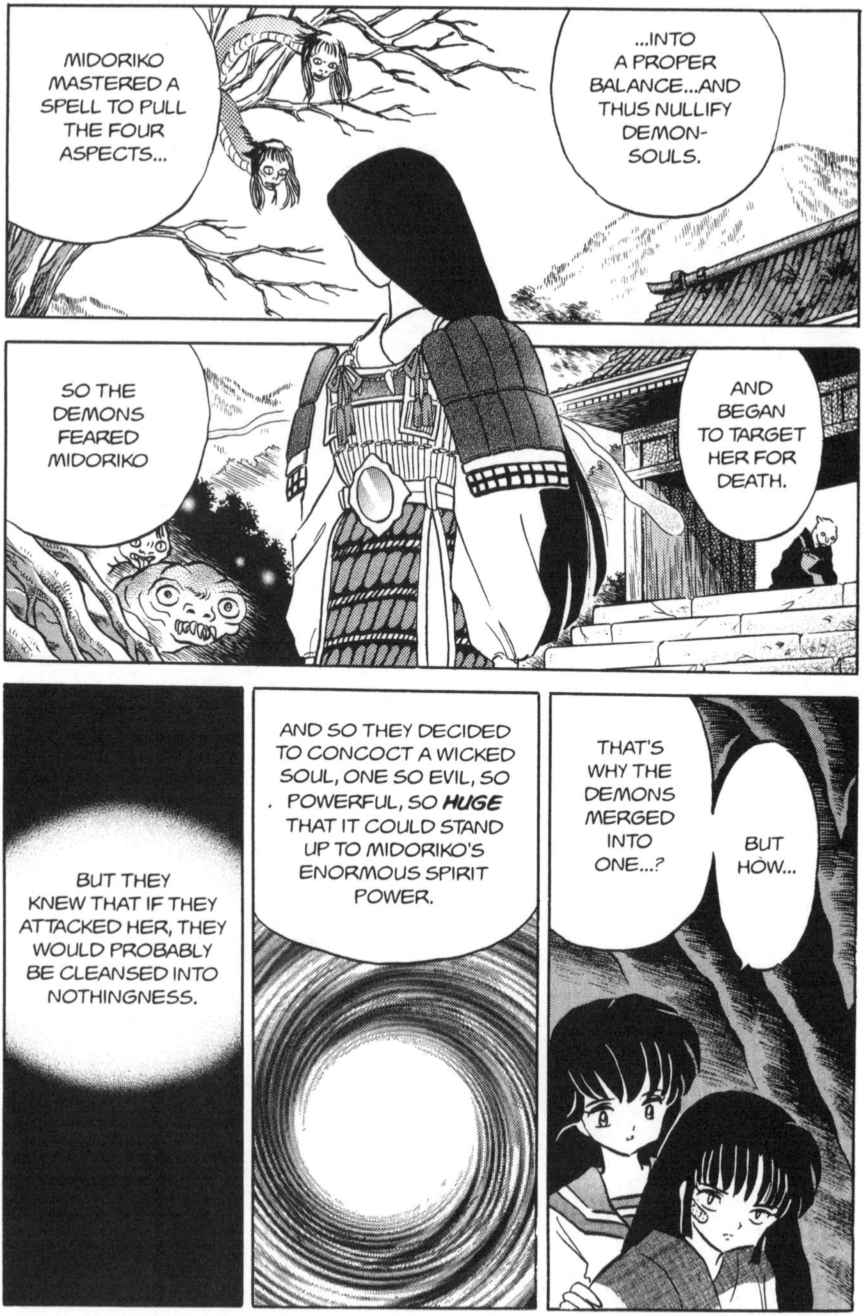
MIDORIKO MASTERED A SPELL TO PULL THE FOUR ASPECTS...
...INTO A PROPER BALANCE...AND THUS NULLIFY DEMON-SOULS.
SO THE DEMONS FEARED MIDORIKO
AND BEGAN TO TARGET HER FOR DEATH.
BUT THEY KNEW THAT IF THEY ATTACKED HER, THEY WOULD PROBABLY BE CLEANSED INTO NOTHINGNESS.
AND SO THEY DECIDED TO CONCOCT A WICKED SOUL, ONE SO EVIL, SO POWERFUL, SO HUGE THAT IT COULD STAND UP TO MIDORIKO'S ENORMOUS SPIRIT POWER.
THAT'S WHY THE DEMONS MERGED INTO ONE...?
BUT HOW...

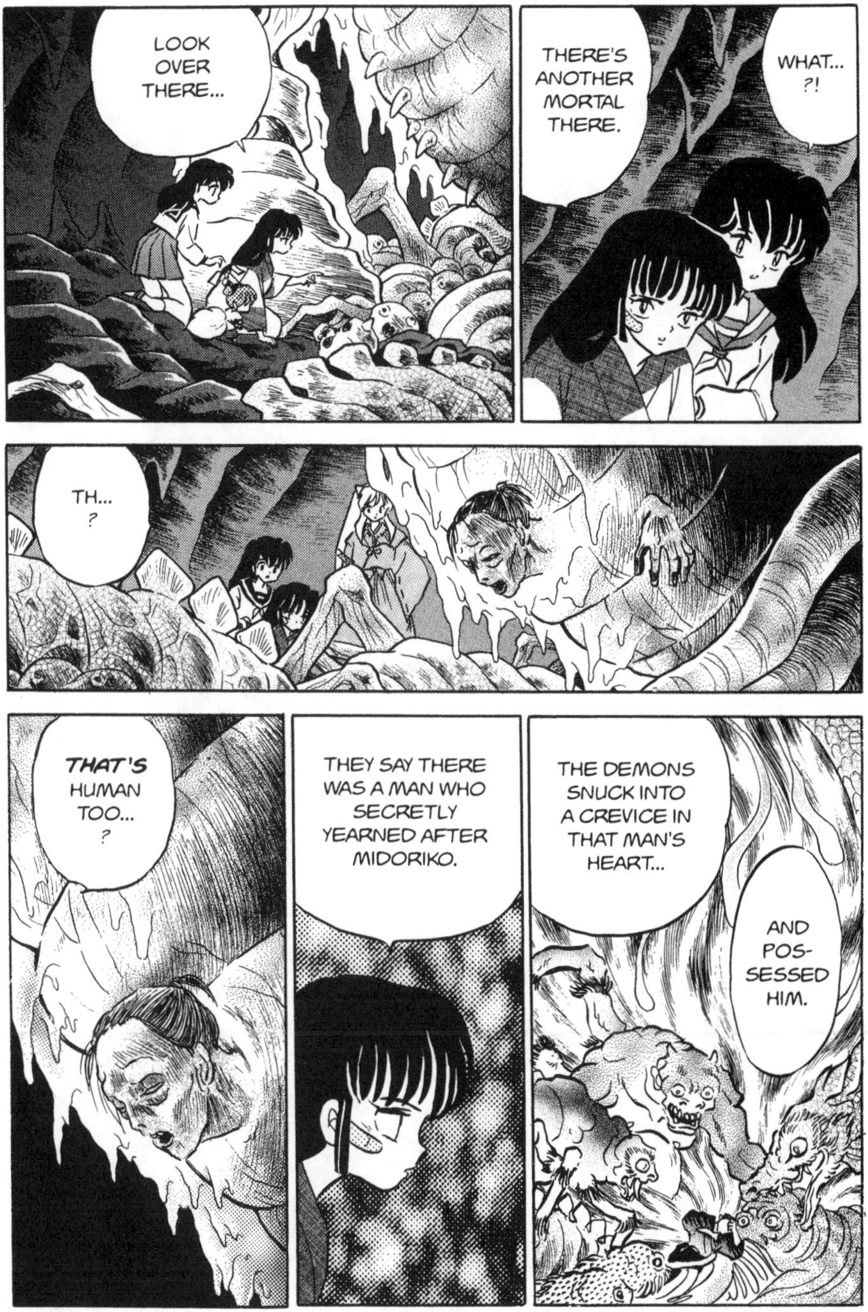
LOOK OVER THERE...
THERE'S ANOTHER MORTAL THERE.
WHAT... ?!
TH... ?
THAT'S HUMAN TOO... ?
THEY SAY THERE WAS A MAN WHO SECRETLY YEARNED AFTER MIDORIKO.
THE DEMONS SNUCK INTO A CREVICE IN THAT MAN'S HEART...
AND POS-SESSED HIM.

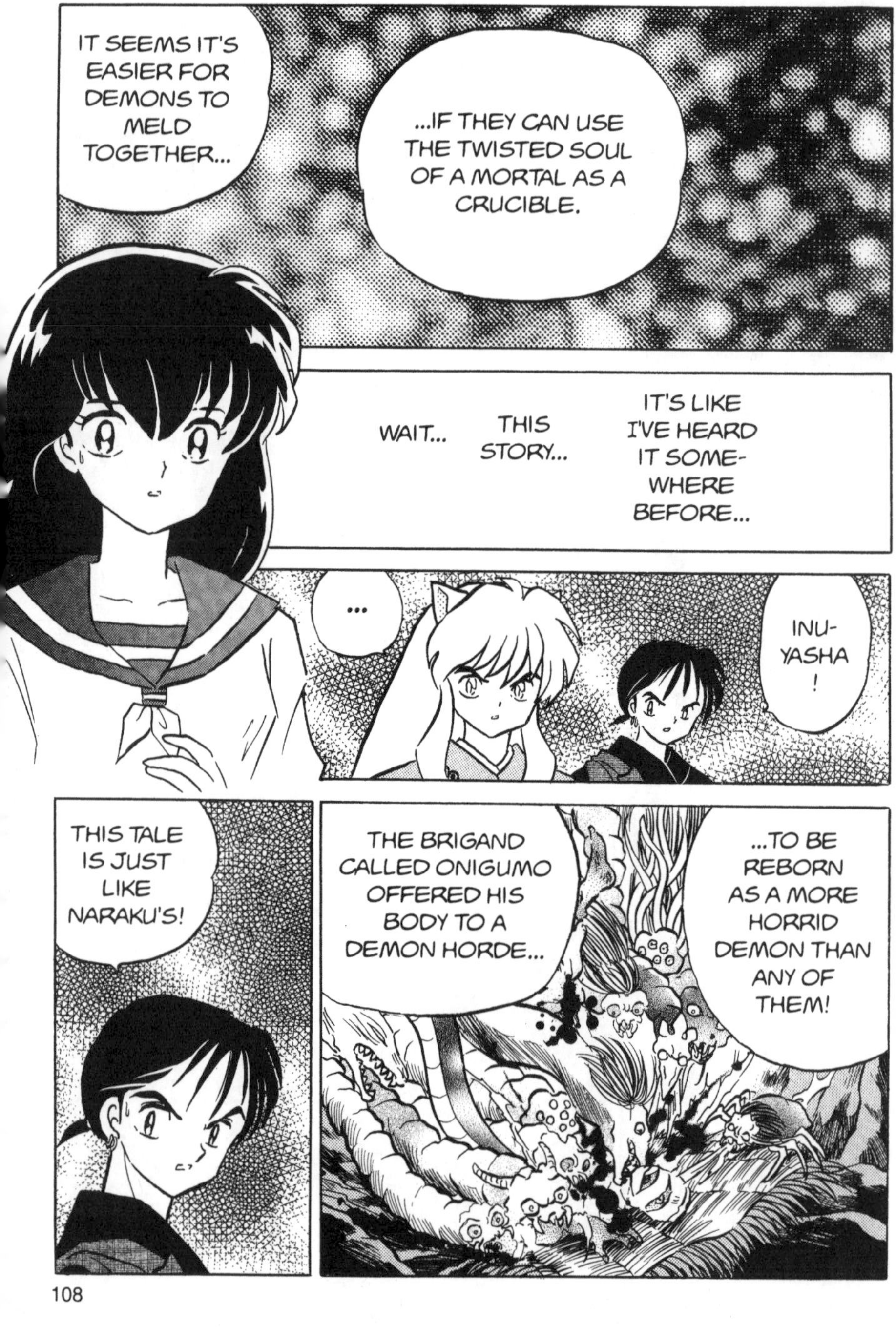
IT SEEMS IT'S EASIER FOR DEMONS TO MELD TOGETHER...
...IF THEY CAN USE THE TWISTED SOUL OF A MORTAL AS A CRUCIBLE.
WAIT...
THIS STORY...
IT'S LIKE I'VE HEARD IT SOME-WHERE BEFORE...
...
INU-YASHA!
THIS TALE IS JUST LIKE NARAKU'S!
THE BRIGAND CALLED ONIGUMO OFFERED HIS BODY TO A DEMON HORDE...
...TO BE REBORN AS A MORE HORRID DEMON THAN ANY OF THEM!

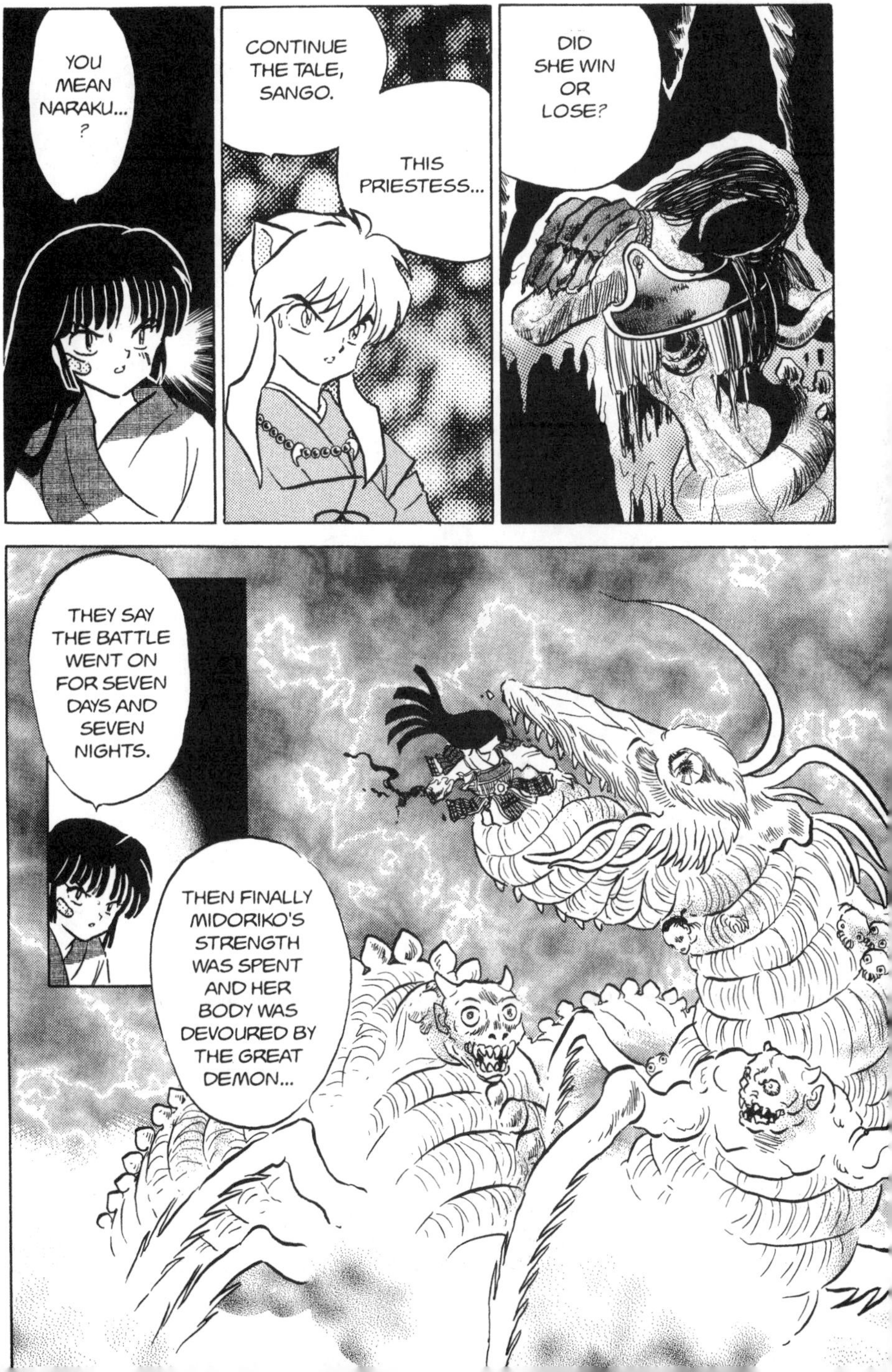
YOU MEAN NARAKU... ?
CONTINUE THE TALE, SANGO.
THIS PRIESTESS...
DID SHE WIN OR LOSE?
THEY SAY THE BATTLE WENT ON FOR SEVEN DAYS AND SEVEN NIGHTS.
THEN FINALLY MIDORIKO'S STRENGTH WAS SPENT AND HER BODY WAS DEVOURED BY THE GREAT DEMON...

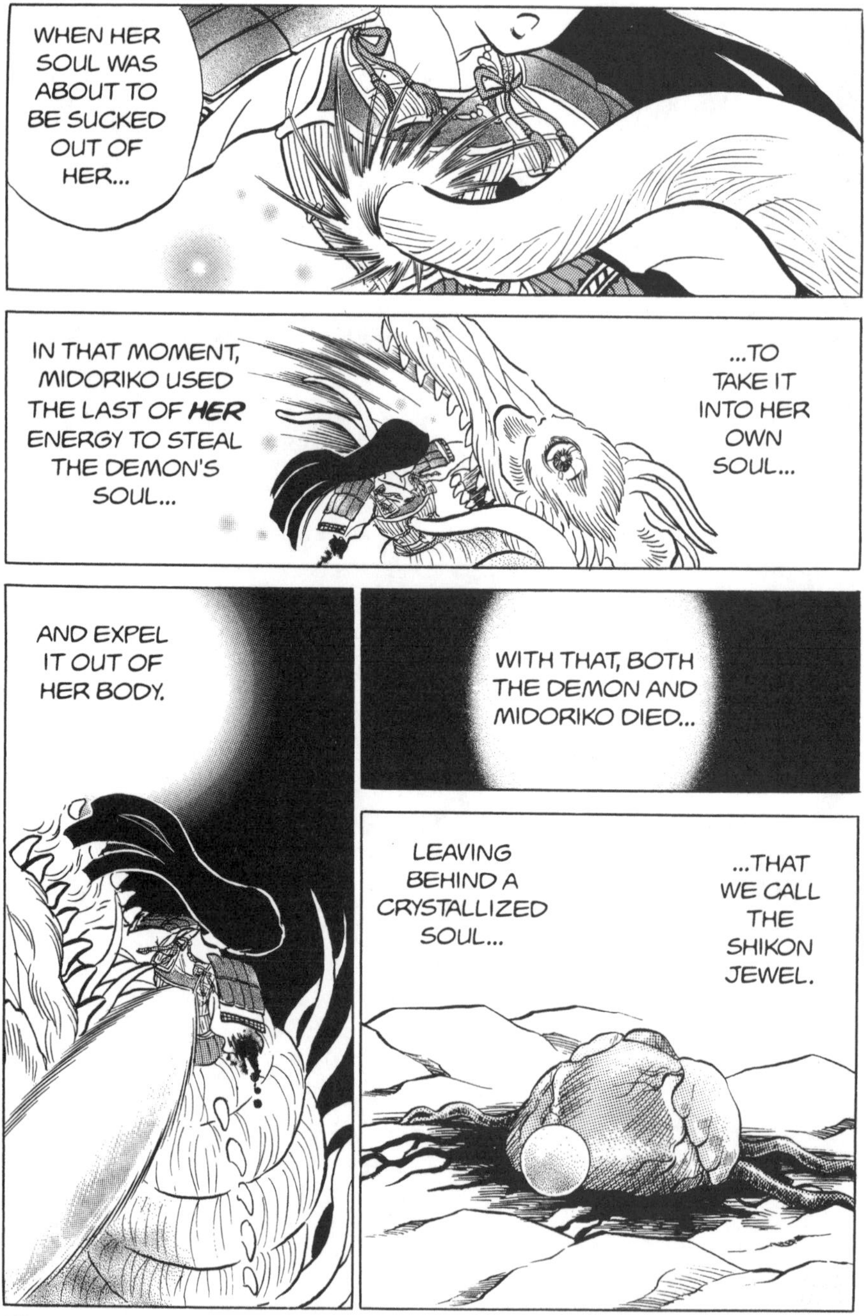
WHEN HER SOUL WAS ABOUT TO BE SUCKED OUT OF HER...
IN THAT MOMENT, MIDORIKO USED THE LAST OF ***HER*** ENERGY TO STEAL THE DEMON'S SOUL...
...TO TAKE IT INTO HER OWN SOUL...
AND EXPEL IT OUT OF HER BODY.
WITH THAT, BOTH THE DEMON AND MIDORIKO DIED...
LEAVING BEHIND A CRYSTALLIZED SOUL...
...THAT WE CALL THE SHIKON JEWEL.

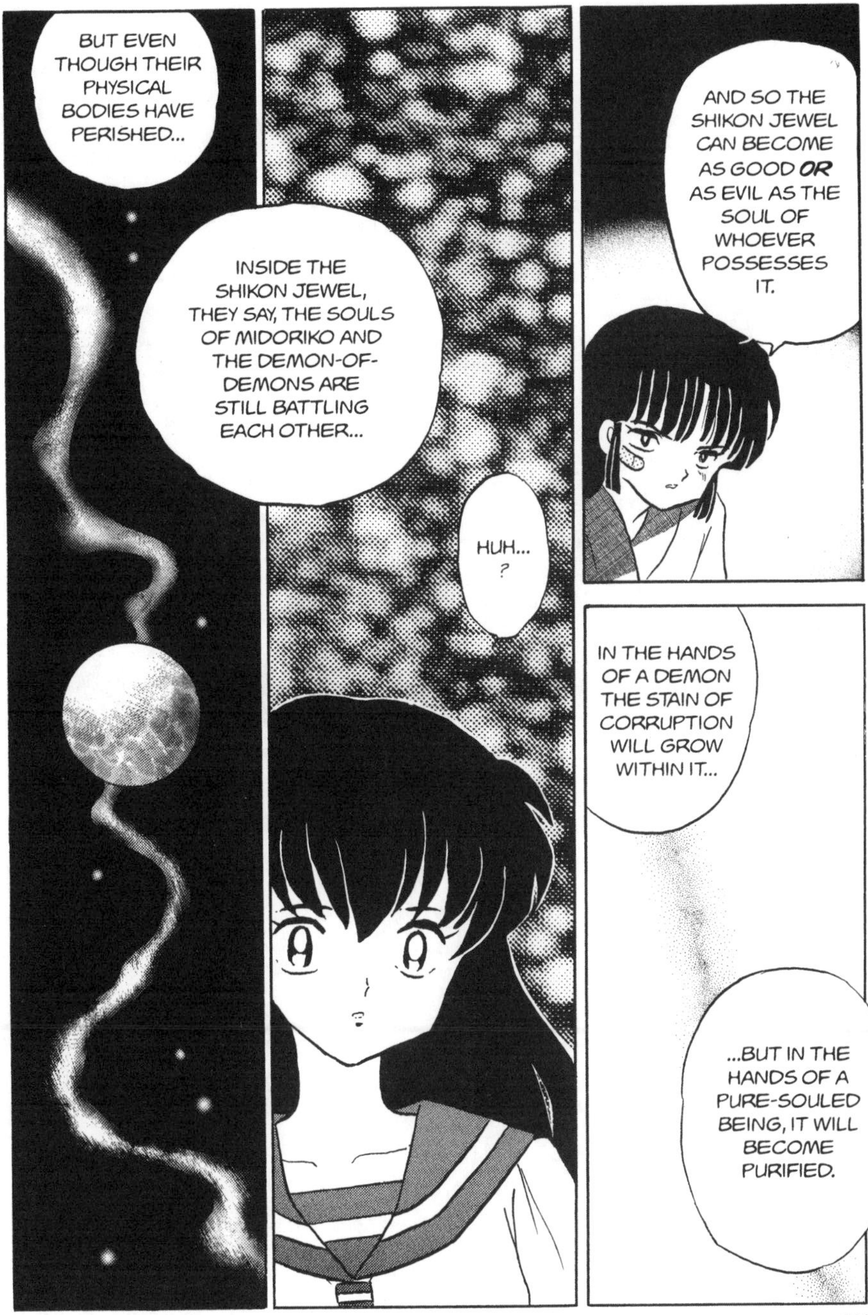
BUT EVEN THOUGH THEIR PHYSICAL BODIES HAVE PERISHED...
INSIDE THE SHIKON JEWEL, THEY SAY, THE SOULS OF MIDORIKO AND THE DEMON-OF-DEMONS ARE STILL BATTLING EACH OTHER...
HUH...?
AND SO THE SHIKON JEWEL CAN BECOME AS GOOD **OR** AS EVIL AS THE SOUL OF WHOEVER POSSESSES IT.
IN THE HANDS OF A DEMON THE STAIN OF CORRUPTION WILL GROW WITHIN IT...
...BUT IN THE HANDS OF A PURE-SOULED BEING, IT WILL BECOME PURIFIED.

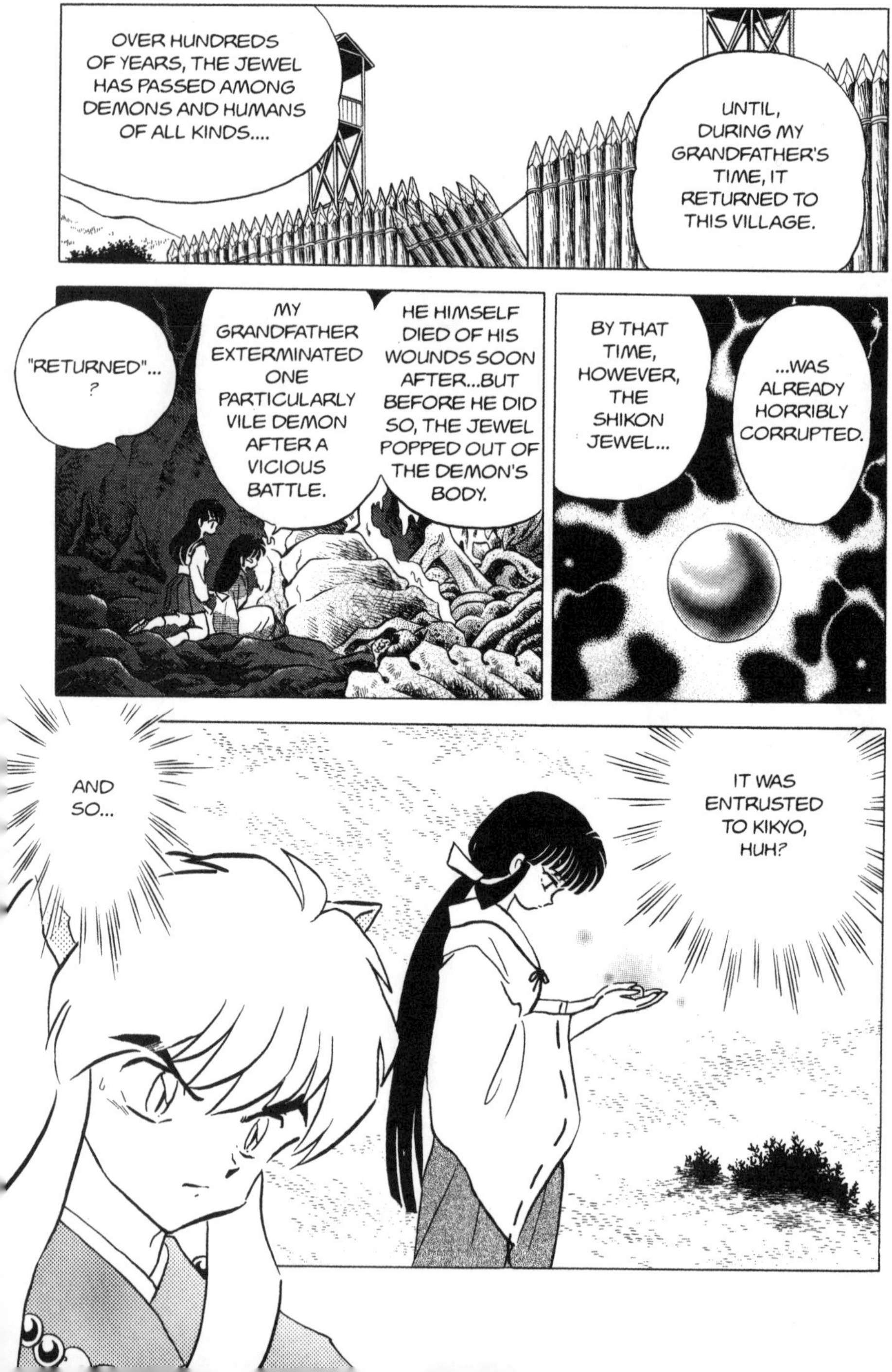

OVER HUNDREDS OF YEARS, THE JEWEL HAS PASSED AMONG DEMONS AND HUMANS OF ALL KINDS....
UNTIL, DURING MY GRANDFATHER'S TIME, IT RETURNED TO THIS VILLAGE.
"RETURNED"...?
MY GRANDFATHER EXTERMINATED ONE PARTICULARLY VILE DEMON AFTER A VICIOUS BATTLE.
HE HIMSELF DIED OF HIS WOUNDS SOON AFTER...BUT BEFORE HE DID SO, THE JEWEL POPPED OUT OF THE DEMON'S BODY.
BY THAT TIME, HOWEVER, THE SHIKON JEWEL...
...WAS ALREADY HORRIBLY CORRUPTED.
AND SO...
IT WAS ENTRUSTED TO KIKYO, HUH?

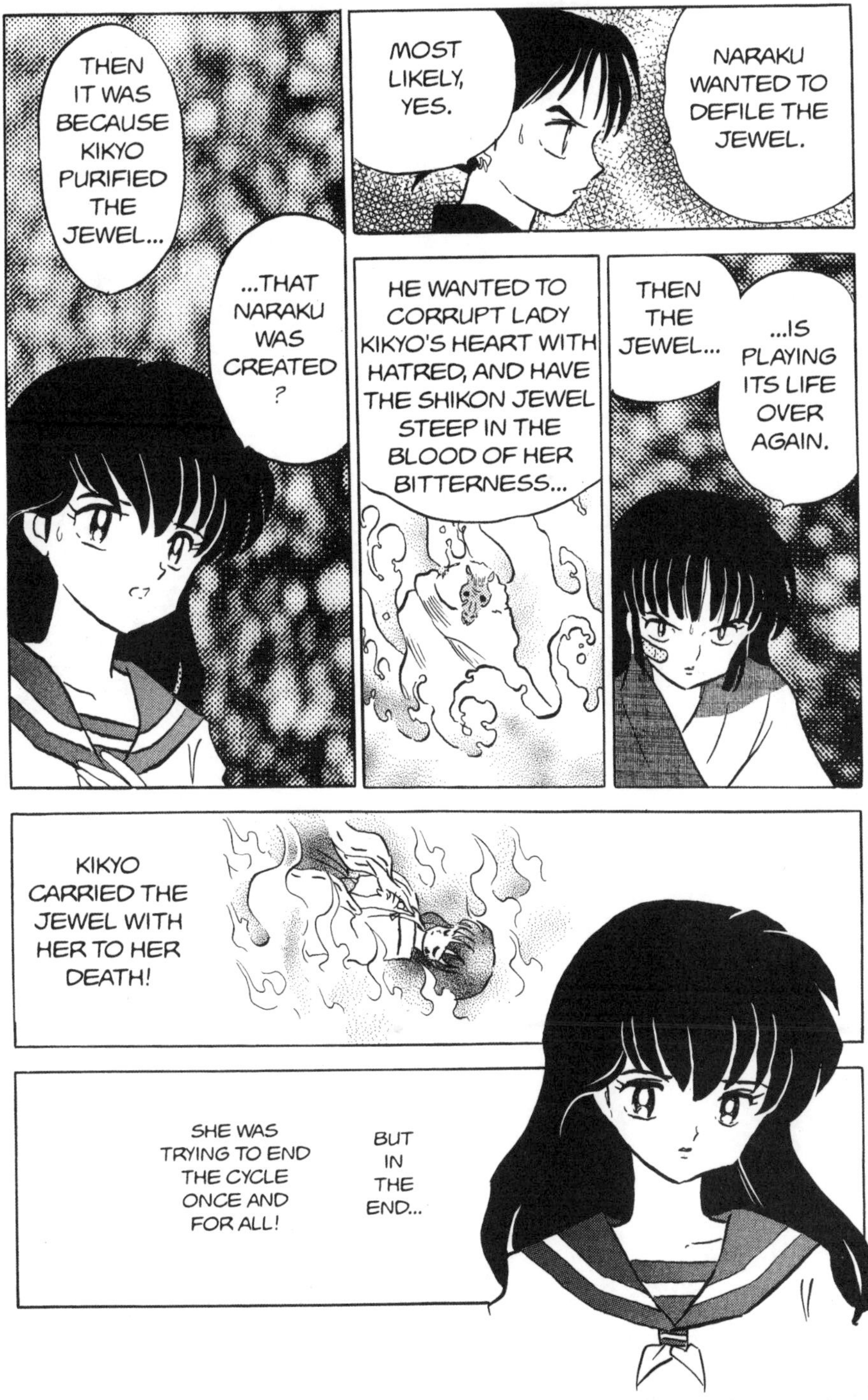
THEN IT WAS BECAUSE KIKYO PURIFIED THE JEWEL...
...THAT NARAKU WAS CREATED?
MOST LIKELY, YES.
NARAKU WANTED TO DEFILE THE JEWEL.
HE WANTED TO CORRUPT LADY KIKYO'S HEART WITH HATRED, AND HAVE THE SHIKON JEWEL STEEP IN THE BLOOD OF HER BITTERNESS...
THEN THE JEWEL...
...IS PLAYING ITS LIFE OVER AGAIN.
KIKYO CARRIED THE JEWEL WITH HER TO HER DEATH!
SHE WAS TRYING TO END THE CYCLE ONCE AND FOR ALL!
BUT IN THE END...

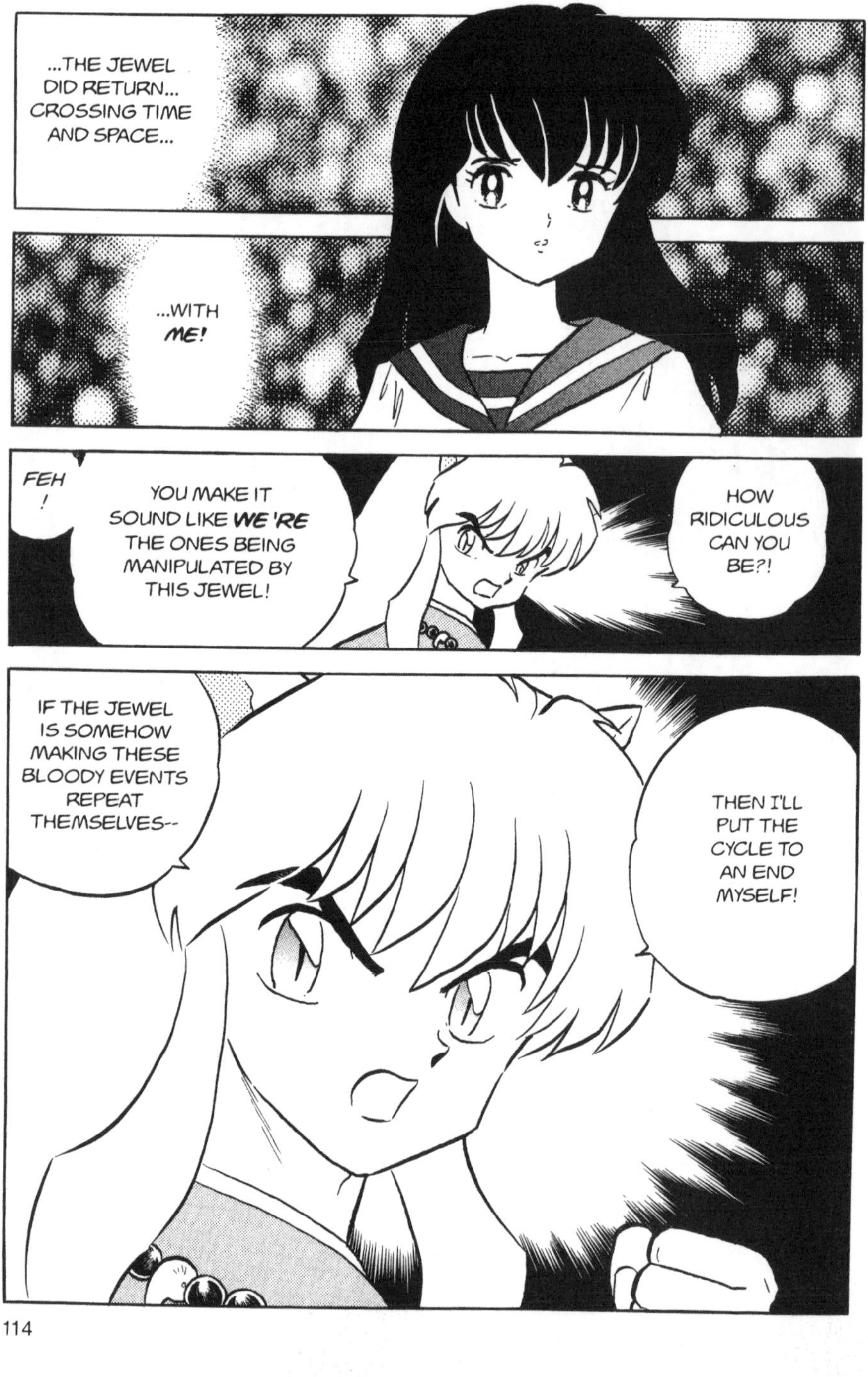
...THE JEWEL DID RETURN... CROSSING TIME AND SPACE...
...WITH *ME!*
FEH!
YOU MAKE IT SOUND LIKE ***WE'RE*** THE ONES BEING MANIPULATED BY THIS JEWEL!
HOW RIDICULOUS CAN YOU BE?!
IF THE JEWEL IS SOMEHOW MAKING THESE BLOODY EVENTS REPEAT THEMSELVES--
THEN I'LL PUT THE CYCLE TO AN END MYSELF!

SCROLL SEVEN

THE WATER GOD

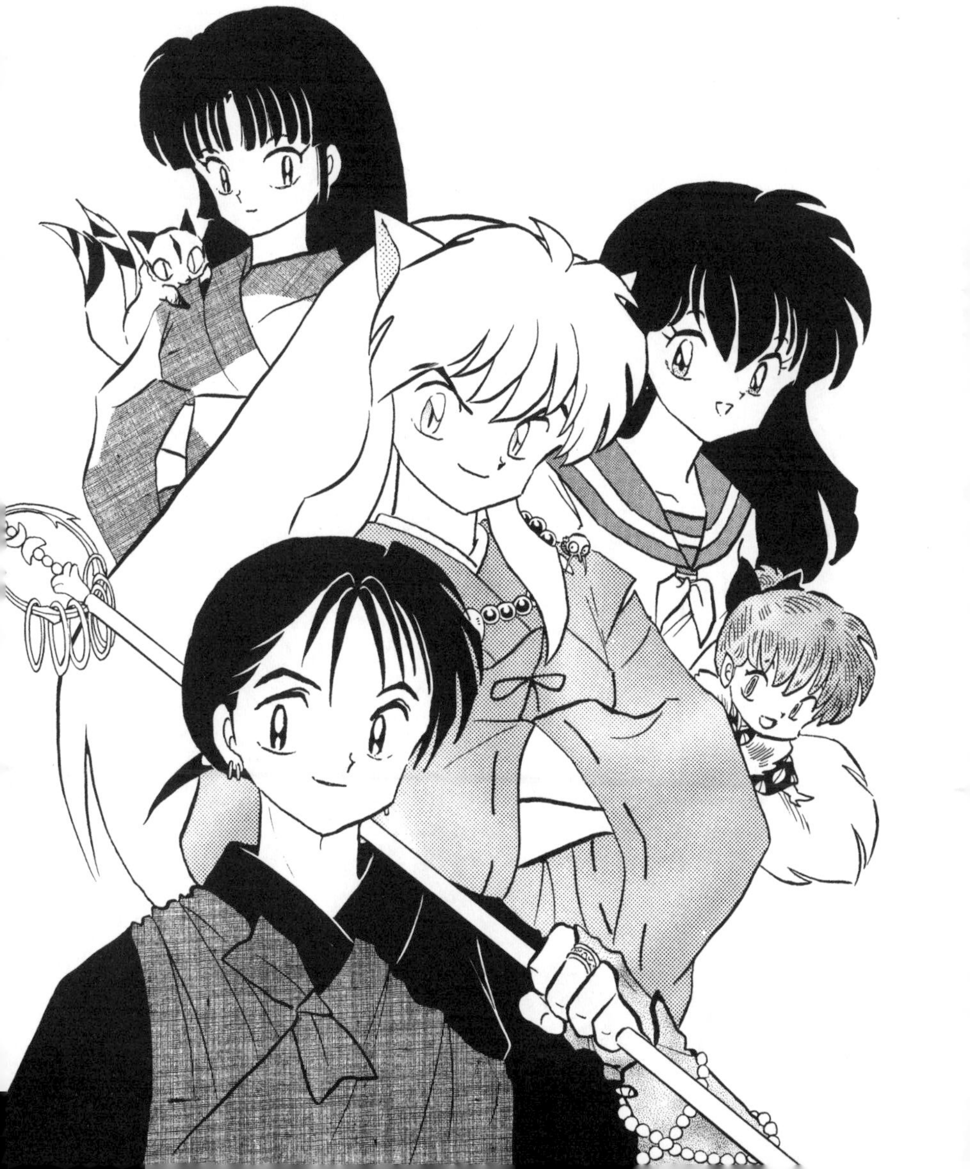

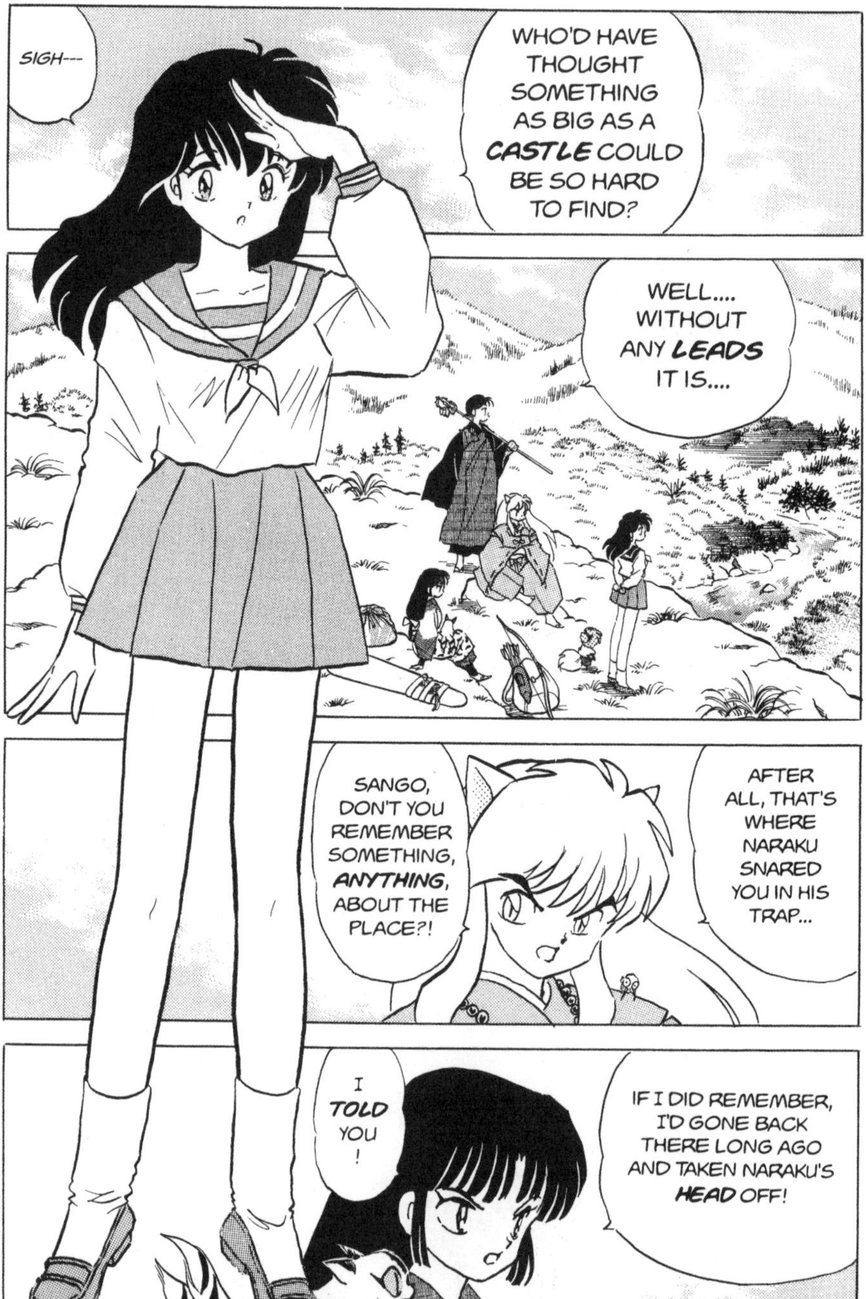
SIGH---
WHO'D HAVE THOUGHT SOMETHING AS BIG AS A CASTLE COULD BE SO HARD TO FIND?
WELL.... WITHOUT ANY LEADS IT IS....
SANGO, DON'T YOU REMEMBER SOMETHING, ANYTHING, ABOUT THE PLACE?!
AFTER ALL, THAT'S WHERE NARAKU SNARED YOU IN HIS TRAP...
I TOLD YOU!
IF I DID REMEMBER, I'D GONE BACK THERE LONG AGO AND TAKEN NARAKU'S HEAD OFF!

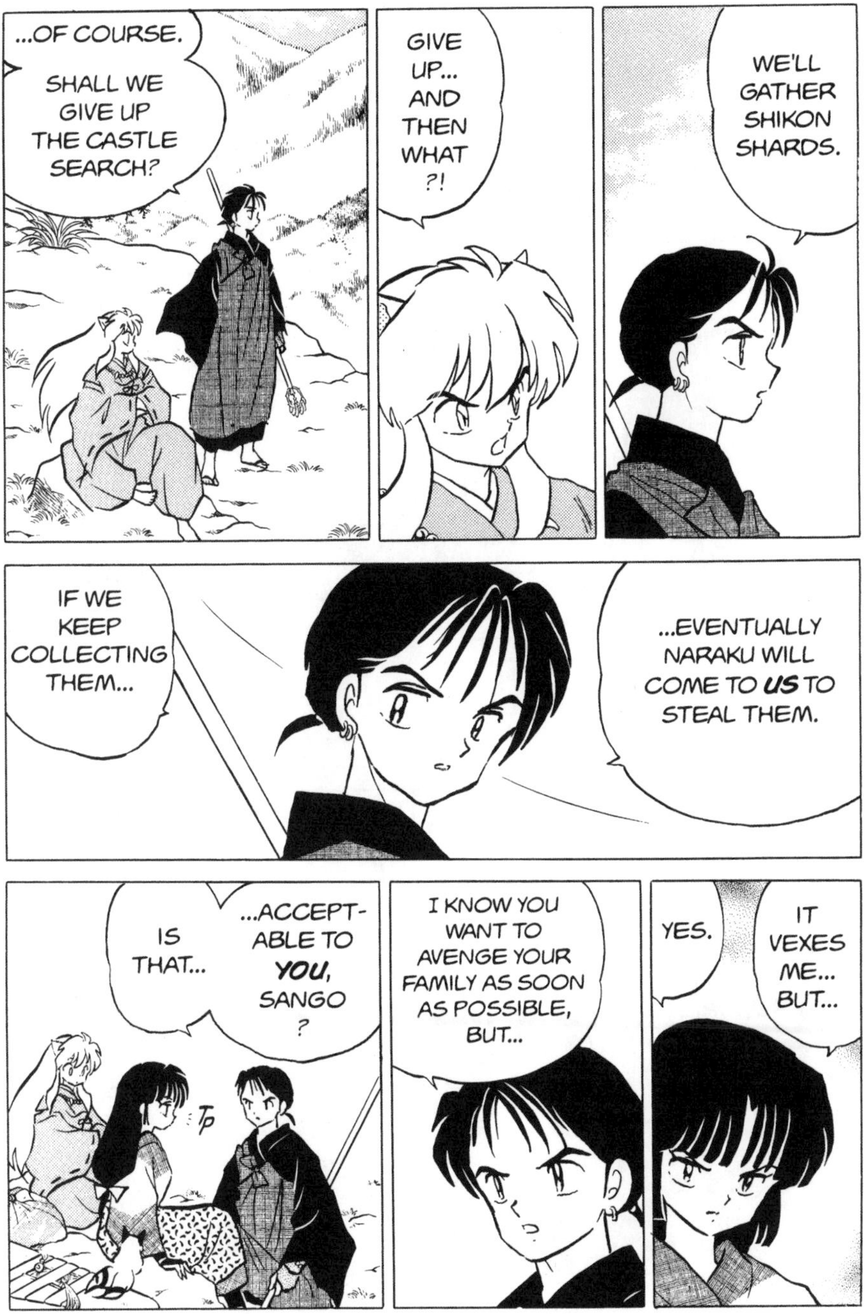
...OF COURSE.
SHALL WE GIVE UP THE CASTLE SEARCH?
GIVE UP... AND THEN WHAT ?!
WE'LL GATHER SHIKON SHARDS.
IF WE KEEP COLLECTING THEM...
...EVENTUALLY NARAKU WILL COME TO *US* TO STEAL THEM.
IS THAT...
...ACCEPTABLE TO *YOU*, SANGO ?
TP
I KNOW YOU WANT TO AVENGE YOUR FAMILY AS SOON AS POSSIBLE, BUT...
YES.
IT VEXES ME... BUT...

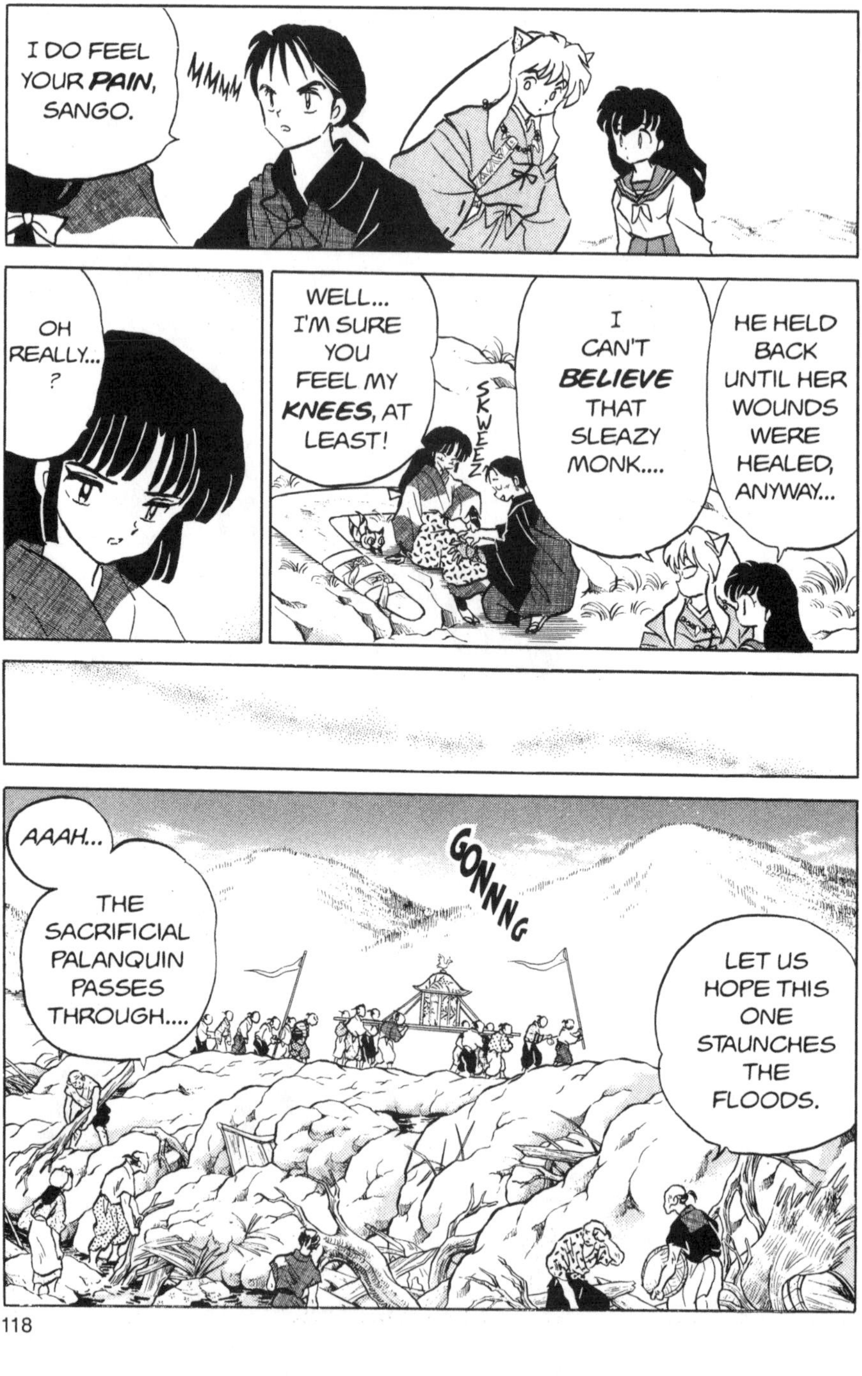
I DO FEEL YOUR **PAIN**, SANGO.
MMMM
OH REALLY...?
WELL... I'M SURE YOU FEEL MY **KNEES**, AT LEAST!
SKWEEZ
I CAN'T **BELIEVE** THAT SLEAZY MONK....
HE HELD BACK UNTIL HER WOUNDS WERE HEALED, ANYWAY...
AAAH...
THE SACRIFICIAL PALANQUIN PASSES THROUGH....
GONNNG
LET US HOPE THIS ONE STAUNCHES THE FLOODS.

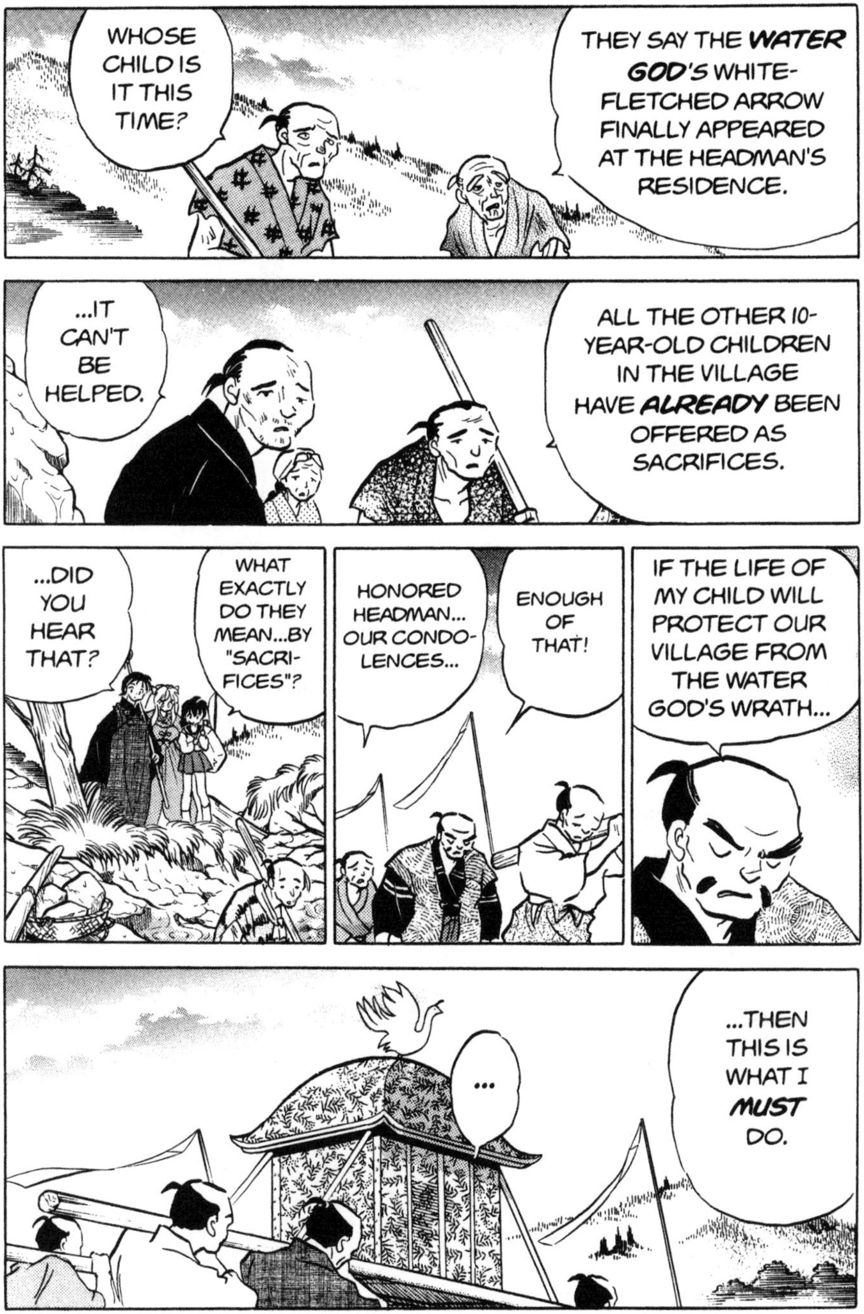
WHOSE CHILD IS IT THIS TIME?
THEY SAY THE *WATER GOD'S* WHITE-FLETCHED ARROW FINALLY APPEARED AT THE HEADMAN'S RESIDENCE.
...IT CAN'T BE HELPED.
ALL THE OTHER 10-YEAR-OLD CHILDREN IN THE VILLAGE HAVE *ALREADY* BEEN OFFERED AS SACRIFICES.
...DID YOU HEAR THAT?
WHAT EXACTLY DO THEY MEAN...BY "SACRIFICES"?
HONORED HEADMAN... OUR CONDOLENCES...
ENOUGH OF THAT!
IF THE LIFE OF MY CHILD WILL PROTECT OUR VILLAGE FROM THE WATER GOD'S WRATH...
...
...THEN THIS IS WHAT I *MUST* DO.

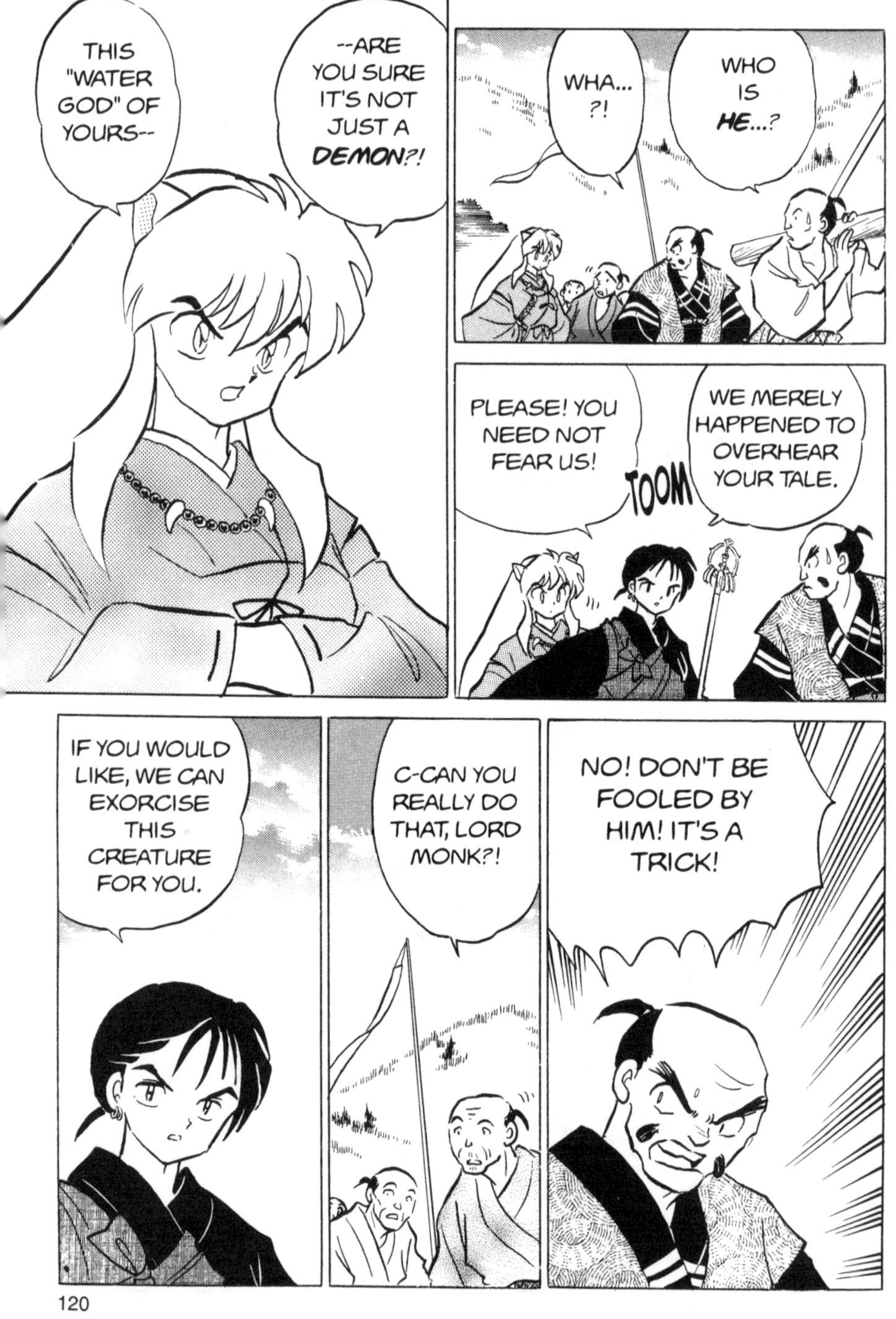
THIS "WATER GOD" OF YOURS--
--ARE YOU SURE IT'S NOT JUST A **DEMON**?!
WHA...?!
WHO IS **HE**...?
PLEASE! YOU NEED NOT FEAR US!
TOOM
WE MERELY HAPPENED TO OVERHEAR YOUR TALE.
IF YOU WOULD LIKE, WE CAN EXORCISE THIS CREATURE FOR YOU.
C-CAN YOU REALLY DO THAT, LORD MONK?!
NO! DON'T BE FOOLED BY HIM! IT'S A TRICK!

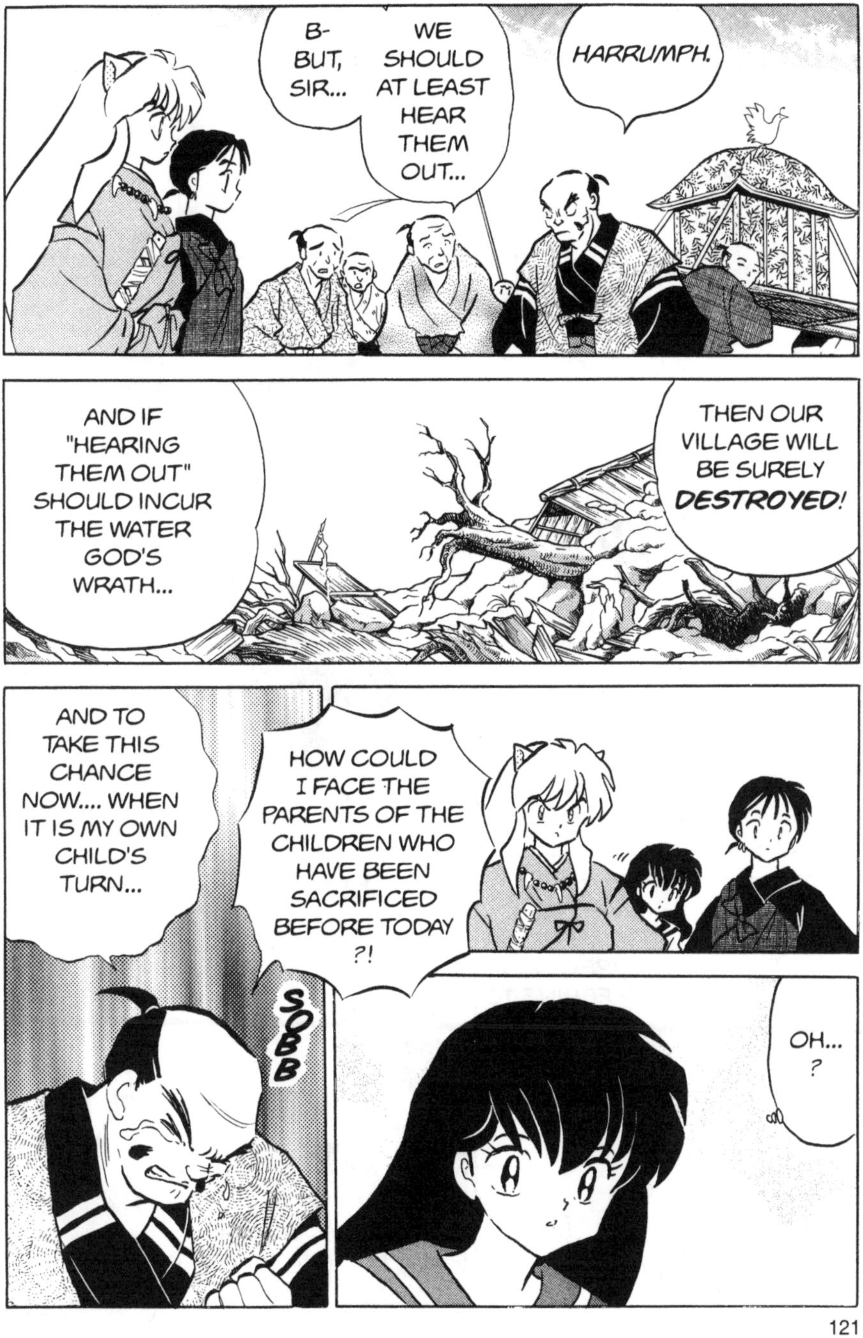
B-
BUT,
SIR...
WE
SHOULD
AT LEAST
HEAR
THEM
OUT...
HARRUMPH.
AND IF
"HEARING
THEM OUT"
SHOULD INCUR
THE WATER
GOD'S
WRATH...
THEN OUR
VILLAGE WILL
BE SURELY
DESTROYED!
AND TO
TAKE THIS
CHANCE
NOW.... WHEN
IT IS MY OWN
CHILD'S
TURN...
HOW COULD
I FACE THE
PARENTS OF THE
CHILDREN WHO
HAVE BEEN
SACRIFICED
BEFORE TODAY
?!
SOBB
OH...
?

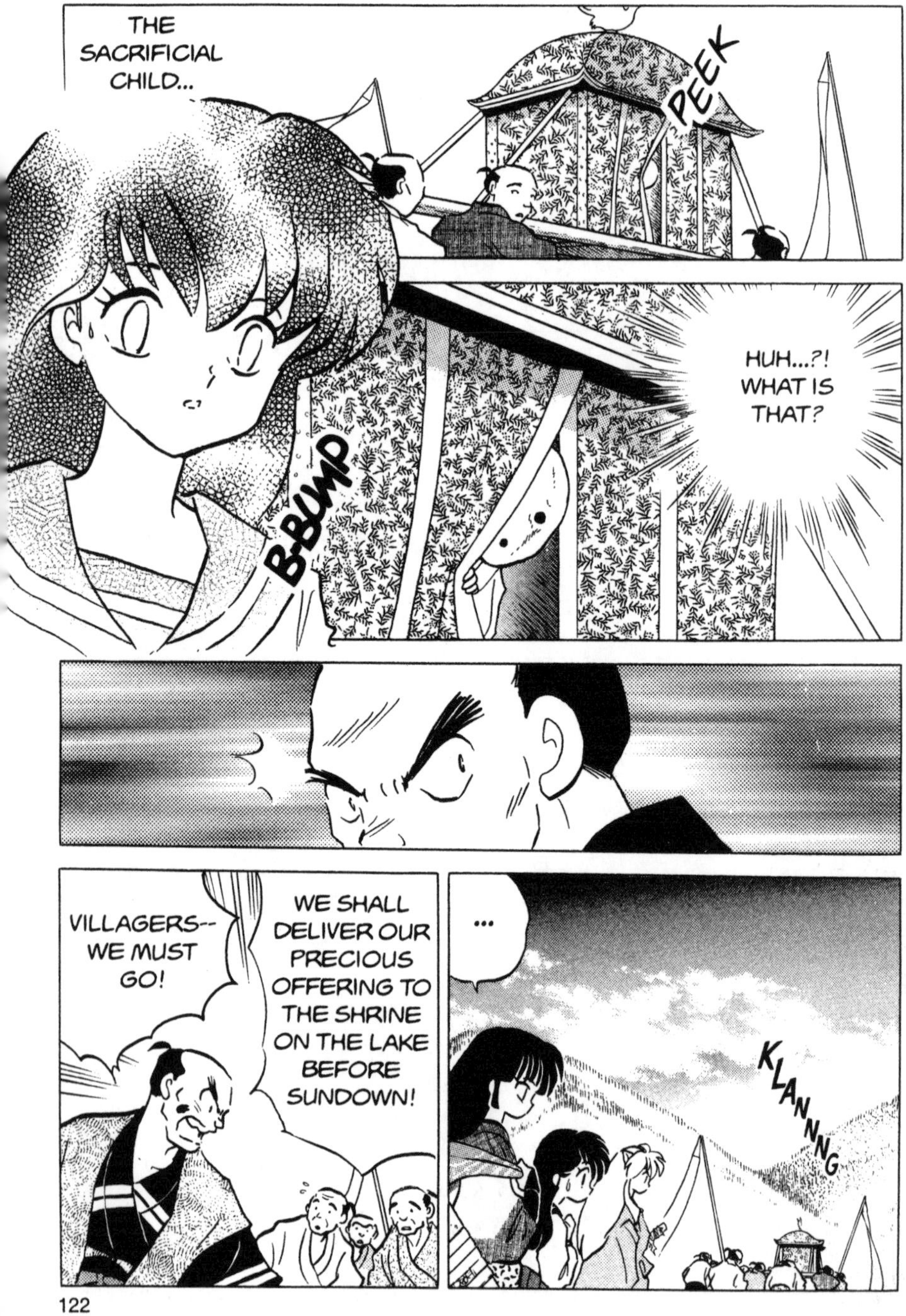
THE SACRIFICIAL CHILD...
PEEK
HUH...?! WHAT IS THAT?
B-BUMP
VILLAGERS-- WE MUST GO!
WE SHALL DELIVER OUR PRECIOUS OFFERING TO THE SHRINE ON THE LAKE BEFORE SUNDOWN!
...
KLANNNG

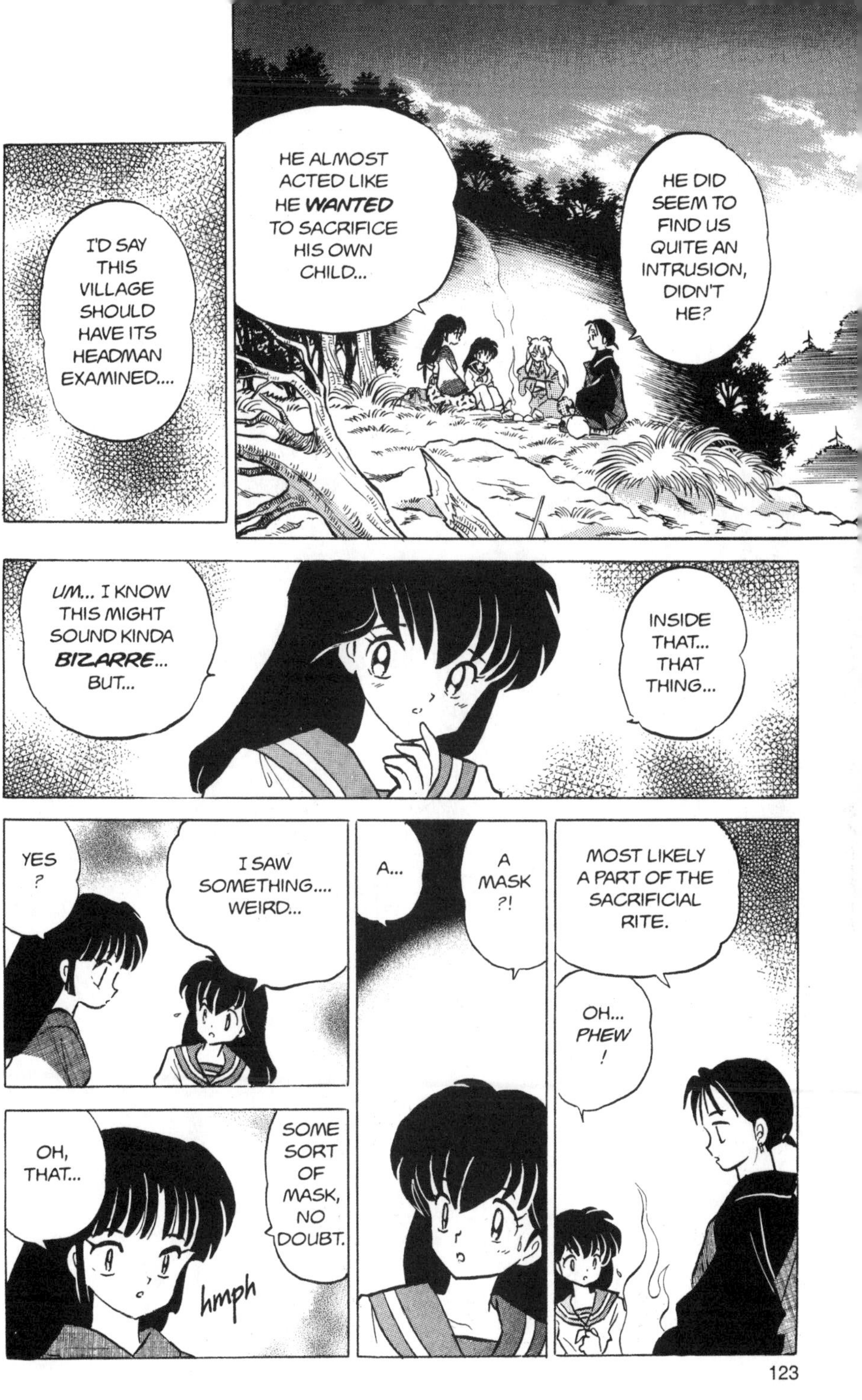

I'D SAY THIS VILLAGE SHOULD HAVE ITS HEADMAN EXAMINED....
HE ALMOST ACTED LIKE HE *WANTED* TO SACRIFICE HIS OWN CHILD...
HE DID SEEM TO FIND US QUITE AN INTRUSION, DIDN'T HE?
UM... I KNOW THIS MIGHT SOUND KINDA ***BIZARRE***... BUT...
INSIDE THAT... THAT THING...
YES?
I SAW SOMETHING.... WEIRD...
OH, THAT...
SOME SORT OF MASK, NO DOUBT.
hmph
A...
A MASK?!
MOST LIKELY A PART OF THE SACRIFICIAL RITE.
OH... *PHEW*!

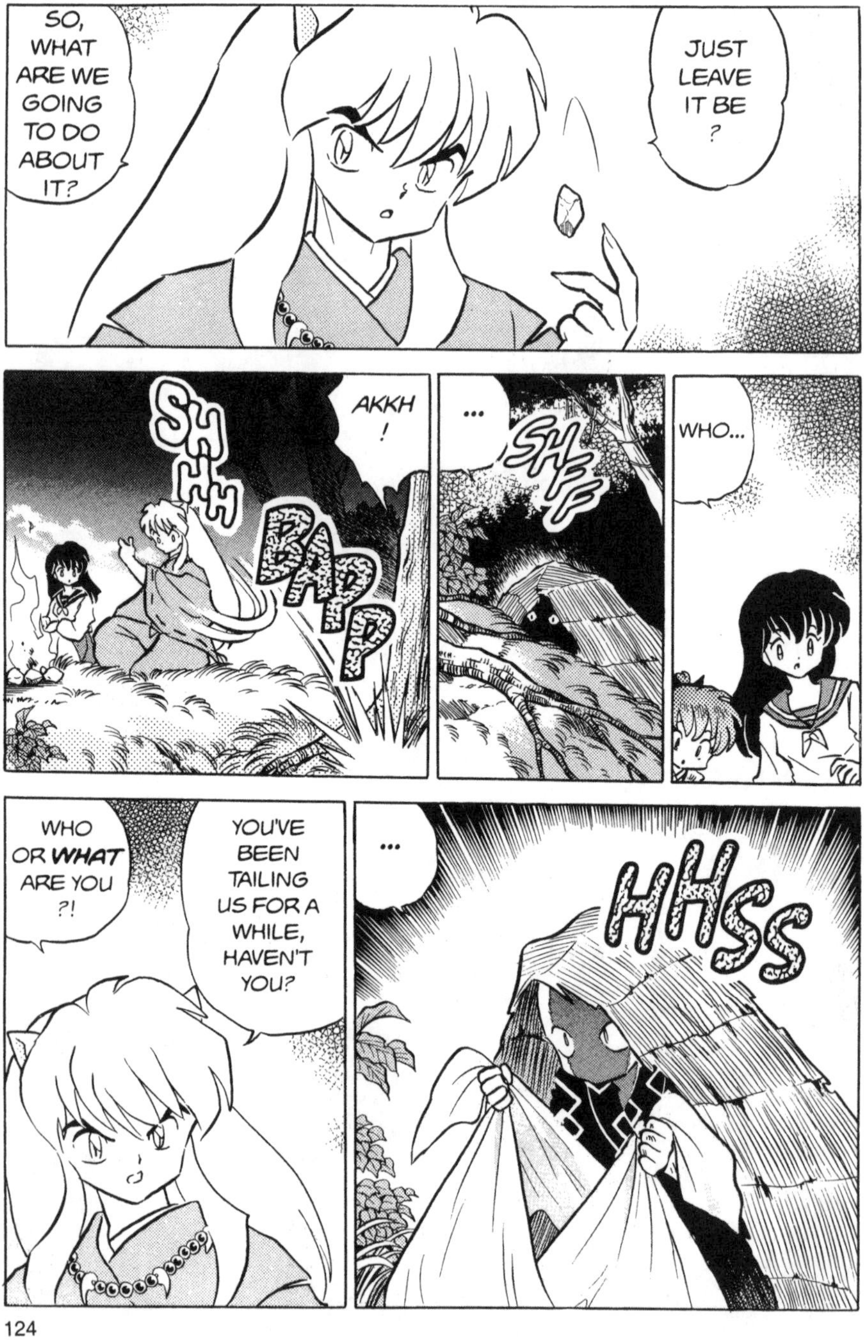
SO, WHAT ARE WE GOING TO DO ABOUT IT?
JUST LEAVE IT BE ?
SHHHH
AKKH !
BADDP
...
SHFF
WHO...
WHO OR **WHAT** ARE YOU ?!
YOU'VE BEEN TAILING US FOR A WHILE, HAVEN'T YOU?
...
HHSS

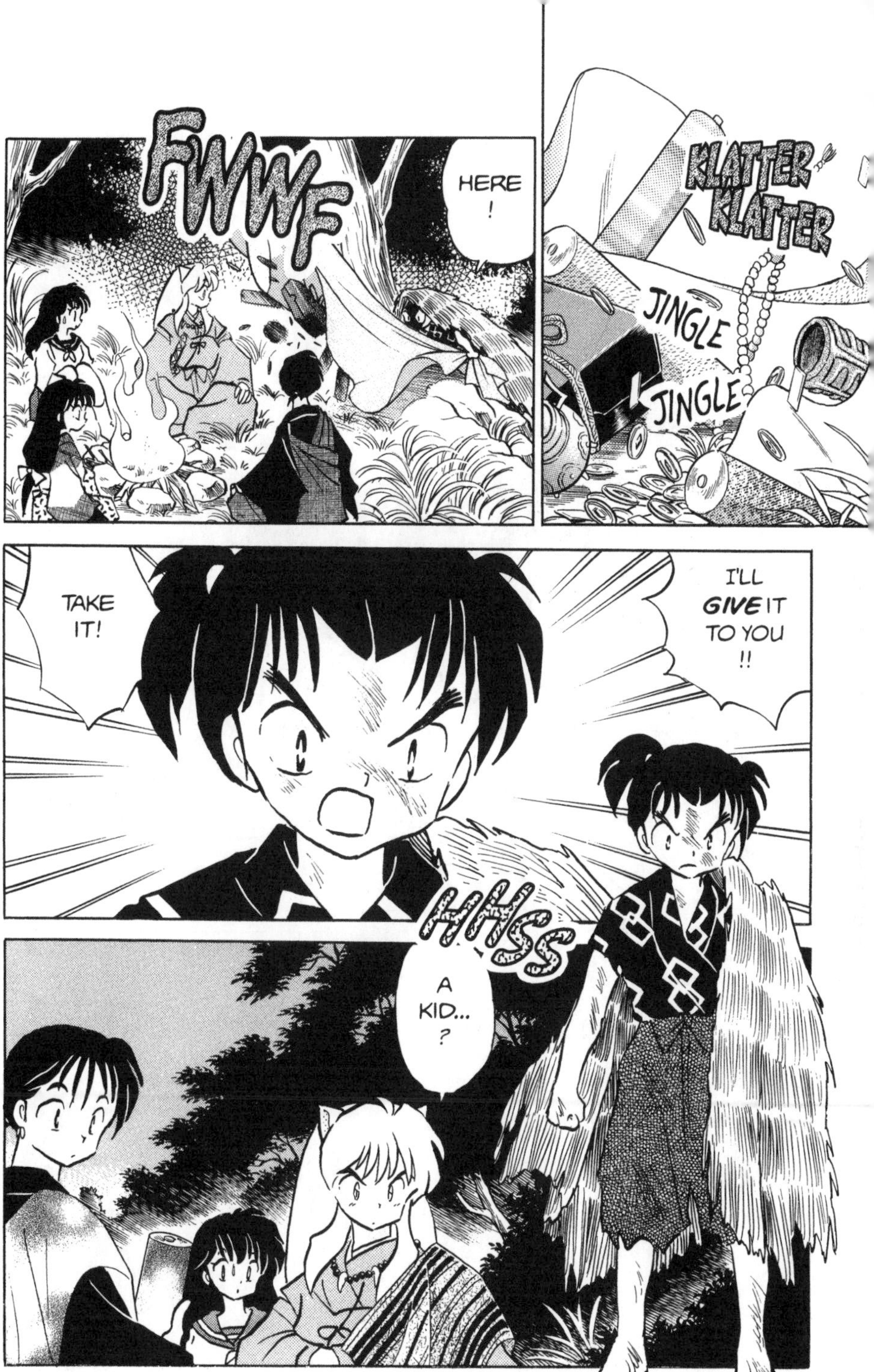

FWWF
HERE!
KLATTER KLATTER
JINGLE
JINGLE
TAKE IT!
I'LL **GIVE** IT TO YOU!!
HHSS
A KID...?

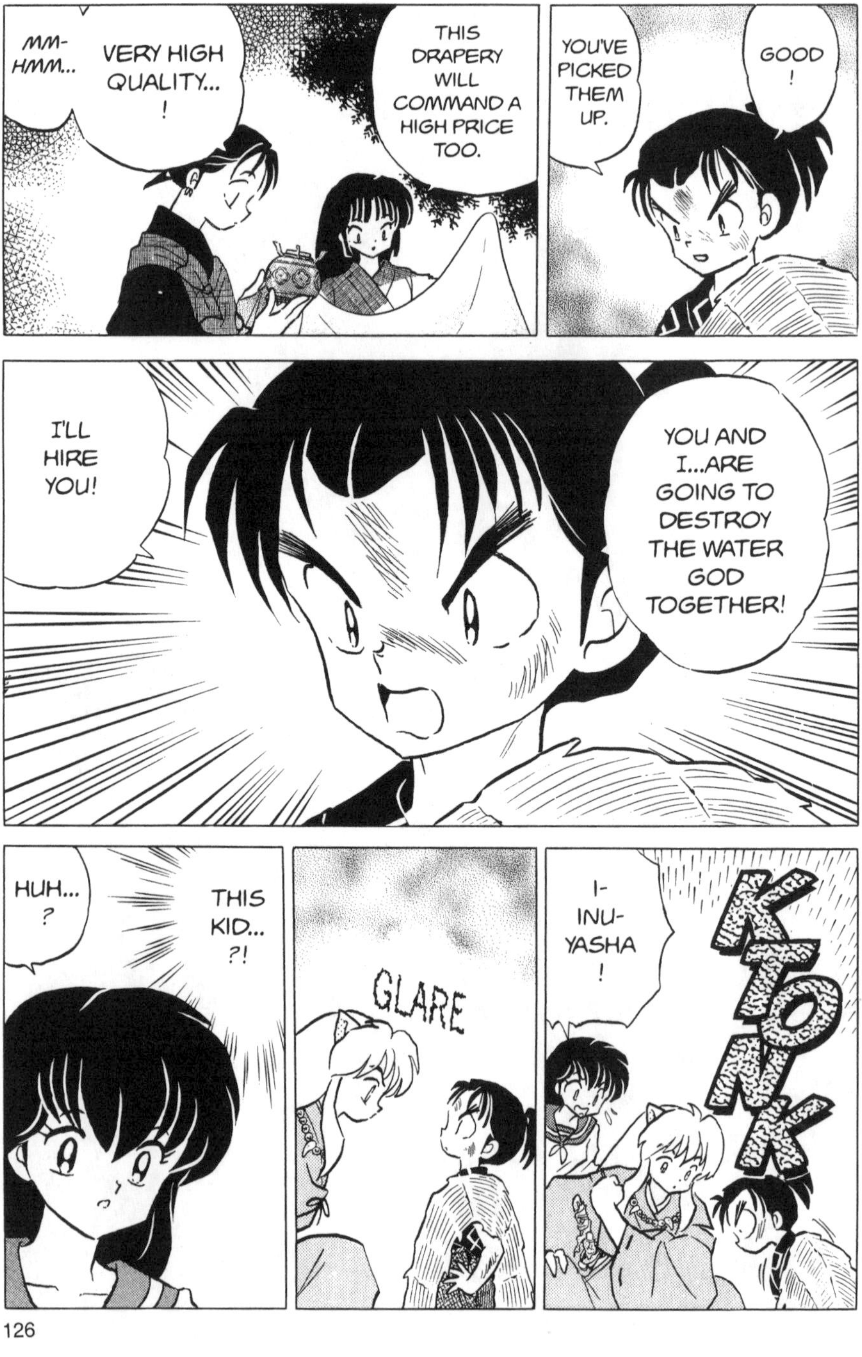
MM-HMM...
VERY HIGH QUALITY... !
THIS DRAPERY WILL COMMAND A HIGH PRICE TOO.
YOU'VE PICKED THEM UP.
GOOD !
I'LL HIRE YOU!
YOU AND I...ARE GOING TO DESTROY THE WATER GOD TOGETHER!
HUH... ?
THIS KID... ?!
GLARE
I- INU-YASHA !
KTONK

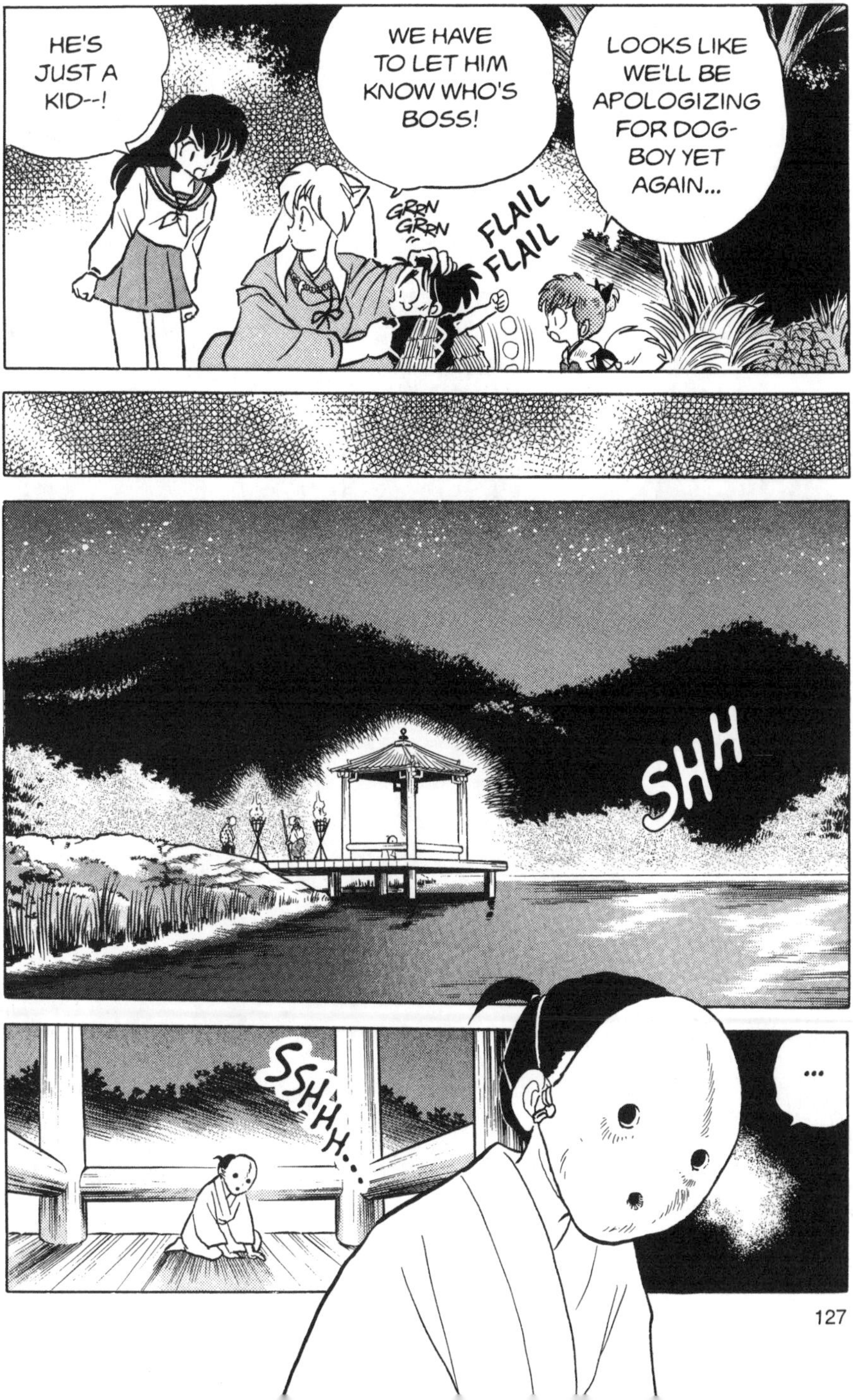
HE'S JUST A KID--!
WE HAVE TO LET HIM KNOW WHO'S BOSS!
GRRN GRRN
FLAIL FLAIL
LOOKS LIKE WE'LL BE APOLOGIZING FOR DOG-BOY YET AGAIN...
SHH
SSHHH...
...

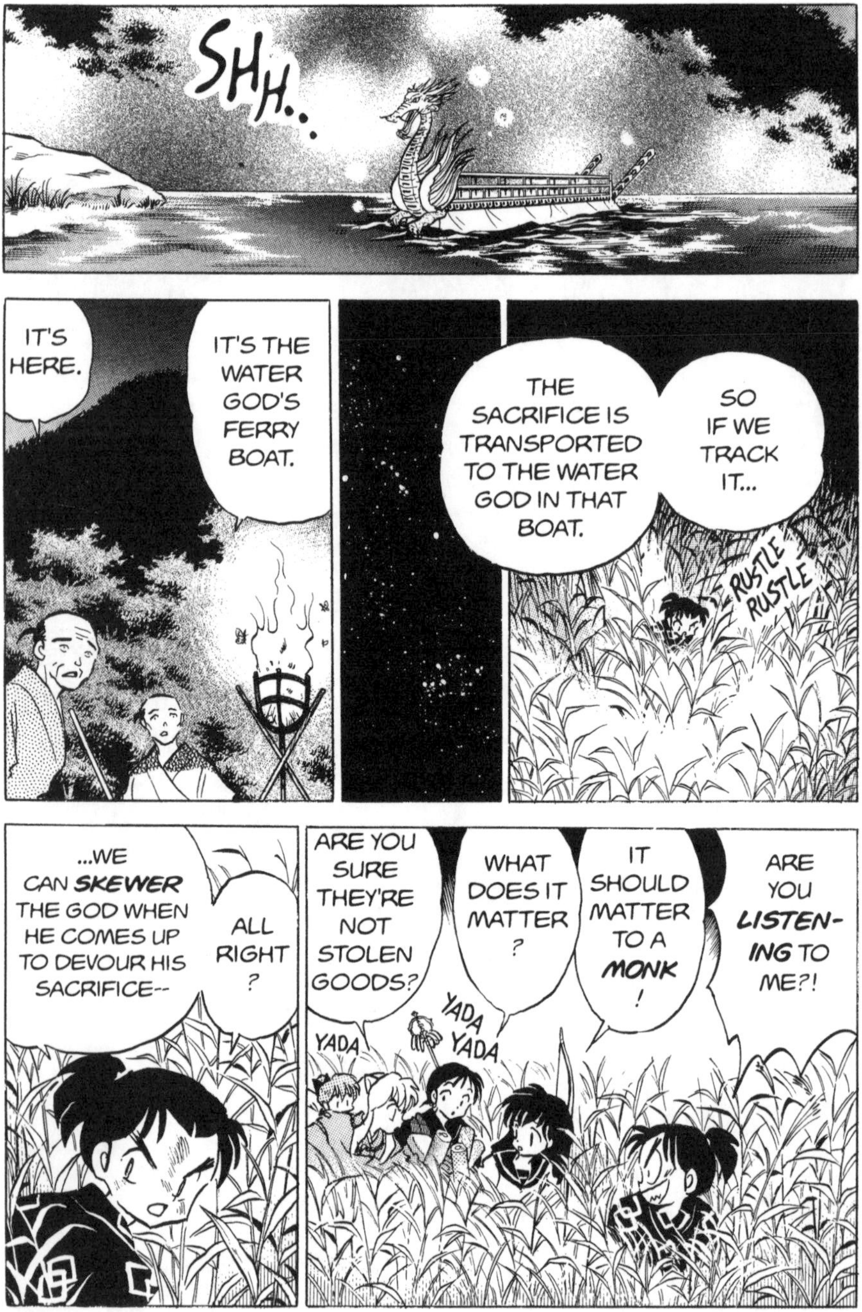
SHH...
IT'S HERE.
IT'S THE WATER GOD'S FERRY BOAT.
THE SACRIFICE IS TRANSPORTED TO THE WATER GOD IN THAT BOAT.
SO IF WE TRACK IT...
RUSTLE RUSTLE
...WE CAN **SKEWER** THE GOD WHEN HE COMES UP TO DEVOUR HIS SACRIFICE--
ALL RIGHT?
ARE YOU SURE THEY'RE NOT STOLEN GOODS?
YADA
WHAT DOES IT MATTER?
YADA YADA
IT SHOULD MATTER TO A **MONK**!
ARE YOU **LISTENING** TO ME?!

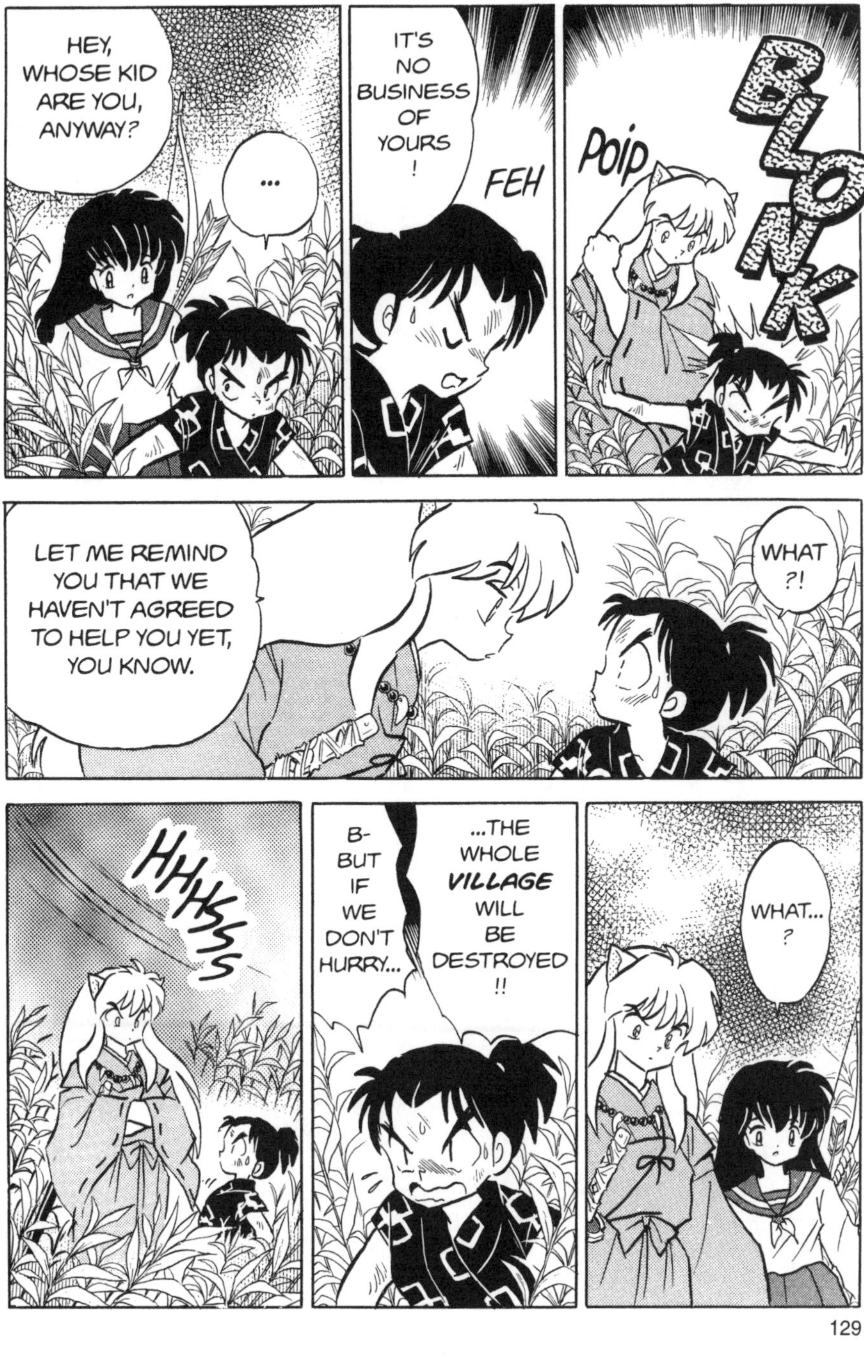
HEY, WHOSE KID ARE YOU, ANYWAY?
...
IT'S NO BUSINESS OF YOURS!
FEH
Poip
BLONK
LET ME REMIND YOU THAT WE HAVEN'T AGREED TO HELP YOU YET, YOU KNOW.
WHAT?!
HHHSSS
B-BUT IF WE DON'T HURRY...
...THE WHOLE VILLAGE WILL BE DESTROYED!!
WHAT...?

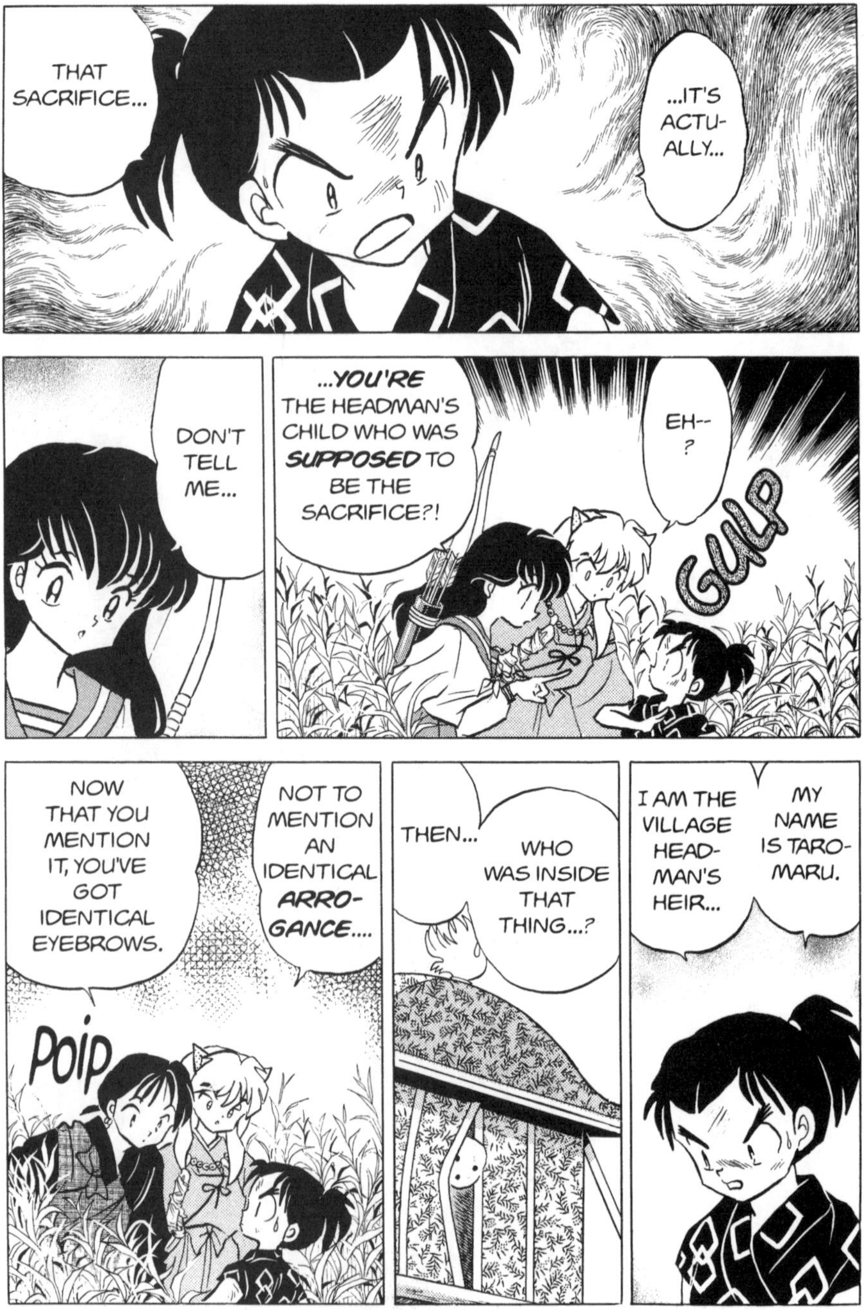
THAT SACRIFICE...
...IT'S ACTU-ALLY...
DON'T TELL ME...
...***YOU'RE*** THE HEADMAN'S CHILD WHO WAS ***SUPPOSED*** TO BE THE SACRIFICE?!
EH-- ?
GULP
NOW THAT YOU MENTION IT, YOU'VE GOT IDENTICAL EYEBROWS.
NOT TO MENTION AN IDENTICAL ***ARRO-GANCE***....
POIP
THEN...
WHO WAS INSIDE THAT THING...?
I AM THE VILLAGE HEAD-MAN'S HEIR...
MY NAME IS TARO-MARU.

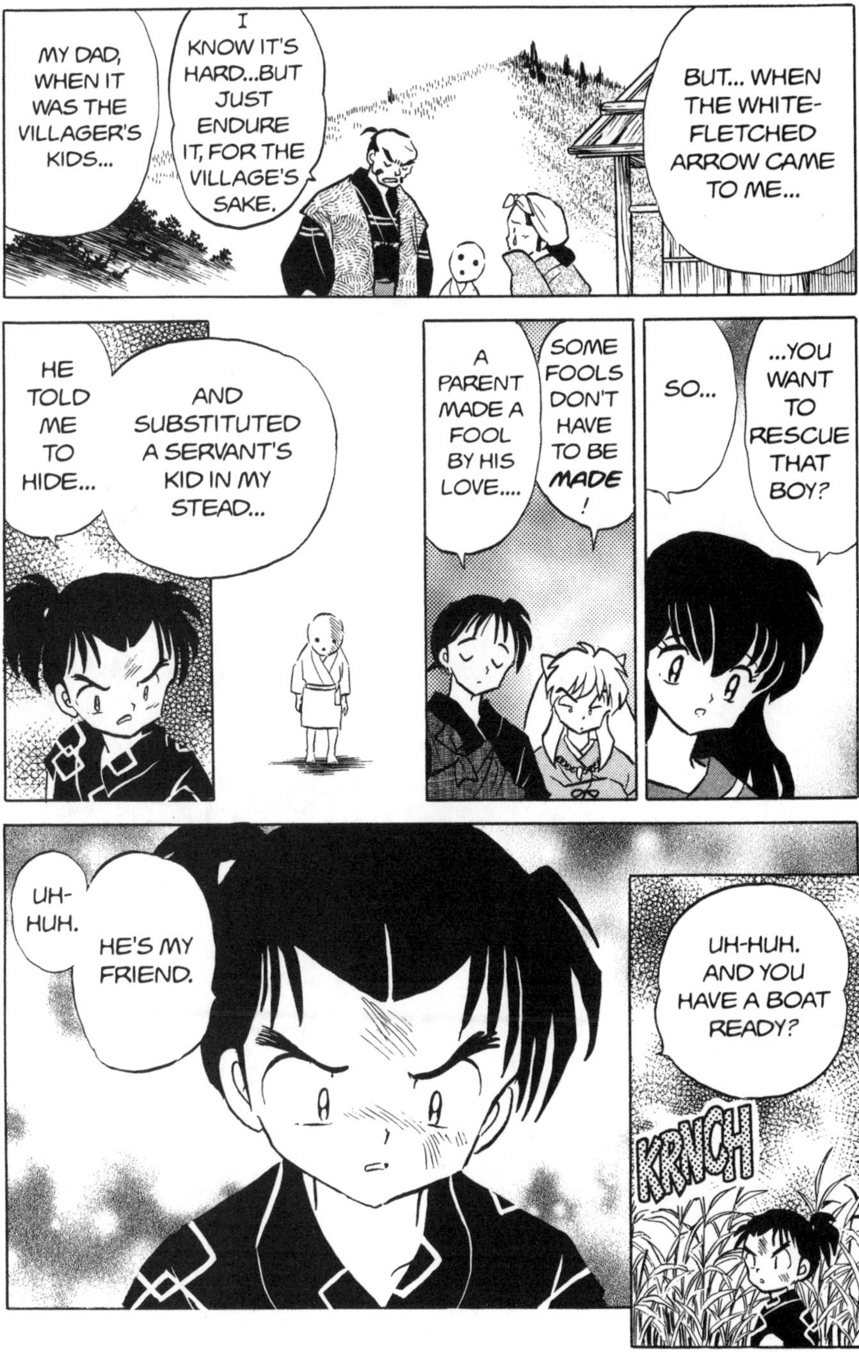
MY DAD, WHEN IT WAS THE VILLAGER'S KIDS...
I KNOW IT'S HARD...BUT JUST ENDURE IT, FOR THE VILLAGE'S SAKE.
BUT... WHEN THE WHITE-FLETCHED ARROW CAME TO ME...
HE TOLD ME TO HIDE...
AND SUBSTITUTED A SERVANT'S KID IN MY STEAD...
A PARENT MADE A FOOL BY HIS LOVE....
SOME FOOLS DON'T HAVE TO BE *MADE*!
SO...
...YOU WANT TO RESCUE THAT BOY?
UH-HUH.
HE'S MY FRIEND.
UH-HUH. AND YOU HAVE A BOAT READY?
KRNCH

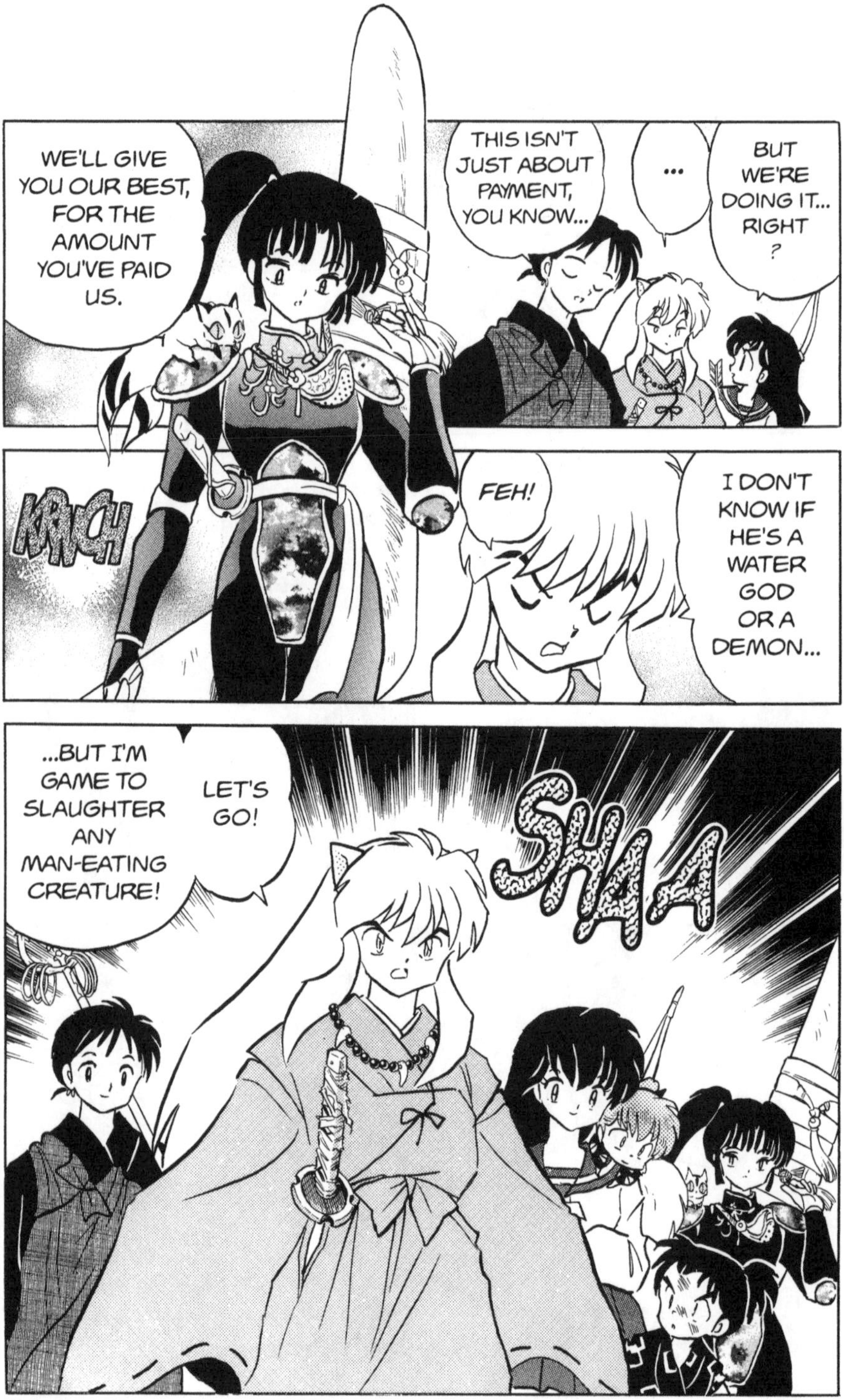

WE'LL GIVE YOU OUR BEST, FOR THE AMOUNT YOU'VE PAID US.
THIS ISN'T JUST ABOUT PAYMENT, YOU KNOW...
...
BUT WE'RE DOING IT... RIGHT ?
KRNCH
FEH!
I DON'T KNOW IF HE'S A WATER GOD OR A DEMON...
...BUT I'M GAME TO SLAUGHTER ANY MAN-EATING CREATURE!
LET'S GO!
SHAA

SCROLL EIGHT

THE HOLY RELIC

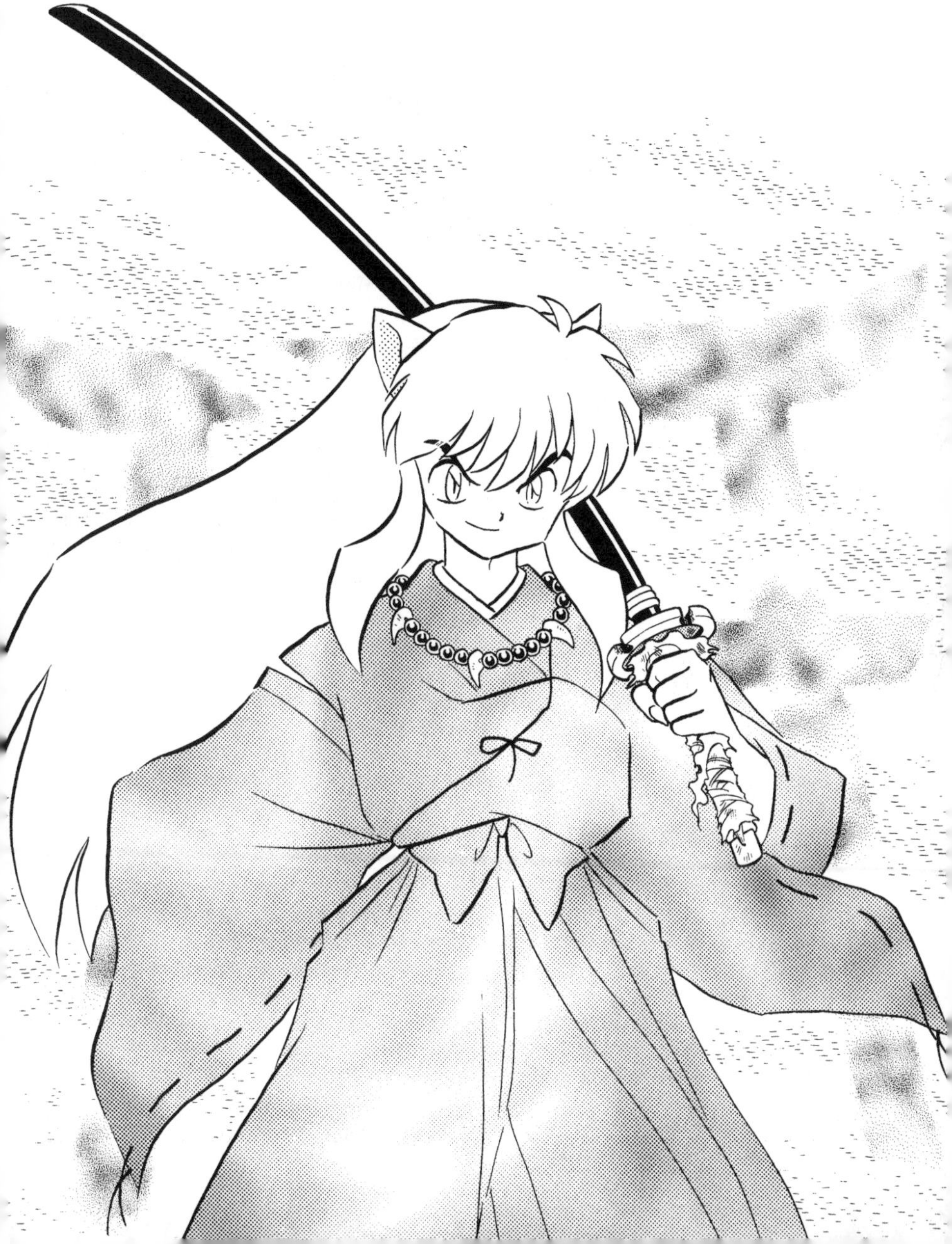

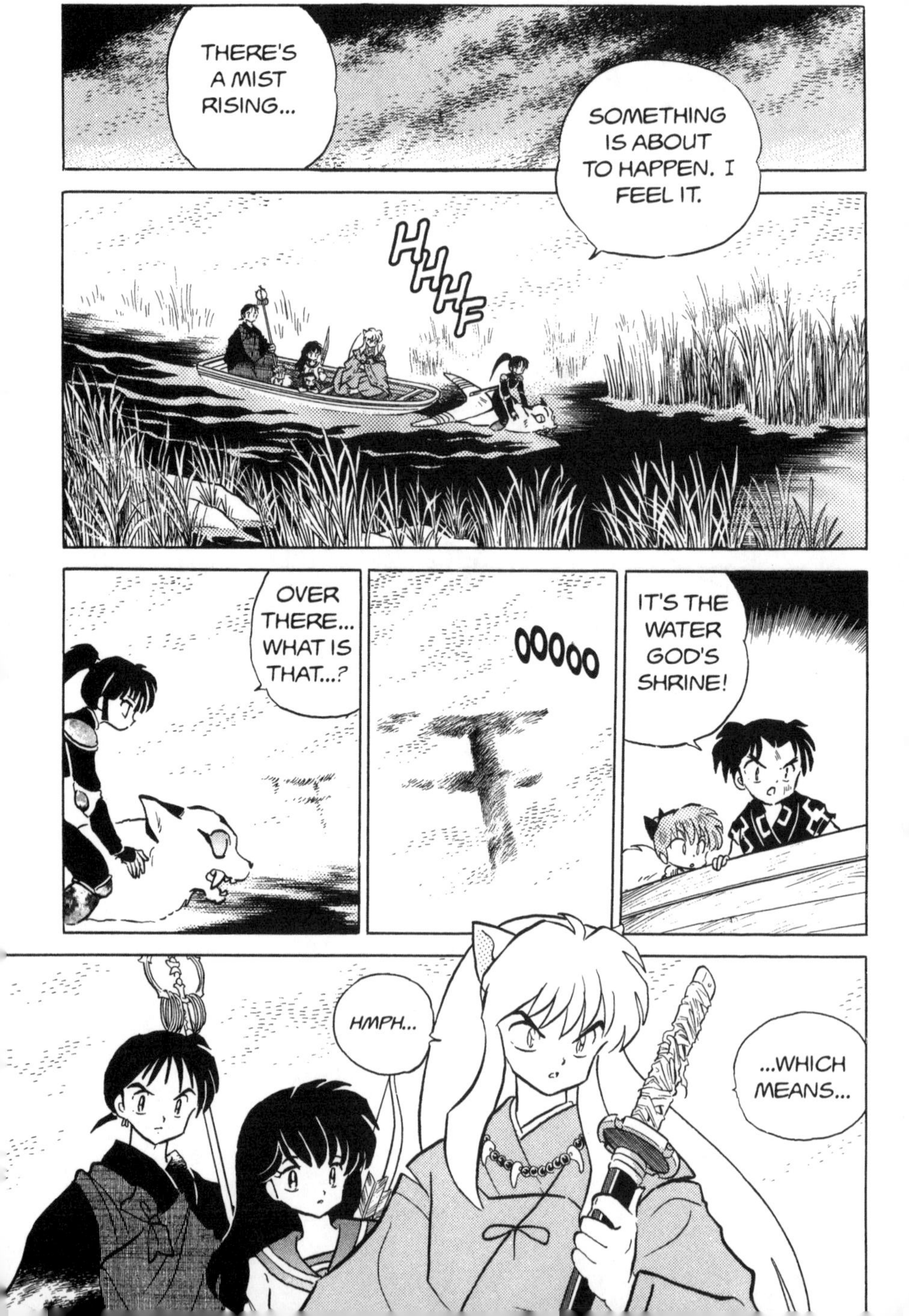
THERE'S A MIST RISING...
SOMETHING IS ABOUT TO HAPPEN. I FEEL IT.
HHHF
OVER THERE... WHAT IS THAT...?
OOOOO
IT'S THE WATER GOD'S SHRINE!
HMPH...
...WHICH MEANS...

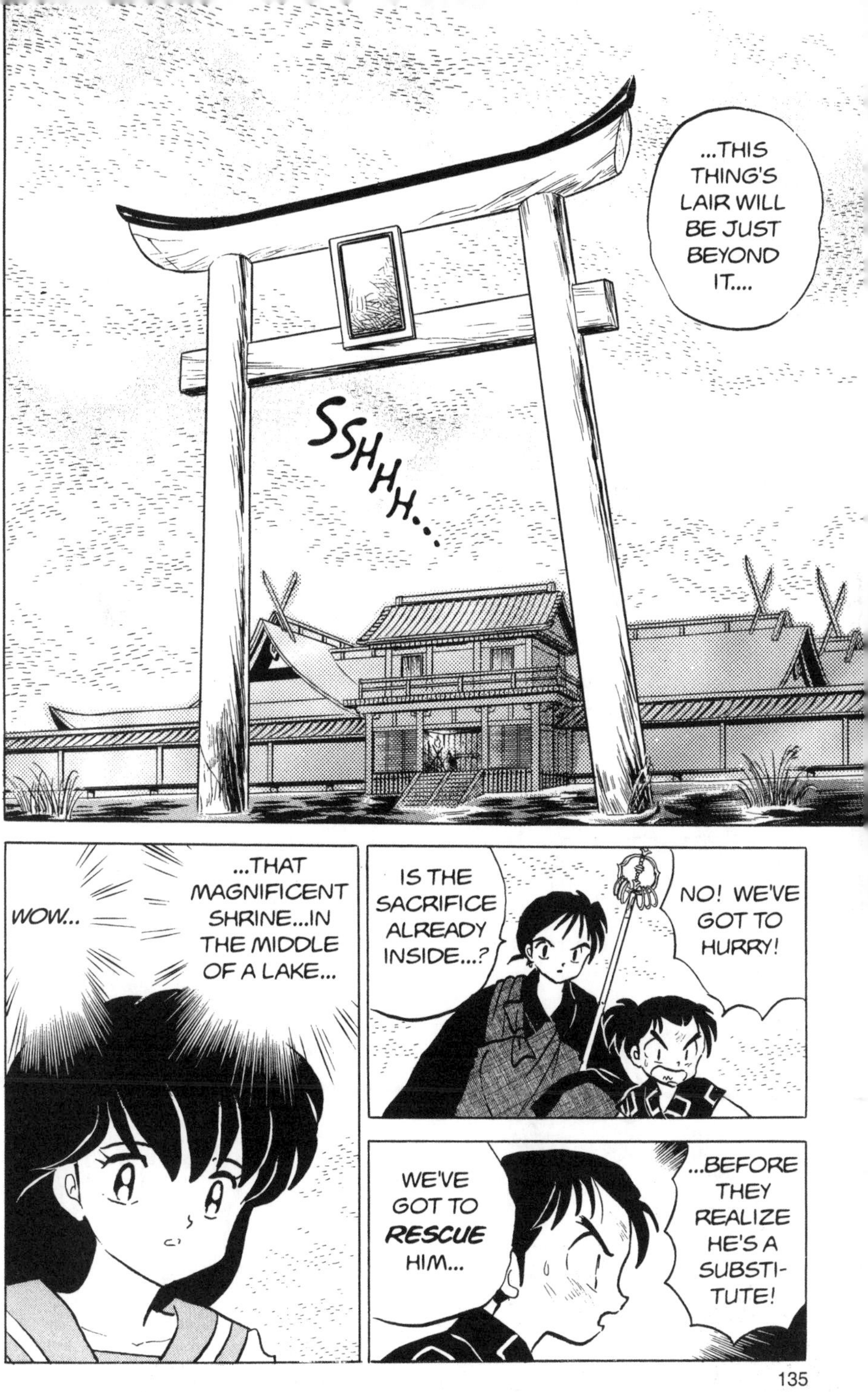

...THIS THING'S LAIR WILL BE JUST BEYOND IT....
SSHHH...
WOW...
...THAT MAGNIFICENT SHRINE...IN THE MIDDLE OF A LAKE...
IS THE SACRIFICE ALREADY INSIDE...?
NO! WE'VE GOT TO HURRY!
WE'VE GOT TO ***RESCUE*** HIM...
...BEFORE THEY REALIZE HE'S A SUBSTI-TUTE!

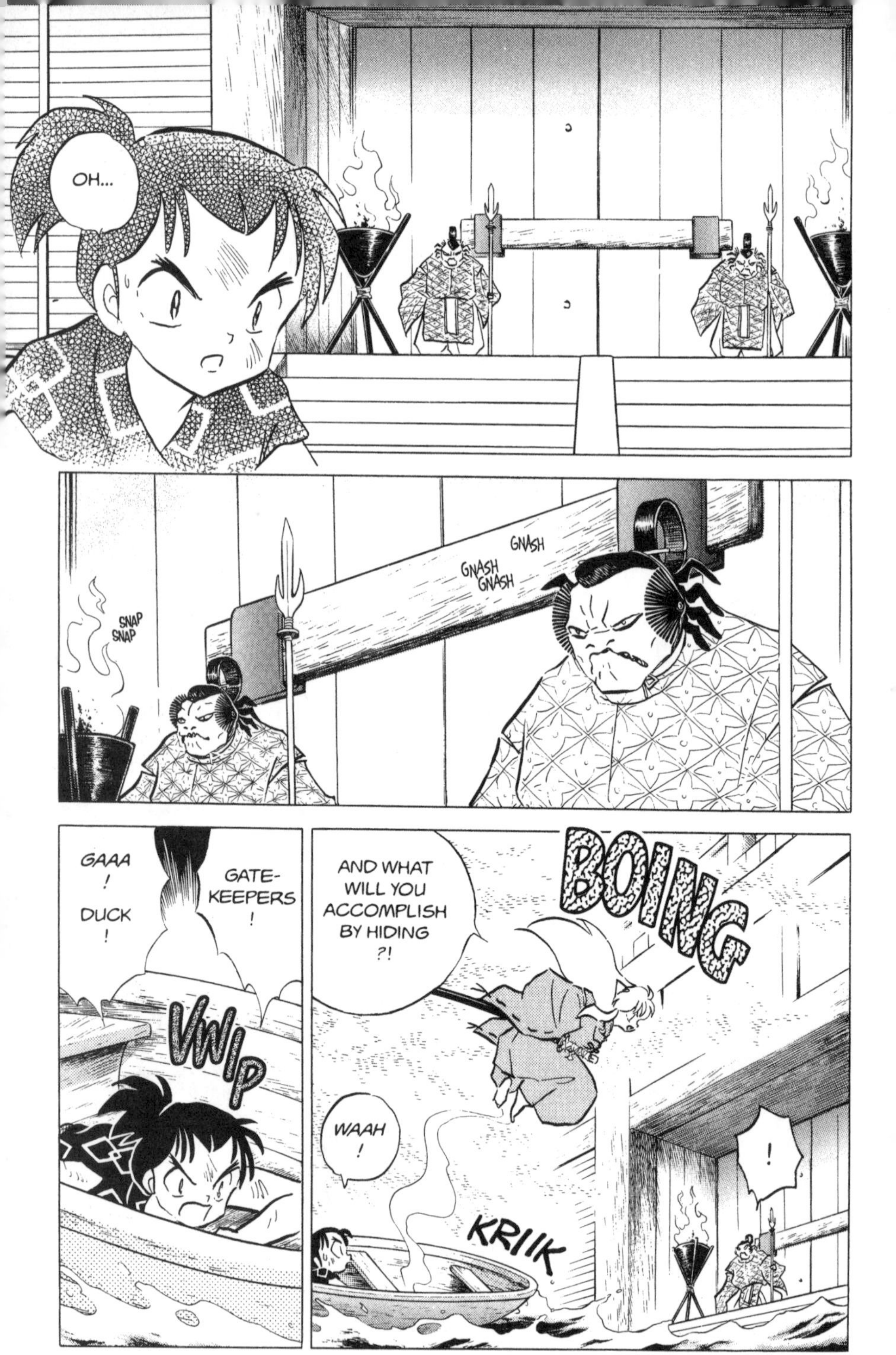

OH...
GNASH
GNASH
GNASH
SNAP
SNAP
GAAA!
DUCK!
GATE-KEEPERS!
VWIP
AND WHAT WILL YOU ACCOMPLISH BY HIDING?!
BOING
WAAH!
!
KRIIK

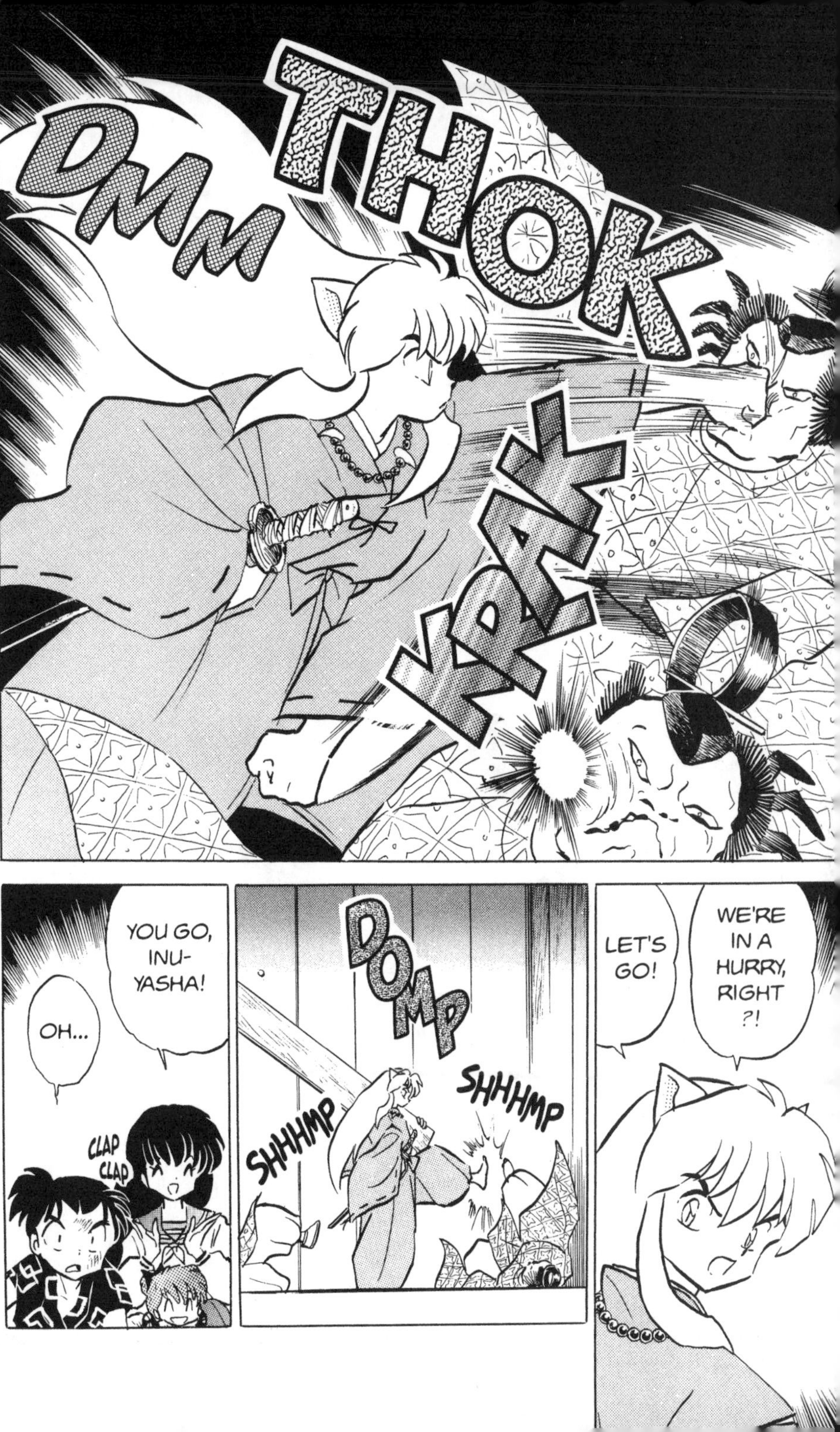
DMM
THOK
KRAK
OH...
YOU GO, INU-YASHA!
CLAP CLAP
DOMP
SHHHMP
SHHHMP
LET'S GO!
WE'RE IN A HURRY, RIGHT ?!

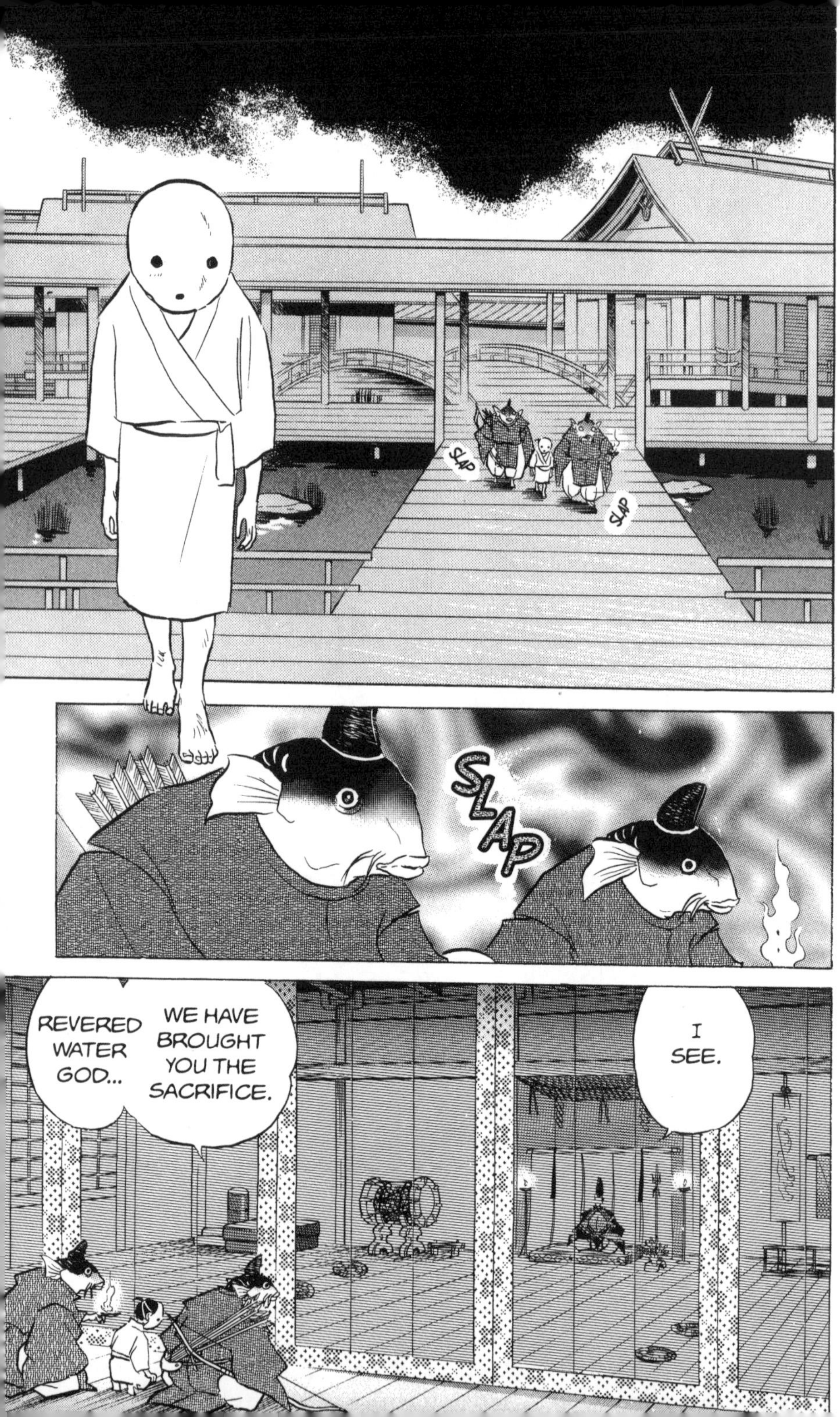
SLAP
SLAP
SLAP
REVERED WATER GOD...
WE HAVE BROUGHT YOU THE SACRIFICE.
I SEE.

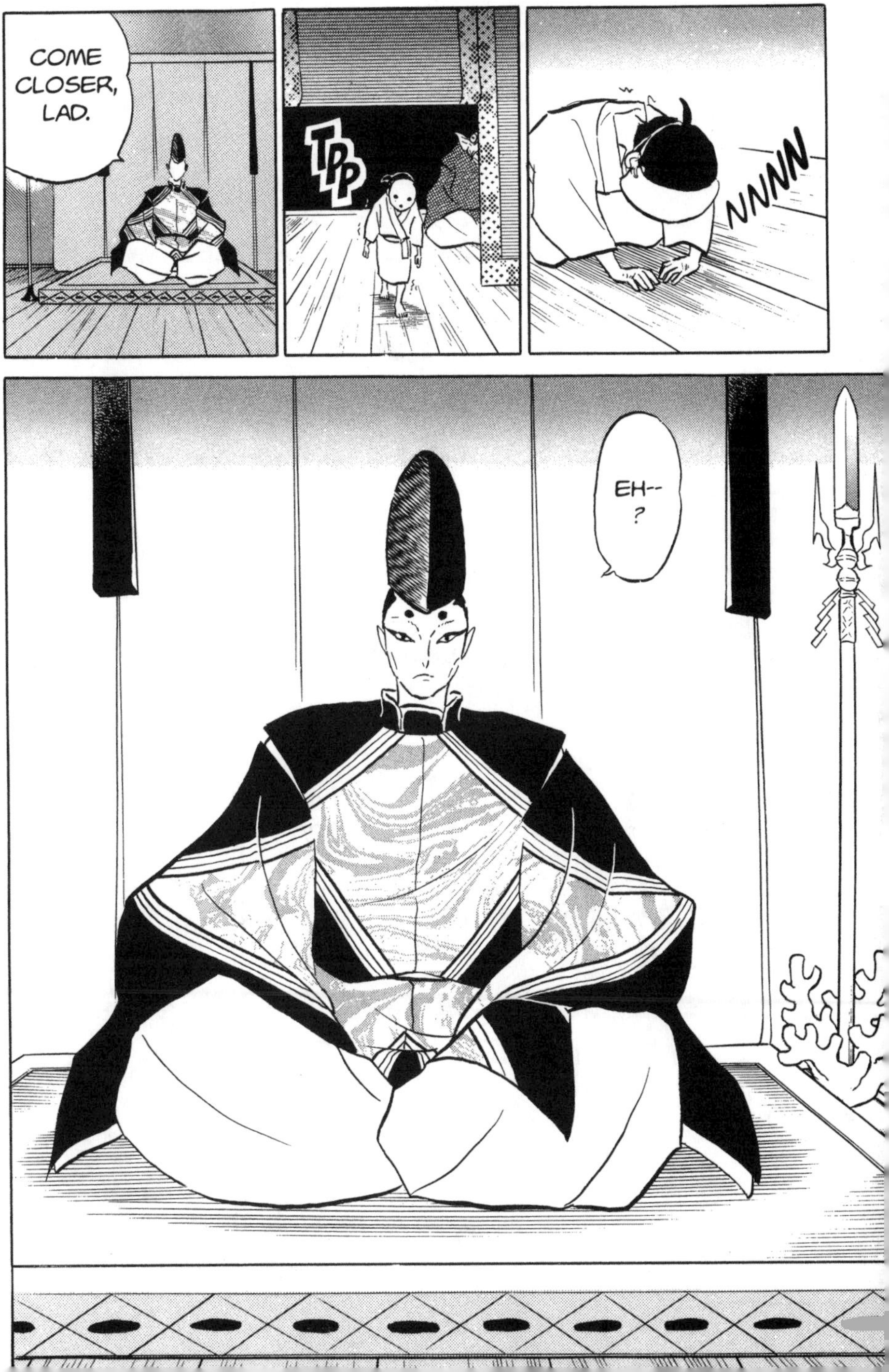
COME CLOSER, LAD.
TPP
NNNN
EH--?

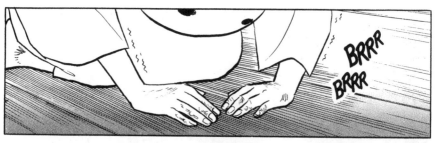

BRRR
BRRR

THESE
FILTHY CORN-
ENCRUSTED
HANDS...

YOU...

...ARE
NOT THE
VILLAGE
HEADMAN'S
CHILD....

FLINCH

WHAT
IS THE
MEANING
OF THIS
?!

SSS

DID YOU
BELIEVE
YOU COULD
DECEIVE A
GOD?!

PLEASE,
LORD
!!

DEVOUR
ME
INSTEAD
!

AND
FORGIVE
THEM
!

SOBB

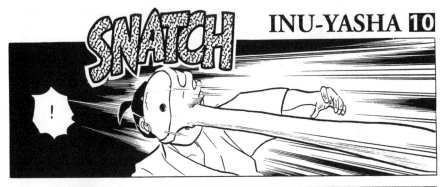

SURELY YOU KNOW THAT I CANNOT FORGIVE *THIS*....

HOW COULD I KEEP MY DIGNITY AS A *GOD?*

...

NNNSH NNNSH

SKWIIISH

DANGLE

SKWRM

SKWRM

THE BLOODY SCRAPS OF YOUR BODY WILL SWIRL IN THE FLOOD I SET LOOSE ON YOUR VILLAGE.

THOK

DM DM DM DM

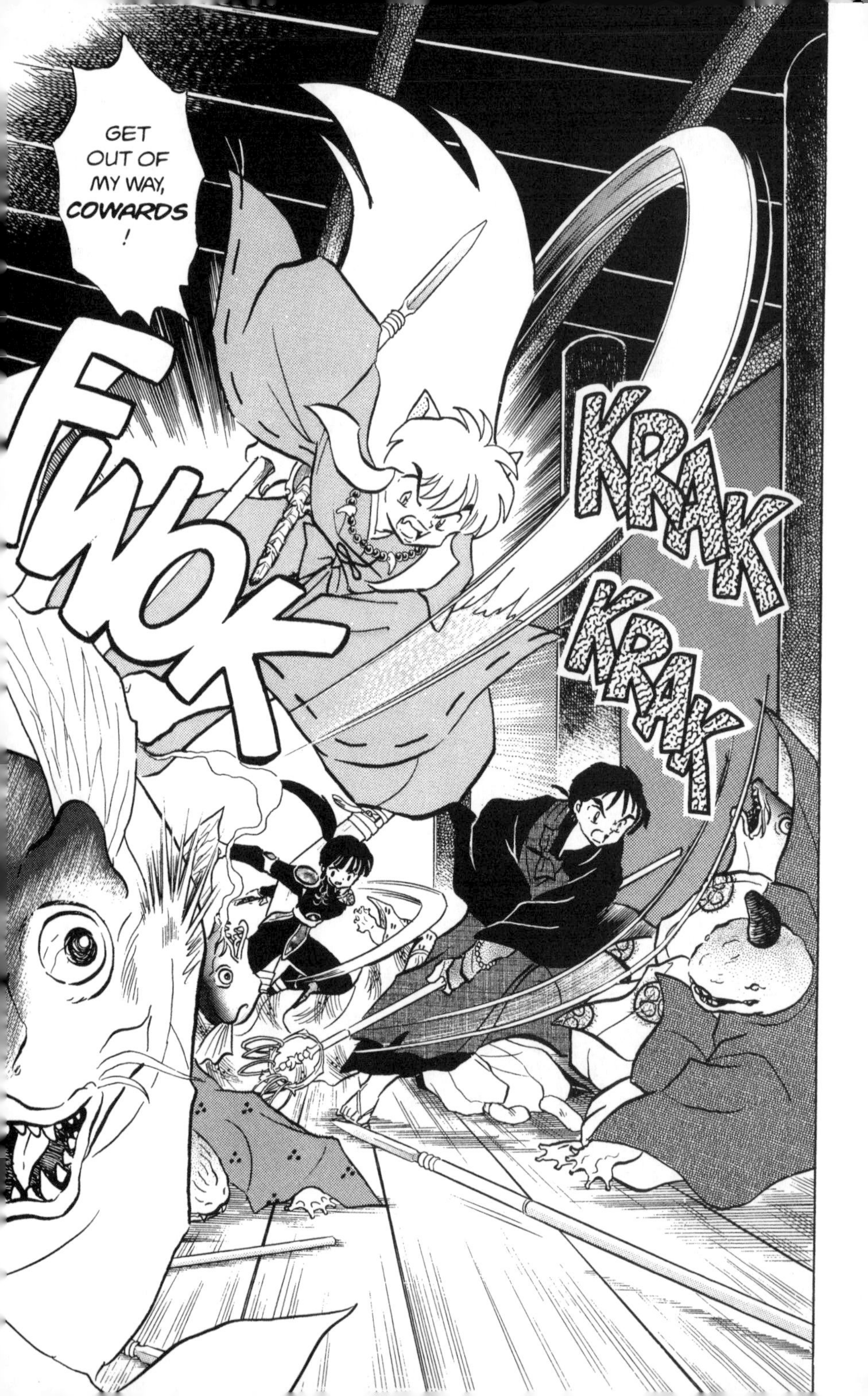
GET OUT OF MY WAY, COWARDS!
FWOK
KRAK
KRAK
KRAK

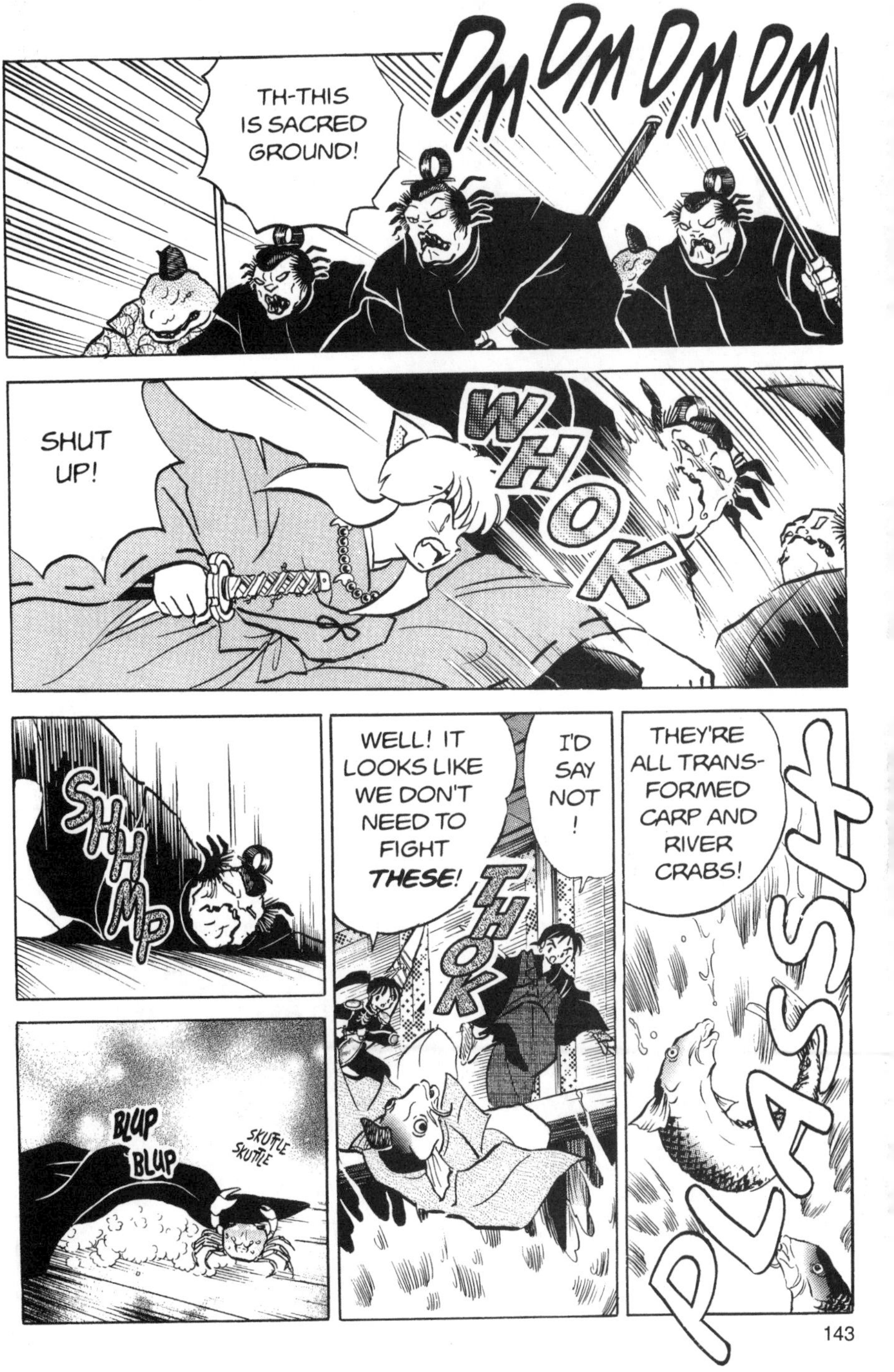

DMDMDMDM
TH-THIS IS SACRED GROUND!
SHUT UP!
WHOK
SHHMP
BLUP
BLUP
SKUTTLE SKUTTLE
WELL! IT LOOKS LIKE WE DON'T NEED TO FIGHT *THESE*!
I'D SAY NOT!
THOK
THEY'RE ALL TRANS-FORMED CARP AND RIVER CRABS!
PLASSH

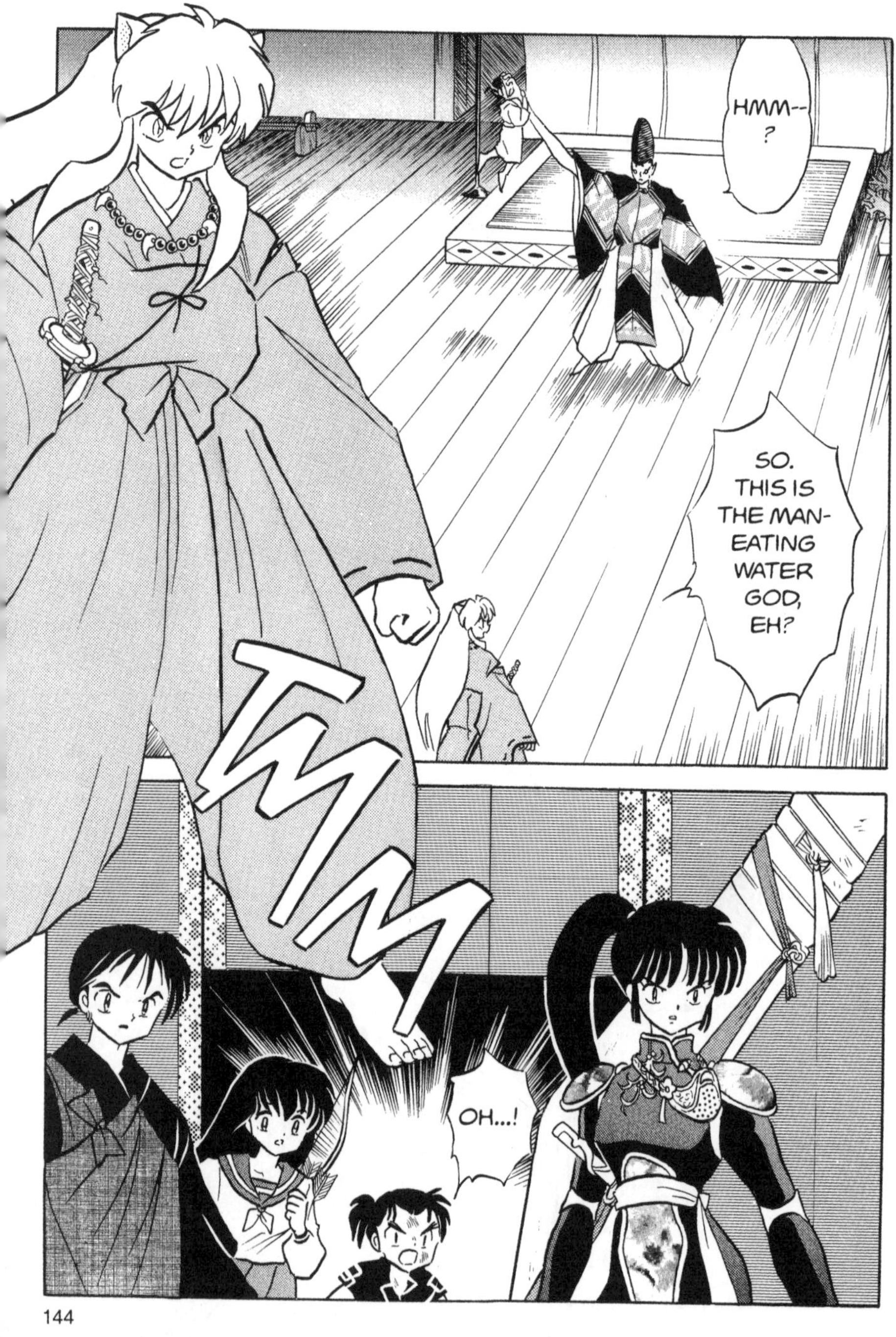
HMM--?
SO. THIS IS THE MAN-EATING WATER GOD, EH?
TMM
OH...!

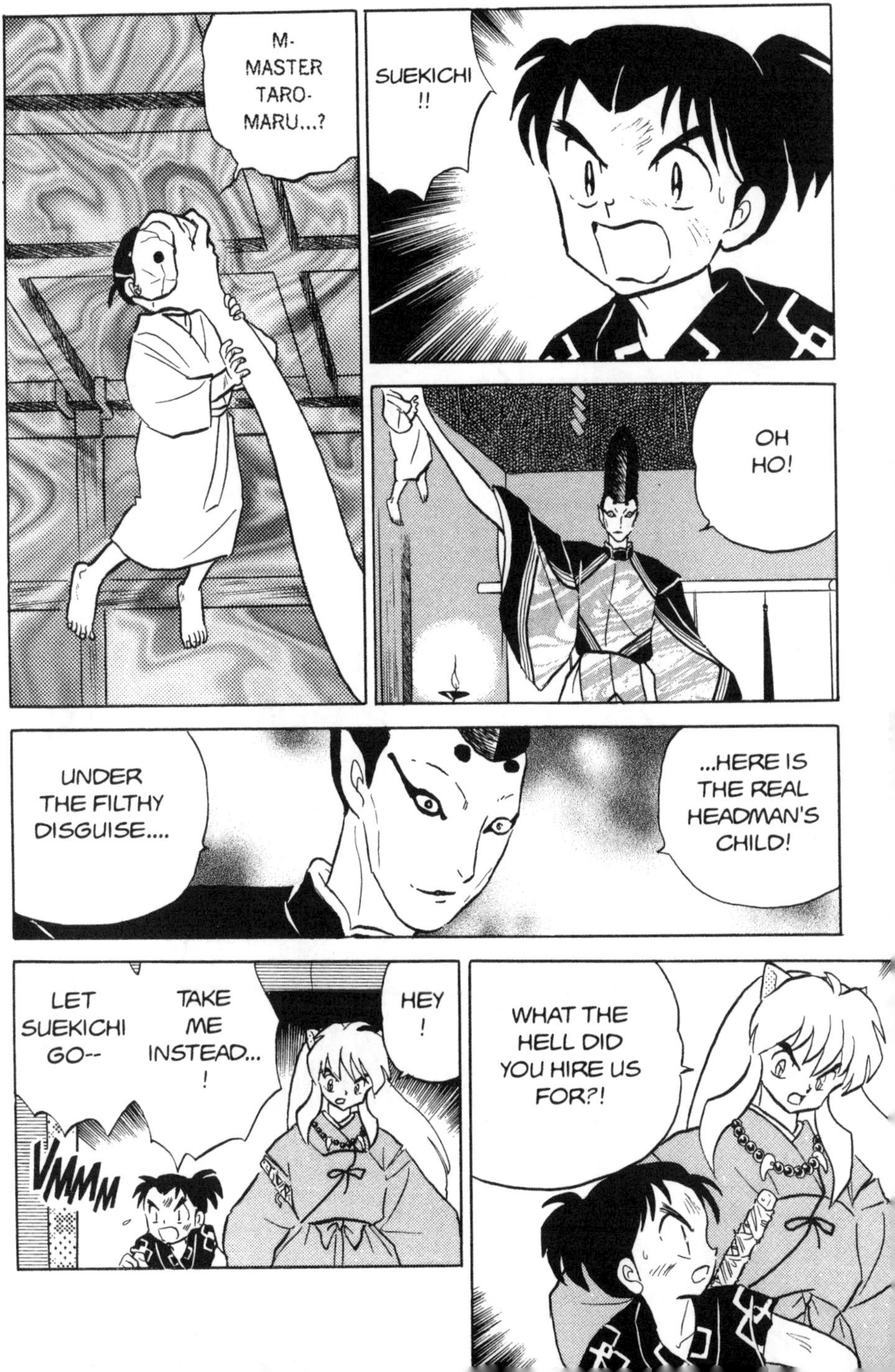
M-MASTER TARO-MARU...?
SUEKICHI !!
OH HO!
UNDER THE FILTHY DISGUISE....
...HERE IS THE REAL HEADMAN'S CHILD!
LET SUEKICHI GO--
TAKE ME INSTEAD...!
HEY!
VMMM
WHAT THE HELL DID YOU HIRE US FOR?!

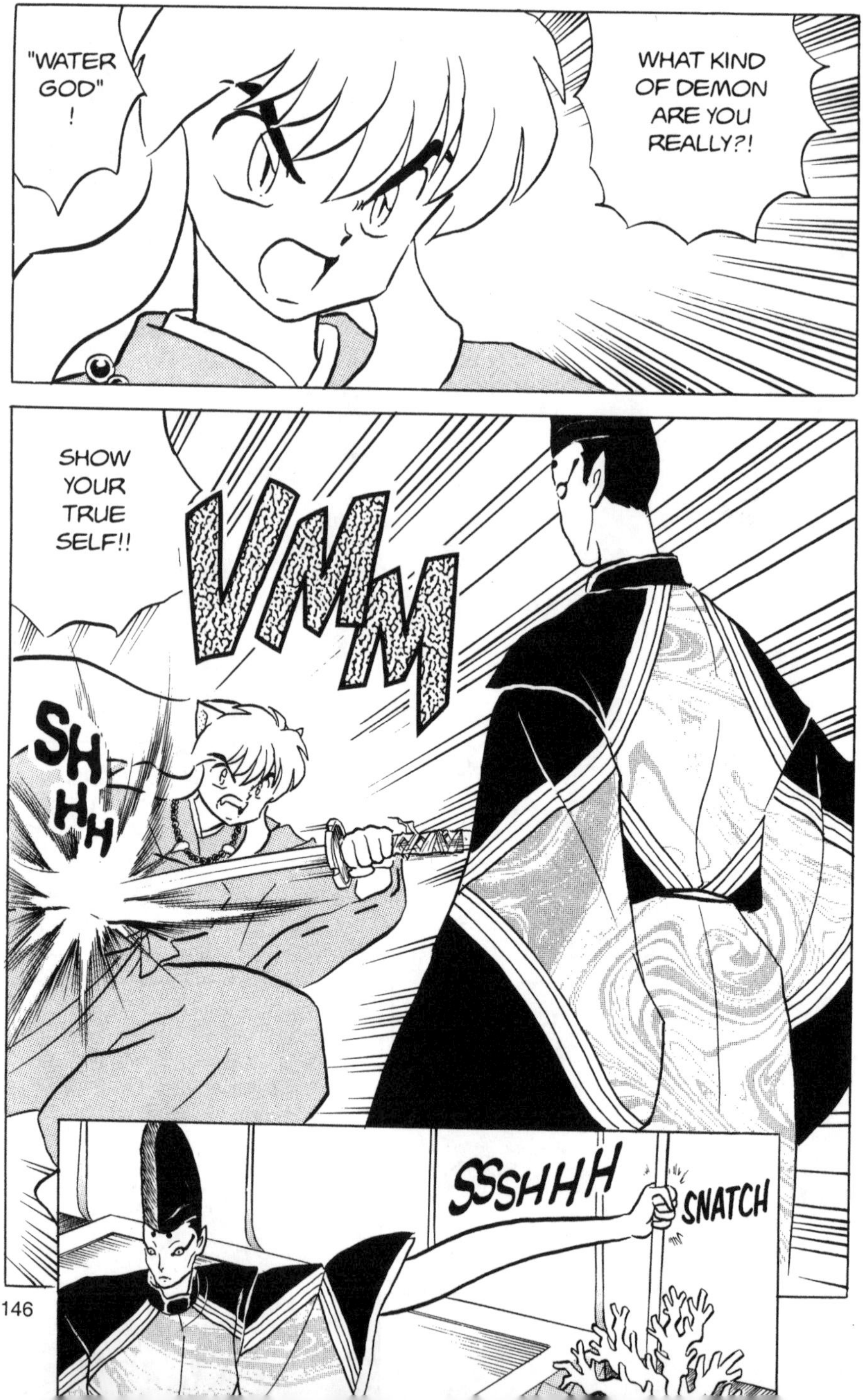
"WATER GOD" !
WHAT KIND OF DEMON ARE YOU REALLY?!
SHOW YOUR TRUE SELF!!
VMMM
SHHHH
SSSHHH
SNATCH

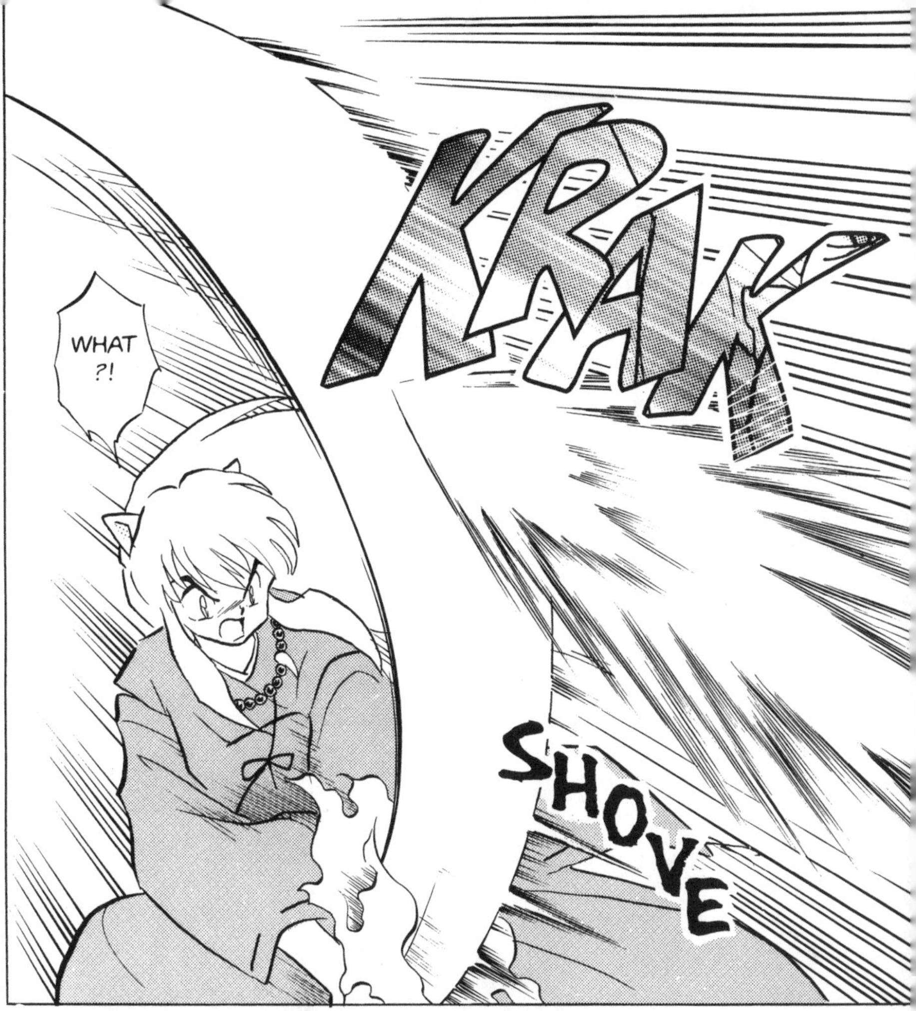
KRAK
WHAT ?!
SHOVE
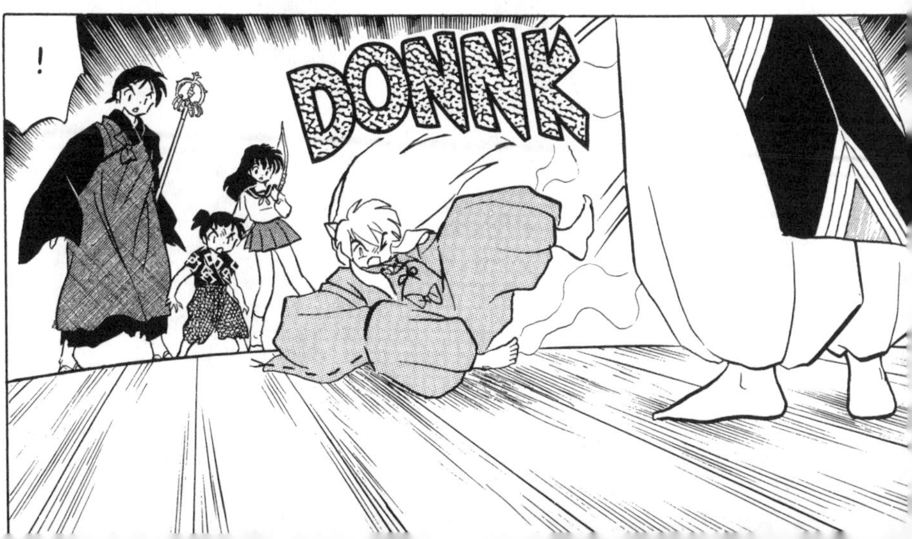
DONNK
!

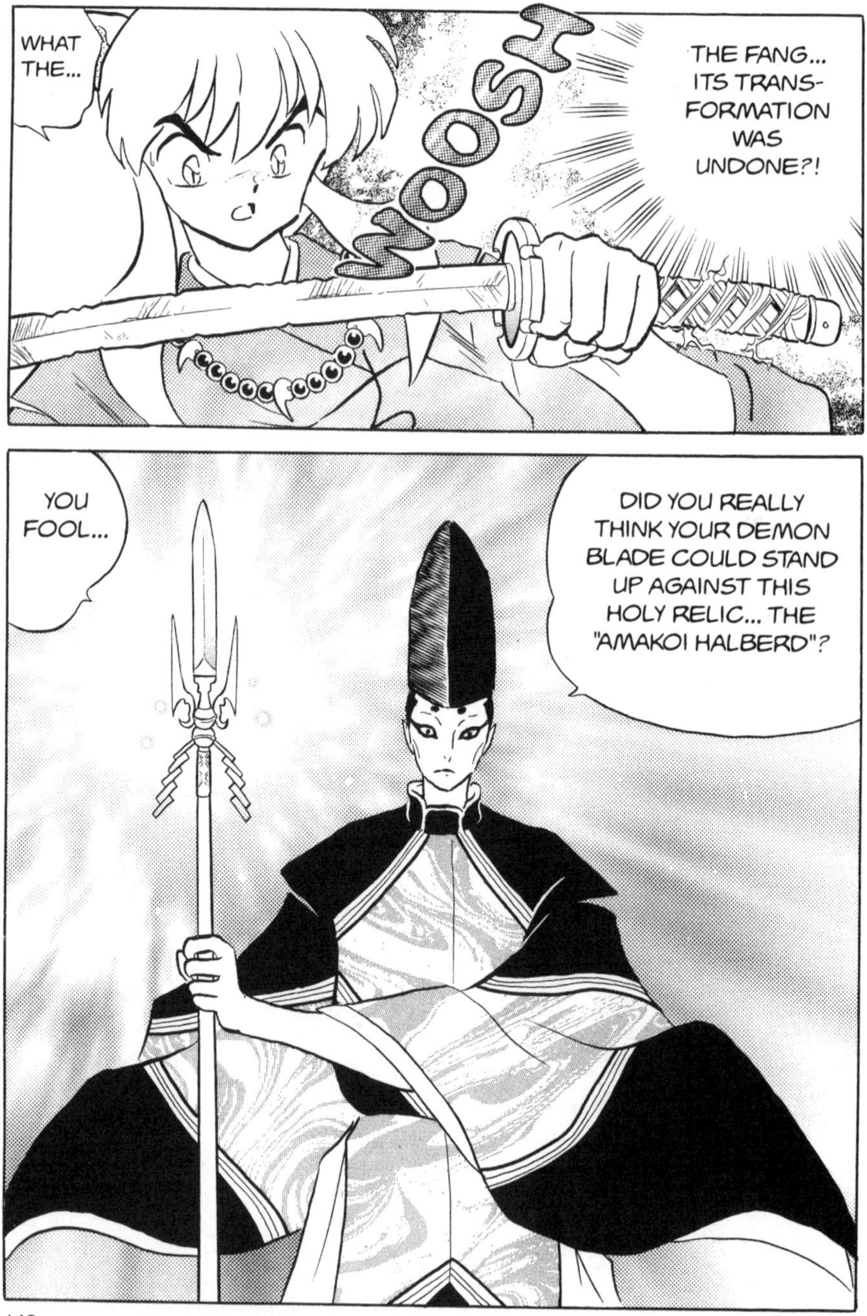
WHAT THE...
WOOSH
THE FANG... ITS TRANS-FORMATION WAS UNDONE?!
YOU FOOL...
DID YOU REALLY THINK YOUR DEMON BLADE COULD STAND UP AGAINST THIS HOLY RELIC... THE "AMAKOI HALBERD"?

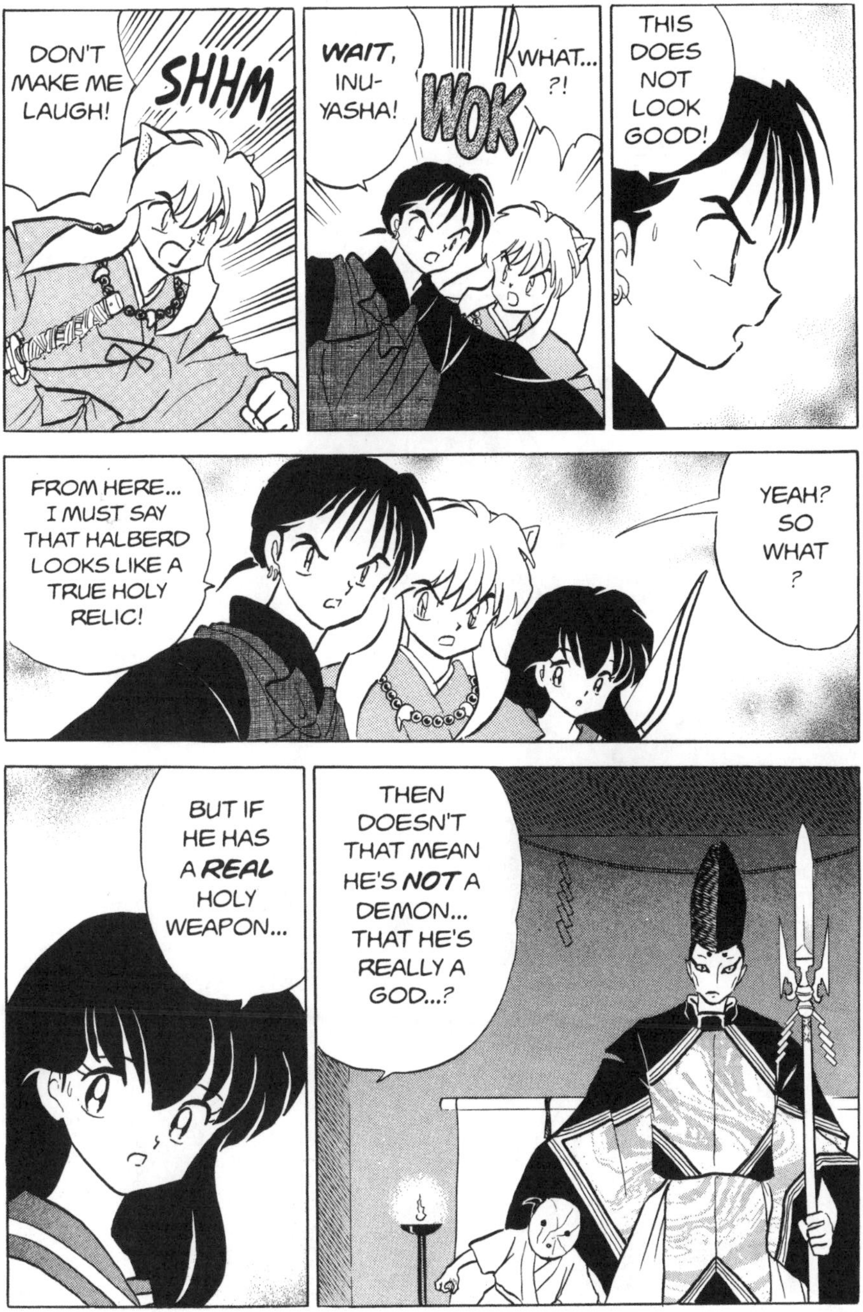
DON'T MAKE ME LAUGH!
SHHM
WAIT, INU-YASHA!
WOK
WHAT... ?!
THIS DOES NOT LOOK GOOD!
FROM HERE... I MUST SAY THAT HALBERD LOOKS LIKE A TRUE HOLY RELIC!
YEAH? SO WHAT ?
BUT IF HE HAS A REAL HOLY WEAPON...
THEN DOESN'T THAT MEAN HE'S NOT A DEMON... THAT HE'S REALLY A GOD...?

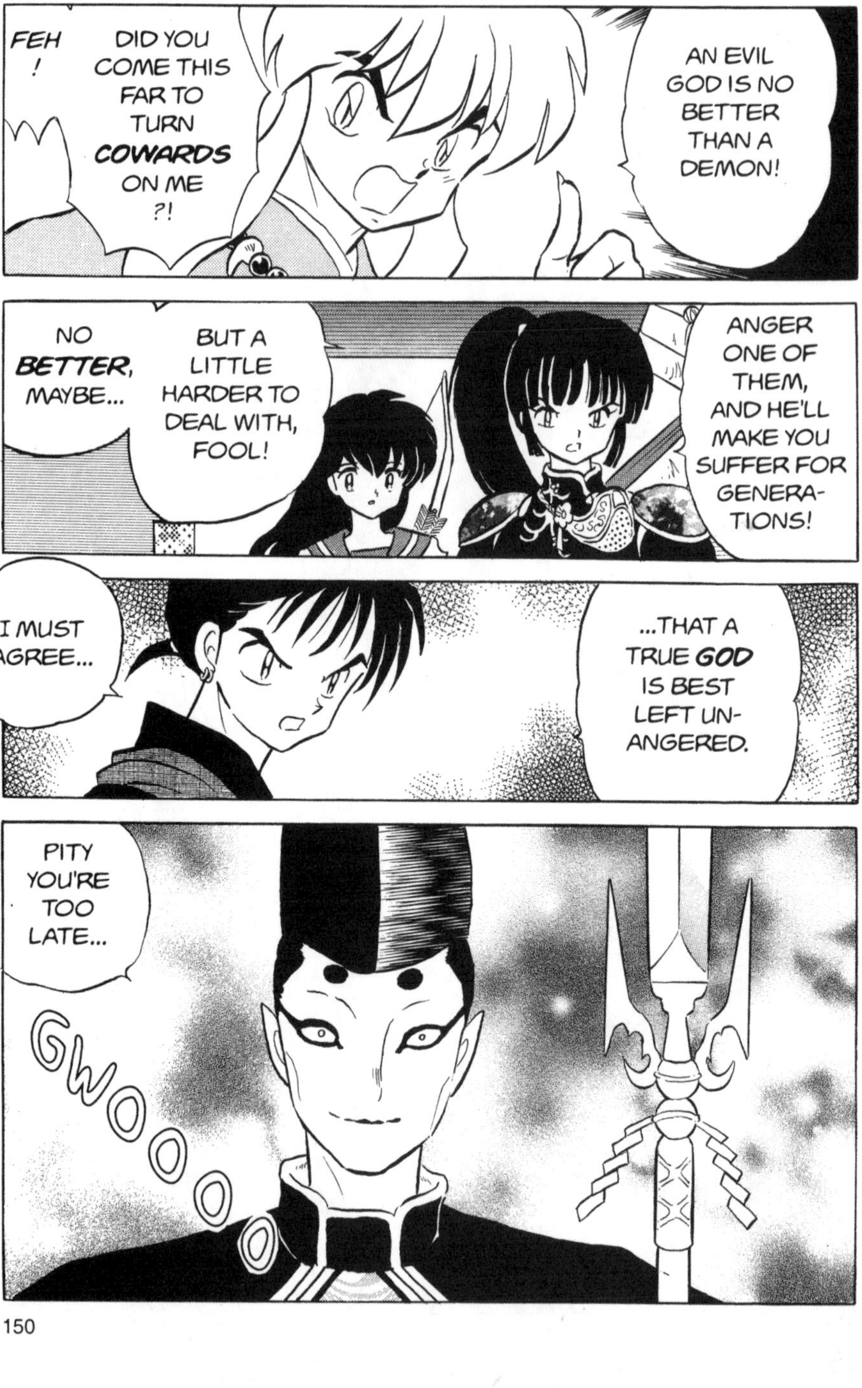
FEH!
DID YOU COME THIS FAR TO TURN **COWARDS** ON ME?!
AN EVIL GOD IS NO BETTER THAN A DEMON!
NO **BETTER**, MAYBE...
BUT A LITTLE HARDER TO DEAL WITH, FOOL!
ANGER ONE OF THEM, AND HE'LL MAKE YOU SUFFER FOR GENERATIONS!
I MUST AGREE...
...THAT A TRUE **GOD** IS BEST LEFT UNANGERED.
PITY YOU'RE TOO LATE...
GWOOOOO

SCROLL NINE

THE GOD'S TRUTH

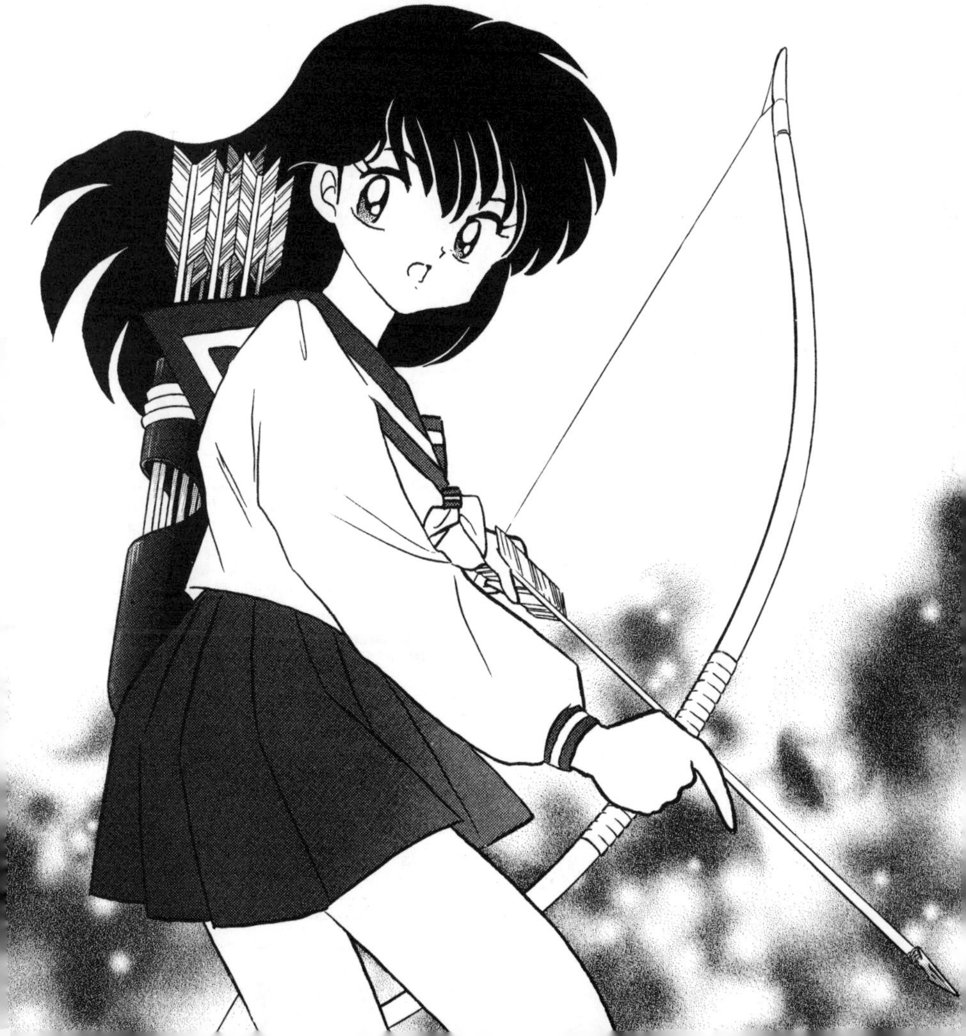

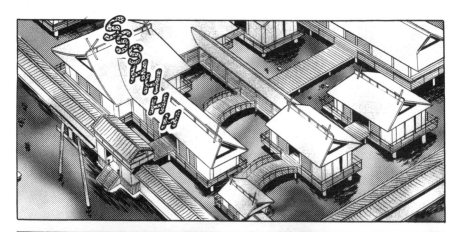

HOOORRRRR

MORTALS...

KNOW YOU THE PENALTY FOR DESECRATING SACRED GROUND?

LET ME GUESS...

IT WOULDN'T BE A *CURSE* NOW, WOULD IT?!

I-INU-YASHA!

DO YOU THINK THIS IS *FUNNY*?!

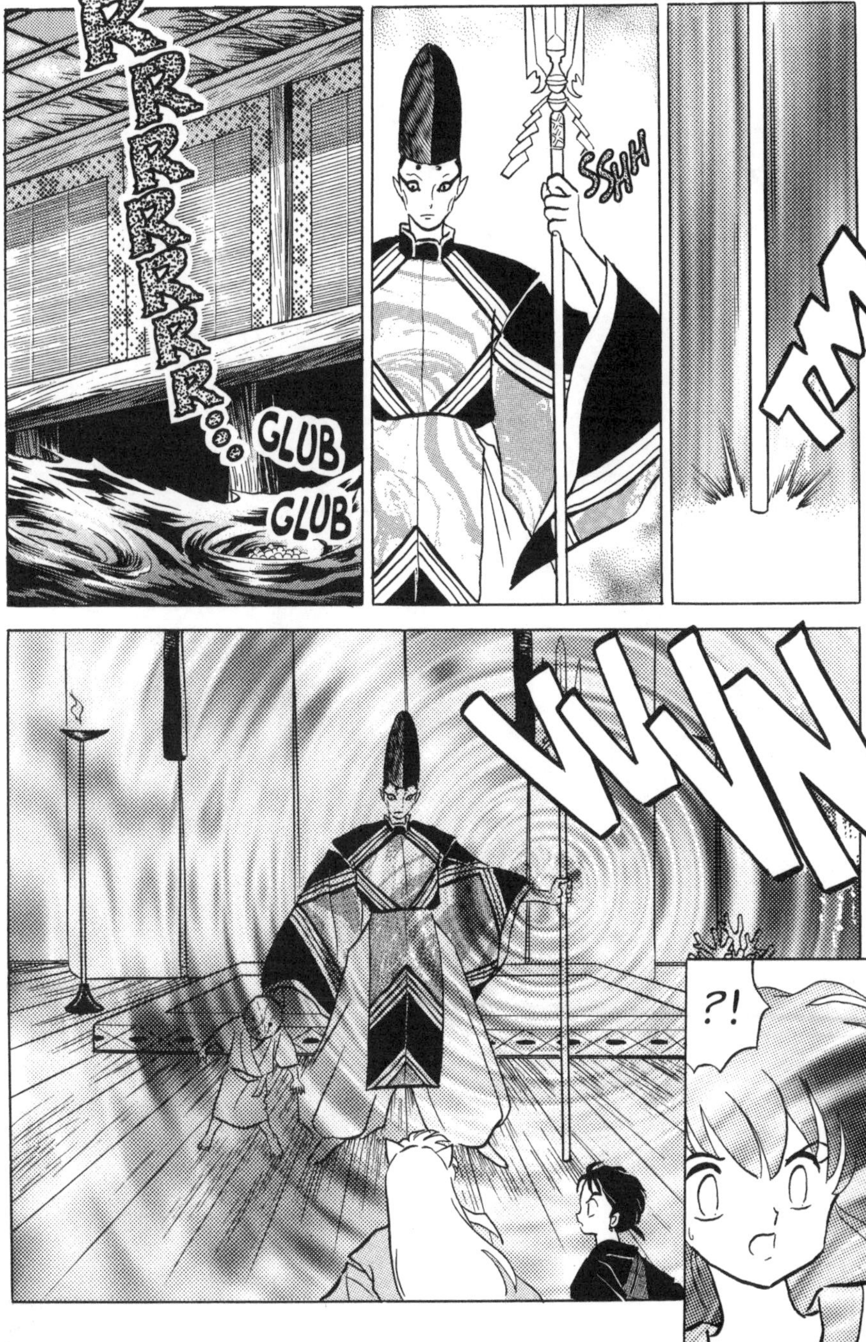
RRRRRRR...
GLUB
GLUB
SSHH
TM
VVVN
?!

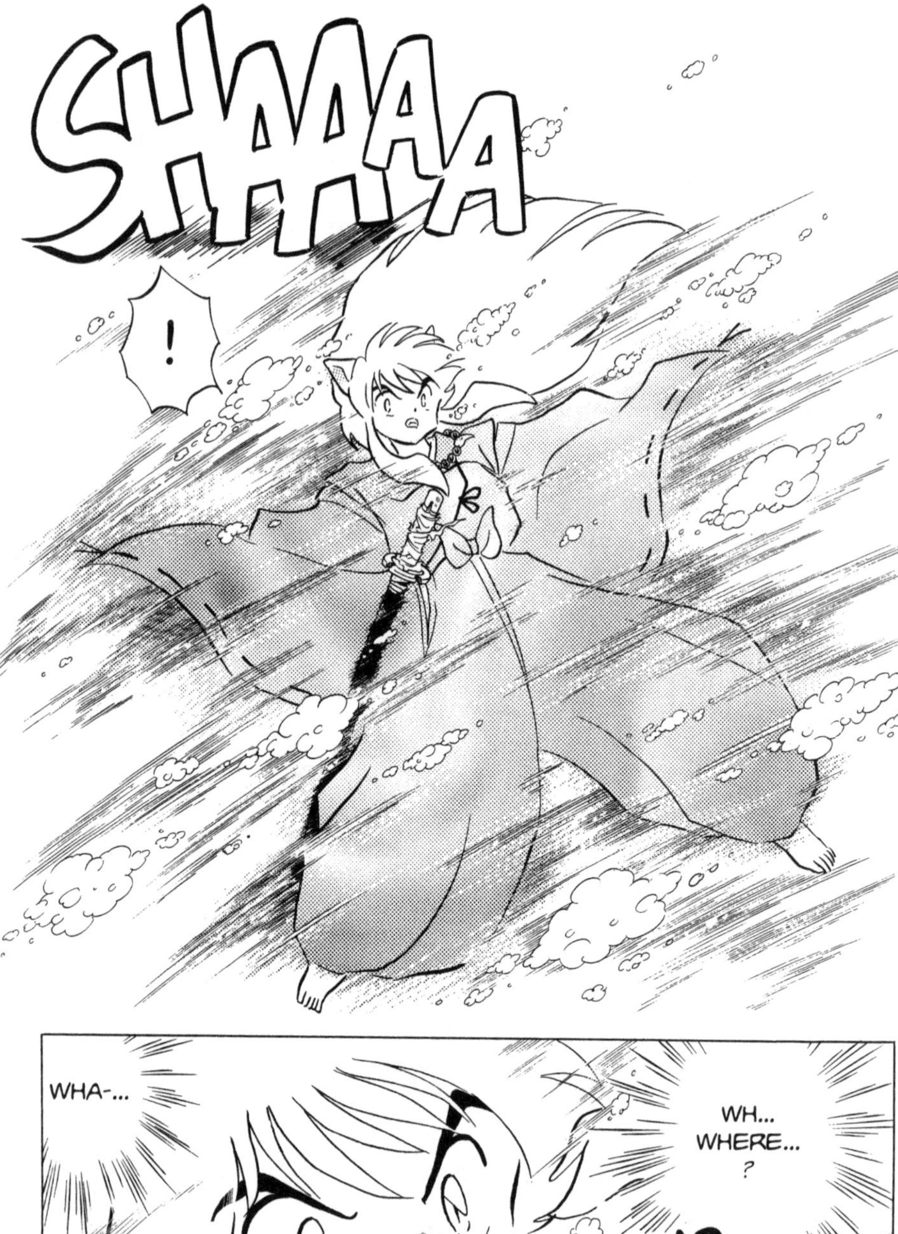
SHAAAA
!
WHA-...
WH... WHERE... ?
GLUB

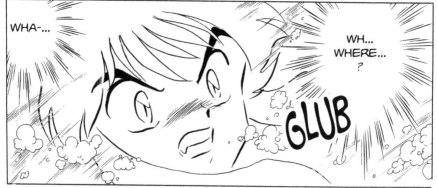

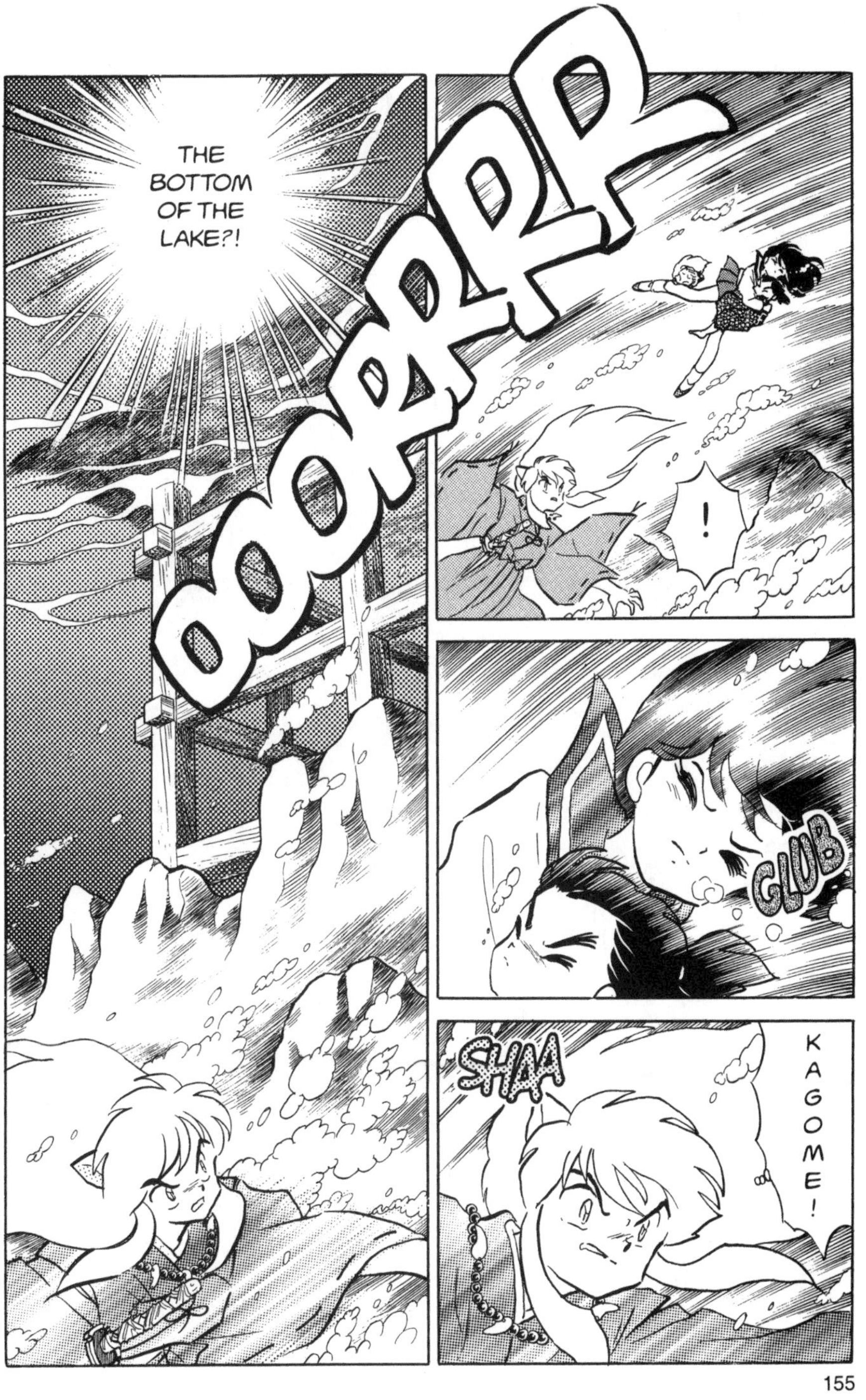
THE BOTTOM OF THE LAKE?!
DOOPPPP
!
GLUB
SHAA
KAGOME!

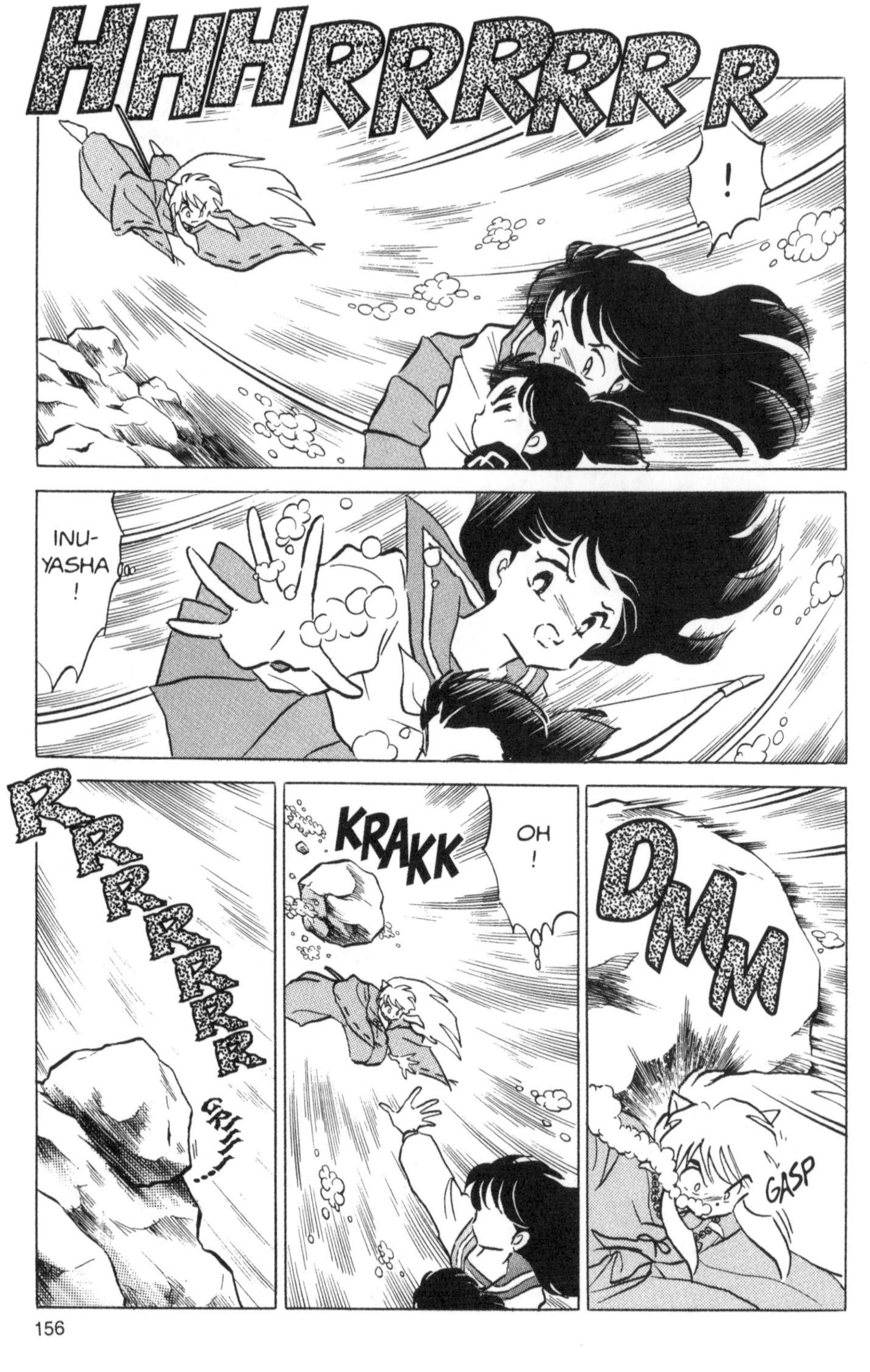
HHHRRRRRRR
!
INU-YASHA !
RRRRRRRR
GRIII...
KRAKK
OH !
DMM
GASP

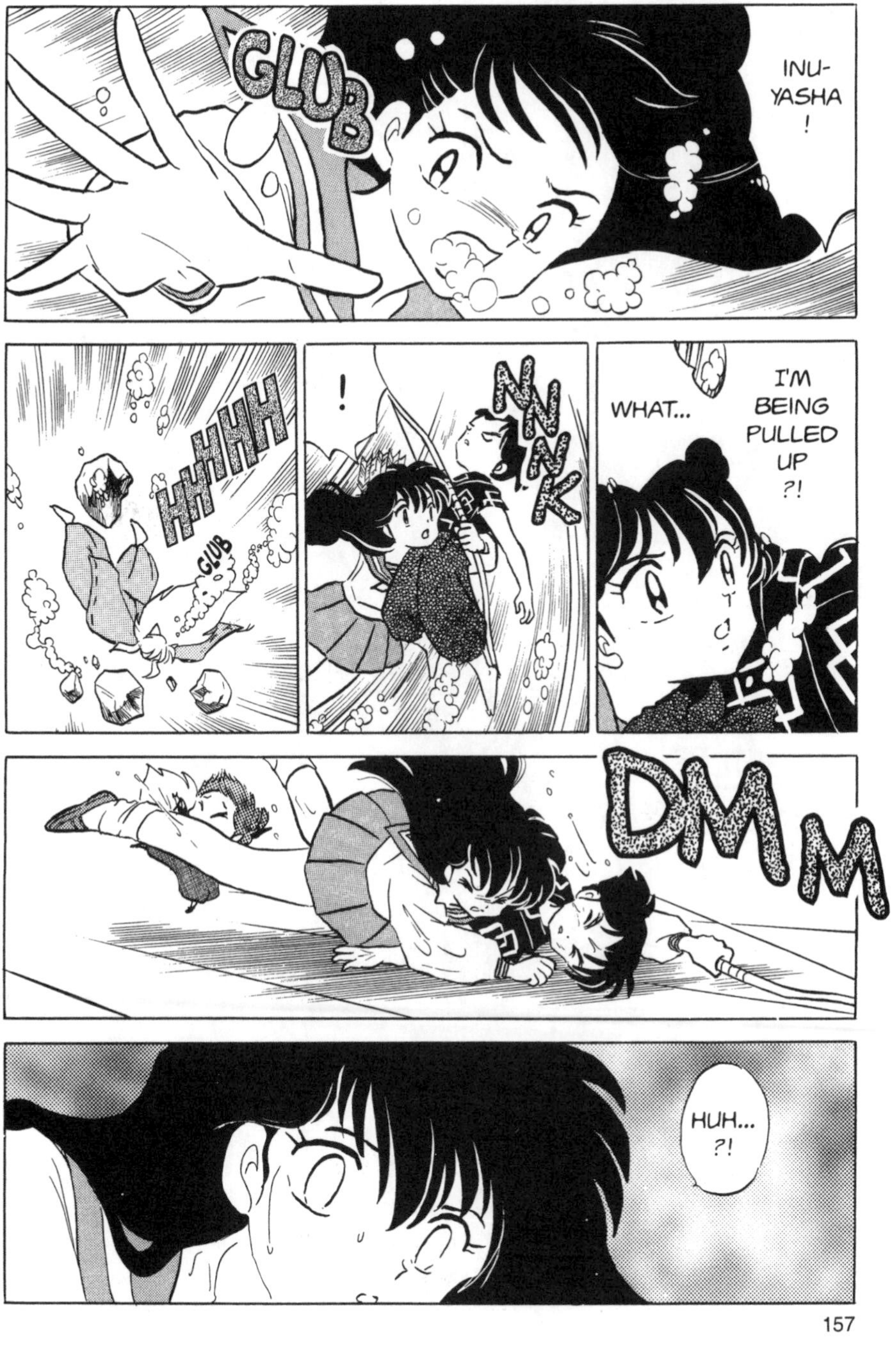
GLUB
INU-YASHA!
HHHHHH
GLUB
!
NNNK
WHAT...
I'M BEING PULLED UP?!
DMM
HUH...?!

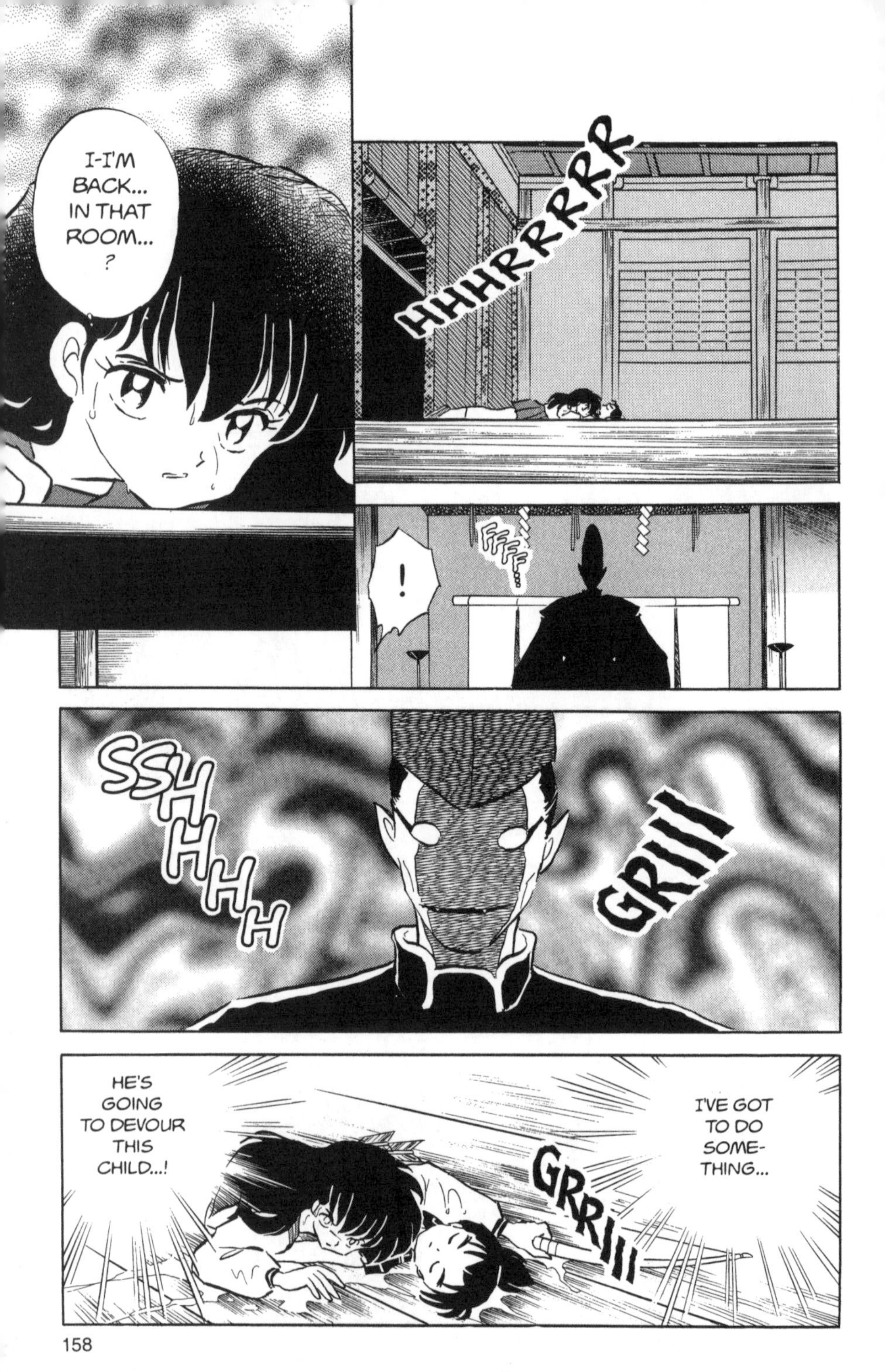
I-I'M BACK... IN THAT ROOM... ?
HHHRRRRR
!
FFFFF...
SSHHHHH
GRIII
HE'S GOING TO DEVOUR THIS CHILD...!
GRRIII
I'VE GOT TO DO SOME-THING...

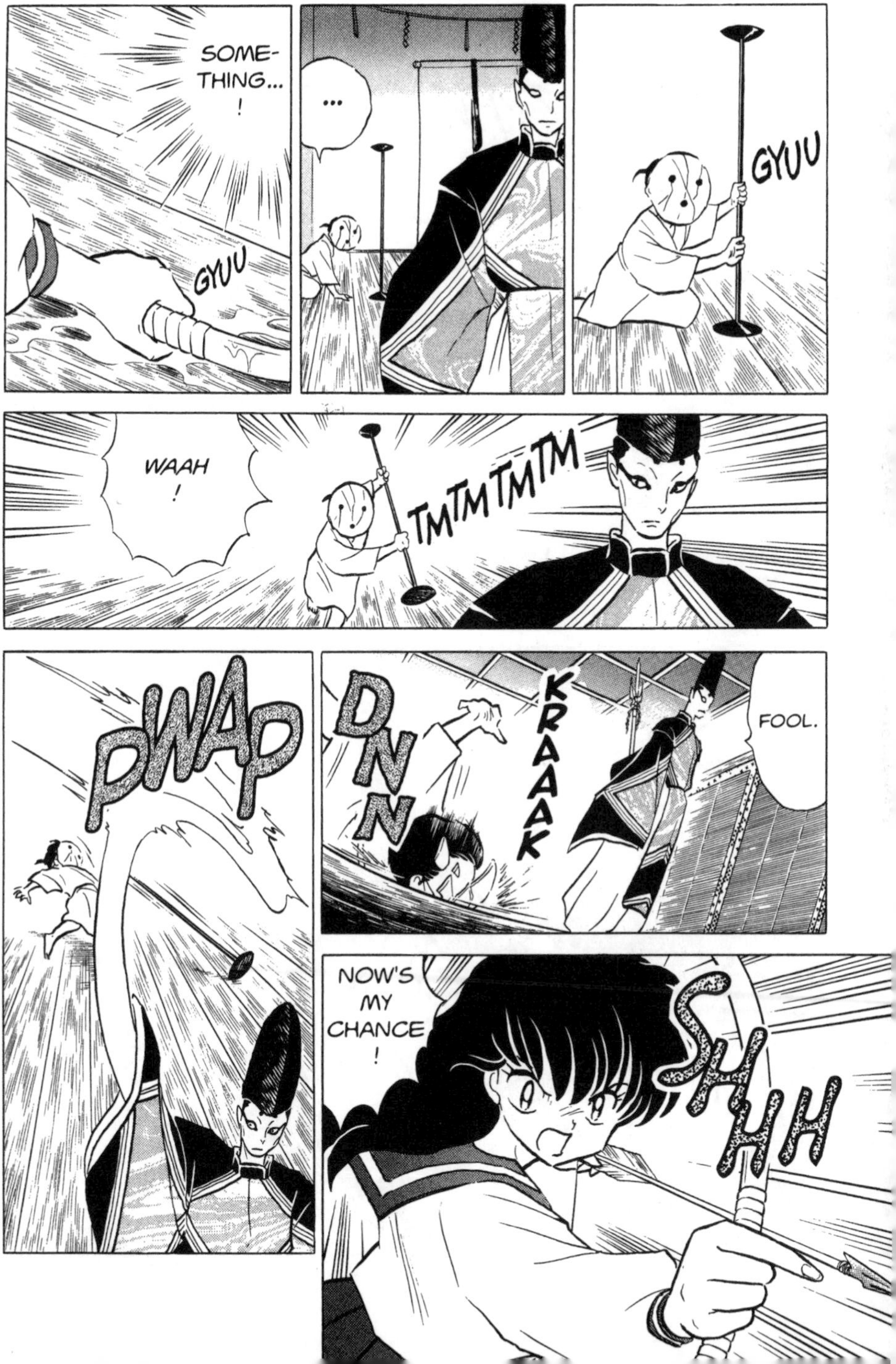
SOME-THING... !
GYUU
...
GYUU
WAAH !
TMTMTMTM
PWAP
DNN
KRAAAK
FOOL.
NOW'S MY CHANCE !
SHHH

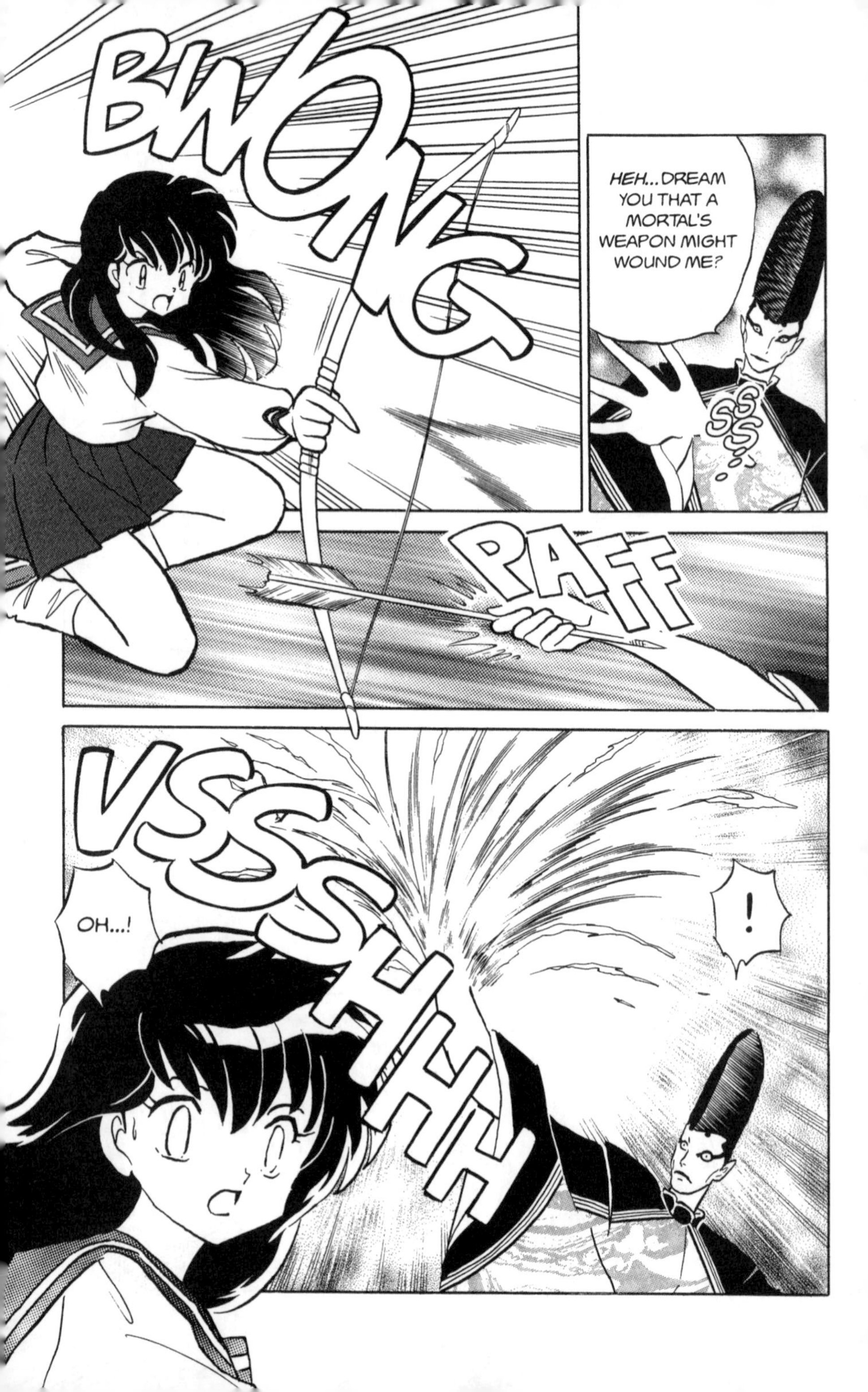
BWONG
HEH...DREAM YOU THAT A MORTAL'S WEAPON MIGHT WOUND ME?
SSS
PAFF
VSSSHHH
OH...!
!

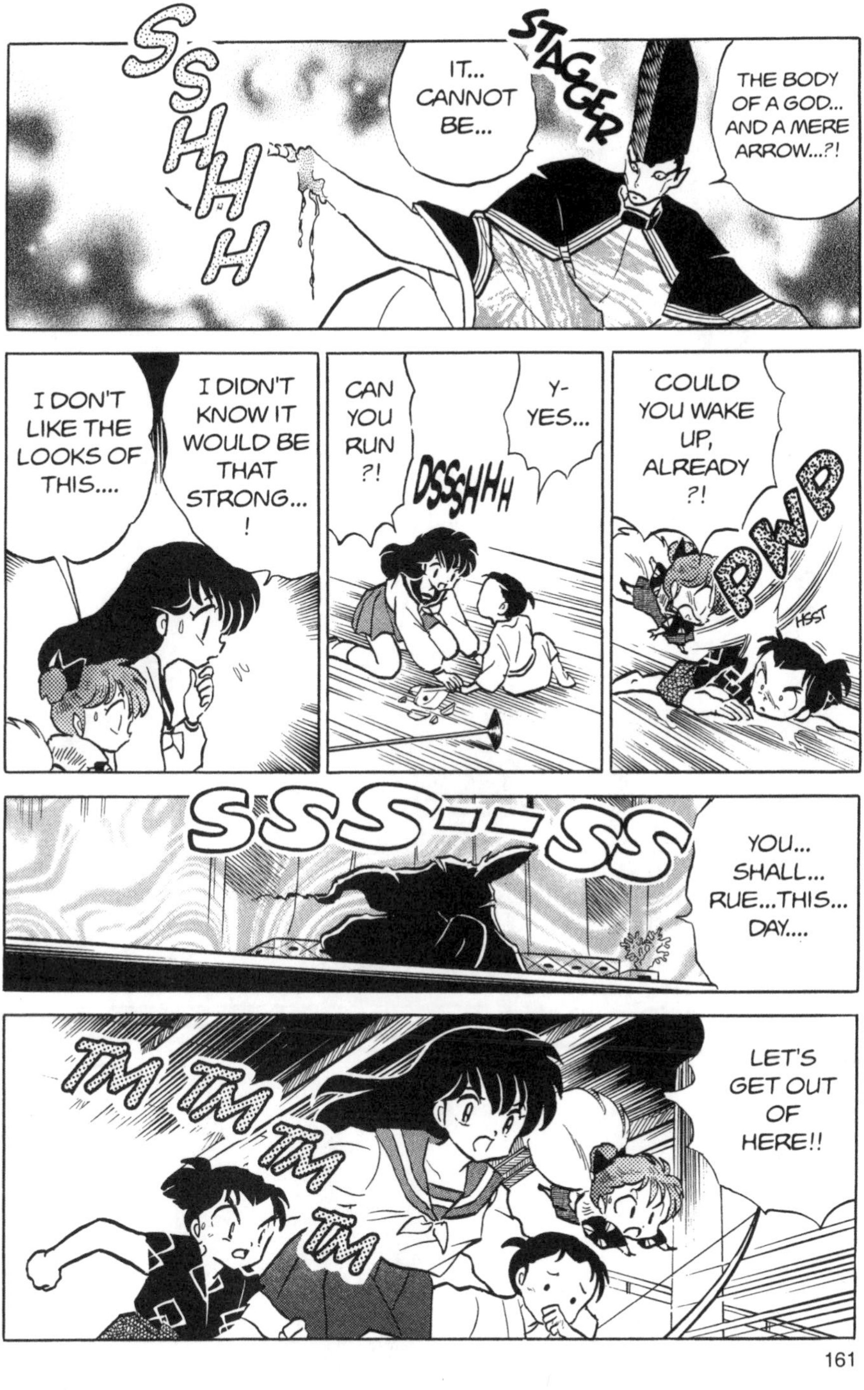
SSHHHH
IT... CANNOT BE...
STAGGER
THE BODY OF A GOD... AND A MERE ARROW...?!
I DON'T LIKE THE LOOKS OF THIS....
I DIDN'T KNOW IT WOULD BE THAT STRONG...!
CAN YOU RUN?!
DSSSHHHH
Y-YES...
COULD YOU WAKE UP, ALREADY?!
DWP
HSST
SSS--SS
YOU... SHALL... RUE...THIS... DAY....
TM TM TM TM TM
LET'S GET OUT OF HERE!!

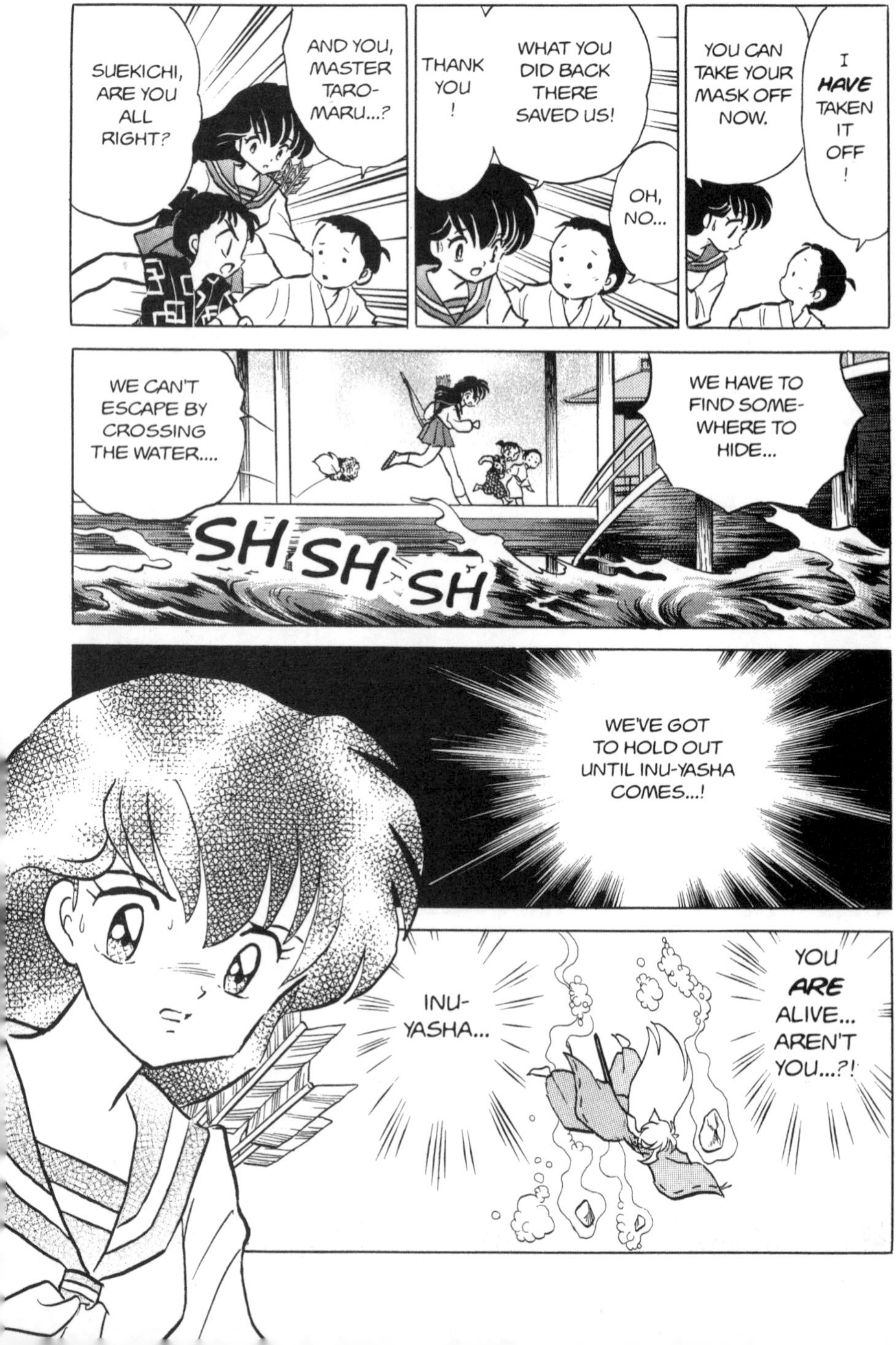
SUEKICHI, ARE YOU ALL RIGHT?
AND YOU, MASTER TARO-MARU...?
THANK YOU !
WHAT YOU DID BACK THERE SAVED US!
OH, NO...
YOU CAN TAKE YOUR MASK OFF NOW.
I **HAVE** TAKEN IT OFF !
WE CAN'T ESCAPE BY CROSSING THE WATER....
WE HAVE TO FIND SOME-WHERE TO HIDE...
SH SH SH
WE'VE GOT TO HOLD OUT UNTIL INU-YASHA COMES...!
INU-YASHA...
YOU **ARE** ALIVE... AREN'T YOU...?!

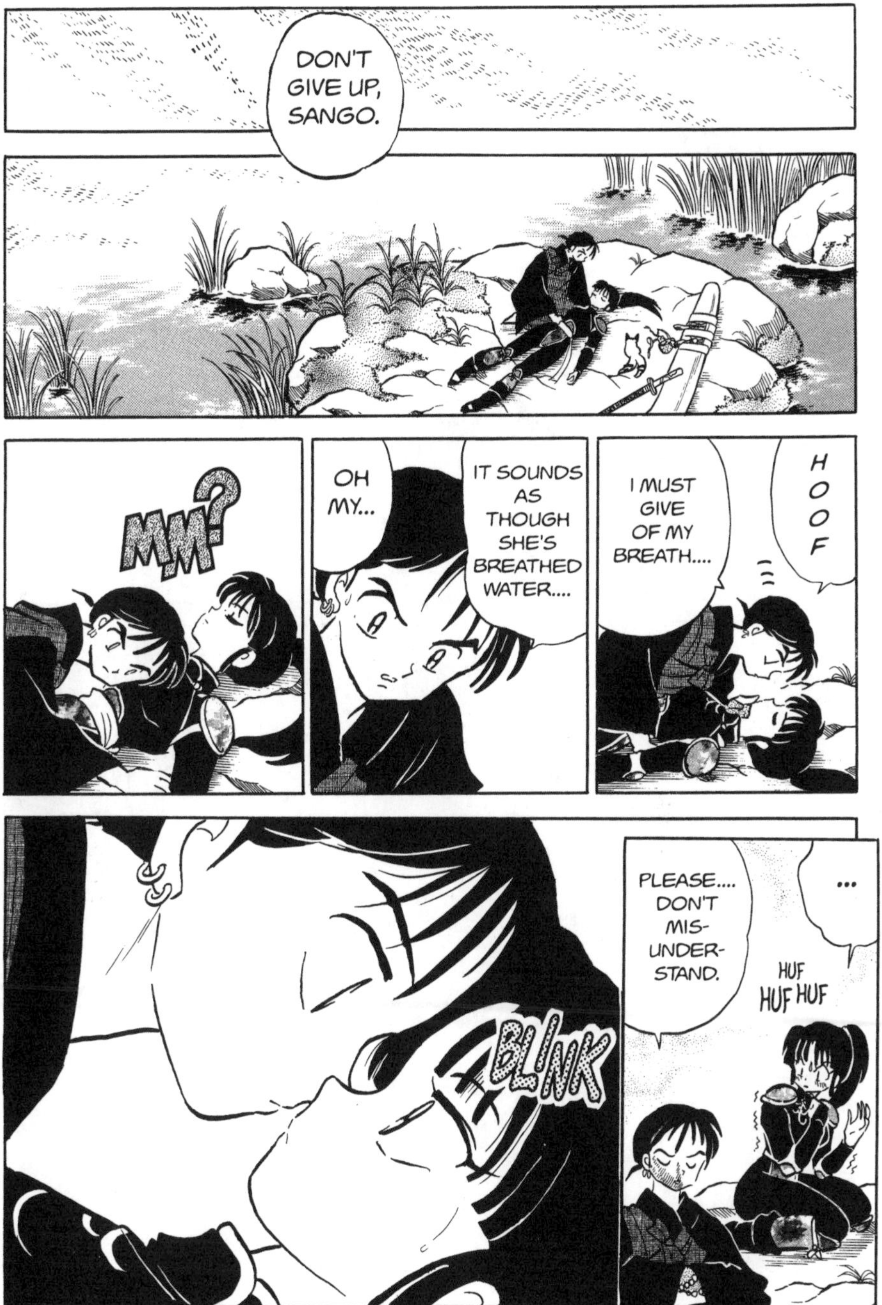
DON'T GIVE UP, SANGO.
MM?
OH MY...
IT SOUNDS AS THOUGH SHE'S BREATHED WATER....
I MUST GIVE OF MY BREATH....
HOOF
BLINK
PLEASE.... DON'T MIS-UNDER-STAND.
...
HUF HUF HUF

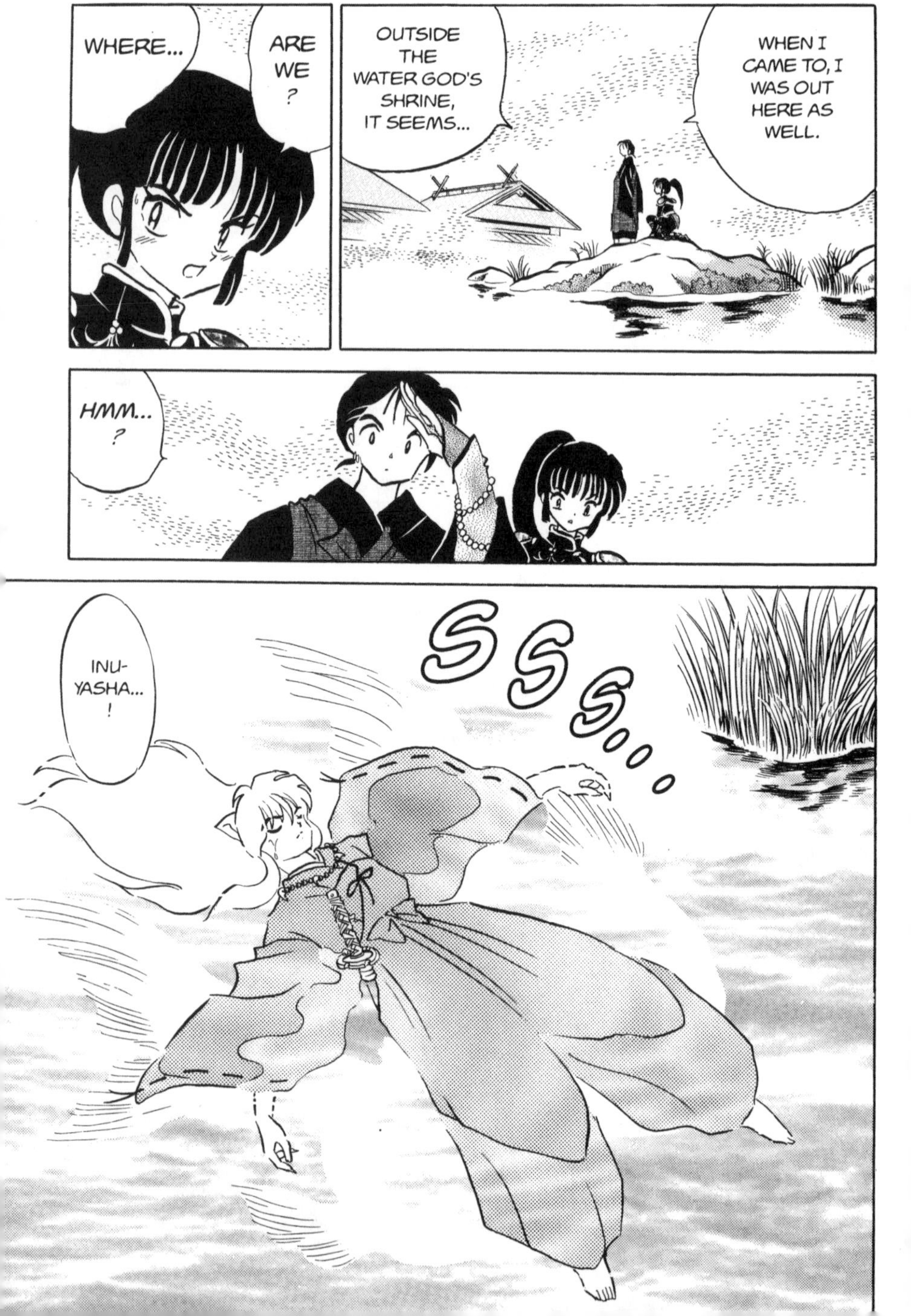

WHERE...
ARE WE ?
OUTSIDE THE WATER GOD'S SHRINE, IT SEEMS...
WHEN I CAME TO, I WAS OUT HERE AS WELL.
HMM... ?
INU-YASHA... !
SSSooo

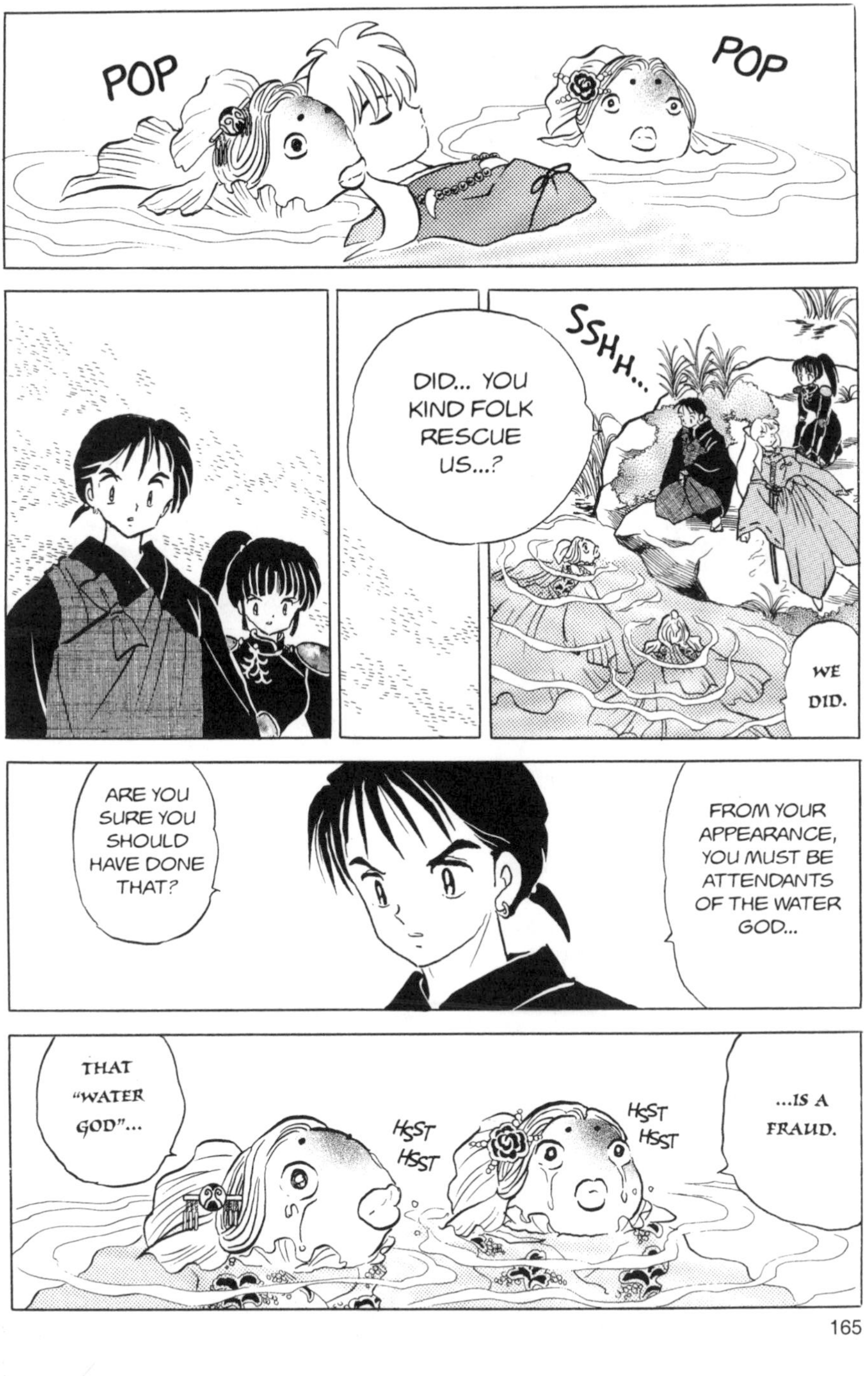
POP
POP
DID... YOU KIND FOLK RESCUE US...?
SSHH...
WE DID.
ARE YOU SURE YOU SHOULD HAVE DONE THAT?
FROM YOUR APPEARANCE, YOU MUST BE ATTENDANTS OF THE WATER GOD...
THAT "WATER GOD"...
HSST HSST
HSST HSST
...IS A FRAUD.

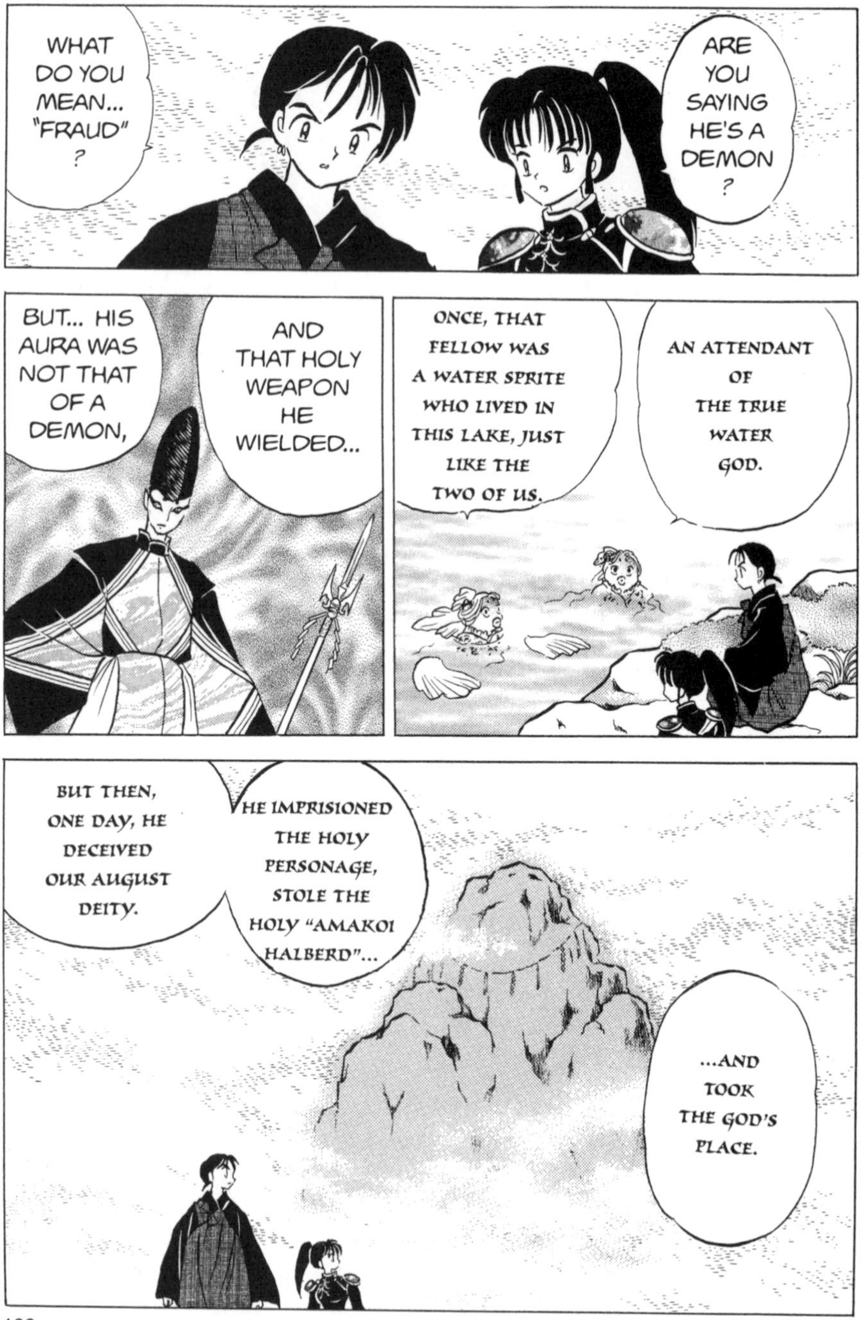
WHAT DO YOU MEAN... "FRAUD"?
ARE YOU SAYING HE'S A DEMON?
BUT... HIS AURA WAS NOT THAT OF A DEMON,
AND THAT HOLY WEAPON HE WIELDED...
ONCE, THAT FELLOW WAS A WATER SPRITE WHO LIVED IN THIS LAKE, JUST LIKE THE TWO OF US.
AN ATTENDANT OF THE TRUE WATER GOD.
BUT THEN, ONE DAY, HE DECEIVED OUR AUGUST DEITY.
HE IMPRISIONED THE HOLY PERSONAGE, STOLE THE HOLY "AMAKOI HALBERD"...
...AND TOOK THE GOD'S PLACE.

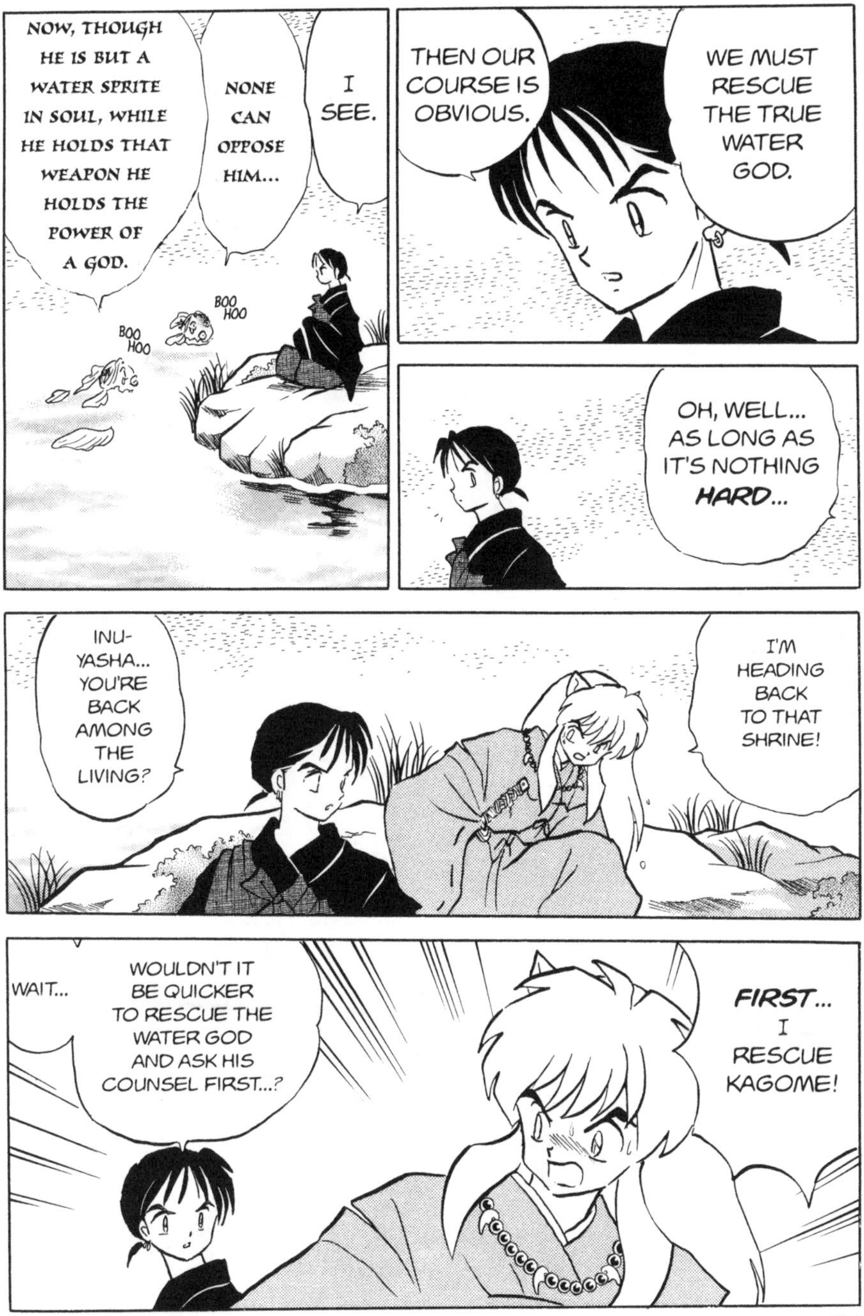
NOW, THOUGH HE IS BUT A WATER SPRITE IN SOUL, WHILE HE HOLDS THAT WEAPON HE HOLDS THE POWER OF A GOD.
NONE CAN OPPOSE HIM...
I SEE.
BOO HOO
BOO HOO
THEN OUR COURSE IS OBVIOUS.
WE MUST RESCUE THE TRUE WATER GOD.
OH, WELL... AS LONG AS IT'S NOTHING **HARD**...
INU-YASHA... YOU'RE BACK AMONG THE LIVING?
I'M HEADING BACK TO THAT SHRINE!
WAIT...
WOULDN'T IT BE QUICKER TO RESCUE THE WATER GOD AND ASK HIS COUNSEL FIRST...?
FIRST... I RESCUE KAGOME!

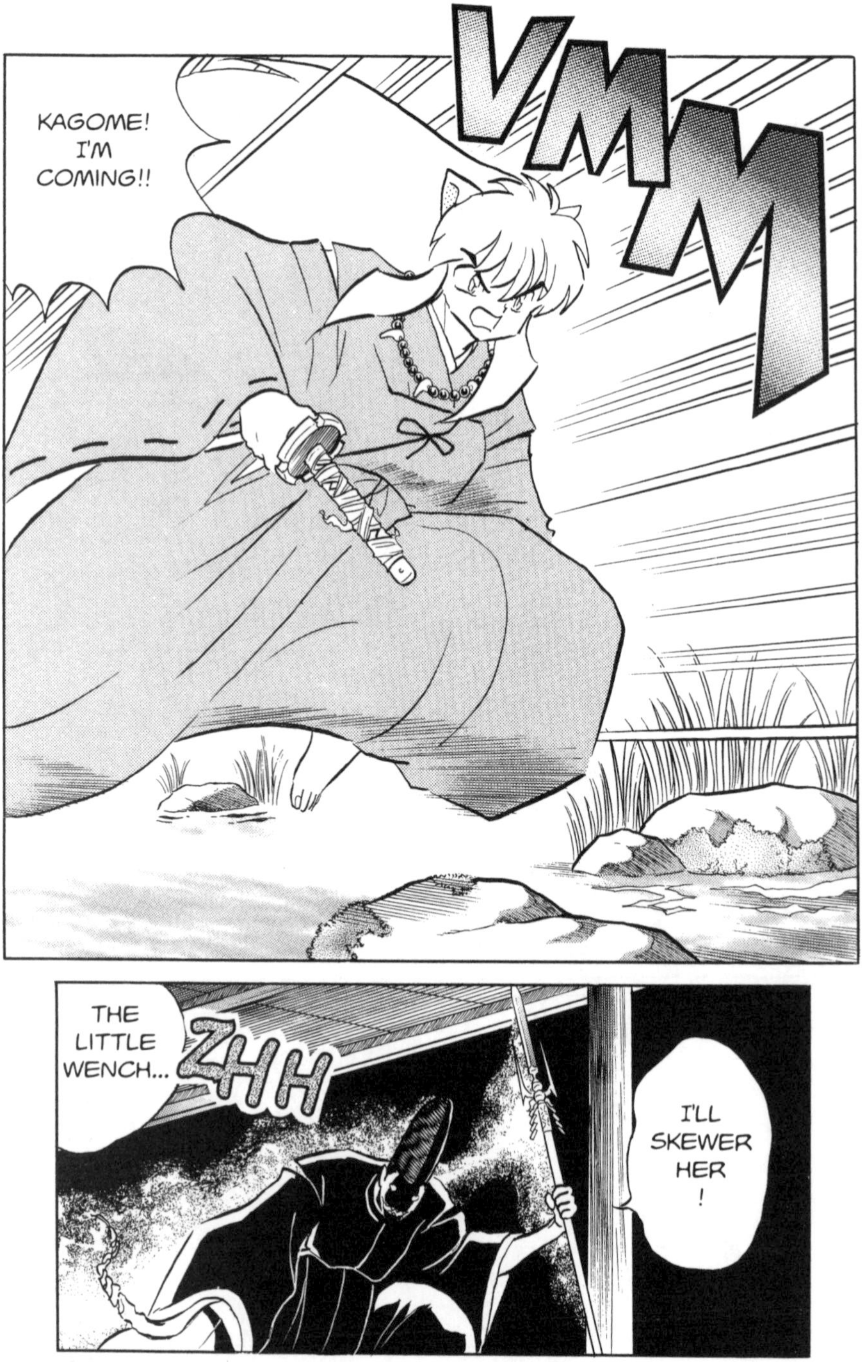
VMM
KAGOME! I'M COMING!!
THE LITTLE WENCH...
ZHH
I'LL SKEWER HER!

SCROLL TEN

THE TRUE GOD

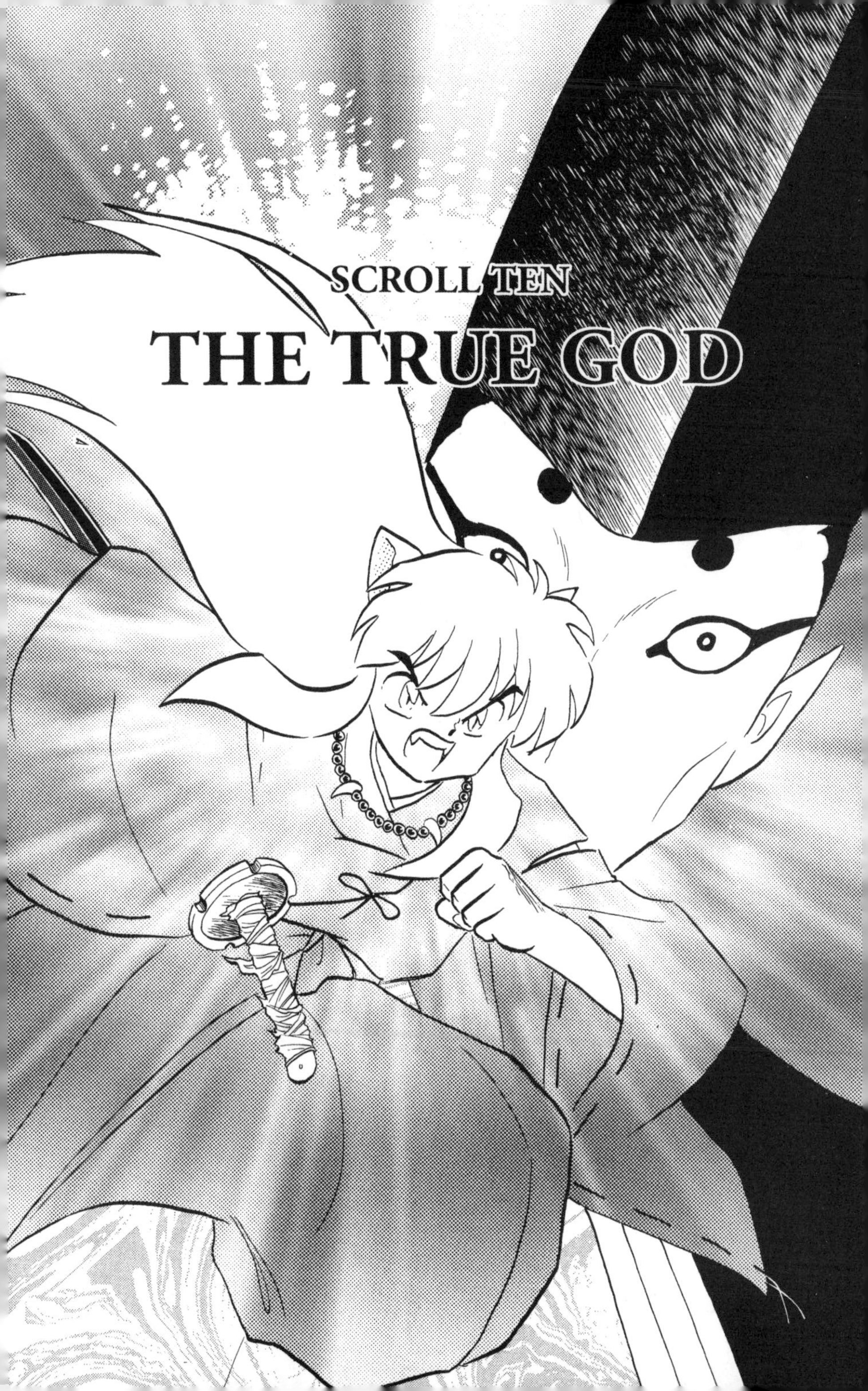

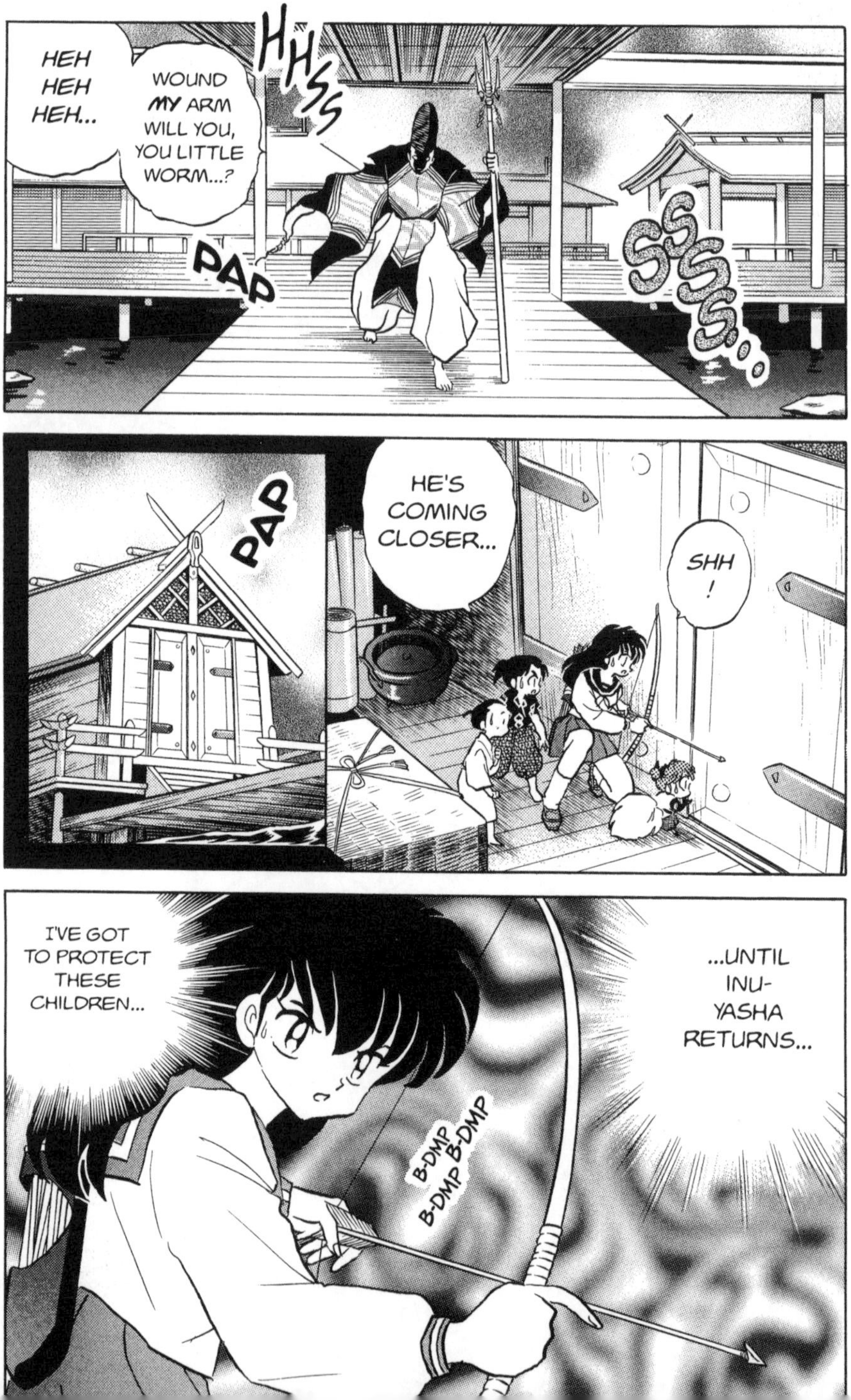
HEH
HEH
HEH...
WOUND MY ARM WILL YOU, YOU LITTLE WORM...?
HHSS
PAP
SSSSS...
PAP
HE'S COMING CLOSER...
SHH!
I'VE GOT TO PROTECT THESE CHILDREN...
...UNTIL INU-YASHA RETURNS...
B-DMP B-DMP B-DMP

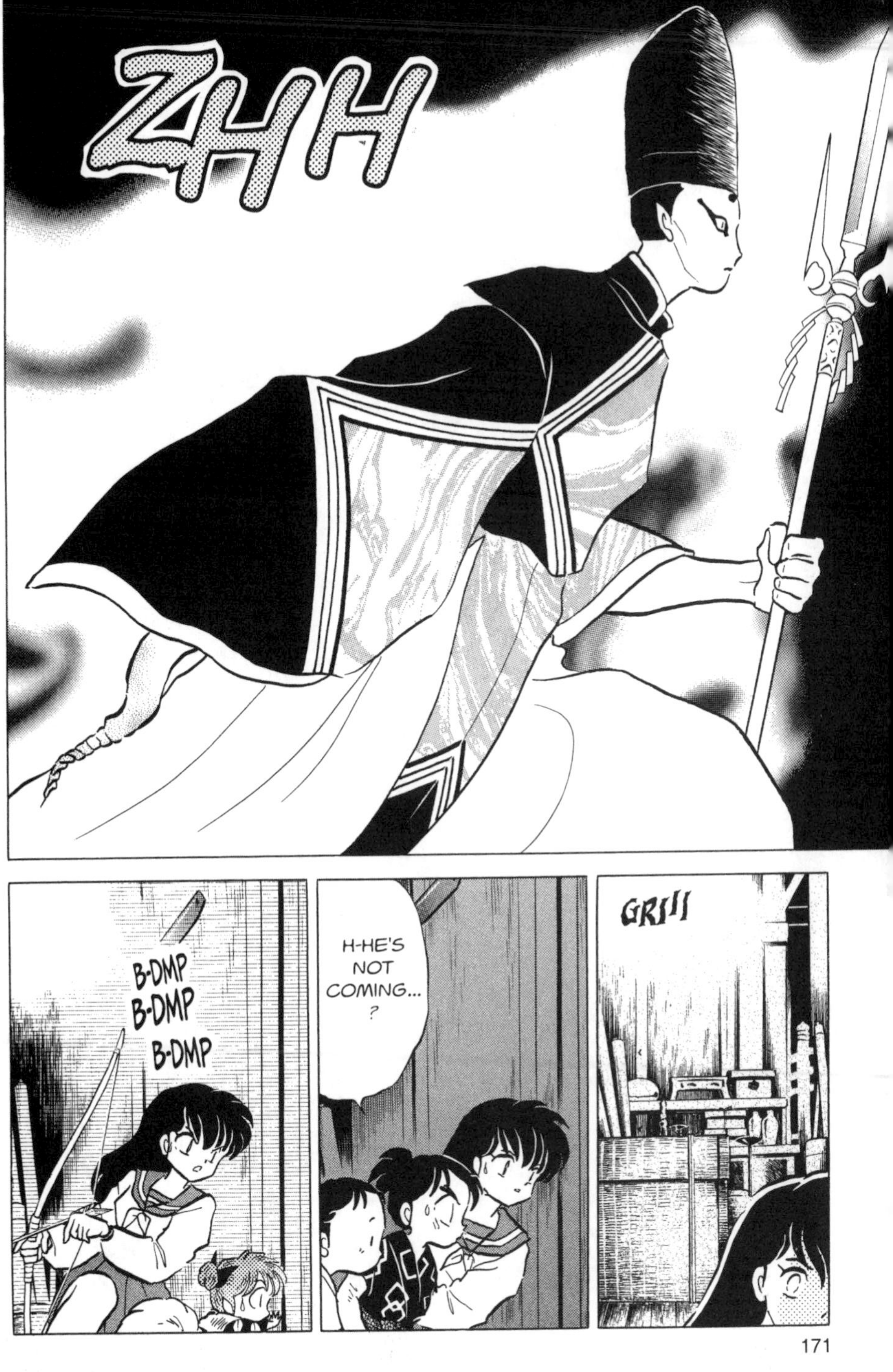
ZHH
B-DMP
B-DMP
B-DMP
H-HE'S NOT COMING... ?
GRIII

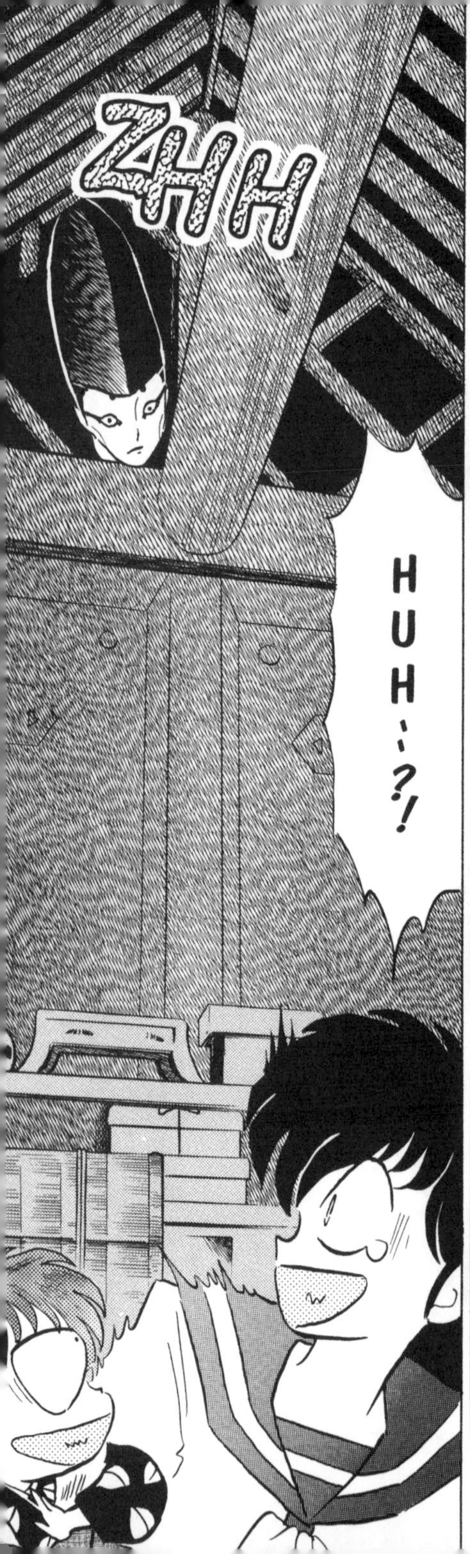
ZHH
HUH...?!
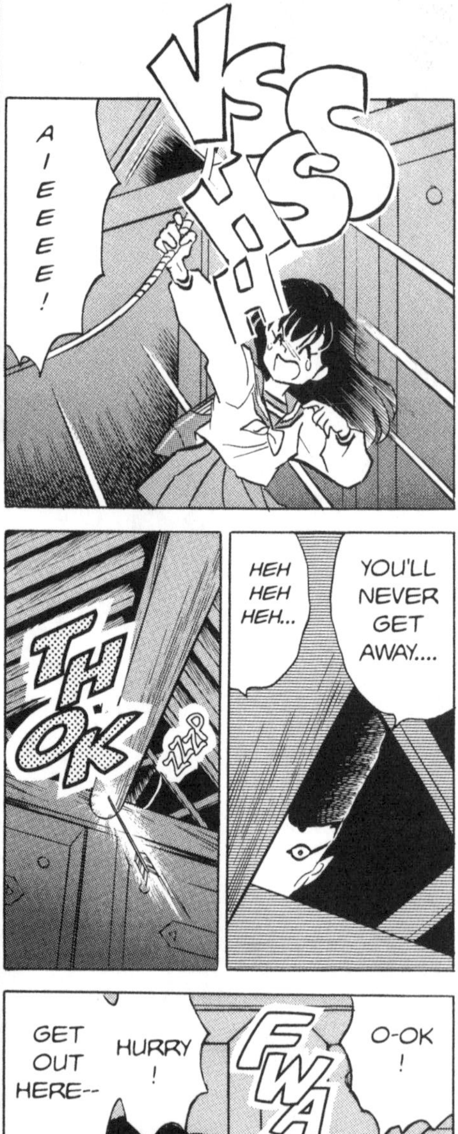
AIEEEEE!
VSSS
THOK
ZZZP
HEH HEH HEH...
YOU'LL NEVER GET AWAY....
GET OUT HERE--
HURRY!
FWAA
O-OK!

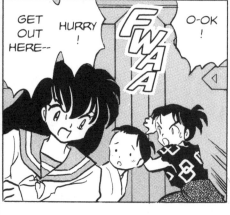

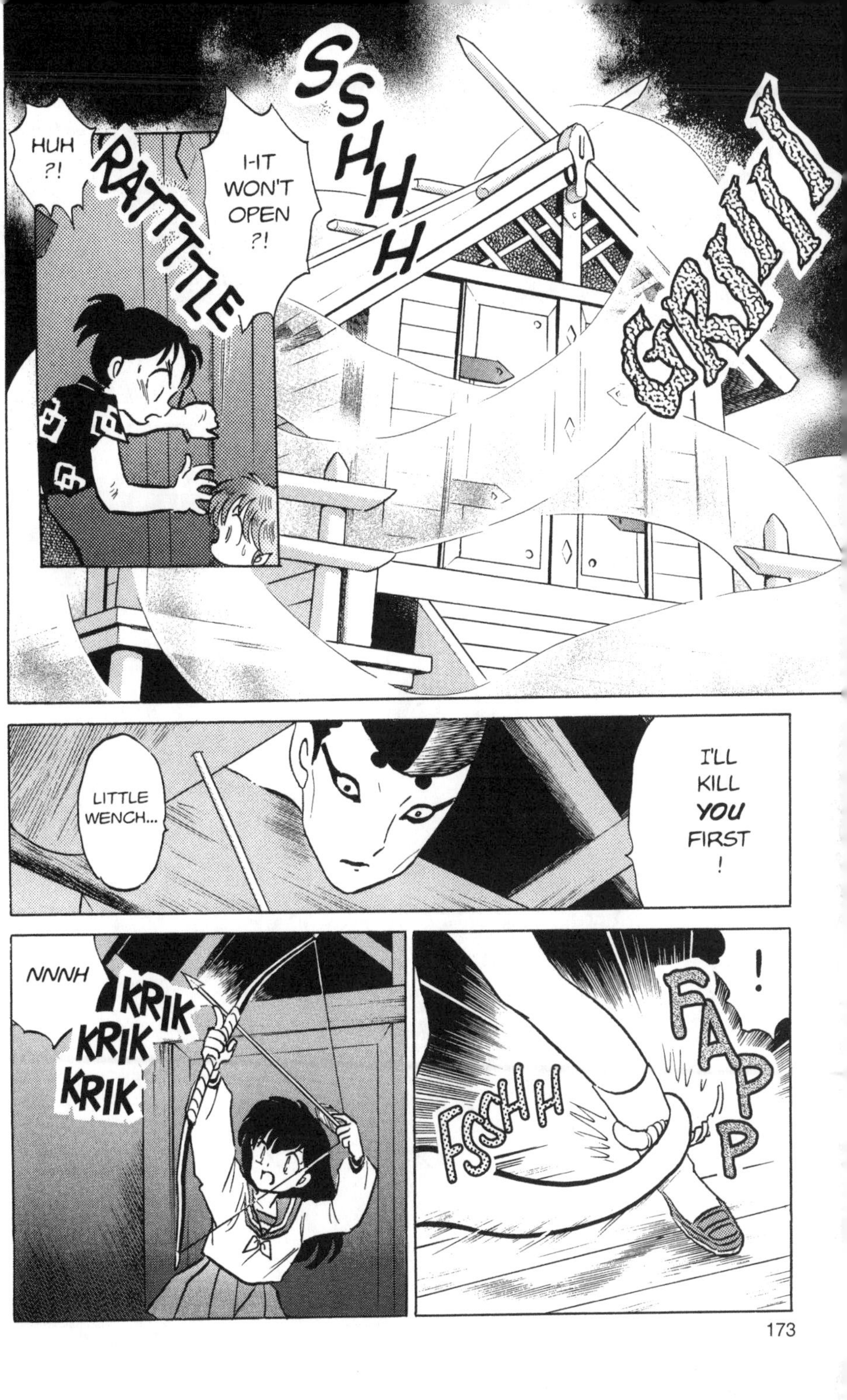
HUH ?!
RATTTTLE
I-IT WON'T OPEN ?!
SSHHHH
GRIIII
LITTLE WENCH...
I'LL KILL YOU FIRST !
NNNH
KRIK KRIK KRIK
!
FSSHH
FAPPP

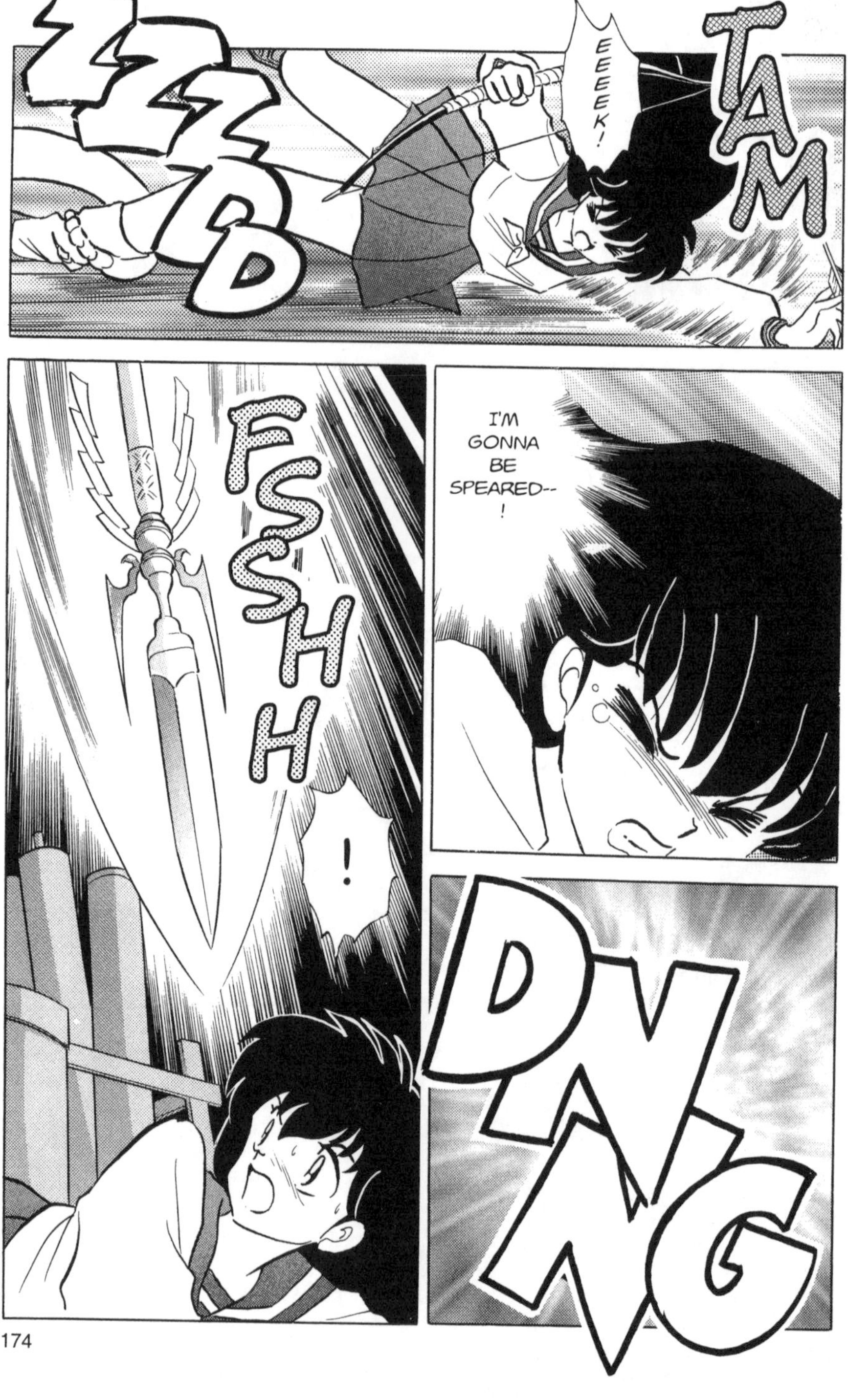
ZZZD
EEEEK!
TAM
FSSHH
!
I'M GONNA BE SPEARED-- !
DVNNG

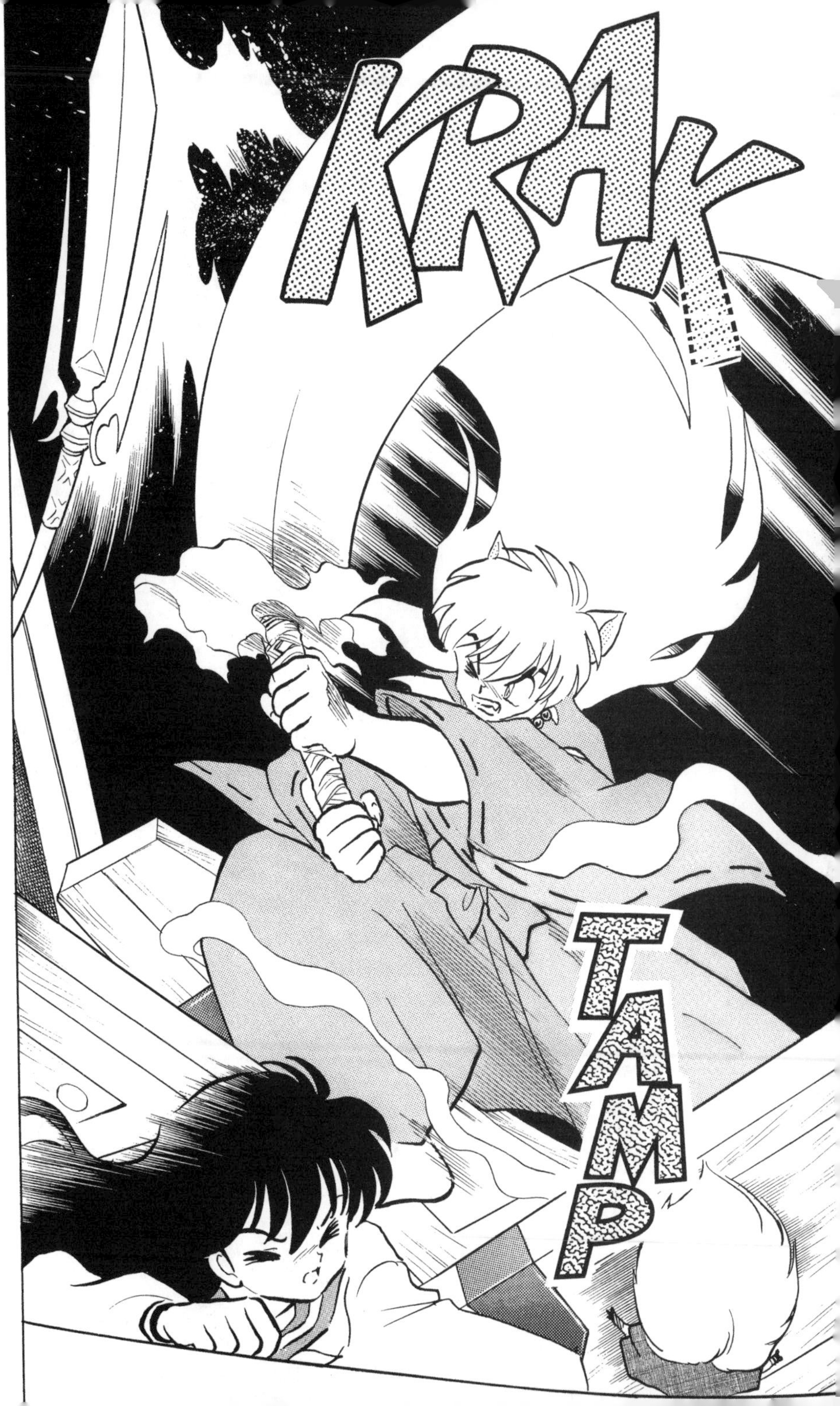
KRAK
TAMP

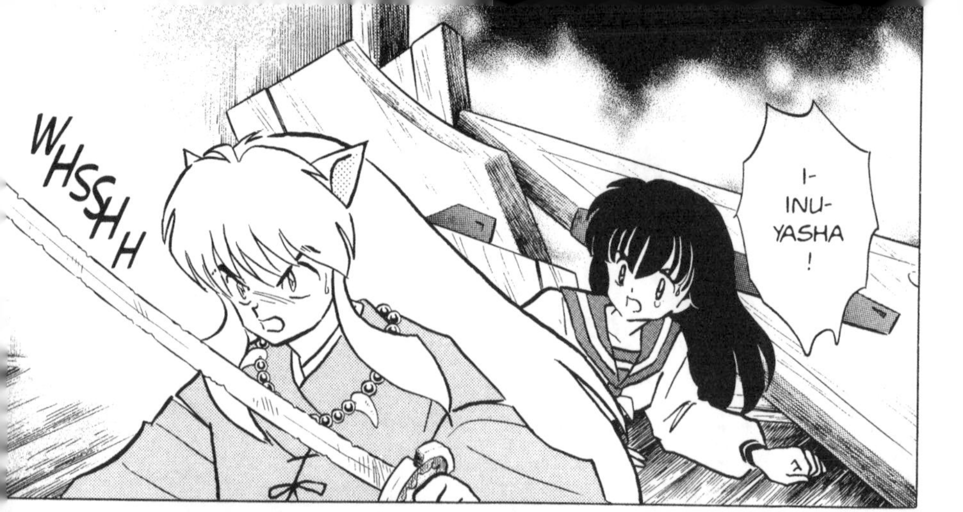
WHSSHH
I-INU-YASHA!

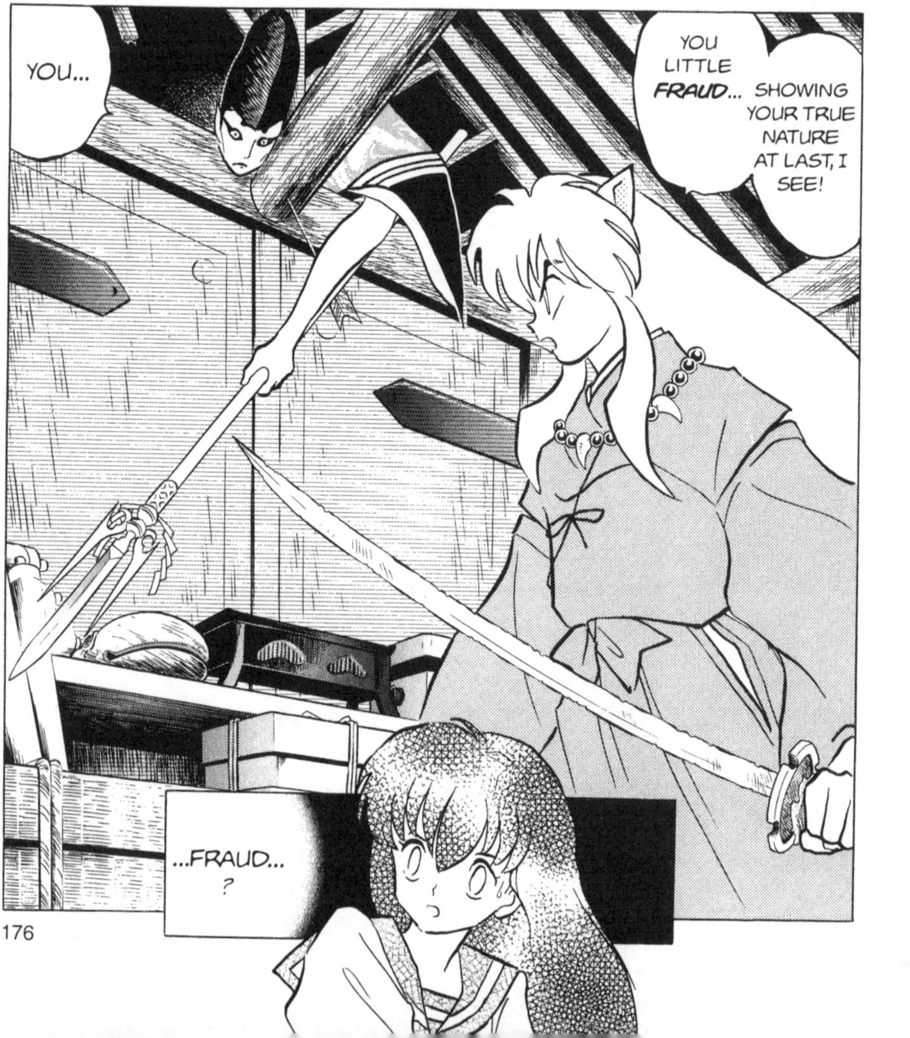
YOU...
YOU LITTLE *FRAUD*...
SHOWING YOUR TRUE NATURE AT LAST, I SEE!
...FRAUD...?

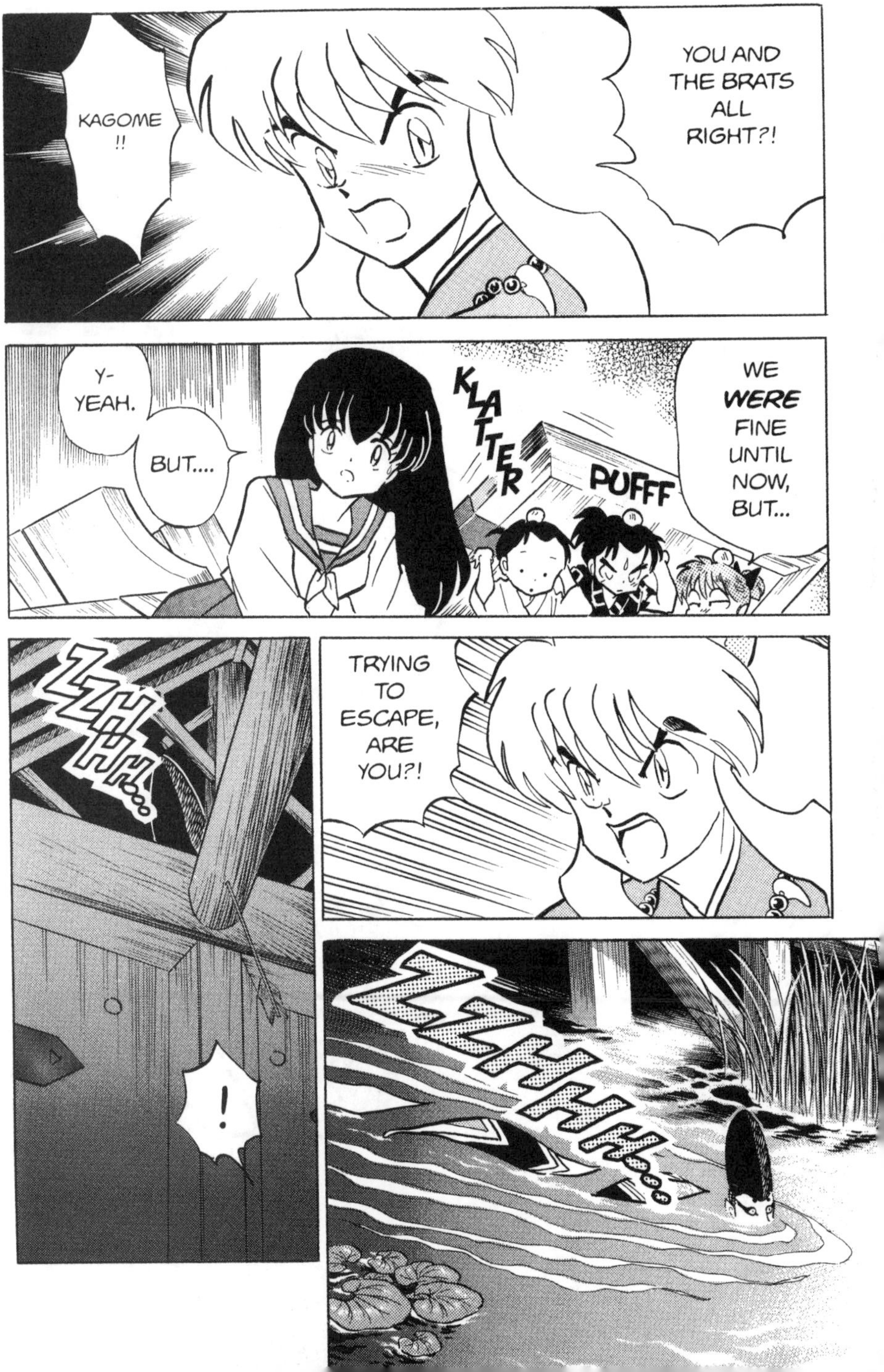
KAGOME !!
YOU AND THE BRATS ALL RIGHT?!
Y-YEAH.
BUT....
KLATTER
PUFFF
WE *WERE* FINE UNTIL NOW, BUT...
ZZHHHooo
!
TRYING TO ESCAPE, ARE YOU?!
ZZHHHHooo

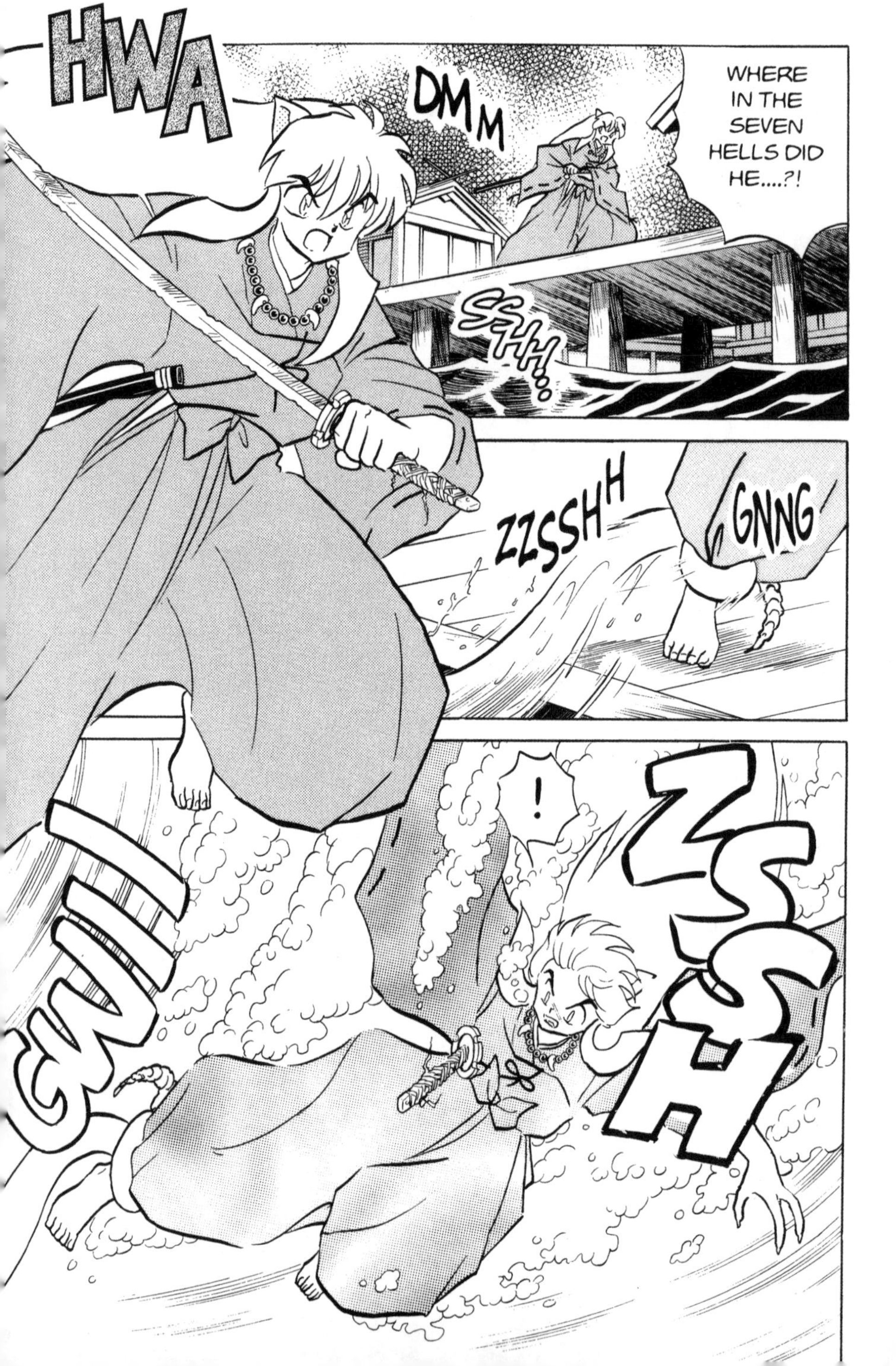
HWA
DMM
WHERE IN THE SEVEN HELLS DID HE....?!
SSHH...
ZZSSHH
GNNG
!
GWIII
ZSSHH

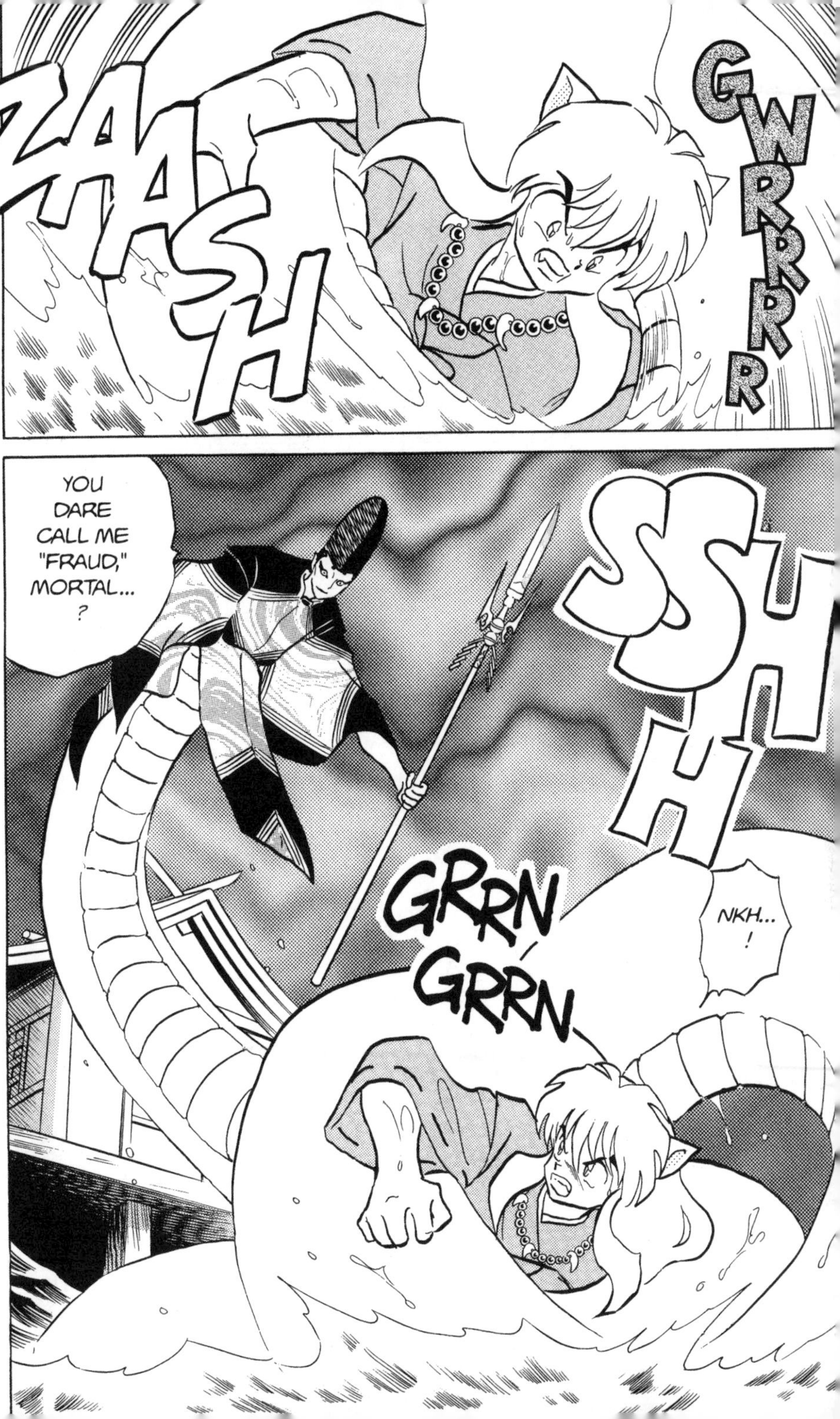
ZAASHH
GWRRRRR
YOU DARE CALL ME "FRAUD," MORTAL...?
SSHHH
GRRN GRRN
NKH...!

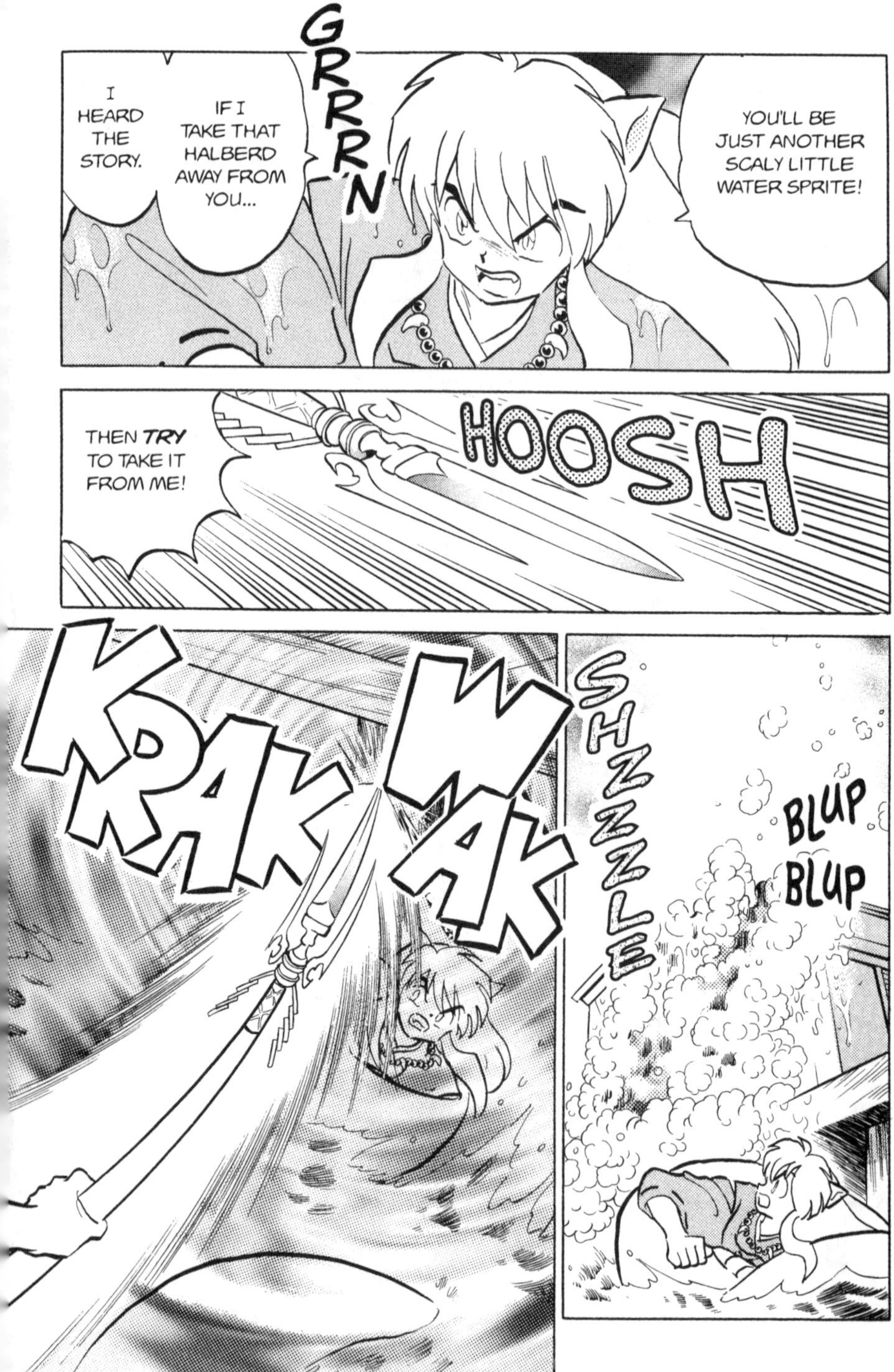
I HEARD THE STORY.
IF I TAKE THAT HALBERD AWAY FROM YOU...
GRRRN
YOU'LL BE JUST ANOTHER SCALY LITTLE WATER SPRITE!
THEN **TRY** TO TAKE IT FROM ME!
HOOSH
KRAK
WAK
SHZZZLE
BLUP
BLUP

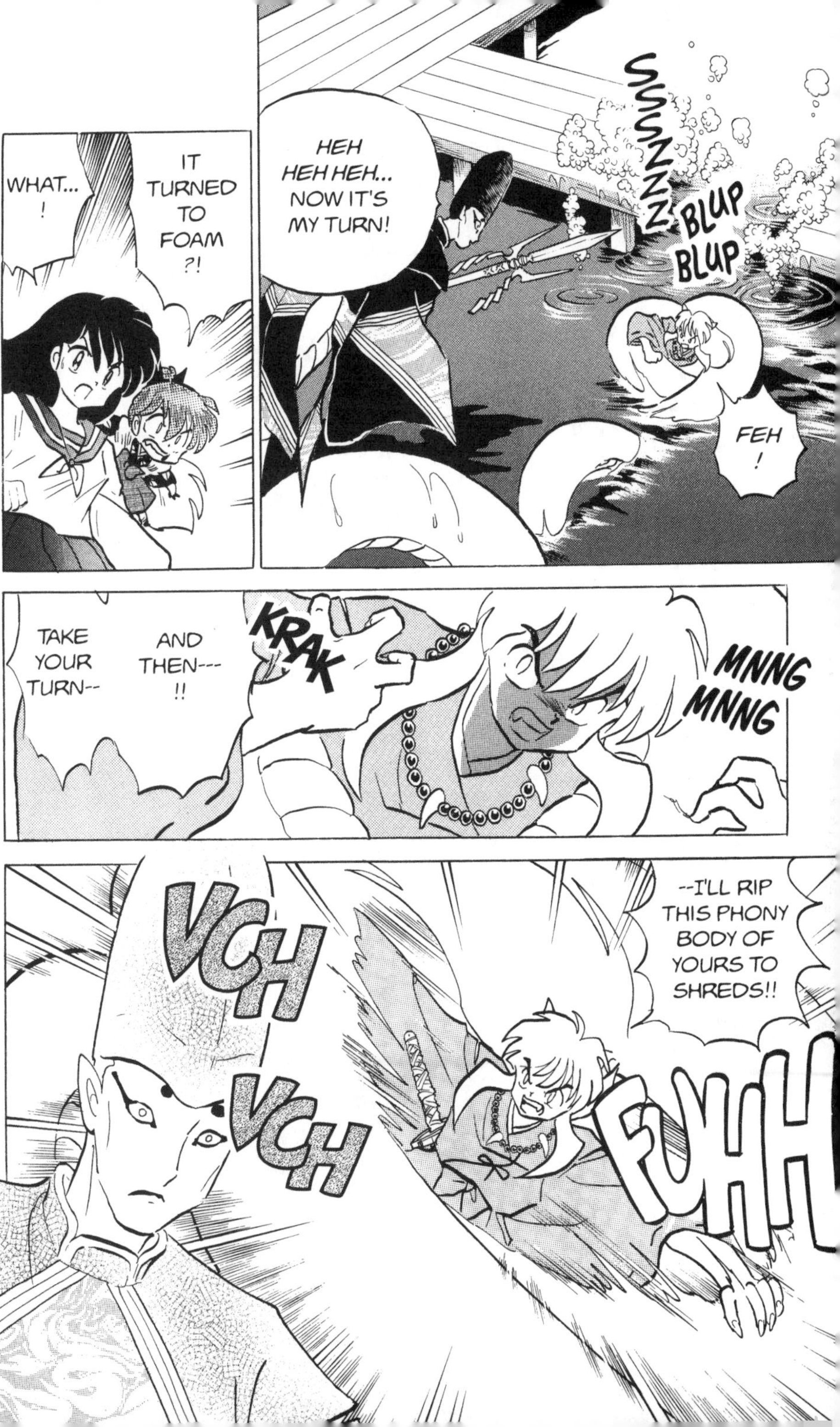
WHAT... !
IT TURNED TO FOAM ?!
HEH HEH HEH... NOW IT'S MY TURN!
SSSZZZ
BLUP BLUP
FEH !
TAKE YOUR TURN--
AND THEN--- !!
KRAK
MNNG MNNG
VCH
VCH
--I'LL RIP THIS PHONY BODY OF YOURS TO SHREDS!!
FUHH

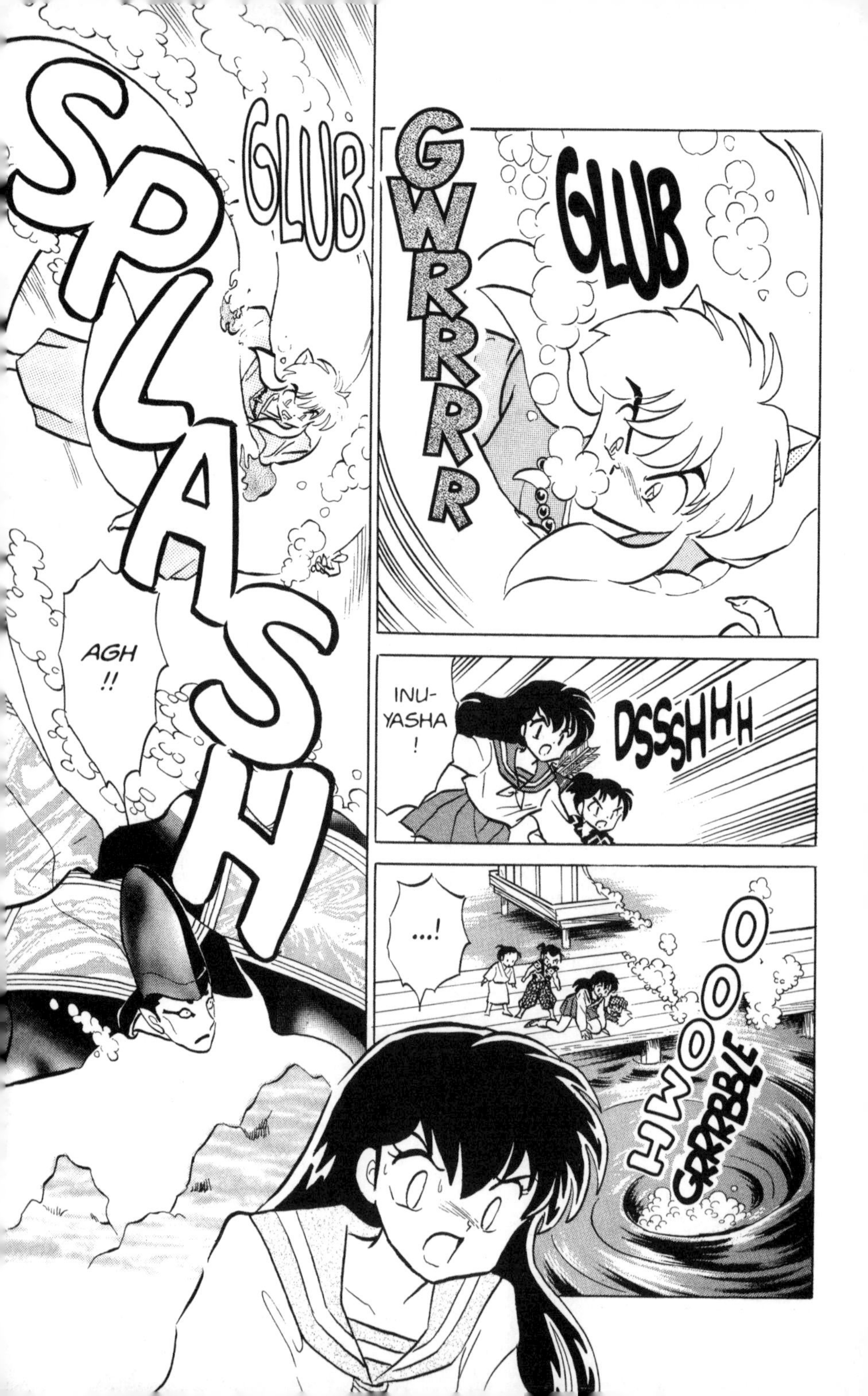
GLUB
SPLASH
AGH !!
GWRRRRR
GLUB
INU-YASHA !
DSSSHHH
...!
HWOOOO
GRRRBBLE

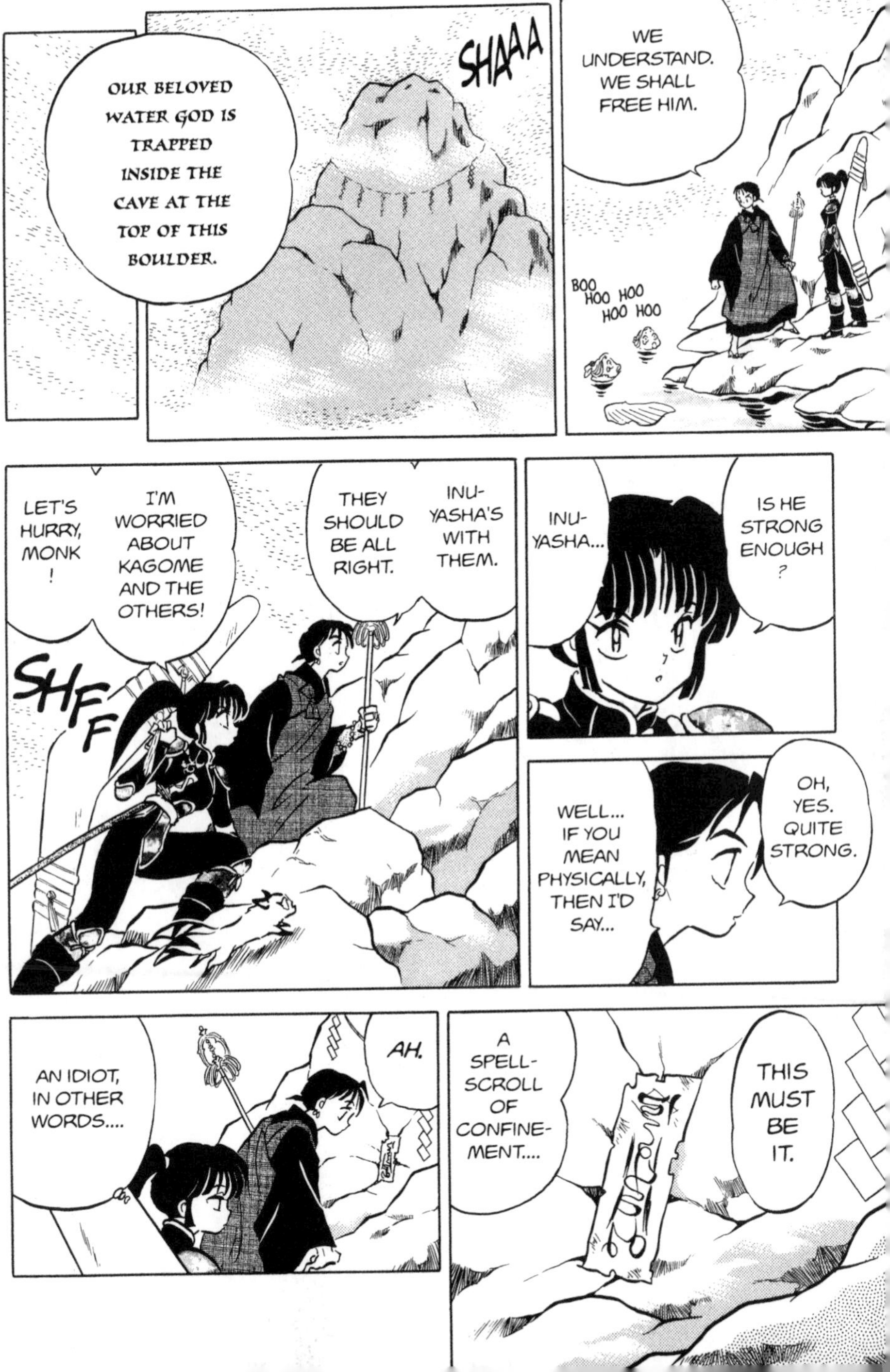
OUR BELOVED WATER GOD IS TRAPPED INSIDE THE CAVE AT THE TOP OF THIS BOULDER.
SHAAA
WE UNDERSTAND. WE SHALL FREE HIM.
BOO HOO HOO HOO HOO
LET'S HURRY, MONK!
I'M WORRIED ABOUT KAGOME AND THE OTHERS!
THEY SHOULD BE ALL RIGHT.
INU-YASHA'S WITH THEM.
SHFF
INU-YASHA...
IS HE STRONG ENOUGH?
WELL... IF YOU MEAN PHYSICALLY, THEN I'D SAY...
OH, YES. QUITE STRONG.
AN IDIOT, IN OTHER WORDS....
AH.
A SPELL-SCROLL OF CONFINEMENT....
THIS MUST BE IT.

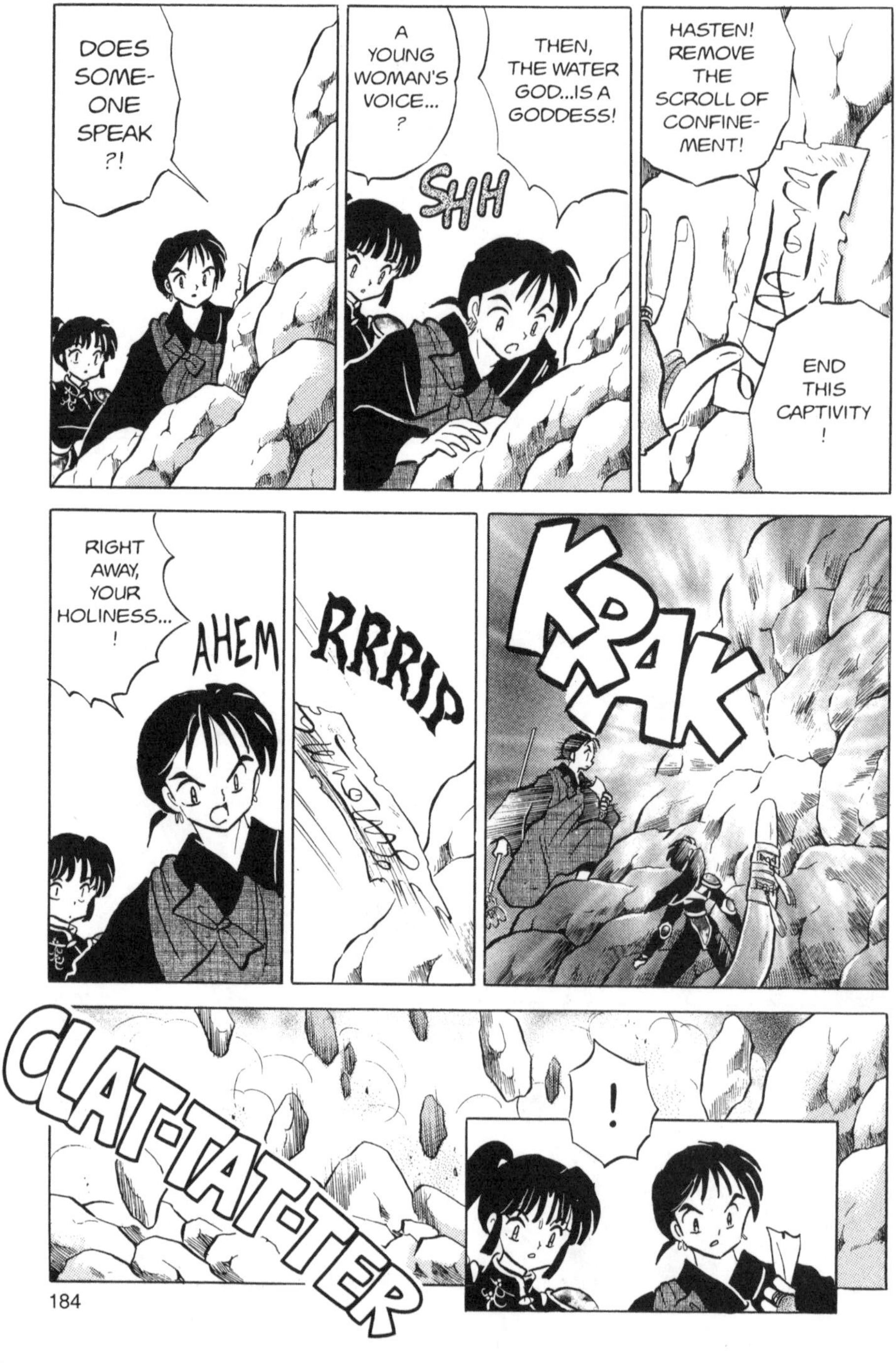
DOES SOME-ONE SPEAK ?!
A YOUNG WOMAN'S VOICE...?
THEN, THE WATER GOD...IS A GODDESS!
SHH
HASTEN! REMOVE THE SCROLL OF CONFINE-MENT!
END THIS CAPTIVITY!
RIGHT AWAY, YOUR HOLINESS...!
AHEM
RRRIP
KRAK
CLAT-TAT-TER
!

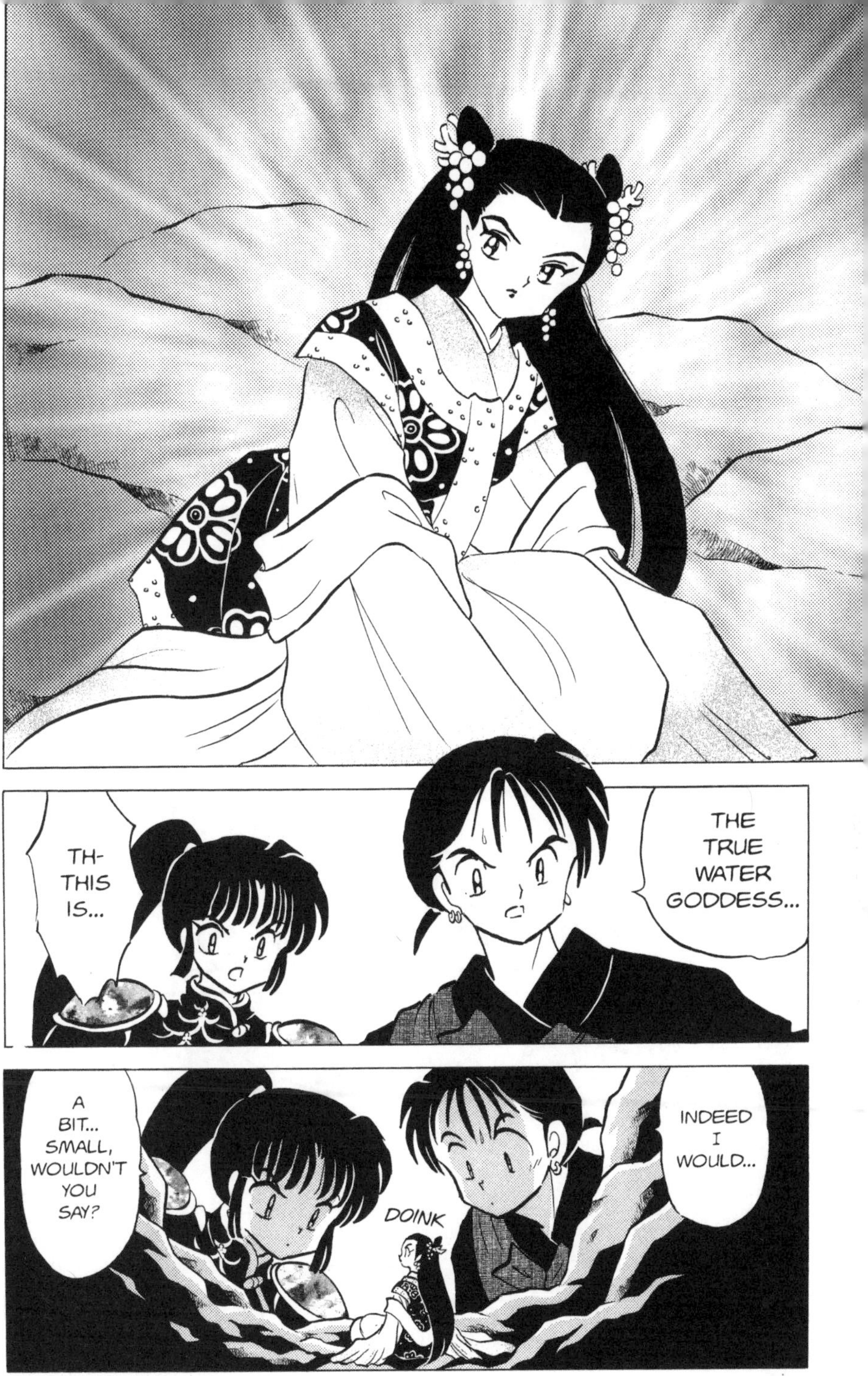
TH- THIS IS...
THE TRUE WATER GODDESS...
A BIT... SMALL, WOULDN'T YOU SAY?
DOINK
INDEED I WOULD...

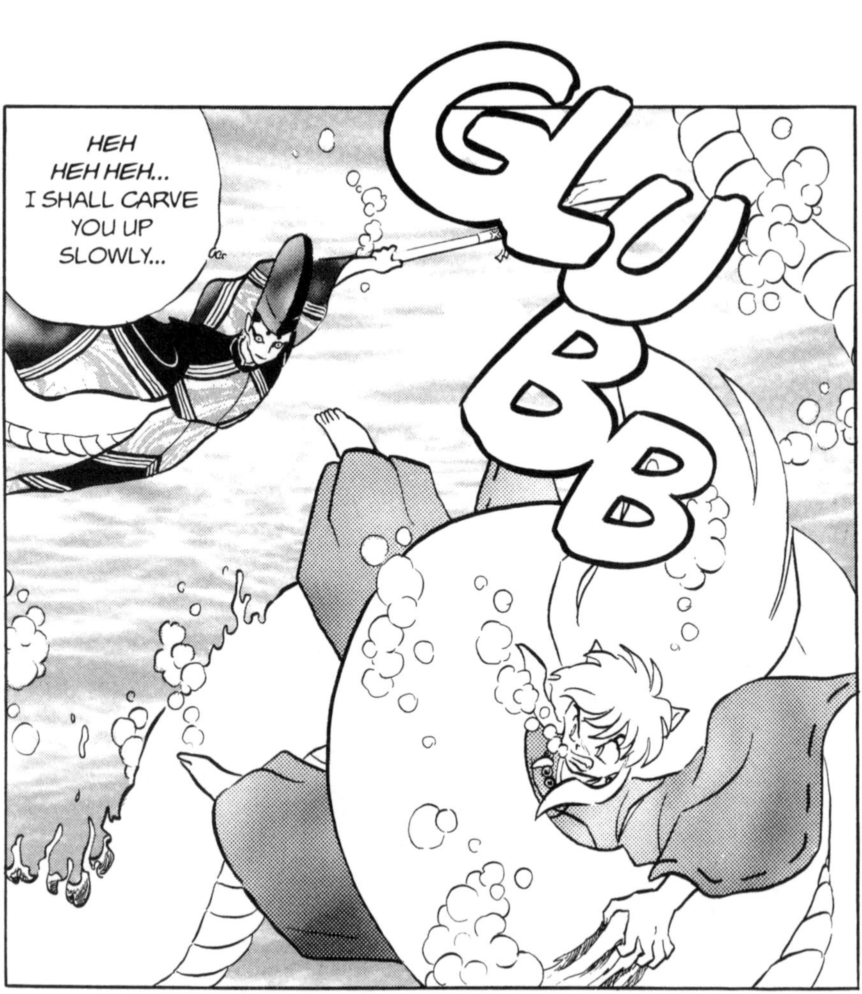
HEH HEH HEH... I SHALL CARVE YOU UP SLOWLY...
CLUBB

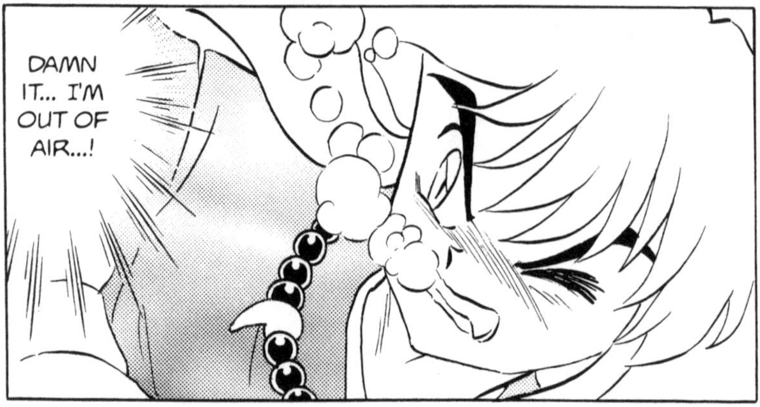
DAMN IT... I'M OUT OF AIR...!

Rumiko Takahashi

Rumiko Takahashi was born in 1957 in Niigata, Japan. She attended women's college in Tokyo, where she began studying comics with Kazuo Koike, author of **Crying Freeman**. In 1978, she won a prize in Shogakukan's annual "New Comic Artist Contest," and in that same year her boy-meets-alien comedy series **Lum*Urusei Yatsura** began appearing in the weekly manga magazine SHŌNEN SUNDAY. This phenomenally successful series ran for nine years and sold over 22 million copies. Takahashi's later **Ranma 1/2** series enjoyed even greater popularity.

Takahashi is considered by many to be one of the world's most popular manga artists. With the publication of Volume 34 of her **Ranma 1/2** series in Japan, Takahashi's total sales passed *one hundred million* copies of her compiled works.

Takahashi's serial titles include **Lum*Urusei Yatsura**, **Ranma 1/2**, **One-Pound Gospel**, **Maison Ikkoku** and **Inu-Yasha**. Additionally, Takahashi has drawn many short stories which have been published in America under the title "Rumic Theater," and several installments of a saga known as her "Mermaid" series. Most of Takahashi's major stories have also been animated, and are widely available in translation worldwide. **Inu-Yasha** is her most recent serial story, first published in SHŌNEN SUNDAY in 1996.

action

THE BATTLE BETWEEN GOOD AND EVIL

- The All-New Tenchi Muyô!
- Bastard!!
- Battle Angel Alita
- The Big O
- Digi Charat
- Excel Saga
- Firefighter!: Daigo of Fire Company M
- Flame of Recca
- Gundam
- Inu-Yasha *
- Medabots
- Neon Genesis Evangelion
- Project Arms *
- Ranma 1/2 *
- Short Program
- Silent Möbius
- Steam Detectives
- No Need for Tenchi!
- Tuxedo Gin
- Video Girl Ai *
- Zoids *

START YOUR ACTION GRAPHIC
NOVEL COLLECTION TODAY!

STARTING @ **$8.95!**

*Also available on DVD from VIZ

www.viz.com

COMPLETE OUR SURVEY AND LET
US KNOW WHAT YOU THINK!

☐ Please check here if you DO NOT wish to receive information or future offers from VIZ

Name: _____

Address: _____

City: _____ **State:** _____ **Zip:** _____

E-mail: _____

☐ **Male**   ☐ **Female**   **Date of Birth** (mm/dd/yyyy): ___/___/_____ (Under 13? Parental consent required)

What race/ethnicity do you consider yourself? (please check one)

☐ Asian/Pacific Islander ☐ Black/African American ☐ Hispanic/Latino

☐ Native American/Alaskan Native ☐ White/Caucasian ☐ Other: _____

What VIZ product did you purchase? (check all that apply and indicate title purchased)

☐ DVD/VHS _____

☐ Graphic Novel _____

☐ Magazines _____

☐ Merchandise _____

Reason for purchase: (check all that apply)

☐ Special offer ☐ Favorite title ☐ Gift

☐ Recommendation ☐ Other _____

Where did you make your purchase? (please check one)

☐ Comic store ☐ Bookstore ☐ Mass/Grocery Store

☐ Newsstand ☐ Video/Video Game Store ☐ Other: _____

☐ Online (site: _____)

What other VIZ properties have you purchased/own? _____

_____

How many anime and/or manga titles have you purchased in the last year? How many were VIZ titles? (please check one from each column)

ANIME	MANGA	VIZ
☐ None	☐ None	☐ None
☐ 1-4	☐ 1-4	☐ 1-4
☐ 5-10	☐ 5-10	☐ 5-10
☐ 11+	☐ 11+	☐ 11+

I find the pricing of VIZ products to be: (please check one)

☐ Cheap   ☐ Reasonable   ☐ Expensive

What genre of manga and anime would you like to see from VIZ? (please check two)

☐ Adventure   ☐ Comic Strip   ☐ Detective   ☐ Fighting

☐ Horror   ☐ Romance   ☐ Sci-Fi/Fantasy   ☐ Sports

What do you think of VIZ's new look?

☐ Love It   ☐ It's OK   ☐ Hate It   ☐ Didn't Notice   ☐ No Opinion

THANK YOU! Please send the completed form to:

NJW Research
42 Catharine St.
Poughkeepsie, NY 12601

All information provided will be used for internal purposes only. We promise not to sell or otherwise divulge your information.

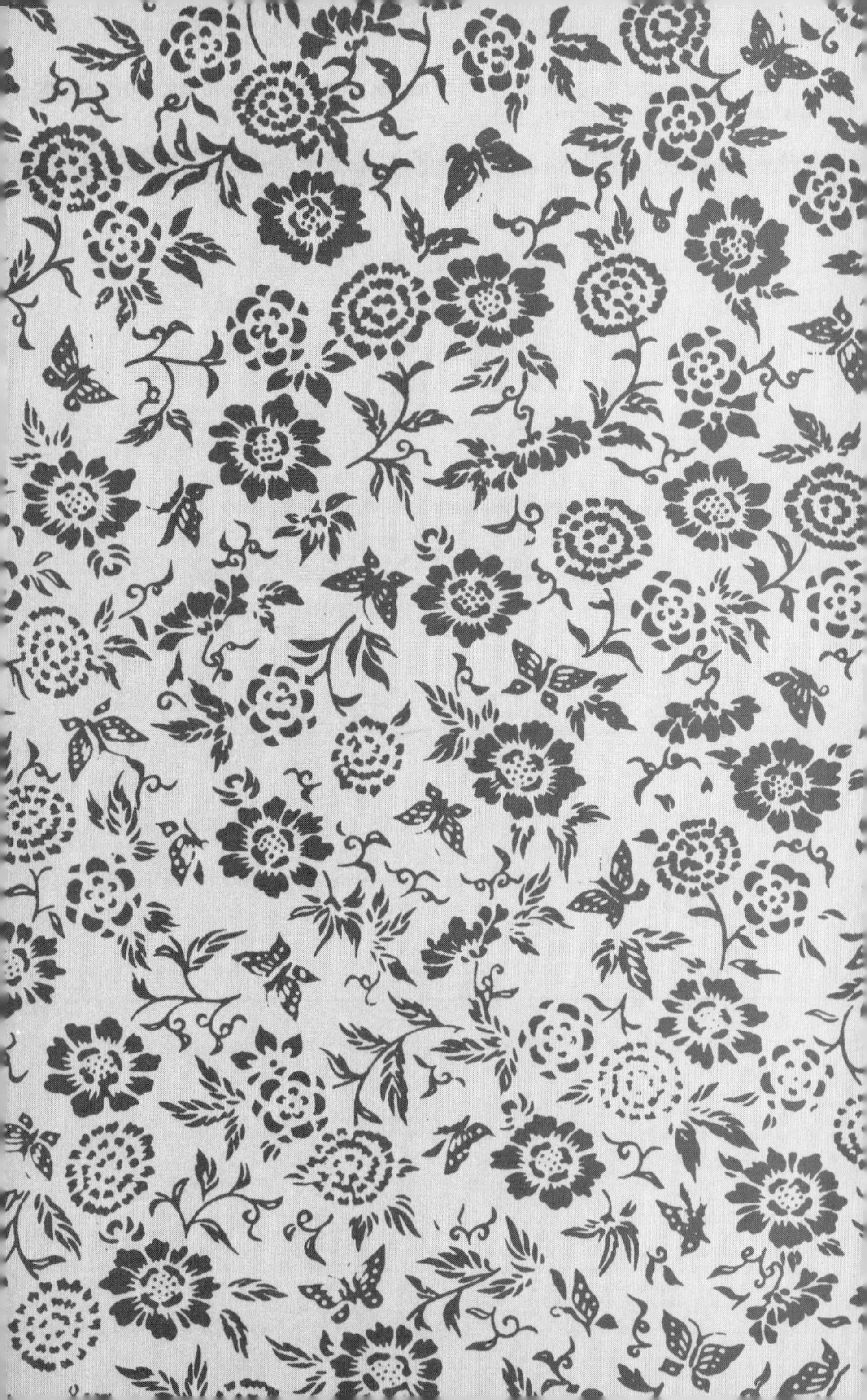